BURNING
DREAMS

Visit us at www.boldstrokesbooks.com

What Reviewers Say About BOLD STROKES Authors

KIM BALDWIN

"*Force of Nature* is filled with nonstop, fast paced action. Tornadoes, raging fire blazes, heroic and daring rescues…Baldwin does a fine job of describing the fast-paced scenes and inspiring the reader to keep on turning the pages." – L-word.comLiterature

ROSE BEECHAM

"…her characters seem fully capable of walking away from the particulars of whodunit and engaging the reader in other aspects of their lives." – *Lambda Book Report*

GEORGIA BEERS

"Beers weaves a tale of yearning, love, lust, and conflict resolution. She has constructed a believable plot, with strong characters in a charming setting." – *JustAboutWrite*

RONICA BLACK

"*Wild Abandon* tells how these two women come to realize that 'life was too precious to be ruled by…fears, by…demons.' While these two women struggle with their issues, there is some very, very hot sex. If you enjoy complex characters and passionate sex scenes, you'll love *Wild Abandon*." – *MegaScene*

GUN BROOKE

"*Course of Action* is a romance…populated with a host of captivating and amiable characters. The glimpses into the lifestyles of the rich and beautiful people are rather like guilty pleasures…a most satisfying and entertaining reading experience." – *Midwest Book Review*

CATE CULPEPPER

"…an exceptional storyteller who has taken on a very difficult subject …and turned it into a spellbinding novel. As an author, she understands well that fiction can teach us our own history." – *JustAboutWrite*

JANE FLETCHER

"*The Exile and the Sorcerer* is a mesmerizing read, a tour-de-force packed with adventure, ordeals, complex twists and turns, and the internal introspection of appealing characters." – *Midwest Book Review*

JD GLASS

"*Punk Like Me*…is different. It is engaging. It is life-affirming. Frankly, it is genius. This is a rare book in that it has a soul; one that is laid bare for all to see." – *JustAboutWrite*

GRACE LENNOX

"*Chance* is refreshing…Every nuance is powerful and succinct. *Chance* is not a novel about the music industry; it is about a woman discovering herself as she muddles through all the trappings of fame." – *Midwest Book Review*

LEE LYNCH

"Lynch, with a dozen novels to her credit dating back to the early days of Naiad Press, has earned her stripes as a writerly elder. She was contributing stories to the lesbian magazine *The Ladder* four decades ago. But this latest is sublimely in tune with the times." – *Q-Syndicate*

JLEE MEYER

"*Forever Found*…neatly combines hot sex scenes, humor, engaging characters, and an exciting story." – *MegaScene*

RADCLYFFE

"…well-plotted…lovely romance…I couldn't turn the pages fast enough!" – Ann Bannon, author of *The Beebo Brinker Chronicles*

SUSAN SMITH

"This disparate duo's lush rush of a romance - which incorporates reincarnation, a grounded transman and his peppy daughter, and the dark moods of a troubled witch - pays wonderful homage to Leslie Feinberg's classic gender-bending novel, *Stone Butch Blues*." – *Q-Syndicate*

ALI VALI

"Rich in character portrayal, *The Devil Inside* by Ali Vali is an unusual, unpredictable, and thought-provoking love story that will have the reader questioning the definition of right and wrong long after she finishes the book." – *JustAboutWrite*

BURNING
DREAMS

by

Susan Smith

2006

BURNING DREAMS
© 2006 BY SUSAN SMITH. ALL RIGHTS RESERVED.

ISBN 1-933110-62-7

THIS TRADE PAPERBACK ORIGINAL IS PUBLISHED BY
BOLD STROKES BOOKS, INC.,
NEW YORK, USA

FIRST EDITION DECEMBER 2006

LIBRARY OF CONGRESS CONTROL NUMBER: 2006935745

CREDITS
EDITORS: CINDY CRESAP AND STACIA SEAMAN
PRODUCTION DESIGN: STACIA SEAMAN
COVER DESIGN BY SHERI (GRAPHICARTIST2020@HOTMAIL.COM)

By the Author

Of Drag Kings and the Wheel of Fate, 2nd edition

Acknowledgments

This book wouldn't exist without the women of the HAG Theatre Company. Cindy Cresap, my brilliant editor, deserves a medal and a raise.

Susan Smith 2006

Dedication

For Morgan, Rowan, Cyd, and Anthony for showing me how to live well, and for being my family.

CHAPTER ONE

There are smarter ways to spend the afternoon, thought
Rosalind Olchawski on the fourth of October in Buffalo, *than
to let a former enemy and rival for the affections of your much younger
lover hold a pointed object to your naked back.* Not that Rhea would
be overcome with a fit of passion and poke her to death. It would take
hundreds of tiny fits of passion, until she died the death of a thousand
paper cuts. Rosalind couldn't picture it. Rhea didn't lose control like
that. And, she had to admit, her relationship with Rhea had grown from
open hostility, past armed truce, and into mutual respect. It helped that
the love object in question, the ridiculously handsome twenty-year-old
girl seated at the counter, was a shared passion for both of them. They
were bound to make peace, once Taryn had made it plain that she was
keeping both her brand-new older lover and her oldest friend. Whom
she just happened to still live with.

Thank God for Joe, Rosalind thought as a mantra. *Good on you,
Joe. You make everything better. You bring calm.* Joe was Rhea's lover,
and had been for two years. A father of a teenage daughter, a masterful
cook, a loving and calm presence in the happy maelstrom of a pagan
queer household. Rhea was occasionally hard to take, but Rosalind
could leave her to the easy stability of Joe and scamper back across the
street to her own house, with Taryn in tow.

Rosalind's hands gripped the back of the chair. Her mouth fell
open.

Focus on something. She'd never been in Rhea's shop before; that would do. A Pound of Flesh was just around the corner from Mariner, down Elmwood from Allen. A green and yellow Victorian converted into a place of business. The shop displayed a small Erie County Health Department permit in the window. Rosalind had hung her coat on the scrollwork coat rack to the left, just inside the door. The shades were drawn over the windows, but illumination came from Rhea's work light and the red and blue candles in ceramic holders shaped like dragons. The scent of sandalwood fought with burning sage, weaving layers of blue smoke in the air. A hand-lettered sign tacked to the door offered tattoos and body art, piercings and jewelry.

Focusing on the details of the room was not working. *Focus on the past?* If she went for the long view, Rosalind thought, it might put her to sleep. Not all that much exciting had happened to her from the age of infancy up until a few weeks before. She had been, until very recently, a mature, collected, responsible, warm sweater and mittens kind of woman, a little nearsighted, rarely without a book, conscious of how other people felt. A perfectly normal thirty-three-year-old divorced English professor.

Until the night she went out to a gay bar with a friend from the theater department to be set up on a blind date with a guy from Poetics. The guy turned out to be a boor and a bore, but the night was not a total loss. The drag show was fascinating. Arousing. Rosalind had taken one look at the girl performing as Elvis and had to have her. It made no sense, in light of her history up until that moment, but, Rosalind reasoned, can we always be bound by history? She had managed to take the drag king performing that night out for coffee.

"Coffee." *I will never think of that word again without quotes. Coffee is never just coffee*, Rosalind thought. Love had snuck up on her. Sex had been waiting at the corner to tap her shoulder. Life itself unzipped, and within a few days, everything that Rosalind knew about herself had been turned inside out. She wasn't just a nice, warm sweater and mittens divorced woman, she was a passionate adventurer, willing to fling herself into the midst of a world she never knew existed. A world of drag kings and transmen, witches, magic, ghosts, and gender transgression where every boundary was only a doorway. There was a lot to learn, but Rosalind wasn't afraid. She knew the secret: Love trumps fear, brings it low and dances on its head. If you can bring yourself to open your arms wide enough, you just might fly.

She should be well used to doing crazy, impulsive, follow your heart and damn the torpedoes sorts of things. The flag of freedom was flying from her gunwales, Rosalind thought. Borders were made to be crossed. What had Taryn said to her, well, growled in her ear just this morning? *Fear is a sign you are doing what you should. If it's easy, everyone would do it.* Needles? Just sharp pointy little things. Nothing much to face, compared to what she'd faced down in the last few weeks. Meeting a twenty-year-old drag king in a gay bar, having a mad, passionate affair? Done it. Accepting that things don't always make logical sense. She'd had to learn a different language. Had to accept that not only did she love this beautiful boy, she'd loved her before. They'd known one another in a previous life. Rhea had told her all that after she'd refused to stop seeing Taryn. The witch hadn't liked her in the beginning; now she knew why. There were debts to be paid, a cycle of pain to be broken. Rosalind's presence meant that Rhea was about to die. In their last lifetime, Rosalind had abandoned Taryn and so broken her heart, she never recovered. That was a lot to face down. Yet they'd done it, all of them, chosen to break the cycle and let Love win. Let everyone live.

Did that mean that they were all free? That there were no more entanglements from the past? The cycle was broken. Rhea lived. She was with Taryn. There was peace in the household.

The woman holding the needle paused, feeling the tension in her subject's back.

"Hurts?" Rhea asked, pulling the metal away from Rosalind's skin.

Rosalind was tempted to lie and not interrupt the ritual, but she knew that Rhea would be able to tell. There is no profit in lying to a witch. "Yes. A little," she admitted. Rhea's hands were cool and sure on her back, a touch that held no fear, only a profound recognition of boundary. Rosalind felt the temperature of the older woman's hands and wondered what she might have been like as a lover. It was hard to imagine Rhea in the throes of passion. How had she ever been Taryn's lover? Taryn was nothing but fire, and from all reports, she was worlds calmer than she used to be. Rosalind glanced guiltily over her shoulder, certain that Rhea had read this errant thought.

"There are two ways we could go. We could stop," Rhea said.

"No." It was immediate. Pain or no pain, this was something Rosalind was determined to do. She remembered the exact moment when she'd made the decision, when the clarity had hit her like the tide. It had been three days after Taryn had shown her the design, the flowering dogwood branch, the golden serpent, and the broken arrow. She hadn't really considered it then. She was simply flattered that Taryn had drawn it for her. But she wasn't the kind of person who got tattoos, so she set the idea aside without truly considering it. She loved the tattoos that covered Taryn's body, the map to her history, a testament to her pain and her sense of humor. She couldn't imagine Taryn's back without the bull dagger, or her right arm without the head of Alexander. It made perfect sense for Taryn, who was, admittedly, very young and very fierce. Rosalind had never, even in her most private moments, considered herself fierce.

They'd been making love on the floor of the living room of her new house; the bed on the second floor was just too far away. The lovely hand-knotted Persian rug she'd chosen to match the tiles on the fireplace was now bunched up under her back, giving her burns. One of Taryn's legs was still caught in her jeans, one boot was off, tossed under the couch. Rosalind's skirt had joined the rug under the small of her back. Her blouse had spit buttons all over the floor in a failed attempt to remove it. Endorphins were throwing a party in her skull, cheering the girl on. Rosalind's fingernails spiked down into Taryn's back in her effort not to scream. She was very aware of her new neighbors, and the windows left open. They would have to get used to the noises coming from Dr. Olchawski's house, but not in the middle of the afternoon.

There she was, skin to skin with her lover, tangled clothing and a faint sheen of sweat between them, and the distance was too much. Even the orgasm that ripped through her, closing around Taryn's hand in a long, possessive embrace, was not enough. With a sense of grief, Rosalind felt her body's climax ebb. Her soul was still reaching out to her, even as her hands slid off her lover's broad shoulders. "No," Rosalind said, the feeling catching in her throat. "It's not enough."

Taryn sat up very quickly, looking hurt. "It's not?"

"Not that, angel." Rosalind brushed the hair away from Taryn's face. "Not my body. My body is very happy right now, as you well know." She reached down and took Taryn's hand, drawing it up her inner thigh. The wetness soothed the hurt look on Taryn's face. She relaxed, flexing her fingers on Rosalind's skin.

"Then what?" Taryn asked, in a voice that threatened to increase the wetness on Rosalind's thigh. Rosalind turned on her side, looking up into the face of her lover.

There were blue shadows under achingly blue eyes, remnants of a highly emotional few days. But the slackness of grief was gone from her face, leaving it vibrant with life. She looked tired, but Rosalind knew that much of the missed sleep hinted at in Taryn's face was of her authorship and could be claimed proudly. The relaxed posture of her body, the ease and speed with which Taryn smiled was also her responsibility, and Rosalind gladly accepted credit. She struggled to put words to how she was feeling, something she rarely ever had to do.

"My body is yours. All you have to do is walk into a room and I get wet. Sometimes it's like I can hear you coming, feel heat from you, before I know you're there."

The corner of Taryn's mouth quirked up into an automatic smile of pride.

"But I want more. I want all of you. I want to take you inside, make you a part of me," Rosalind said.

"I am a part of you, Rosalind."

It was the way Taryn said her name that did it, the final push. There was such passion layered into the syllables, she felt the blood come to the surface of her skin, reaching out. "I want to wear you on my skin, all the time. I never want to be away from you."

Taryn's eyebrows rose. "You sure? It's not the kind of thing that goes away."

"Neither is how I feel about you," Rosalind said, and the warmth moved from her heart outward, making the distance between them unbearable. She pulled Taryn back down into her arms.

Rhea had been approached and asked to do the tattoo. The raised eyebrow and Mona Lisa smile were the first answer Taryn and Rosalind got. "Took you long enough. I've been planning this for days."

So Rosalind found herself in A Pound of Flesh, too distracted by the bite of the needle to enjoy the name of the shop. Rhea had taken one glance at Taryn's design and predicted three sessions. This was the first, the outline of the tree and the serpent. From the way it felt, Rosalind wasn't sure she could go through with it. Rhea seemed to hear this thought, or read it from her body. "I can do this another time," she said, quietly pulling the needle away.

"It's fine. No, really. I took ballet for years. You call this pain?" Rosalind said, and forced a laugh.

"I could block your pain. It's a simple matter of pressure points."

Rosalind heard the hesitation in Rhea's voice. "But? It's not just a matter of blocking the pain, is it? What's the catch?" Had Rosalind been looking over her shoulder, she might have seen the complex look of approval that Rhea shot across the shadowed room at the girl who leaned against the counter. She did hear the note of pride in Rhea's voice when she spoke.

"I say this to you as one of the family, not as anyone I might do work on. Pain is a form of communication. If you can keep a sense of place, of stillness, during the experience, you'll learn what it has to tell you on the other side. Especially with a mark like this one. It's your first. It's bound up with your symbols of power, and it was drawn with the hand of love. I advise you to go through the pain and see what is there, but it is your choice."

"Let's do it," Rosalind said with determination. Her body, now expecting the bite of the needle, tensed like a bowstring. Rhea shook her head and placed the palm of her hand on Rosalind's shoulder.

"There are ways of staying aware without wallowing in it. Taryn?" Rhea said, summoning Taryn to push off the counter and lope across the floor, moving from the light of the candles to the circle of Rhea's work lamp. Rosalind's attention shifted immediately to Taryn, delighting in her approach. Rosalind never tired of looking at Taryn, of absorbing the shock of her presence in a room.

Electric blue eyes under coal black brows gave her a brooding, intense look, at once dangerous and enticing. Her face, a study in planes and angles, was wrinkled with concern she hesitated to voice. It was a face that men glanced at, drawn by the strength, that women glanced at, then returned to, lingering. There was something about the blending of characteristics too hard to be called pretty but too striking to be ignored. It was a face that raised questions, that unsettled and aroused. On first look, she might be called interesting, on second, beautiful, if the beholder had time to allow that word to ripen into an embrace of character. Boy or girl, both or neither, Taryn was simply sexy, thought Rosalind, watching her walk, unconsciously moistening her lips.

Taryn dropped into a crouch in front of the chair, her eyes level with Rosalind's. Rosalind looked into the endless fields of blue, forgetting the pain, the needle, even her own name. There was only the recognition she felt every time she and her lover locked eyes. *I could drown in here and never regret a moment*, Rosalind thought, unaware of the smile that lit up her face.

"Hey," Taryn said, her voice warm.

"Hey," Rosalind answered, aware now of the size of her smile. *Lord, I hope she has this effect on me when I'm fifty. I'll be the old lady with the lithium grin roaming the streets of Buffalo.*

"Hurts, huh?" Taryn asked, interrupting Rosalind's fantasy.

"What hurts?" she asked. The needle touched her back, making her shoulder jump. "Oh, that. Yes, a bit. But you did warn me."

"Just stay here with me. That's it. Look at me. That's my girl," Taryn said, her voice a caress.

"Damn right. Don't you forget it. I don't get my body inked for just any chick I'm dating," Rosalind said, and frowned at her.

Taryn cocked her head thoughtfully. "I'm the first chick you've dated."

"Technicality." Rosalind felt Rhea begin the work on the dogwood flowers, and grimaced.

"Hey. Tell me a story," Taryn said, drawing her attention back.

"Now?"

"Why not?"

"What about?" Rosalind asked, the muscle in her shoulder jumping.

"Tell me about your home. Where you grew up," Taryn said, and there was no resisting that tone. It melted the tension from Rosalind. She found it easy to start speaking, to focus on nothing but her lover's eyes.

"Once upon a time there was a town folded away between low green hills. Outside of Poughkeepsie, along Freedom Road, out by the border where the farmland started, was a house. That house was yellow and brown, surrounded by mulberry and pine trees. There was a dogwood tree in the very back of the yard, near a stand of bamboo. On the other side of the yard—it was kind of L-shaped—was a garden. In that garden grew vegetables, flowers, the normal garden stuff. There was a great mystery to the garden. The green beans that grew there would vanish overnight. But only halfway. Now, in this yellow and brown house lived a boy, who isn't important here, but he threw fits if he was left out of anything, even this story. This boy had an older sister, a very wise and thoughtful girl."

"Bet she was gorgeous, too," Taryn said.

"Oh, perhaps someday somebody might think so. For the time of this tale, we'll say she was in her awkward years. Say between ten and thirty-three," Rosalind said lightly.

"No. We say she was gorgeous, because she was," Taryn insisted.

"Fine, fine, I won't argue with you. She was a looker, boy, a regular Jayne Mansfield. It doesn't matter for the story."

"It always matters. She was gorgeous. Say it." The look in Taryn's eyes gave a new definition to stubborn.

"All right. She was gorgeous. But it would be a long time before she knew it. Okay? Where was I? Ah yes, wise and thoughtful. This girl decided to get to the bottom of the green bean mystery. Since nothing odd happened in the garden during the day, she reasoned, it must be something that came at night. Could be an animal, sure, but this girl hadn't grown up enough to forget the supernatural. So the heroine of our tale knew what she would have to do. The window in her bedroom overlooked a slanting roof that ran down to the woodpile. A pine tree grew between the pile and the house, providing a makeshift ladder. With the right amount of balancing, it would be possible to leap from roof to tree, and then down the woodpile.

"This undertaking would need help, so the girl considered. Her little brother would blurt out the plans the minute he was confronted. She needed someone who would do anything she asked and never say a word if they got caught. She decided on her best friend, the next-door neighbor she'd grown up with. He was informed of the plans and agreed to meet her at night by the woodpile and help her jump down.

"The girl took the red flashlight from the kitchen drawer to bed with her. When she was pretty sure her parents were asleep, she eased the window open and crawled out on the roof." Rosalind paused, enjoying the look of interest on Taryn's face. That focus and attention were for her. She had the feeling that no one had told Taryn stories as a child. It was a pleasure she came to only as an adult.

"You get busted?" Taryn asked.

"I'll get there. Her friend was waiting, just as he said he would be. At night the space between the end of the roof and the top of the woodpile looked like an abyss. The trunk of the pine tree looked miles away. She'd never made this kind of leap, only imagined it. She thought about turning back. The lure of the mystery drew her on, and her sneakers started to slip on the tiles. So she closed her eyes and leapt out into the dark.

"She felt the rough bark grab at her hands and slide through. Her feet hit the top of the woodpile. The wood gave way, cascading down onto her friend, who waited to catch her."

"Did you get hurt?" Taryn asked.

"No. The friend stood his ground and cushioned the fall. The woodpile was scattered, the noise woke everyone in the house, and they got an all-night talking-to."

"I want to know what happened to the guy," Taryn said.

"Paul ended up with a fractured ankle. Poor boy, he was just following my lead, but he saved me from getting crushed."

There was a subtle change in Taryn's face. The set of her jaw firmed with the mention of the name, but Rosalind missed it as Rhea pulled the needle away.

"Done," Rhea said, setting the needle aside. Rosalind twisted around in the chair, looking at her shoulder.

"That's it?" she asked, incredulous.

"For this session. I have the tree and the snake done. We can do the color next time."

"But it didn't hurt nearly as much," Rosalind said.

"You were distracted. You had help. It made the pain manageable. You still went through it." Rhea pulled off the rubber gloves. "I'm going to clean up. Sit still for a few minutes. Let your body calm down. The endorphins will start hitting you soon."

"Does this count as a special occasion?" Rosalind asked Taryn as soon as she saw Rhea's back vanish into the hallway. The candlelight was flickering oddly in front of her eyes, forming shapes of galloping horses and dancing women.

"You bet. You feel like celebrating?"

Rosalind crooked her finger, summoning Taryn closer. Taryn obligingly leaned in, tilting her head to the side. She found Rosalind's hand and rolled into the caress. "I'll tell you how I'm feeling. I want you to go home, put on your harness, and bring the toys over to my place," Rosalind purred into her ear.

"Thought you had office hours this afternoon," Taryn said with feigned detachment. The motion of Rosalind's hand was underscoring her request in the most convincing way.

"I'm about to come down with the flu. Care to join me?" Rosalind punctuated the question by biting Taryn's ear.

"I'm feeling it."

"That's my boy." Rosalind grinned. Her nerve endings were returning from the gulag they'd been exiled to and were starting to throw a coming-home party. The lines of fire Rhea had trailed across her skin kept up a banked heat, moving from pain to sensation. There was something interesting about how it felt, Rosalind thought, as the tide came in, lifting her up with it. It wasn't so bad now, like giving blood. A sting, then that floating feeling. Only there had been a thousand stings, and the floating was levitation. Taryn was right. This might be worth the experience after all. The background hum she'd just started to detect in the room sounded like bees waking up. She saw Taryn turn her head, and for a moment, there was a trail of blue fire left in the air, an afterimage.

Rhea clicked the electric lights back on. Jealous, Rosalind thought fuzzily, mentally sticking her tongue out at the older woman. Rhea looked right at her.

"Some. But that's to be expected," Rhea said, cleaning up her work area.

"What?" Taryn asked, standing up from her crouch.

Rosalind shook her head. You couldn't think too loudly around Rhea.

"Answering a question. It wasn't directed at you," Rhea said calmly. She set a patch of gauze on Rosalind's shoulder. "Leave this here for twenty-four hours. Taryn can teach you how to care for it. Are you ready to move?"

"Yes," Rosalind said, experimenting with standing up. It was a wonderful thing, the way her muscles responded to her thought, even if everything felt like it was in slow motion. She slid her arms back into her shirt. "Thank you, Rhea."

"You're welcome. I have to run. There's going to be company at the house tonight. I have to get more food and wine." Rhea picked her black shawl up off the counter.

"I didn't know we were expecting anyone," Taryn said.

"We're not. But someone is coming, and I expect him to get here late and in need. Taryn, you can lock up."

Rosalind walked up Elmwood Avenue toward the corner of Allen. The air had started to cool. It felt like water over her skin. October proved noticeably colder than September, hinting at the onslaught of winter. It amazed her that Taryn still walked around in a T-shirt, refusing to wear a jacket. *Too butch to feel the cold?* Rosalind thought, and snorted. *We'll see how tough she is the minute she gets sick.*

Rosalind had proposed a game. She would walk at a casual stroll up Elmwood to Allen, then down Allen to Mariner. Taryn had to go down Elmwood to Virginia, then up Mariner. If she made it to 34 Mariner, fetched the toys, and beat Rosalind home, she won. Taryn stood still on the porch of A Pound of Flesh, as if considering the offer. Rosalind expected Taryn to ask what the prize would be, but she didn't. One moment she was standing there, the next she was vaulting over the porch rail and tearing down the street like her boots were on fire.

"That's what I like about you, kid. Your enthusiasm," Rosalind called out after the vanishing Taryn.

Even at a reasonably paced stroll, Rosalind made it to the porch of 41 Mariner without any sign of Taryn. She sat down on the steps and waited. It didn't take long for the front door to 34 to slam open and for a figure to vault off the porch and dart across the street, a red nylon bag swinging from her fist. Taryn bounded up the steps, the flush to her cheeks from the crisp air, or the game.

"Beat you here," Rosalind said.

Taryn held up the bag like a string of fish supporting an alibi. "I had to find something to carry the toys in. I ended up stealing the bag Joe packs his sleeping bag in when he goes camping."

"Taryn, you didn't."

"He won't notice. When was the last time he went camping? So you won. What do you get?" Taryn asked with a disarming grin.

"You," Rosalind said. She held out her hand, and Taryn pulled her up.

The room Rosalind had chosen as the bedroom was on the second floor, with a set of bay windows overlooking the backyard garden. The light came in through the windows in the afternoon, making an inviting rectangle of heat on the bed. Taryn walked up the stairs, bolted toward the bedroom, and launched herself onto the bed. Rosalind mentally winced, hearing the protest of the springs under this attack. There was a can of WD-40 under the sink in the back bathroom. She made a note to treat the springs as soon as the weather was nice enough to leave the windows open. Taryn sat up, pulling her legs under her, and started to fight with the drawstring on the nylon bag. Rosalind sighed.

While Taryn was becoming more civilized through contact with her, some things didn't change. Taryn had started to pick the towels up off the bathroom floor after she showered, didn't stand quite as long in front of the refrigerator with the door open, and rarely smoked in the house. Rosalind had never said a word, but Taryn saw what Rosalind did and how Rosalind reacted to her. She was like an animal learning the new territory by experience. She rarely made the same mistakes twice, except for the quilt.

Rosalind's mother had made the quilt by hand as her going-away gift when she went to Ithaca to do her doctorate. It had been on every bed she'd slept in since, even at the foot of the bed she'd shared with her ex-husband Paul. She had never mentioned that to Taryn, but Taryn seemed to sense it, and reacted to the quilt like it was an enemy. During the night the quilt would find its way to the floor or be bunched into a corner of the bed by the seemingly innocent, sleeping girl. The rivalry between them extended to Taryn's refusal to remember to remove her boots before vaulting onto the bed.

It bothered Rosalind enough that she'd actually mentioned it, asking Taryn if she would take the boots off before jumping on the bed. Taryn would comply for a day, then forget completely. Rosalind reminded herself that this was a luxury, in a fashion, because of who wore the boots and her eagerness to spring into her bed. That didn't exactly work, though the part about Taryn's willingness to spring onto the bed was gratifying.

Taryn felt Rosalind's look and glanced up. She dropped the bag and looked at her feet, like a dog caught tipping over the garbage can. She ducked her head, muttered an apology, and unlaced the boots hastily. She tore them off her feet and tucked them under the bed. The sight made Rosalind laugh. Who would ever believe that a single glance from her would make Taryn react so quickly?

"What's so funny?" Taryn asked, fighting with the knot on the bag.

"Nothing. I just like you." Rosalind sat down next to Taryn on the bed. "You hate the quilt, don't you?"

"Uh, no, not…I mean it's…" Taryn said, shrugging.

"Stand up," Rosalind said. Taryn did, and Rosalind took the edge of the quilt in her hands and tore it away from the bed, sending pillows everywhere. She bunched it into a ball and tossed it into the closet. "No more quilt. Can I give you a hand with that knot?"

Taryn upended the bag, spilling the contents across the bed. There were toys of various sizes and hues, some realistic, some outlandish, a bottle of lube, a handful of condoms in silver foil wrappers scattered like coins in the pile of black leather straps and buckles. Rosalind picked up a condom and turned it, the metallic wrapper catching the light.

"Why? You don't exactly need one," she asked.

"Always a good idea if you want to play well with others. Besides, they're fun," Taryn said and grinned.

"Honey, I've had to use them since high school, and they were never fun," Rosalind said gently. She knew how Taryn could bristle at any mention of her sexual past, associating it primarily with her ex-husband. *Not too far off the mark,* Rosalind thought. *I never was much of an adventurer. I must be making up for it now.*

"No. Use them like that, and they suck. Use them with me, and they're fun." There was a gleam of challenge in Taryn's eye.

Rosalind decided that she must have looked skeptical, because Taryn snatched the condom back from her.

"I'll show you. I'll go get geared up and come back in." She took the pile of leather straps and a few condoms in her right hand, and stuffed most of the toys back into the bag.

"What should I do?" Rosalind asked.

"Take off all your clothes. Sit there and try not to think about anything," Taryn said as she ducked out the door.

Rosalind folded her hands in her lap. That was unfair, she thought. Get naked and not think of anything? Was there something snide in the way Taryn had said it, a glimpse of a smirk? Of course she could sit here and not think of anything. Foolish thing for the arrogant boy to ask. It wouldn't be more than a few minutes, anyway. How long did the harness take to put on? She'd seen Taryn wearing it but had never seen her put it on. Taryn liked the mystery of showing up already packing.

There had been that one night when they'd gone out to dinner with Rhea and Joe. Taryn had worn her gray suit, held the chair for her like a perfect gentleman. When Taryn sat down, Rosalind had put her hand in its accustomed spot on Taryn's thigh. Naturally her hand drifted during the course of the meal, lazily caressing the smooth gray fabric and the leg underneath. She'd been in the middle of a sentence, talking to Joe, when her hand wandered across Taryn's inner thigh. She stopped dead. Rosalind knew that particular spot like the back of her own hand. This was new. She faltered, fishing for the end of her sentence, while her hand identified the shape through the trousers.

"Uh …well…" she'd said in response to Joe's question about her class.

"Yes?" Joe asked, trying not to smile.

Taryn had shifted in the chair, giving Rosalind's hand more territory to explore. Taryn's smile was all innocence, her arm casually resting on the back of Rosalind's chair. Mercifully, the waiter came around with coffee, saving Rosalind from having to form a complete sentence. Taryn was beaming at Joe. Rosalind promised herself that Taryn was in for it later. And she had been.

How long did it take to put on the harness? It had to have been a few minutes already. It couldn't be all that difficult to manage. It looked rather like a bridle when it had tumbled out of the bag, a mass of straps and buckles. Reminded her, in fact, of summer camp when she was fourteen.

She'd had to tack a horse for the first time. Rosalind had been able, through determination and luck, to avoid actually getting on a horse up till then. The truth of the matter was the things scared her.

They were far too large for her to believe that a slip of metal in the mouth would do more than annoy them. Her instructor had handed her a shapeless mass of leather straps and told her to put it on the horse's head.

This posed a problem. Rosalind was a good deal smaller than the horse, and from the way it kept rolling its eyes at her and laying its ears back, it wasn't about to cooperate. It wasn't like a dog. You couldn't just tell it to sit. How did you reason with a ton of flesh? She tried grabbing at its head, but the horse just tossed it up and snorted, sending her skittering a few steps back. It wasn't like Black Beauty at all, or the Black Stallion, where riders had a mystic communication with their noble steeds. She was lucky the damned thing didn't step on her.

Okay, thinking about nothing wasn't working.

Rosalind was an adult. She could acknowledge that. Taryn was probably out in the hall, having a good laugh about it, knowing how her mind worked. What was taking Taryn so long, anyway? You'd think she'd have this down to a science. It couldn't take this long. She just had to put on waist straps, and leg straps…did she leave them buckled, and step into it, or adjust it after it was on?

This thought led quite naturally to picturing Taryn stepping out of her jeans and stepping into the harness. Rosalind pictured Taryn's hands pulling the strap tight against the muscle of her thigh with the economy of long practice. She imagined Taryn selecting a toy from the bag, considering it, weighing it in her palm, then shaking her head. The right one would make her grin that feral smile she had when she was pleased with herself. Taryn would hold the steel ring in her left hand and slide the toy in with her right, not even needing to look. One smooth motion. Her hand would drift back, adjusting it so that it hung just right…Rosalind glanced around the room and wondered if she should invest in a ceiling fan. It was warm for October.

A suspicious thought crept into Rosalind's brain. It was all part of the game. Taryn was taking so long just to play with her, to get her to imagine everything that she was imagining. Part of the big seduction routine. Well, it wouldn't work. She could think about other things. She was an extremely well-read person.

It didn't help that her skin was reacting to the tattoo, sending very specific messages to her brain. But wasn't that always the way,

Rosalind thought. The flesh warred with the intellect. She had years and years invested in the intellect's side of the battle. It was almost unfair. After all, what hold did the flesh have on her? A few weeks of passion and madness, balanced against a lifetime of...well, not restraint. There was no reason to restrain herself. She'd never felt anything that overwhelmed her senses, flooded her mind, made sitting still impossible. Not until that night in the bar, when Ellie had hauled her in to see a drag show...The lights had gone down. Out of the darkness came that slim, broad-shouldered form in the jet-black suit.

Rosalind crossed her legs and looked at the clock. She could think about work. Next week she was wrapping up *King Lear* and starting her students on *Romeo and Juliet*. That didn't help at all. There were fireworks going off all over her skin, slamming bolts of energy from brain to groin and back again. Rosalind shut her eyes, took a deep breath in, held it, then exhaled slowly. *I can do this,* she thought. *Just because my blood is currently being microwaved doesn't mean a thing. It's just like yoga class. Clear your mind. Let any thought that drifts across the mind go. Become One with the Universe.* But dammit, it wasn't the Universe she wanted to become One with. The sound of wood creaking snapped her eyes back open.

Rosalind took another deep breath, but not out of serenity. *Does she have to look like that?* she thought helplessly.

Taryn was leaning against the door frame, arms folded across her chest. There was the barest hint of a smirk on her lips, infuriating and enticing. Her eyes were smoldering, dangerous. Taryn unfolded her arms slowly and hooked her thumbs in the pockets of her jeans, drawing Rosalind's eyes down. There, where her hands rested against the curve of muscle in her thigh, was a suspicious bulge in her jeans.

The long fingers were relaxed, slightly curled, framing the patch of denim that took on a great interest for Rosalind. Taryn's hand moved closer to the inside of her thigh. Even with her penchant for wearing her jeans low and loose, it was evident that she was packing. *She hangs to the right*, Rosalind thought, the incongruity of it not stopping her pulse from speeding up. She watched Taryn's hand cup the bulge suggestively. Rosalind glanced up into her face. Taryn knew that she was being bad and that it was working.

"Come over here and kiss me," Taryn demanded, the corner of her mouth quirking up.

Rosalind got off the bed and walked very slowly toward her lover. She could feel the connection between them spark to life. The look her boy was giving her was only a part of it. She knew that they were playing, but if she asked for anything, she would have it. Taryn shifted her weight, pushing her hips forward.

The denim stretched over the bulge in her crotch, presenting it for Rosalind's inspection. It was the knowledge of what was coming that was making it hard to restrain herself, Rosalind thought. The way Taryn wore the toy was an announcement of intent, pure, sexual, and explicit. Taryn had put it on for her, at her suggestion. The power she had in the moment burned through Rosalind.

She hooked an arm around Taryn's neck and leaned up to kiss her, her lips parting automatically. She felt herself open to Taryn, her body, her heart, reaching out to draw her in. The brief shock of their lips meeting was the shock of how much separation from Taryn hurt and how much pleasure there was in rejoining. She could never get close enough to Taryn. The agony that they were just meeting, that they had been apart so many years, was eased by the welcome Rosalind felt from Taryn's body.

Taryn kept her relaxed slouch against the door frame, minimizing the difference in their heights. Taryn held Rosalind's waist in her hands, keeping a small distance between their bodies. Only their lips met, in a kiss that made Rosalind forget that she was standing up. She pressed against Taryn's hands, seeking to move into her arms, but was held back. It was clear that Taryn wanted the kiss to be their only contact. It was more than a little frustrating, but Rosalind decided to play along and focused her attention on the kiss.

There are kisses that communicate desire, kisses that are born in hunger of the flesh, ones that offer up the soul like a sacrifice. That kiss was the dance of the soul in ecstasy, the breaking down of barriers, the primal force of obliteration of distance between the self and the beloved. In that kiss Rosalind became one with the object of her desire, lost all distinction of herself as separate. She felt her blood running in Taryn's veins. It was enough to make her believe, all over again, in the existence of the divine.

In that moment, in the heightened state, Rosalind quickly learned why Taryn was moving so slowly. The tattoo had slapped all her nerve endings awake. Now even the bliss of drowning in her love for Taryn was interrupted with pangs of insistent desire. Her body wasn't about to be ignored. The lazy trailing of her lover's tongue through her mouth went from heavenly to maddening. Rosalind was torn. The kiss could go on for hours, from the way Taryn set the pace, and while that was good, it was no longer enough. Rosalind pressed against Taryn's hands with her hips and felt the resistance give, felt herself be drawn into her familiar place against Taryn's body. It was amazing how much better it felt having Taryn's arm close around her, completing the circle. Rosalind sighed and went back to the kiss.

Their hips were level. It took only a moment to connect thought to action. She slid her hand over Taryn's ass, pulling them together. She was nestled up against the toy. Rosalind experimented with pressing forward, then easing back, her hands finding purchase on her hips.

Taryn kept her stance. Rosalind took this as an invitation to explore. She moved her hand up to Taryn's hip, fondling the straps of the harness through her clothing. Rosalind's hand moved to the top of Taryn's jeans, then to her fly. When she lay her palm against the crotch, Taryn sighed. Rosalind stroked the toy, and Taryn moaned against her open mouth. This was Rosalind's dance.

"I want to see you wearing it," Rosalind said, not recognizing her own voice.

"Go ahead," Taryn said, her voice betraying her uneven breathing.

Rosalind undid the buttons on Taryn's fly, one by one. The part of her brain that watched the movie of her life extended congratulations all around and had a cigarette.

Taryn's jeans were down around her knees; her boxers quickly followed. Rosalind hadn't forgotten how long it had taken, at first, to get Taryn out of her boxers. It was still a triumph, how willing Taryn was to shed them. It spoke of the trust between them, the faith Taryn had in her as a lover and a friend.

The harness was stark, achingly black against Taryn's pale skin. The tattoo of the yin-yang was framed by the waist and leg straps. Rosalind ran a finger across it and watched Taryn's hip tremble. The boxers caught on the toy, and she had to reach in and free it. Rosalind's hand closed over it, feeling the warmth from its resting place against Taryn's thigh. It was a shock, that warmth, from the latex in her hand. She caressed it as Taryn leaned her head back against the wall. Taryn closed her eyes, rolling her head to the side. Rosalind was getting acquainted with her new friend.

Taryn leaned sideways, one long arm groping for her jeans. She managed to snag them with two fingers and reach into her pocket. She straightened back up, managing not to interrupt Rosalind's exploration. Taryn lifted the packet to her teeth and ripped the foil open. "Here. Put this on," Taryn said, handing the packet to Rosalind.

Rosalind took the packet in her left hand, glancing at it.

"It's an act of sweet imagination," Taryn said and kissed her.

That kiss brought Rosalind's soul to her mouth, seeking to rejoin its other half in the body of her youthful lover. It was that easy, and that profound. Rosalind surrendered to it, let down the barrier between the sacred and the profane. There were no boundaries she wouldn't cross for this girl, especially not when she leapt to the top of them and held out her hand.

The toy was a piece of latex, held in place with a steel ring and leather straps. It was also a part of the girl she loved, who wore it for her pleasure. Rosalind rolled the condom down the length of the toy with her left hand, her right hand spread against Taryn's hip. It was the blatant declaration of what was coming, and it surprised Rosalind how much she enjoyed it. It was like claiming the space, announcing her desire. She felt the coursing of power along her veins. She was doing something simply for her own pleasure, not because it made any sense. It made her feel light-headed.

When Taryn lifted her up and carried her to the bed, she tripped on her jeans, nearly falling. They landed with little grace. Taryn laughed. "That was suave," she said, kicking the jeans away.

Rosalind felt a bolt of love go through her, out from her heart. There was room in their passion for this, for laughter, for awkward moments without fear. It nearly made her cry. "If you don't get over here right now, I think I'll die," Rosalind said.

Taryn's head turned, her breath caught. She climbed over to her lover, covering her. Rosalind wrapped her arms around Taryn's back, slid her heels down Taryn's thighs. They started kissing again; the flare of nerve endings blossomed out from the tattoo on Rosalind's shoulder, involving all her skin.

"I need you inside me. Please, baby," Rosalind said, her nails digging into Taryn's back.

Taryn groaned. Rosalind felt her hips move, felt the toy slide against her thigh. She felt Taryn's hand snake down and guide it. Her head arched back against the pillow. It was exquisite, it was agony, and if Taryn ever stopped, she would kill her. Rosalind felt her hands sliding off Taryn's moving hips and grabbed for the harness. That was better. It allowed her to communicate through pulling. Words were beyond her right now. Her hands held the straps in a death grip, urging her on.

The toy was slipping in its ring, guided by the splendid twist of Taryn's hips. She felt something in her heart crack and leak gold like Vulcan's forge. Taryn was yelling. Rosalind might have screamed something. She wasn't sure.

They came to rest, Taryn sprawled on her, one arm around her back, drawing her close. Rosalind kissed the side of Taryn's sweaty neck. "God loves me." Rosalind's voice took on a drunk meandering, leaving words soft and unfinished, blurring into one another. The feeling expanded out from her skin, filling the room. At that moment, she loved all the world.

"I love everything," Rosalind added.

"You must get tired," Taryn murmured, her face halfway into the pillow.

"Don't you see? Everything is gorgeous. You are gorgeous." She hugged Taryn fiercely, then kissed her neck again.

"I love you, and I say this from love. You should get tattooed more often," Taryn said, rolling off onto the mattress with a sigh.

"I should spend my life in bed with you."

"I'm ready."

"Do you have any idea how good you make me feel?"

Taryn reached out and brushed her fingers over Rosalind's breast. "Yeah. You always let me know. I feel like a rock next to you. You express everything so easily."

Rosalind laughed. "You have no idea. I haven't always been the debauched dilettante you see before you, lost in a pleasure haze. My whole life, I was not what you'd call expressive. More Mother Teresa than Susie Sexpert."

Taryn snorted.

"What was that?"

"I don't buy the goody-two-shoes crap. You've been waiting to be a troublemaker."

"Baby, I have a confession to make." Rosalind's voice got very serious. Her face lost its drunken look. Taryn froze.

"What?"

Rosalind dropped her eyes, then raised her chin. "This is hard for me to say." She knew she was playing havoc with Taryn, from the set expression on Taryn's face.

"You can tell me anything. You know that."

"It won't change your opinion of me?"

"Not even death will change my opinion of you. You're the best person I know."

Rosalind's head tilted to the side, her smile tender and distracted by Taryn's response. "I was kicked out of the Girl Scouts," she finally said.

Taryn was silent for three full heartbeats. "That's it? That's the big secret?"

"Aren't you going to ask me why?"

"Okay. Why?"

"For eating a Brownie," Rosalind said solemnly.

Taryn moved like a cat hit with a water gun. She snatched the pillow out from under Rosalind's head and hit her with it squarely on the stomach.

"Hey! Brute," Rosalind yelled, curling away from the attack.

"Liar." Taryn aimed a shot at her lover as Rosalind rolled to the edge of the bed.

"Republican," Rosalind said, ready to vault off the bed.

Taryn's hand froze midswing. "That's low."

"Sorry, baby. Truce?" Rosalind managed to make her eyes as big around as she could, and even batted them. It worked. Taryn dropped the pillow immediately. Rosalind wondered if Taryn knew how easy she was, but thought it best not to tell her. She crawled back up onto the bed, up the length of her body, and settled herself against Taryn's chest.

"I love you, you know?" she asked softly.

"I know," Taryn said. "You're lucky you're all cute. You deserve a pillow thrashing." Taryn exhaled heavily, shaking her head.

"I'm lucky it's against the butch code of honor."

"Chapter three, page twenty-six. Right after rescuing kittens from trees and helping ladies across the street," Taryn said.

"Did you get a lesbian starter kit, too?" Rosalind asked, drawing her fingers along Taryn's collarbone.

"Nah. Butches are expected to rough it for a few years before they mail you your copy of the code of honor."

"Funny. You'd think lesbians thrived on oral history."

The phone on the nightstand rang, making Rosalind jump. She reached for it, but felt Taryn's arms hold her back. "Fuck 'em. Let it ring," Taryn said, pulling Rosalind back down.

The phone rang again. Rosalind looked at it. "It might be Ellie. I told her to call if any of my students showed up for office hours with a real problem."

"Remember the last time you got up out of bed with me to answer the phone? You stayed on for half an hour," Taryn said, her eyes narrowing.

"I just feel so bad for those poor telemarketers. She was going along with her spiel. I couldn't interrupt."

The phone rang again. She gave Taryn the sad look.

"Fine! I'll answer it. I'm not afraid to tell people to go to hell." Taryn reached for the phone. "Hello," she said, her voice as low and grim as she could make it.

Rosalind giggled into Taryn's shoulder. From here, she could hear the bewildered man's voice come over the line. "Um, hello? Hi. Is this Rosalind Ben—I mean, Olchawski's address?"

"What do you want?" Taryn said, her tone flat.

"I want to speak with Rosalind." There was something stubborn and familiar about the voice, but Taryn shifted away so Rosalind had trouble hearing.

"You can speak with me. I'm her husband," Taryn said and grinned at Rosalind.

There was a moment of shocked silence while Taryn held the

receiver. She looked down at the phone, then extended it to Rosalind. "He says he's your husband, too."

Rosalind sat up and took the phone. "Paul?" she asked, her voice calmer than she felt.

Taryn reacted immediately. She rolled off the bed at the mention of his name and grabbed her boots. She was down the hall before Rosalind could speak.

"Ros? Is that actually you?" It was Paul's voice.

"Yes, it's me," she said, listening for the sound of the front door slamming open. So far, Taryn hadn't fled the house.

"Who the hell was that answering your phone? You're not remarried, are you?" Paul asked. It brought Rosalind's divided attention back to the phone in her hand.

"No, I'm not remarried," she said, wanting to put the phone down, wanting to go see if the silence downstairs meant Taryn was waiting for her.

"I called your office at work. The voicemail left this number," Paul said.

"Paul, why in the world are you calling me?" Rosalind asked. She heard the front door open.

"I need to talk to you, Ros."

"Now is not a good time," Rosalind said. Boots clomped down the steps. Taryn was gone.

"We haven't spoken in months. What kind of welcome is this? I know things didn't work out with us, but I thought we were still friends, Ros." He sounded hurt. Rosalind recognized that tone. It brought her frustration level down. She took a deep breath and tried to sound more available.

"We are. But I haven't heard from you in months, and you caught me at a bad time. Why don't we make an appointment to talk?"

"I'll be in Buffalo tomorrow night. I need to see you," he said immediately.

"In Buffalo?" Rosalind repeated, hating how stupid it made her sound. What in the world was he doing in western New York?

"In Buffalo. Have dinner with me. I can meet you at your office at six. Your voicemail said you don't have a class tomorrow night. All right?" Paul asked.

"All right," Rosalind said.

"Great! I can't wait to see you." He hung up, and Rosalind dropped the phone back into its hook.

She dressed quickly and ran across the street, her mind full of shards of glass. If Taryn reacted like this to Paul calling her, how would she take the news that he was coming to town?

CHAPTER TWO

Rosalind jogged up the steps to 34 Mariner, listening for telltale sounds. If the stereo was blasting from the second-floor windows, Taryn would be up punching the heavy bag. That would be a bad sign, but not the worst. If her anger was still energetic, Rosalind knew she was more prone to talking about it. It was when Taryn's anger cooled and hardened that she became impossible, as sulky as Achilles in his tent. If, however, Patsy Cline or Melissa Etheridge was leaking out of the third-floor windows, Rosalind knew she would find Taryn sitting on the floor, her back to the wall, next to the stereo. That was bad. Her brooding spot and her brooding music. Rosalind wondered if there was some indicator of a still darker mood, music she had yet to hear, actions she had yet to see. The thought of it chilled her like a wind off the lake.

Music was playing, but it was coming from the first floor, from the back of the house. Rosalind lifted her head, puzzled. What in the world was this racket? She walked down the hall to the kitchen and caught sight of Joe. He had his back to the door and hadn't heard her with the noise from the radio. He plucked a skillet from the wooden dish drain and tossed it end over end, catching it deftly. He threw back his head and bellowed something unintelligible in a very bad English accent. Rosalind walked very carefully to his right, entering his line of sight out of range of the juggling skillet. He saw her and promptly fumbled. He dropped the skillet into the sink and reached for the radio.

"Jesus, Ros, you scared the hell out of me. You interrupted my impression of Sid Vicious doing 'My Way.' Think T would put me onstage for her show?" he asked, grinning.

The warmth of his smile, the way the skin crinkled at the corners of his brown eyes extended his unfettered welcome. He looked at her face, his smile fading as he read her mood. "But that's not what you came here for. What's up?"

"Joe, is Taryn upstairs?" Rosalind asked.

Joe shook his head. "I thought she was with you. She left me some half-assed note about my camping gear," he said, looking more closely at her. "Uh-oh. You and T had a fight."

"How can you tell?" Rosalind asked, relieved that it was Joe she'd encountered. She didn't think she was feeling up to seeing Rhea right now, even with how well they'd been getting along. There was a warmth to Joe that she badly needed right now. It nearly made her cry how easily he assessed her mood.

"'Cause you look like you just lost your best friend. Sit down. I'll make the coffee. Start at the beginning."

"She's not here? She just ran out of my house, not ten minutes ago."

"Nah, I've been here. I just put the music on, so I don't think I missed her. Taryn in a bad mood is not a subtle thing," Joe said wryly.

"Where would she go?" Rosalind asked.

"Maybe to Spot, maybe to the Towne, maybe up Elmwood. I know she's got rehearsal tonight, but beyond that, your guess is as good as mine." Joe set the kettle on the flame.

"Shit," Rosalind said, sinking into a chair. "I really need to talk to her."

"You want some unsolicited advice?" Joe asked, reaching for the blue glass mug. The mug was Taryn's and she was very territorial about it, but after she'd declared to the world that Rosalind was her girl, the household automatically put it out for Rosalind when she came by.

"Whatever advice you have would be much appreciated," Rosalind said, and meant it.

"If T doesn't want to be found, you won't find her. She doesn't do this often, but I've seen her do it when she and Rhea used to fight. Taryn will take off for a few hours and cool off. She's just being a punk. She'll come around again by morning."

"Morning?" Rosalind said, tears starting to spill. She couldn't bear the thought of not talking to her lover before morning.

"Aw, hey, Ros. Don't listen to me. That was when she was fighting with Rhea. I'm sure she'll come around a lot faster with you. She can't live without you," Joe said, crouching down by the chair and handing her a dish towel.

Rosalind dabbed at her eyes with the towel. "Thanks. It's just… we left things badly. I wanted to see her and make sure she's okay."

"Tell me what happened. Don't worry about shocking me. I'm the parent of a teenager," Joe said solemnly.

"Well, we were…in bed. Just talking, but…" Rosalind hesitated. Joe waved her on.

"I can fill in the rest. What happened?"

"My ex-husband called."

"Oy." Joe stood up and went to the stove.

"I was on the phone with him for a minute, but Taryn grabbed her boots and took off. I thought she'd be here. I have to head out to school. I have a class at six," Rosalind said, twisting the dish towel in her hands. Joe walked over to her and gently took the towel away, replacing it with the blue glass mug.

"Hang out here for a minute and drink your coffee. If she comes in when you're at school, I'll have her call your office. Okay?"

"Have her call me the second she comes in. Tell her I need to talk to her. Tell her…"

"I'll tell her you love her. And I'll armlock the little punk until she calls you."

Rosalind sat at her desk and cradled her head in her hands. It was a bad day. There was no getting around that, no matter how brave a face she put on it. Class had been bearable. She'd been able to slip into teaching mode and leave her emotional turmoil at the door. Time had obligingly stood still until class was done. But as soon as the last student left, as soon as she was alone in her office, the emotion came back with a vengeance.

Rosalind put the phone down. She'd checked her voicemail half a dozen times. Joe hadn't called, and Taryn hadn't called. That meant she hadn't come home yet. It was getting late. Had she gone directly to rehearsal? This was ridiculous. Taryn's moody departure was ruining her whole evening. "This is why you never date someone thirteen years your junior," she said to the picture of herself in Renaissance Festival garb. "Because they insist on acting like it."

She felt herself reach for the phone and halted the movement. "Have to get her an e-mail account. Then I can waste time futilely checking another electronic source for no messages," Rosalind mumbled.

Taryn would come around. If she wanted to be alone, Rosalind could grant her that space. She wasn't possessive, or clingy—oh, she knew the contempt with which Taryn spoke the word *clingy*. Like there were few sins greater than that evidence of dependence. Rosalind felt a flush of embarrassment. She was acting like a teenager herself. She could be cool, show Taryn how easy it was to let her go brood for the night. More than likely she'd show up before morning.

Her hand was dialing before she realized it.

"Joe? Ros. Yeah. Has she—? No? Okay. I'll be here for another forty-five minutes or so, finishing up a few things. Yes, please do. Thanks."

Rosalind hung the phone back up and gazed mournfully at her desk. There had to be something to distract herself with. Grading papers—no, too much effort. Shakespeare—too close to home.

"Dammit! Shutting me out is not an effective means of communication."

The door to her office opened. Rosalind all but jumped out of her chair. Ellie poked her head in, the light from the hallway turning her hair into a helmet of gold, chased with silver. The high collar of her black shirt gave her a severe look, reminding Rosalind incongruously of a priest.

"Saw your light on. What are you doing?" she asked, taking the chair opposite Rosalind's desk.

"Torturing myself."

"Oh, sounded like you were talking to someone. You don't exactly look like your normally cheerful self."

"I'm not," Rosalind said, feeling a weariness settle on her.

Ellie held up her hand. "If you're fighting with lovergirl, don't tell me. You two need to be my romantic role models right now. I can't bear for you to fight."

"Why now?" Rosalind asked, intrigued. It was good to be drawn out of herself. Ellie was excellent at that.

"I broke up with Bill," Ellie said in a voice fit for a funeral oration.

"Ellie! Why?" Ellie had been dating Bill for months. They seemed to get along well and had never fought, to her knowledge.

Ellie looked at her, askance. "It's all your fault."

"Mine? Goodness. Have I led you on?"

"Nope. You went ahead and fell in love for real, right in front of me. Now, I'm a sensitive person, given to fits of grand emotion. What in the world am I supposed to do with a romantic example like you and Elvis parading right in front of me?" Ellie said, the words more serious than the tone she used to carry them.

"I thought you liked Bill," Rosalind said carefully.

"Exactly," Ellie said, flinging her hands up.

"I'm not sure I follow your logic."

"I liked him. We got on well. We had some fun. But he never looked at me like Taryn looks at you. And I never felt like looking at him like you look at her." Ellie finished with a sigh, sinking into the chair.

"Oh, Ellie." Rosalind knew the look Ellie meant, remembered the first time she'd seen it, from the stage at the auction. The naked look that offered her the world. For all her defenses, there were times when Taryn was so raw in her emotion, she was unable to mask it.

"Don't you sound sad on me. I made a bold step into the brave new world of dateless bitches. The least you can do is cheer me on. What's on your plate tonight? Let me guess. Brooding, sighing, reading depressing poetry, waiting for the phone to ring…" Ellie's voice trailed off into a sublime silence, tinged with self-pity.

"That sums it up."

"Come to rehearsal with me. You and lovergirl can work out whatever tiff you're having. Fire and floods wouldn't keep her away from rehearsal. You really should see her work. It's astounding. Has she talked about rehearsals yet?" Ellie sat up in the chair.

"She's been very closed mouthed about the whole thing. I was thinking of asking her if I could crash one just to see what's going on."

"Perfect. I'll sneak you in the back. You can watch for a while. The boys are working tonight. You'll love it. They hang on T's every word, follow her around like a pack."

"You're calling her T now?" Rosalind asked, surprised.

"Picked it up from the show. They're all T's boys now," Ellie said, grinning.

Urban space likes to be recycled. It prevents the loneliness of abandoned buildings. It confirms the material world's belief in reincarnation. Nothing is ever wasted; it is simply reborn as a new thing.

At the corner of Main Street and Halbert there was a sprawling angled building that had once been a hairpin factory. Inside, it was carved up into rental space for small businesses and nonprofit organizations. On the fourth floor of the old hairpin factory, the echoingly empty space had been transformed. Plaster walls had been thrown up, lighting added, space divided and reused.

Like all good arts organizations, ArtSpace was perpetually underfunded, undermanned, overstressed, on the brink of extinction, and surviving with sheer stubbornness. This particular brand of stubbornness had lasted for twenty years, garnering a reputation for excellence. ArtSpace now boasted a gallery, a film and video theater, and exhibition and performance space.

Rosalind liked to think that she was a fairly well-rounded individual. She adored theater, had a fondness for painting and photography, a passing brush with dance, a smattering of music. Something about going to ArtSpace still intimidated her. Perhaps it was the air of insider cool she imagined, the understanding of modern art that all the black-turtleneck-wearing crowd seemed to have. She pictured Ellie sailing in the door in her usual somber finery, greeted by crowds of pale, wan men and consumptive women, all gazing in deep reflection at empty frames—the final ironic comment on materialism and culture. Rosalind was afraid she just wasn't hip enough. She voiced some of this to Ellie as they climbed the stairs to the freight elevator.

"Oh, sweetie. You are way hip enough. It's just art. It doesn't bite back. We'll have to wade through an art opening in the gallery before we get to the theater, but just follow my lead. Walk up to a painting, look deeply at it, grunt, and grab a glass of wine. Everyone will leave you alone," Ellie said as the doors to the freight elevator opened on the fourth floor.

Rosalind looked down at what she was wearing. "Ellie, I look like a teacher. I can't go in there."

"You look great," Ellie said over her shoulder.

"I'm wearing color. I'm going to stand out like neon," Rosalind said. Green. What had possessed her to wear green? She couldn't look less like an undertaker if she tried.

"Neon's very hip." Ellie was halfway down the hall.

"If every other person in there is wearing black, I'm turning right back around."

The double doors were thrown open to the waxed concrete hallway. Loud conversation was fighting with a single piano being played indifferently. Ellie breezed through the doors, a queen reentering her demesne. Rosalind took a deep breath and followed her. The crowd wasn't what she'd expected. True, the women were all in black, but it was black eveningwear. The men were all in suits and ties, balancing tiny paper plates loaded with cut vegetables and exotic cookies. Everyone had plastic cups of wine.

Ellie moved with perfect confidence right up the center of the room, between the bar and the gallery. The crowd gave way. Rosalind followed. She glanced off to the left and saw a young woman dressed as Ellie was, in a high-collared black shirt over a pair of jeans. Her dark hair was pulled back in a braid. She was listening to a woman in a black dress and a man in a gray suit speak, one into each ear. The man pointed to one of the paintings. She nodded, bemused.

Rosalind risked a look at one of the paintings. It was recognizable. A young man seen from the back with what looked like an ax resting on his shoulder. Ellie was at a door, under a sign that read Black & Blue. "We'll sneak in and sit in the back," Ellie whispered.

The house was dark. Ellie took Rosalind's hand and crept to the back. They picked the end seats in the last row, in front of the tech booth. The lights were bright on the stage. Rosalind saw a splinter of light from a half dozen rings as Linda Alejandros gestured. She was facing four young women who stood in a half circle around her. Rosalind searched automatically for Taryn, but her lover wasn't onstage. Rosalind recognized the tall, handsome black girl as Roberta, Laurel's new girlfriend. The others were unfamiliar, but they looked very young to her.

"Good! But get into character while you are finding your walk. It's more than just strutting, Wolf. What are you telling the audience with your walk?" The director pointed to a girl who stood with her arms folded over her chest.

Her hair glowed a deep purple in the stage light, like the blood of an anemone. She wore multiple earrings in each ear and three chains around her neck. A flannel shirt was tied low around her hips; her jeans sagged over unlaced work boots. "That I know how to fuck?" she said, deadpan. She rolled her eyes to the girl standing next to her.

Linda looked her over with exaggerated care. "Do you have a problem with the exercise?"

"This is bullshit. We're supposed to be doing drag, not walking in circles. When do we get to put on beards and shit?" Wolf said.

"Your strongest instrument onstage is your body. Not your costume. Taryn?" Linda asked.

Rosalind felt her pulse speed up. Taryn appeared out of the front row, folding herself out of the darkness. Taryn stood next to Linda, weight on one hip, hands in her pockets. Rosalind saw the others quicken when Taryn stepped onstage, standing up a little straighter. Even Wolf unfolded her arms.

"Would you walk for us?" Linda asked politely. "Like you know how to fuck," she added, looking at Wolf.

Taryn nodded. She took her hands out of her pockets and centered her weight over her hips, then started strolling. The stage was suddenly smaller. She ate it up with her stride. Her shoulders were tight, controlled. Her hands fell naturally to her sides. It was confidence made flesh. Quiet, controlled, majestic. Every movement was eloquent of restraint, of coiled strength, a paring down of motion into a shorthand. It made Rosalind think of the afternoon, of the harness, of holding back just enough to drive the watcher mad. Taryn walked like there was a promise of something more, if you could pierce her shell.

Her head was up. Her eyes swept the space in front of her,

claiming it before she moved into it. Her hips retained just a hint of fluidity. When her path came close to one of the girls, the girl stepped back automatically.

"There. You see how Sam stepped back even though Taryn didn't touch her? T was convinced that the space was hers, and she convinced Sam. T doesn't walk like that all the time. It's a choice, an exaggeration of certain qualities. You want to pick what type of masculinity you want to project," Linda said.

Taryn came to rest, hands in her pockets, gazing mildly at Wolf. "Try it," Taryn said quietly.

Wolf's head went back, either an aborted nod or a response to a challenge. She pushed Sam out of the way with a sweep of her arm and started walking. Linda glanced at Taryn, then took a step back. Taryn watched Wolf cross the stage, her eyes narrowed. When Wolf turned around, Taryn walked over to her. "You been downtown when the Sabres win?" Taryn asked her.

"Yeah," Wolf said.

"Walk like a guy from South Buffalo when the Sabres just won."

"Do I have to wear those stupid stripy pants?" Wolf asked.

Taryn looked at her steadily until she started walking. Taryn paced alongside her.

"You just got off work at the Ford plant. You got a six-pack of Molson and drank it in the parking lot with your buddies. You had Sabres tickets. The Dominator was hot tonight. The Sabres won, man! Nothing else matters. Not your fight with your girlfriend, not the bills you can't make. Right now, you're the king of the world, like that jerk who made that chick film your little sister cries over." As Taryn spoke, she slowed her pace down. Wolf matched her stride, adding a swagger, rolling her shoulders, leading with her upper body. "That's it. You're not angry. You're not scared. You own the whole goddamn world."

Rosalind watched, amazed, as the purple-haired girl began to disappear. The arrogance began to pare down. Her elbows relaxed. Her stride came more from her thighs. Wolf started to roll in her step, just a little, like a guy who'd had a few beers. Taryn continued to walk next to her as she found the character. When they reached the edge of the stage Wolf stopped and grinned at Taryn. "Better, right?"

Taryn shrugged. "A little. Sam! Come over here." The girl Taryn called was not much over five feet tall, and heavy. She wore her hair cut short on the back and sides, longer on the top. It was a rich brown, and curled over her forehead like grapes spilling over an arbor. She smiled when Taryn spoke to her, a smile of embarrassment and pleasure that took over her whole face. She wore a man's shirt, buttoned to the collar, that hung off her shoulders and stretched across her breasts. She walked across the stage hesitantly, shoulders hunched in.

"You try it. Same thing. Guy from South Buffalo," Taryn said more gently.

"I'm not sure," Sam said, but Taryn's hand on her shoulder halted her.

"Just walk. Don't think about it beforehand. Get into it. Then find the guy, make him part of you."

Sam took a deep breath and started walking. Her head was down, watching her feet. Taryn walked alongside her, hands in her pockets, shoulders back. Sam glanced up at Taryn, then adjusted her posture to match. She shifted her shoulders back with effort and raised her chin. Taryn smiled at her, a quick flash of a grin, just as soon gone. Her face went back to a cool, neutral look.

"Good. Don't be afraid to take up space. Guys use much more space than they need, and they never apologize for it. Make eye contact with me. Good. Wait for me to flinch away first. Don't smile. A smile is an apology. It's a girl thing. Just keep a straight face. Good." Taryn stopped walking. "You're getting it. Robbie, you next."

Robbie stepped forward and walked without hesitation, a cool, rolling walk, with a glance to the side to acknowledge that everyone was watching.

"Look at that. She already knows that she's the hottest thing to ever hit the stage. She's got the presence, and she's working it," Ellie whispered in Rosalind's ear.

It seemed so to her. The absolute confidence of the handsome girl was striking, similar to Taryn's. Robbie turned at the end of her walk and flashed a mile of white teeth at the house.

"She'll have the audience howling," Ellie said.

"Get off the stage, you dog," Taryn said, shoving Robbie in the back. "Grace, try it out."

The last girl caught Taryn's signal and started her walk. She wore her red-brown hair in a ponytail, exposing the delicate bones of her face. Her stride was confident and quick, but she held her arms tight to her sides, her shoulders stiff. Taryn shook her head. "Loosen your arms. Let your elbows fall out a bit. Good. You're getting it."

When Grace came to rest, Taryn turned to Linda. "Can I suggest something?" she asked.

The director smiled. "Go right ahead. They're already miles better than five minutes ago."

"You're getting bits and pieces down, but it isn't all coming together. Know what we need?" Taryn asked, addressing the group.

Wolf shrugged and looked over at Robbie, who looked at Sam. Taryn smiled, turning on the charm. "A night out with the boys. We'll get geared up, and I'll show you what it's like to walk the walk."

"You mean do drag in public?" Sam asked, fear and interest fighting in her voice.

"Yeah. Just like you wanted, Wolf. Passing drag. Come over to my place at seven tomorrow. We can get ready together. Cool?" Taryn said.

"You sure you don't have to call your girl and ask her permission to go out for a night?" Wolf said, her grin taking the edge from her words.

"Hey, if I had a woman like T has at home waiting for me, I'd be asking all kinds of permission," Robbie said evenly.

Taryn's face went cold. Wolf glanced at her in the silence that followed Robbie's words. There was a glimmer of real anger in Taryn's eyes. Rosalind could read it from the back of the house. Then Taryn smiled and it passed, pushed away under her public persona. "I don't ask for permission," she said, her tone flat. Taryn waited for three heartbeats, letting Wolf shift uncomfortably before she added, "I beg for it."

"You all have a lot to learn about women. Well, maybe not you… Go on. Rehearsal's over. Run for your lives," Linda said, waving them out.

Wolf let out a whoop of joy and grabbed her leather jacket. "Got a smoke, Robbie?" she called as she banged out the door. The other four took their belongings and followed her out. Sam hesitated in the open door, looking back over her shoulder.

"Seven, right, T?"

"Yeah. I'll see you then," Taryn said. Sam beamed and closed the door.

Linda waited until she heard the latch click before speaking. "It's a good idea for the number, T, but are you sure? They are going to be a handful."

"Robbie's got it down. Grace and Sam just need some confidence. Wolf needs to be kicked around a little. It's cool. I'll take them somewhere dark and noisy, like the Old Pink. Nobody will care if they get spotted." Taryn walked to the edge of the stage and balanced, rocking back on her heels.

Linda watched her, then started gathering up her books. "It's not like you to hang around after rehearsal. You need a ride tonight? Joe busy?"

Taryn glanced over her shoulder at the director. "Felt like walking. Maybe I'll take the subway. But thanks."

Linda slung the strap of her backpack over her shoulder and wrapped her Argentinean scarf around her neck. "None of my business, T, what goes on at home. But your energy was way down tonight. You want to go get a beer, maybe talk it out?"

Rosalind knew that she was eavesdropping, that Linda and Taryn hadn't realized that they weren't alone in the theater. The look of pain that passed over Taryn's face clenched at her heart. She had to restrain herself from calling out. She wanted to hear Taryn's answer. She wanted to comfort her, take that look of pain away. She had been, inadvertently, the cause of it, and she was about to bring down more. The thought kept her silent.

Taryn raised her head, her eyes shadowed as Linda snapped off a row of the stage lights. "No. I—"

Linda cut her off gracefully. "Another time. Got it. I'll see you tomorrow at seven."

Ellie's chair creaked, the sound amplified in the darkness of the house. Linda and Taryn both turned, startled. "Think we have company. Come out. You've been spotted," Linda said, amused. Ellie gave Rosalind an apologetic look, then called out toward the stage.

"Yoo-hoo! I was so mesmerized by your work, I forgot to announce myself."

"Ellie, that's not like you at all. Come on down here. Why are you hiding up in the last row? You usually sit front and center," Linda said.

"You make me take notes when I sit in the front. I was feeling like being pure audience tonight. Well, come on, sugar. Face the music." Ellie held out her hand to Rosalind.

"Pay the ferryman," Rosalind muttered.

They walked down the aisle into the light. Linda smiled when she saw Rosalind following Ellie. "I was wondering when we'd get you here for a rehearsal. I keep asking T to invite you," Linda said warmly. Rosalind looked past the director to Taryn.

Taryn stood with her hands in her pockets, her eyes guarded. It was a look so different from the welcome Rosalind had come to relish from her that it hurt, as if Taryn were treating her like a stranger.

"You know, there is this painting I can't wait to show you, Linda. Come with me," Ellie said, taking the director's arm.

"Painting? What do I care about painting? You're tripping."

"You'll like this one. It's a study of two women who know when to make an exit." Ellie hauled her off toward the door.

Rosalind stood with her coat folded over her arm, looking up at Taryn. She wanted to take Taryn in her arms. She wanted Taryn to apologize for ruining her night with her abrupt exit. She wanted to know why Taryn was being so cold. The hurt at Taryn's lack of a welcome won out.

"You ran out on me."

"You were busy," Taryn said lightly.

"Honey, knock it off. I'm not a teenager. I don't need this shit. I didn't know Paul was going to call me. I was naked in bed with you at the time, remember?" Rosalind said, annoyance bleeding into her voice. Why did Taryn have to act, well, her age?

"You don't need this shit? Right, like I'm fucking up your schedule. You managed to stay on the phone with him. You didn't come after me," Taryn drawled, stepping down off the stage.

"That's ridiculous! I spent all afternoon and half the night trying to track you down. I've Joe worried to death, combing the city for you. You took off without a word!" Rosalind said, her voice rising with frustration. She knew Taryn, inside and out. She knew that Taryn was hurting, was burned by any mention of her ex-husband, was terrified that Rosalind wasn't serious about their relationship. That knowledge was hard to hang on to when Taryn gave a half shrug and looked away. It made Rosalind more furious, Taryn's angry pose. It triggered her worst nightmare. She transformed into her own mother, right down to the delivery of the words. "I don't appreciate being treated this way."

It got an immediate response from Taryn. She curled her lip as if she'd been slapped. "You don't like how I treat you?" she said dangerously.

Rosalind felt the ground tilting away under her feet. What was going on? She was angry with Taryn, but it was anger mixed with relief that she was all right. It was the desperation to mend the breach between them before it got any bigger. Rosalind took a deep breath and tried again. "I'm sorry, baby. I turned into my mother there for a minute. I was worried sick about you all afternoon. I was going out of my mind not being able to find you. Ellie found me in my office reading gloomy poetry aloud. I love how you treat me. I love you. It makes me crazy to see you hurt." She held out her arms and waited.

Taryn crossed the floor in a single stride and grabbed her, nearly crushing the breath from her lungs. She felt Taryn kissing the side of her neck, her shoulder, her cheek. "I need that. I need to know you love me, all the time," Taryn whispered.

Rosalind closed her eyes at the naked sound of Taryn's voice. She let herself forget, for a moment, the news she had to give, and stayed in Taryn's arms. The new tattoo on her shoulder burned, reminding her of the bond she'd accepted with Taryn.

"I do love you," Rosalind whispered back.

"Come home with me," Taryn demanded.

"Honey, I—" Rosalind was cut off as Taryn bent down and kissed her. She tried again, and Taryn kept kissing her, refusing to let her speak. When Taryn pulled back, there was rawness to her, unsettled by their separation.

"No. Come home with me."

Rosalind did.

Chapter Three

There were plenty of good reasons not to do exactly what she was doing. Ellie reviewed them as she drove to 34 Mariner. First, Taryn and Rosalind were fighting, and from the look on her friend's face when they'd left the theater, the drama wasn't over. She was holding Taryn's hand, though, and that was a good sign. Rosalind had been distracted when Taryn hauled her off toward the elevator, distracted enough that she'd forgotten her appointment book. Ellie hefted it in her hand, considering. She could just give it back to Rosalind tomorrow at school, drop by her office, leave it in her mailbox. She wouldn't be needing it tonight. Ellie smirked at the thought. Taryn wouldn't be letting Rosalind do any work tonight, from the look on Taryn's face as they left.

Linda Alejandros had poked her in the ribs and indicated the handsome girl plowing through the crowd in the gallery, trailing her lover possessively. "I haven't seen her project that much determination all night," Linda said wryly.

"It's this weird effect they have on each other. It's like watching lightning strike, over and over," Ellie said, looking after her friend.

"Well, I hope they have some way to ground. That much energy burns everything near it."

Funny that Linda had said that. It was like that sometimes, being around them. Ellie could feel the sparks jumping back and forth between them, fueled by every look Taryn gave Rosalind, every touch Rosalind returned. Ellie cheerfully admitted to her own voyeurism and enjoyed the show. Maybe it was Linda's odd comment that had her thinking this way, but she could almost see an afterimage when they passed by, lost in one another. Like the flare of the sun, it left her blinking. An unsettled feeling gripped her. Ellie was in the habit of indulging any mood that came her way, even ill-defined ones. Her sense told her to take the book and follow Rosalind to 34 Mariner, and gave her an excuse to do so.

Rosalind's Saturn was parked in front of 34. The house was dark on the upper floors; maybe she'd been in time to catch them before they slipped upstairs and were no use to anyone. Ellie had become a regular visitor at 34 Mariner since Rosalind had started seeing Taryn. It was a pleasure to get to know Taryn's companions. Every visit to the house had been momentous. Joe had granted her immediate status as Rosalind's best friend in a way that made Ellie feel like an extended member of the family. He had an excellent sense of the complex ways people find their family. Ellie had expected Rhea to be disapproving, considering her initial conflicts with Rosalind, but the witch had looked her over and never said a cross word to her. Well, the past month had been full of surprises. She was an expert in taking everything in stride.

Ellie jogged up the steps, waving Rosalind's appointment book like a passport. "Yoo-hoo! Anyone home?" The door was open, the screen letting in the crisp October air. She let herself into the hallway. There was a light on in the kitchen. Ellie headed for it and tripped. She knocked into the wall under the coat hooks, swearing. Ellie crouched, feeling around for the object she'd tripped over. One of Taryn's combat boots in the middle of the floor? Ellie's eyes rose suspiciously to the stairs, where she saw the boot's mate, halfway up the flight. Rosalind's jacket was flung over the rail nearby. A trail of outerwear marched up to the second floor.

"Boy, you guys don't waste any time," Ellie said, dropping the boot.

She'd missed them. Ellie shrugged, a little disappointed. She could leave the book on the kitchen table, along with a note. There was a yellow notepad on the counter under the wall of coffee mugs and a pen partly tucked into the paws of the massive calico asleep next to the phone. Ellie slid the pen out of the cat's grip. The cat shifted, stretched its legs out, then folded back into sleep. "Must be nice to be that comfortable," Ellie whispered to it. She dashed off a quick note and set it under Rosalind's book.

There was a sound like an army charging the house, boots galloped up the porch steps, the door slammed back. Ellie called out "Taryn?" as she walked down the hall, expecting such a riot of an entrance to belong to Taryn. But Taryn's boots were on the stairs. She and Rosalind had already gone up to the third floor.

Ellie's first thought was that the person had been hit by a car. Another two steps, and Ellie saw a man, dirty and doubled over as if in pain, bracing one arm against the wall. His leather jacket was covered in mud and looked as if it had been dragged down a mile of pavement. A patch the size of her fist was missing from his right elbow. His hair was an indeterminate brown, matted and lank, hanging in his eyes. She saw a three-quarter view of his face, his skin a pale gray-green under two days' growth of beard. His eyes were hidden, dark as empty sockets under lowered brows. He had the build of a man who made his living with his hands, but his flesh seemed to hang on his bones. Every muscle was weighted down. The jacket added bulk to his frame, but when he turned, Ellie could see that his red T-shirt hung on his frame, as if he'd recently lost a great deal of weight. The light in the hall caught his eyes. They were as dark as Rhea's but looked to her as flat as a toad's eyes.

"Not Taryn," he said. His voice a rasp.

He coughed, then pushed away from the wall, fumbling in his pocket for a crushed pack of cigarettes. He lit the last one with a cheap plastic lighter, crumpled the pack, and tossed it down the hall.

"Can I help you?" Ellie asked, thinking about the objects in the hall, what she might be able to use as a weapon if need be.

An unexpected smile crossed his face, a twist of his full lips. "No. You can't help me."

He started to walk past her into the living room. "Excuse me, I know the residents of this house, and you don't live here. You either tell me what you want or I call the cops," Ellie said, following him.

He looked over his shoulder at her, as if surprised to find her following him. He sighed heavily and ran his hands through his long hair. "You're Taryn's new kill? You will not be around long enough to learn who I am. Run along and wait for the kid to get home, and leave me."

"Been a while since you been here, hasn't it?" Ellie said and folded her arms. It was interesting to be taken for Taryn's girlfriend of the month. Part of her wanted to play it out, see what this man wanted. He seemed to know at least one resident of 34 Mariner, so her guard went down slightly. Taryn and Rosalind were within screaming distance, and that helped her relax another notch.

Anger sprang up in his face; he wasn't expecting to be challenged. "You think fucking the kid makes you special? You're not even her type. I have reason to be here that you will never have. Leave me alone." He turned his back on her as the door opened.

Joe walked in, midconversation with Rhea and Goblin. "At least you had the sense to call me when you got stranded. What kind of friends—" He stopped dead in his tracks when he saw who was in his living room. "Misha? What are you doing here?" Joe asked, looking over the man as if he were a ghost.

"Been a while, brother-in-law. You look good. I was just talking to Taryn's kill here," Misha said.

"That's not Rosalind. That's Ellie," Goblin said as she set her backpack down on the couch.

"No, Rosalind and Taryn are upstairs. Ros forgot her appointment book. I left it for her on the kitchen table," Ellie said to Rhea and Joe.

"Then who are you?" Misha asked, pointing at Ellie.

"Rosalind's best friend. Long story," Ellie said.

"Misha, what are you doing here? Are you all right?" Joe asked, stepping closer to the man. Misha looked at him with haunted eyes.

"Enough," Rhea said firmly. "We will hold this discussion in the kitchen. First, Misha, go up and wash up. You will find some of Joe's clothing folded on the shelf above the window in the bathroom. You remember the way. Joe, please start heating the wine. Goblin, put your books away."

"Am I being exiled to my room?" Goblin asked.

"No, you can come down for the talk. Misha is family. Ellie, if you would, please stay."

"Listen, I was just dropping off the book for Ros. I hate to intrude on a family matter—"

Rhea looked at her for a long moment.

"Did you say hot wine? Okay, I'll stay," Ellie said, feeling distinctly uncomfortable. What had she gotten herself into now?

Joe was busy adding mysterious things to the pot of wine, all from memory. His hands moved in a blur, adding a palm full of a yellowish powder, three grains tapped out from an uncorked glass jar, a pinch from an apothecary's mug. Ellie, not knowing what else to do, sat down at the table. Rhea had gone down into the basement, followed by the calico Ellie had seen earlier, a gray tabby, and a slim black cat with an oddly long tail. The cats had perked up the moment they heard Rhea open the door, and all dashed to follow her. "You keep their food down there?" Ellie asked.

Joe shook his head and pointed at the food bowls under the sink. "Mice?" Ellie asked.

"Not many. Doubting Thomas—the tabby—cleans them out as quick as they come in," Joe said. He set the lid on the pot and turned the branching flame down to a small yellow leaf.

"So why'd they make a beeline for the door when Rhea opened it? Stash of catnip?" Ellie asked, refusing to be put off by anything cryptic. Rosalind had told her many stories about this kitchen. It was her turn to experience it.

"Oh, that. They caught a whiff of Rhea's intent. They get excited whenever there is a healing. They sit around and soak up the energy like a patch of sunlight. Greedy little bastards. Would you help me set out the wineglasses?" Joe said calmly. He wiped his hands on a dish towel and opened the cabinet.

The glasses were all mismatched, a collection of goblets, water glasses, flagons, and fast-food cups. Joe pulled the table away from the wall so he could set out more chairs. "Put the red glass out for Rhea. She likes it. Give Goblin a flagon. She hates the Snoopy glass," he said.

"Snoopy for your surly friend?" Ellie asked.

"He's earned it. I'd say give him the green glass, but he isn't ready. Was he unbearably rude to you before we came in?" Joe asked.

"No, just rude enough. He thought I was Taryn's disposable femme du jour. I managed not to brain him with the coat rack. We actually got on quite well," Ellie said, amused.

Joe nodded ruefully. "He hasn't regained any of his charm. If it helps, he used to be quite pleasant, even entertaining." Joe lifted the lid off the pot. The scent of cloves and cinnamon drifted across the kitchen, mingled with a sweetness Ellie couldn't place.

"He's your brother-in-law?" Ellie asked, trying to sound nonchalant.

"More or less." Joe sighed. He glanced at the door to the basement then back to Ellie. "I think I have a minute to fill you in. The shower sounds like it's still running. Have a seat. Our family relationships can get a little complex. Misha is the brother of my ex-husband's lover. After my husband and I divorced, when I was transitioning, he started seeing Stephan. We still spent a lot of time together. Goblin goes to see her dad every other weekend, so we got to know Stephan well. And Stephan and Misha are two sides of the same coin. Very close. So we got to know Misha."

"Okay. I may be out of line, but he didn't look well when he came in. Why didn't he go to his brother?" Ellie asked.

"Because his brother is dead," Rhea said. Ellie jumped. She hadn't heard the stairs creak, or the door to the basement open. The cats wove around Rhea's ankles, lifting the hem of her dress.

"Stephan had AIDS. He died in February. I haven't been able to contact Misha since before the funeral. I heard he was up in Canada for a while, but I never got word from him. We might be the only family he has now," Joe said softly.

Goblin came down the stairs with a bouncing step. "Rhea, I knocked on T's door, but there was no answer."

Rhea looked toward the stairs for a moment, her eyes unfocussed. "Ellie? Would you go up and ask Rosalind and Taryn to come down?"

"I think they're…busy," Ellie said. She felt Rhea's eyes focus on her.

"Not anymore. Now they're just talking."

"Okay then. I'll just trot on up and pry them out of their conversation."

It wasn't nearly long enough a walk up to the third floor to convince Ellie that she was doing the right thing. In a way, it didn't matter. The thrill of adventure was humming along her veins; the magic of the house was singing to her. Rosalind and Taryn might well just be talking. She wouldn't put it past Rhea to see through walls. Just in case, she marched with copious noise up the stairs and knocked on the door to the love nest.

"Yoo-hoo! Get yourselves decent. You have company."

She heard her own name repeated back to her, both in Taryn's low rumble and Rosalind's honeyed tones, the postcoital voice she was getting used to hearing from her dear friend.

Ellie stepped into the attic, took a long look at the bed, and promised herself that she'd find a twenty-year-old of her own. Rosalind was reclining with her head and shoulders in Taryn's lap, lazily accepting Taryn's strong fingers combing through her hair. Cleopatra couldn't have looked more self-satisfied. "Aren't you just the postcard? Visit Buffalo, the best kept romantic secret on the East Coast," Ellie said.

Rosalind smiled and stretched like a cat in front of a fireplace. "Ellie. What are you doing here?"

"Long story. Rhea wants you both to come down. The house has a guest. T knows him. Misha?" Ellie let her voice rise into a question on the end.

The reaction from Taryn was gratifying. She sat up as if she'd been hit with a bolt of electricity. "Misha? Here? Did Joe see him?"

"Saw him and let him come into the kitchen."

"Thought he'd have slugged him. Joe's too nice of a guy," Taryn said, shaking her head.

"Who's Misha, baby?" Rosalind asked, stroking Taryn's arm.

Ellie took charge of the moment. "No. All explanations will happen downstairs, where Rhea can oversee them. She's clearly got something in mind. You two are a part of it, and Lord help me, so am I. So. We all put on our clothing and march down to the kitchen."

The hot wine had made the first round of the table by the time Misha creaked down the back stairs. He walked into the kitchen shaking droplets from his hands, reminding Ellie of a priest casting holy water for an exorcism. She had to admit that he cleaned up well. His hair was sleek as a seal's coat, hanging down heavy and straight like a warrior's mane over his shoulders. There was a lucidity to his dark eyes she didn't remember seeing when she'd found him in the hallway. Joe's clothing suited him. The chamois shirt draped on him as if it had always been his. He'd shaved. The face now revealed was younger than she expected, no more than thirty, worn from grief rather than years. He walked to the table, casting a look at the counter where Taryn sat on her favorite bar stool with Rosalind standing between her knees.

"T. Been a while. This must be Rosalind, who I keep hearing about." He extended his hand. When Taryn ignored it, Rosalind took it and shook it lightly.

"Yes, I'm Rosalind. Nice to meet you, Misha."

"No, it isn't. But you are nice enough to lie about it. Taryn's tastes have changed," he said evenly.

Rosalind felt the girl shift under her, the first sign of growing anger. She looked at Rhea. The witch held out a chair. Misha took the hint and sat down at the table. Joe poured him wine. Misha held up the glass and frowned. Rhea took up her goblet, tipped a few drops of the wine out on the floor as a libation, then sipped from the glass. The wine looked black as old blood through the red glass, but smelled as sweet as summer nights. Misha took his glass and downed it in three gulps, not tasting anything. Joe refilled it.

Misha tipped back the glass again in a gesture of pure habit, as if he'd been burned in the mouth and could not remember how wine tasted. It struck Rosalind as a shame, the wasteful way this strange man drank. The wine was exquisite. She sipped at it with a mouth still bruised by love and felt a sweetness slide over her tongue that echoed her lover's embrace. She felt pity for Misha and wondered if he knew what he was throwing down like offal.

Misha sprawled in his chair, spinning the Snoopy glass between his hands. Everyone else drank in silence. Even Goblin sipped at the single glass of wine Joe had allowed her. He started up as if resuming a conversation they'd been having a few minutes ago, his eyes roving around the room, unable to rest. "Been up in Toronto last few months. I was working a road show. The stage manager knew this guy on *Phantom*, got me a gig. I'd felt like slowing down. I hadn't worked in one city for a few years. I figured, can't be bad. Steady work, rent a place, maybe buy a goldfish. What the hell? It was just normal stuff at first. Couldn't eat. Figured that was normal. How long had it been since I cooked anything not out of a can? I had culture shock, not being a nomad anymore. Couldn't sleep. It wasn't a new hotel every week, so that was normal. You have to get used to the sounds of a new city. I'd start sleeping soon."

He paused long enough to drain his glass. He held it out absently with a small move of his elbow. Joe looked at Rhea, who touched his arm.

"It's all right. He belongs to Dionysus right now. He'll only be able to talk through the drunkenness. He won't move to rage."

Joe took Misha's glass and refilled it from the pot on the stove.

"Listen to the witch. She knows. Everything. Stephan knew. He believed in you. I never did. Has he married you yet, witchy woman?" Misha leaned on the table toward Rhea.

"Are you offering for me if he hasn't?" Rhea asked.

Misha rolled back in his chair, his arm up in a guard posture. "I'm not man enough for the woman who loved Taryn, then Joe. Average Joe. You always wanted to be an average Joe. Now look at you." He took the glass back from Joe with a wide smile.

"How long has it been since you slept?" Rhea asked.

"Few days. Last I remember was…Thursday? Yeah. There was this girl from the show. A little company on a cold night, you know? We were at my place. I thought it'd be fine. I might even sleep. She got up in the middle and ran right out of the flat. She said something came in and sat down on the bed and kept looking at her. She could feel it."

Misha turned his eyes on Rhea. "I couldn't feel him. I couldn't see him. I can't…I didn't go in to work. I stayed in the flat, trying to see. I haven't slept. I've gone blind from trying to see, but all I've got is a headache. Today, I walked to my bike, and here I am. At the house where everyone can see. Be my eyes, sister-in-law."

"I can only be your eyes if you do as I say. No questions. No fighting," Rhea said, setting her wineglass aside.

Misha let his head fall forward, his hair covering his face.

"Well?" Rhea asked, her voice firm.

"Yes," Misha said, his head coming back up, his dark eyes hooded.

"Very well. You will live here with us until I tell you that you are ready to leave. Joe's study can be made up with a bed. You'll need to work. It's too vital to your sense of who you are for you not to. I'll find something suitable. Until then you can help Joe with the electrical work around here. You can descend into Dionysus's realm to excess, but there will come a time to set it all aside. You'll know that better than I will."

Misha nodded, in exhaustion or drunkenness, his limbs losing all strength. He pushed his arm out on the table and lay his head down on it.

"Rosalind, would you please take a look at Misha?" Rhea asked politely.

"Look at him? I'm not sure—" Rosalind said.

"Tell me what you see," Rhea said as if the man they were discussing had left the room. Rosalind wasn't sure what Rhea was after, so she did as Rhea asked and just looked at the man collapsed on the table. What was there to him that Rhea was asking her to see? He was exhausted. Anyone could see that. He hadn't been eating well. By his own admission he hadn't slept, and now he was passed out from all the wine. Rosalind looked at him and gasped. Rhea looked at her expectantly.

"There's a bruise covering his face, over his eyes. Like a shadow," Rosalind said.

"Good. You see it too. You'll help me with the healing." Rhea pushed her chair away from the table. "Joe, would you put Misha to bed? I think he'll be sleeping for a while. Goblin, it's time for you to go up as well. School tomorrow. Ellie, would you walk to the front of the house with me?"

Ellie shrugged at Rosalind and Taryn and followed Rhea out of the kitchen.

"Poor guy seems flattened," Ellie said to Rhea as Joe slipped Misha's arm around his shoulders and helped him to the stairs.

"He's carrying more grief than he can bear. It's time to set it down, or go blind," Rhea said.

"Sure. You, ah, certainly seem to have everything under control."

"I have nothing under control. Only Misha can decide if he's going to be healed." Rhea stopped at the foot of the front stairs and showed no signs of further movement.

"I hesitate to ask, but why are we walking to the front of the house?"

Rhea tilted her head and appeared to be listening down the hallway. "Because Taryn and Rosalind are about to have a fight. They'll need both of us. Give them a moment. They'll be here."

There was a shout from the kitchen, a mingling of incoherent rage and disbelief. It was followed closely by a crash that rattled Ellie's teeth.

"Whaddya think, chair breaking or door being kicked in?" Ellie asked Rhea, trying to make light of the noises coming down the hall. Rhea didn't seem disturbed in the least.

She tilted her head as if assessing the sound. "Bar stool being thrown across the room. The door would have more of a splintering sound to it."

Voices overlapped the sounds of destruction, rising. Ellie made out a few words, none of them good, all in Taryn's fierce, anger-threaded tones. She heard Rosalind answer, protest something in a voice that was sounding frayed with frustration.

"That was a mug being smashed," Rhea said, glancing down the hall.

"Boy, how does anybody ever get any sleep around here?" Ellie asked.

"Emotion is a messy thing. This house has a releasing effect on people. They lose their restraint while here," Rhea said.

"You don't seem all that unrestrained, if you don't mind my saying." Ellie looked into the witch's steady dark eyes and thought she saw a spark of humor.

"I've made exceptional progress in the past three years," Rhea said, deadpan.

"What are they fighting about?" Ellie asked. There was a hush from the kitchen, a quiet that made her nerve endings jangle. The storm was still coming.

Taryn exploded up the hall, slamming her fist into the wall as she came. Rosalind was right on her heels, swearing in a way Ellie had never heard. "Don't you dare run out on me again!" Rosalind shouted at Taryn's broad back. Taryn ignored Ellie and Rhea, shouldering past them to the door. Rosalind looked at Ellie, her face red, and threw her hands up in a gesture of disbelief. Ellie took the hint. She jumped out in front of Taryn her arms spread wide.

"No, no, no. You're playing this all wrong. Taryn, you live here, so Rosalind should be storming out. Taryn, you come back here by Rhea..." Ellie took Taryn's arm and hauled her away from the door. "Good, good. Now, Ros, you go stand by the door. Don't open it yet. We'll work on the exit line. Great! Now, action," Ellie said with a flourish and stepped back.

Taryn was furious. Every line of her body was vibrating with it. Ellie thought she must have been lucky to grab Taryn and not have her explode. Taryn's eyes were on Rosalind, ignoring everything else around her, hot as coals. Rosalind came up the hall and stood next to Ellie, giving her friend a quick look of gratitude. Taryn and Rosalind faced off, but they didn't speak. Ellie stepped between them. She couldn't stand the weight of that silence, where she could hear the thews of their relationship straining. "Okay, so what is going on here? I thought everything was all patched up between you two."

Taryn's lip curled up in a snarl. "Ask your friend."

"I told Taryn about Paul," Rosalind said in a voice struggling for balance.

Comprehension flickered on Ellie's face. "Oh."

Taryn's head went up, her eyes narrowed. "Tell the rest. About you meeting him for dinner tomorrow night."

"I know this hurts you. If I had had a chance to think about it, I might not have said yes. You'd just stormed out. I wanted to get him off the phone and go after you. Taryn, I know you're upset, but I gave him my word. He may be my ex, but he's still my friend. He asked for my help. I couldn't say no." Rosalind stepped closer to Taryn as she spoke, her voice softening.

Ellie could see her setting her anger aside, see her all but holding her arms out to Taryn. She saw Taryn flinch and look away, turning her head in profile. It looked like it caused her physical pain, having Rosalind move closer. For a moment there was silence. Rosalind reached out to touch Taryn's hand. Ellie held her breath, hoping that the calm was true.

Taryn's head turned, her eyes slitted. "What the fuck do you want me to do, cheer you on?"

Rosalind took a step back as if she'd been slapped. "No. I want you to try to understand." For a moment Rosalind could see Taryn soften, see some internal structure start to give way. She saw Taryn's hand tremble and almost reached out to hold it. It was like a cold wind blowing down the hallway when Taryn shrugged and jammed her hands into her pockets. Taryn turned her back and walked down the hall toward the kitchen.

"You go out with him. See if I understand."

"Oh, it's all right for you to live with your ex-lover, but not for me to have dinner with mine?" Rosalind yelled, exasperated.

Her only answer was the sound of boots stomping up the back stairs.

"She's going to be the death of me, so help me—" Rosalind said to Ellie.

"Easy, killer. I'm on your side," Ellie said, patting Rosalind's arm.

"Let me talk to her. There's more going on here than I thought. Rosalind, did you see Taryn's back?" Rhea said, gazing down the hallway.

"She made sure of that, walking away from me while I was talking to her." Rosalind paced in the confined space like a lion in his first cage.

"No. Did you look at it?" Rhea asked.

"I thought it was poor lighting. A shadow," Rosalind said, slowing down.

"You saw it. Well, Hecate knows, all things come in threes. You'll help with that healing as well. I'd ask anyway. You are her lover, but your vision will come in handy. I suspect the third will show up soon," Rhea said in her dry, cool voice.

"I didn't understand a thing you just said," Rosalind admitted.

"The Rule of Three. First Misha storms into town, in need of a healing. Ghost-ridden. Now Taryn's showing signs. That shadow has wrapped around her throat. It came on fast. It doesn't seem like a ghost, but something has her. I expect it will be connected with the next one to show up. I will need to heal them. You will assist me."

"Is she acting like this because she's sick?" Rosalind asked.

"Taryn's acting like this because she's Taryn. But she will have to find peace with something before she can shrug the mood off." Rhea smiled as she spoke, a smile of affection and sadness.

"I should go talk to her." Rosalind glanced up the stairs.

"No. Leave her be tonight. Let me have a few words with her."

The door at the top of the stairs was shut. Rhea tapped once with her knuckles, then walked in. Taryn was sitting on the windowsill, looking out over the street, and didn't turn around. "She left," Taryn said, her voice flat. She tapped out a cigarette and threw the pack toward the bed.

"She did," Rhea said, walking toward Taryn.

Taryn hauled against the unpainted wooden frame, cracking the window open. She lit the cigarette, then snapped the silver lighter shut with a flick of her wrist. It was a flash of light on metal, a fish leaping out of water, just the fragment of a moment, but it carried a memory along with it. Rhea had given that lighter to Taryn years ago, when Taryn had first moved in. It had been a love token, given on no occasion but from her own need to give something to the teenager who'd entered her life like a storm. She knew the careless way Taryn had with most of her possessions, the manner of an angry child who had never owned anything of value. Rhea touched her hand to her chest, just for a moment, seeing that girl again.

Taryn had changed so much during the past three years, and Rhea was honest enough to acknowledge her place in that. It had been her source of fierce pride, being Taryn's guardian, bandaging wounds she had never caused, making a home for someone who had no experience with what a home could be. It hadn't been easy. Taryn was all raw emotion, as careless with herself as she was with possessions. The year that they had been lovers Taryn kept her eye on the door, and it took Rhea the entire year to realize she was waiting not for a chance to flee, but to be told to leave. She couldn't simply accept love. She'd never learned how.

It was after they were no longer lovers, after Joe had moved in, that Taryn truly seemed to relax, seemed to accept 34 Mariner as her home. Joe had a lot to do with that, Rhea knew. The man could make anyone feel at home. It was his gift, the grace of acceptance, the seemingly casual touch of caretaking. It had been a revelation for Rhea to see Taryn begin to respond to such an approach, to see her accept Joe's parental attention. Once, she had come home from closing the shop and found Taryn, sullen, clotted with rage, sitting in the kitchen. Taryn had rebuffed all attempts to talk, muscles bunching in the corners of her jaw around what she couldn't say.

Hours later she found Joe in the kitchen making coffee, with a still-silent Taryn perched on her bar stool, watching him like a cat. The silence between them was eloquent to Rhea. Joe must have come in and seen the state Taryn was in, but he hadn't asked. He went about making coffee as if Taryn had every right to brood uninterrupted. It was this silence that eased the coiled tension in Taryn, eventually letting her speak. Rhea still didn't know what the trouble had been, only that Joe had been the one to give Taryn what she needed this time. It had been the hardest thing she had done since ending her relationship with Taryn, letting another person become that anchor for her. As much as she loved Joe, jealousy had knifed into her, seeing them. It was the first time she had to face that there were places in Taryn Rhea could not go, that other people would become as important as she was in Taryn's life. She'd managed to retreat without them seeing her.

Years passed, and in the parade of Taryn's sexual contacts, there had been no rival for her. No matter how many days Taryn vanished from the house, she always came home. To her. Seeing Taryn sit by the window now, as drunk with anger as she'd ever been, Rhea knew. Taryn was in need, but she was no longer the one to heal her. Rhea had accepted Rosalind with resistance and little grace, it was true. She'd come to approve of Taryn's choice, even thank the gods that these two had found one another, through all the rivers of time and death and rebirth. Rosalind could give Taryn what Rhea no longer could, a chance to grow, a bridge to the future. With Rhea, Taryn had learned to love. Now, perhaps there were other lessons to learn, other places she needed to go.

"She left because I asked her to," Rhea said.

"Why would you do that?" Taryn asked, the cigarette hanging from her fingers, the fire climbing slowly toward her flesh.

Rhea sat down on the edge of the windowsill, perching like a hawk watching for prey, the uneasy waiting of a woman who knows her own limits. "I wanted to talk to you alone," Rhea said, smoothing her hair back with an impatient gesture.

Taryn had stilled to a polished silence, her listening sharp edged in the quiet of the room. It was nearly Rhea's undoing, the perfect attention Taryn focused on her. She remembered other nights, when those same eyes had slid away from hers with the carelessness of youth, the inability to stay still for even a moment.

Taryn had changed; even the past few weeks had wrought new things in a person Rhea thought she knew to the core. This new stillness she had never seen. Was this the product of time with Rosalind? *It must be, surely*; Rhea didn't remember ever feeling the weight of the stone blue gaze as she felt now. Rosalind had taught her this. Rosalind's love had slowed her down, given her dancing spirit an anchor. For a moment, Rhea felt tears prick at the back of her eyes. She set them aside.

"Why are you so angry?" Rhea asked, surprised to hear the words come out. This wasn't the question she had intended to ask Taryn, but she found that she wanted to hear the answer.

There was a twitch in Taryn's cheek. A muscle jumped. "She shouldn't go see him. She should have stayed with me."

It was Taryn's voice, but not hers. Someone older spoke those words. Rhea could hear it clearly. It was a voice she had never been around to hear. The tones of youth passing on into adulthood. It was the part of Taryn she never got to know, that she was always drawn away from before it happened. *I have always loved you*, Rhea thought in dull shock, *but I have never known you beyond this moment. My time was always up. I don't know you anymore. Everything that comes from here after is new.* The knowledge was sharp, but Rhea stayed with it. She had to balance it against the information she now had to hand Taryn.

"She was his wife. She is his friend. She had to go to him. You knew full well that she would."

Rhea wasn't prepared for Taryn's reaction. She tossed the cigarette out the window and walked away, her stride clipped. "Taryn?"

Taryn leaned her hand on the dresser, facing the altar. "I don't care."

Rhea saw the teenager come forward again, the rawness of emotion unalloyed by humor. "Yes, you do."

"I don't. She's not his anymore. He shouldn't be here. This is my home."

"You've gotten lucky, this time around. You get to keep your lover. I am still alive. Now it is time to pay the price for your good fortune and continue to grow."

"I don't like what you're saying."

"It doesn't matter. Have I ever spared your feelings when you need to know the truth?" Rhea asked.

Taryn shook her head sullenly.

"If you love Rosalind, he comes with the package. You will bloody well have to learn to live with him. As she had to embrace your people. You don't get to choose a person's past for them. You love them entirely or not at all."

"He was her husband. It doesn't matter if she loves me, if she's with me now. I'm not stupid, Rhea. It's like she's on vacation now, from everything she's been. That'll be fun. It'll be different for a while. But eventually vacation gets tiring, and you start wanting to go home."

Taryn picked up her wallet from the dresser in a blind motion. "I'm going out. Don't wait up."

CHAPTER FOUR

It was three in the morning. Rosalind had passed from nervous exhaustion into a trance state nearly an hour ago and now sat with the remote control pointed at the window. She raised it experimentally and clicked, but the view from her solitary bed didn't change. She tossed it aside with a sigh. This was ridiculous. She was an adult. Rhea had made a perfectly reasonable request in asking for time alone with Taryn. It had been a long night. She didn't need to make it any longer by sitting up until she hallucinated.

"I didn't get all the angst in high school, so now I make up for it?" Rosalind asked the clock. It couldn't simply be that she could no longer sleep without Taryn next to her. "It hasn't been that long. A few weeks. And we have spent nights apart," she said, this time to the dresser. The silence seemed argumentative.

"We have! There was…that one night she first had rehearsal. We spent the night apart."

Except the night had gotten so long, and she'd gotten restive. Finally, at five a.m., she'd crept across the street and up to the third floor of 34 Mariner. Taryn was sprawled out on top of the bed, her boots still on. She'd pulled them off, with Taryn barely registering awareness. When she'd crawled into bed and pulled a blanket up over both of them, Taryn had opened one eye. Rosalind had a perfectly good explanation ready, but Taryn didn't say a word. Her eye drifted closed. She'd smiled, taken Rosalind's arm, and pulled her down, falling promptly back asleep. No questions, no walls. Just that small smile of joy and the welcome home.

How was an empty bed ever going to compare to that?

"Great. Now I've gone and done it," Rosalind said. She was out of bed and across the street before she cast a thought to what she was doing.

It was dark in the house, but Rosalind knew every inch of the old wood, where the stairs creaked, where a lover might rise and not give herself away. The door to the third floor was open. Goblin's bedroom was right next door to the stairs. She didn't want to wake her. Barefoot, she climbed up to Taryn's bedroom. She pictured Taryn's reaction, the smile she might get, and felt the warmth flush her entire body. The fight didn't matter. The lateness of the hour was of no concern. She could always come home to Taryn.

There was a dull glow from the windows. Rosalind felt a wave of affection for Taryn's careless habits and resolved to buy her shades. The altar on the dresser top was in disarray, like someone had swept an arm across it. Rosalind paused and set the statue of Kali Ma upright. Taryn's passion for ritual had given her some feeling for altar space. She knew that it was bad for the house to have it be unsettled. Rosalind glanced toward the bed and saw only darkness. Her back was to the window. She figured that she must be blocking the light. Rosalind pulled the covers back and slipped like a thief into the bed, reaching out for the sleeping form of her lover. Her hand kept on reaching. The bed was as empty as her own.

The alarm went off at eight, shredding the leaden sleep that had finally claimed her. Rosalind felt the dislocation of not knowing where she was, or who she was, for a moment. It came back to her after she slapped the alarm off. She'd made a late-night visit to Taryn's bed and found it empty. She'd gone home, abashed, and now her alarm clock was unmercifully reminding her of her morning class. *Great*, she thought. *I feel like* Night of the Living Dead*, and I have to lecture on* Henry IV.

It wasn't fair to feel hungover without having had enough to drink. The shower didn't help inject life back into her protesting body. Breakfast seemed like an abomination. Her last, best hope—coffee— was inert in her cup. The memory hit. Taryn had thrown her blue mug across the kitchen, shattering it.

The phone rang, startling Rosalind into dropping her cup. The coffee spilled out over the floor tiles, staining them a dull brown. She jumped, swore, grabbed for a dish towel and the phone. The phone dropped from her hand as soon as she jerked it off the hook, falling into the coffee. "Mother of God!" Rosalind plucked the phone up, swabbing at the spill.

"Hell-o!" She half yelled into the phone while trying to stop the coffee from spreading under the table.

"Hey."

The voice made her weak. She chose to drop the towel and grab at the phone with both hands. "Hi."

"Did I wake you?" Taryn asked, her voice distant, an echo coming from a wasteland.

"No, I was up. Nine o'clock class. You know that." Rosalind reached awkwardly behind her back, feeling for support. She found the kitchen cabinets and sank to the floor, leaning on them.

"Yeah. I know."

"Honey, are you all right? I stopped by last night. You weren't home." Rosalind admitted it and got it out of the way. There was nothing normal about Taryn's tone. She wanted to get past it and find her.

"I went out. I'm okay. Listen, I'm sorry about yesterday. It's cool if you go see him." Taryn spoke without any particular emphasis, as if she'd rehearsed the words until they could be bland.

"Taryn?"

"I have the guys from the show coming over tonight. I have to do this drag king field test stuff with them. So I'll be out late. You'll have the evening free, you know? And I kinda wanted to spend some time with Joe and Misha. So it's all good."

"Baby, please tell me what's going on."

"Nothing's going on. I'll be busy tonight, and you have plans. I'll call you tomorrow."

"You in the kitchen?" Rosalind asked, drawing air in between her teeth.

"Yeah," Taryn said, sounding puzzled.

"Good." Rosalind slammed the phone down.

Her bathrobe flared out like a cape as she stormed across the street. She was wearing a pair of Taryn's sweatpants, the pair Taryn had given her to wear after their first night together. They belled like a Scythian's trousers around her bare ankles. Rosalind didn't bother with the front door. Her stride ate up the path around the side of the house, past the woodpile with its quietly rusting hatchet, the wreckage of clay pots and trowels.

Rhea usually left the back door open so the cats could come and go as they pleased. Rosalind took the stairs in one leap, tore the screen open, and came like the rage of Kali into the kitchen. Taryn was still at the counter next to the phone. The look of surprise on her face was gratifying to Rosalind. Taryn hadn't planned on seeing her.

She looked like she'd been up all night. Blue shadows carved out the hollows of her face. Her hair was standing out at a half dozen angles. Her eyes were rimmed with blood, from smoke, or alcohol, or crying. More likely all three, Rosalind thought. It wasn't just the ravages of a bad night. Rosalind had seen Taryn greet the dawn on more than one occasion and still be shining like new bronze, daring the sun to match her. The weariness on her face, the slump of her body against the counter spoke of grief, of the weight of a thought that came down like a millstone.

"Rosalind..." Taryn said, her composure showing fine cracks, branching out.

Rosalind didn't answer. She took Taryn's worn face in her hands and kissed her, hard. Rosalind pressed her body against Taryn's, pinning her to the counter. She only pulled away when Taryn softened and returned the kiss. Taryn's hand was in the small of her back. Rosalind took it and pulled impatiently until Taryn wrapped her whole arm around her.

"Don't you lie to me if I ask you what's wrong. I'll always know better."

Taryn ducked her head. "I know I can't fool you. I thought I could fool myself."

"Hey. Look at me," Rosalind said softly. "Not good enough. Give me your hand."

Rosalind took Taryn's hand and opened the fingers gently, as if readying her to receive a gift. The knuckles of that hand were seamed with tiny white scars, the palm creased with calluses. Rosalind rubbed the palm lightly with her thumbs, massaging the pad of flesh, the tendons that wrapped around the wrist, the edge of bone. Taryn was watching her, quiet under her attention, soothed by it.

Satisfied that Taryn was with her, that she had stopped hiding, Rosalind opened her robe. She took Taryn's hand up inside her T-shirt, cupping it against the curve of her left breast. Taryn's eyes shut, then opened slowly. Her mouth hung open. Rosalind's heart started to drum. "Feel that?" Rosalind asked, seeking her eyes. Taryn nodded, mute. "That's for you. I know you go away sometimes, not just in bed. I'm asking you to come back here with me and tell me what's going on."

Taryn nodded, an abbreviated toss of her head.

"You know how there are things you just know about yourself?" Taryn said. "When you're good at something, everybody would say so, and you have no trouble believing it. We haven't been together that long, you and me. Sure, it's been great. A real roller-coaster ride. I specialize in that, you know? Sweeping women off their feet, showing them a good time, and leaving them with a smile on their face. But I haven't left you. And it's not just a good time anymore. I'm not sure I know how to do all that other stuff, how to be solid all the time, like Joe. I saw something yesterday. You know when he called? He said he was your husband."

"He was. That was over before I met you, baby."

"Rosalind, I'm not just some dumb kid you've been banging. I know you. I know the kind of person you are."

"What kind of person do you see?" Rosalind asked, feeling her heart trip. Taryn felt it too. Her hand moved subtly against Rosalind's skin.

"I see a very brave woman, breaking out, trying all sorts of things she never thought she could. I see a woman finding a part of herself on a grand adventure," Taryn said.

"That's true. I am finding a part of myself."

"But the rest was already there. The part you're vacationing from right now, that wants a house. Wants to settle down. Wake up with the same person every morning. Maybe have kids. I know you've never said any of that, but I see it. It's been a great couple of weeks. You've thrown yourself into my life. The rest is still there, and one day you're going to want it again. I can't give any of that to you."

Taryn looked at Rosalind for a sign and saw the tears on her cheek. The sight caused her an immediate, agonizing pain, like a large hand punching into her chest and pulping her heart. She was hurting her lover, and she couldn't bear it. "Don't cry," she begged, ready to say anything to make Rosalind smile.

Taryn moved her hand away from Rosalind's heart, unable to stay close to that beating. It came to rest awkwardly on Rosalind's hip. There. She'd done the damage, she'd let Rosalind know she couldn't give her what she'd need. It was all over but the details. The weight on her back doubled, then doubled again, all but snapping her bones. If only Rosalind wouldn't keep looking at her like that, even though she'd started to cry harder. Taryn hauled her into a rough bear hug, not knowing what else to do.

"What did they do to you?" Rosalind asked, pressing her face into Taryn's chest.

"Who?" Taryn asked, her throat constricted. With her arms around Rosalind this way, she couldn't imagine giving her up, no matter the consequences.

"All of them. Everyone who taught you to be terrified of someone loving you. I know you, baby. When it gets too close, your survival instinct kicks in and you try to push away."

Taryn blinked. Was that what she was doing? The woman curled up to her had, with a few simple words, shifted her perspective. The night started to look less like a disaster and more like a fight. The grip of her melancholy relaxed, she glanced around the kitchen, surprised. The sun was up. She hadn't slept. Rosalind was crying against the front of her smoke-stained shirt.

"It won't work," Rosalind said, curling her arms around Taryn's waist.

"It won't?" Taryn asked, her own voice sounding strange to her ears.

"No. I'm not letting you go. Live with it, pretty boy." Rosalind lifted her head. The tears had stopped. She pulled down the collar of Taryn's shirt and kissed her neck.

Taryn closed her eyes and felt a wave of peace wash over her.

It made no sense, but standing there in Rosalind's arms quieted the voices in her head, made her fears fall back into silence. It took her a moment to realize what she was feeling was joy. Subtle, profound joy. She opened her eyes. "Thank you," Taryn said, tightening her arms around Rosalind. They stayed leaning against the counter in silence, until footsteps thudded down the back stairs.

Joe came trotting into the kitchen with a basket of laundry in his arms. He spotted them, did a double take, and tried to pivot on his heel and leave again. Taryn laughed. "It's cool, man."

He raised his eyebrows at Taryn, who allowed Rosalind to push away and wipe her face.

"It's fine, Joe. I was just—"

"Stopping by to borrow a cup of sugar. Which it looks like you got. Don't mind me. I'm just on my way down to the laundry room. Completely involved in this laundry. Didn't see a thing." Joe walked past them with exaggerated care, looking out the window.

Rosalind glanced at the clock over the stove. "Damn! I've got to run or I'll never make class. We okay here?" Rosalind asked, tugging on Taryn's shirt.

"Yeah. We're okay."

"No more crazy talk? Good. I'm not quite done talking to you. What you said was true. But it was only a part of the truth. Of course I want that stuff. Who doesn't? You left out the most important thing. I know who I want to wake up next to every morning for the rest of my life. I've had the house and the proper marriage, Taryn. Without the right person it means nothing. It's all smoke and ashes."

"I'd lose my mind if you left me," Taryn said softly.

Rosalind paused with her hand on the door. "You keep saying things like that to me, I'm just gonna marry you and get it over with." Her tone was light, but the look on her face was adoring. She blew Taryn a kiss.

Rosalind had expected the day to crawl by, filled with anxiety, but the afternoon had grown wings. The lightness was due in no small part to the reconnection with Taryn. Rosalind kept the memory of the last look at Taryn before she'd left, one of the moments when all her shields were down and emotion was raw on her face. She knew how Taryn fought against being vulnerable, how naked she could be when she was. It was like drunkenness the way she approached her own emotions, angry, lurching, and finally a wholehearted surrender that left Rosalind breathless. How could she stand to feel so much and not be consumed by it? She'd thought that, given time, the intensity of her connection with Taryn would ease. The sharpness would blunt with the weight of days. It hadn't. The connection had grown deeper as they discovered one another, as they fell into a balance that made everything else pale. She could feel it even in the glance Taryn had thrown at her, her head turned back over her shoulder, her eyebrows raised, a core of vulnerability showing through the hardness of her face. There was a question there that would take years of devotion to answer, coupled with a look of such love it took her breath. Rosalind replayed that memory all afternoon, keeping it like a hard candy under her tongue, sweetening every moment.

It got to be five thirty before she had time to worry. Rosalind picked up her phone and dialed a number she knew better than her own.

A hollow voice answered in a tone of world-ending despair. "Existential Central. The abyss stares back into you."

"Very funny, Joe."

"Thank goodness it was you. Someone who doesn't have to ask me what *existential* means. I was explaining it for half an hour to the gas company when they called." Joe's voice was rimmed with humor. Rosalind could picture him standing in the kitchen next to the wall of coffee mugs. She let herself feel the stab of longing for the house, then set it aside.

"Getting all ready for tonight?" Rosalind asked.

"Yeah. Your boy is setting out the spirit gum and scissors in the living room. I didn't think we had that many mirrors in the house. Lucky me, I get to chaperone a roomful of novice drag kings on their first outing. New Age Boy Scouts? Nah."

"I saw them rehearse the other night. They looked like a handful. Most of them are younger than Taryn," Rosalind said.

"Can you just picture a roomful of Taryns? Brrr," Joe said.

"You'll have fun. They worship her. They won't be any trouble. You'll both be good role models for them."

"Where are my manners? I'm stealing all the time with you. You want me to get her?" His voice moved away from the phone on the end of the sentence.

"Actually, I wanted to talk to you for a moment," Rosalind said quickly.

"Be still my heart. But what will we tell Rhea and Taryn?" Joe asked, whispering into the phone.

"Joe, can I ask you for a favor?"

"Name it."

"Look after her tonight. She should be fine during your outing, and I know you would anyway, but...I'm just worried. I know how she can get."

"She gives cosmic despair a new definition. Not to worry. Misha and I will be taking your boy out after the drag king field test. Rhea wanted us to go do a male bonding night. She said it would be good for Misha and Taryn both. I'll look after her for you."

"Thanks, Joe."

"What's family for? Hang on. I'll call Elvis."

Rosalind could hear the thud of familiar boots on the kitchen floor and counted the steps. Then she was there, with the low-voiced greeting that still tied her insides in knots.

"Hey."

"I love you, you know that?" Rosalind closed her eyes, picturing herself in the kitchen, picturing Taryn's long body slouching against the kitchen counter.

"I know."

"You better not forget," Rosalind said.

"Death wouldn't take that from me. If we only get to take one memory with us, that'd be mine."

"Don't be morbid. I miss you." Rosalind twisted the phone cord around her finger.

"All the romantic poets you like talk about death all the time. I miss you too. Is jerk boy there yet?" Taryn kept her tone bitter but light, showing a practiced sense of humor. Rosalind took it as a good sign.

"He's not—oh, never mind. No, he isn't. Another fifteen minutes or so. When are your boys getting there?" Rosalind asked.

"Another hour."

"You excited?"

"Yeah. I think they'll do good. Robbie is gonna breeze through it. Hey, Laurel is actually coming back to the house tonight. Joe was gonna hang a For Rent sign on her bedroom. She's been over at Robbie's every minute since they met." Taryn's voice took on a new energy, betraying her excitement.

"I can't imagine behaving like that in a new relationship. Can you?" Rosalind asked.

"Nah. Animals. We're gonna be great tonight. Too bad you'll miss it."

"Joe said you and he and Misha are going out afterward."

"Yeah, to Buddies. If you get done with jerk boy, you might find us there. Not that I'm asking or anything," Taryn said, and Rosalind could picture the shrug that went along with it.

"Will you come over tonight when you get done?" Rosalind asked. There was a sound in the hallway. Footsteps.

"If you want."

"I want you in my bed every night. How much plainer do I have to make it?" Rosalind turned in her chair, cupping the phone.

"I'll be there." The answer was low and vibrant, conveying poorly veiled pleasure.

"Somebody's at the door. Have a good time tonight, sweetheart. I love you."

"Love you too. I'll see you tonight."

Rosalind set the phone down as the door to her office opened. Her past walked in. He'd changed. It was the first thing she thought when he opened the door, that his hair had thinned. His face had taken on a weariness she didn't remember. He had always had a boy's face under a shock of light brown hair, but there were lines carved around his mouth now that no boy would have. The Boy Scout grew up and became a businessman. It was October. Rosalind realized with a sense of missed obligation that his birthday had just passed. How could she have forgotten that? He was thirty-four now.

He had on his blue suit, the one he wore to every conference, but she didn't recognize the tie that was loosened at his throat. The questioning look on his face was familiar, the readiness to apologize if he'd chosen the wrong office. Paul had always walked through life with an apology in waiting. That timidity brought out her maternal instinct when they were children. He needed her protection, and she reveled in it. Eventually, when they were engaged and in grad school it began to frustrate her, his hesitancy. She didn't want to be standing in front of him, taking life on for him. It made her less graceful with him as they grew apart.

Rosalind stood up. He saw her and his face changed. He was a different man, recognition transforming him back into her old friend. Rosalind wondered what he saw when he smiled at her, what changes the past year had made in her face. "Paul." She spoke his name, not knowing what else to say.

"Ros! It is you. You look fantastic." He opened his arms and moved to hug her. Rosalind hesitated, then met the greeting with her upper body, patting him on the back.

"You look good too. Did you have any trouble finding me?" Rosalind asked.

"Not too much. You have no idea how good it is to see you. This campus is nothing like Ithaca, is it? But you like it here. You must. You look like a million bucks. Glowing." Paul stepped back and put his hands in his pockets, his eyes traveling over her in a way that Rosalind couldn't quite place. Under the genial, hearty greeting she sensed urgency, even desperation, that was wholly unlike the man she remembered.

"You must love it here. Look at you. You look happy. But that was always your strength. Your mom always said, 'drop Rosalind off in a room full of strangers, come back in an hour, and meet all her new best friends.' It worked in preschool and hasn't failed you since. I always knew to let you go into a room first and soften it up. I don't think I'd have made it through high school if I hadn't followed you around."

"Paul…everything isn't all right, is it? You didn't come to Buffalo to stand in my office and reminisce about high school," Rosalind said.

"Good old Ros, cutting right to the heart of things. A demon with the language. There's an Italian place not far from here. I got it out of a guidebook. You must still love Italian. Some things don't change. Come have dinner with me. We'll talk."

She waited until he'd driven her to the suburban restaurant, until he'd led her to the table, until he'd ordered a bottle of wine. He seemed happier away from the campus, falling back into the routine of holding the door and walking her into public space as if they were still a couple.

Surely that's how it looked, Rosalind knew. Two people in their thirties, professionals, a man and a woman. The way they selected a table, the way they sat, anyone watching would have no doubt they'd known one another for many years, and had less of a need for words.

The opposite was true. Rosalind yearned for Paul to start speaking. She'd forgotten how easy it was to hide under people's assumptions, from the hostess who'd shown them to their table, subtly but professionally flirting with Paul, to the waiter who handed the menus to him first. It started to feel claustrophobic. Rosalind told herself to be calm. This was just dinner. Naturally, everyone would treat them like a couple. They were a man and a woman. It made perfect cultural sense. So why did it feel like a betrayal when Paul ordered the drinks without consulting her, when the waiter simply bowed and disappeared without glancing at her?

She knew that she was comparing the moment to something he couldn't possibly know, what the reception in the restaurant would be like had she come in with her lover. She couldn't hold him responsible for the waiter's assumptions, for the suburban setting, for the way the air was starting to get thick. So why was her blood heating with anger? Why did she feel a sense of guilt?

"I wish you wouldn't do that," Rosalind said, unable to stop herself.

"What?" Paul asked, baffled.

"Order for me. You didn't ask me what I wanted."

"You always have white wine to start. I thought I'd save us some time," Paul said.

"Paul, you haven't seen me in months. Did it occur to you that my tastes might have changed?" She knew how she sounded as soon as she spoke, and regretted it. He had no idea what was going on. Could she blame him?

Paul froze, knowing that she was annoyed, not knowing why. "I'm sorry. I didn't think it'd be a problem."

She softened toward him immediately. "I'm sorry. Long day at school. I'm in another world. Forgive me?"

He smiled and relaxed. "Don't worry. Come on, Ros. You can't have changed that much. Tell me you don't drink white wine anymore. Scare me."

"I don't, actually. I've been drinking a hot, spiced wine lately."

"Hot wine? I can't imagine that being good. It seems too strong for your taste," Paul said, creasing his forehead.

"You'd be surprised." Rosalind pictured the pot on the stove, Joe stirring, the smell of summer grass and endless afternoons under changing skies. She tasted again, pouring over her lips the sweetness made for a tongue that had just come to rest from an act of love. In that moment was the taste of the wine suspended, between afterglow and moonrise, an echo of the heated mouth that had bruised her with kissing. There was no way to tell Paul about the wine.

He asked about Eric. She regaled him with stories of her brother and Sandhya. He spoke with warmth of the card Mrs. Olchawski sent him for his birthday. The mixture of wistfulness and desperation was unsettling. Rosalind couldn't relax into his storytelling. She knew that Paul had never had an easy time with his emotions, that this lengthy prelude was vital if she was going to get him to speak at all.

She admitted to herself that she'd gotten used to a more headlong emotional style. This drifting talk made her yearn for the immediacy of rage, the molten look of unguarded love.

She gathered bits of what his life was like now. He was still teaching. He had been seeing Kathy, the woman with whom he'd had the affair. It wasn't in his nature to be a serial monogamist, even with the end of his marriage. It didn't surprise Rosalind that he'd stayed with Kathy. Some part of him would feel an obligation to make a relationship work. If not his marriage, then the next best thing. There was some sort of trouble between them. Rosalind got the impression that Kathy had left him.

He asked a few questions about her work and deflected her answers with an outburst of memories. Remember when we, and hey, didn't that guy remind you of the time…It caught her up, in a way, the evidence of their shared past, but not as strongly as it did Paul. He laughed longer at his own stories, chuckled with mirth at what crazy young people they'd been. In his nostalgia, he didn't recognize Rosalind's silence.

"Paul, tell me what's going on," she said at the end of one of his remembrances.

It seemed to drain all the blood out of him. He shrank down in the chair. His face lost the sheen of humor. "My father died," he said, naked as a skull.

"Arthur? My God, Paul. When?" Rosalind asked, stunned. She'd always loved his father, an energetic, endearing man given to expansive emotion, so unlike his quiet son. Paul had worshiped his father, never losing the small boy's conviction that his dad was immortal. No wonder Paul looked green. She wondered how he'd been able to survive that.

"Stroke. Two months ago. Dropped dead. Snap! Just like that. After all those years of telling us to eat our vegetables, never smoking, Mr. Marathon Runner keels over at fifty-seven. We might as well be smoking ten packs a day and never getting off the couch for all the sense nature makes."

Rosalind reached out and touched his hand. "I'm so sorry."

Paul shook his head, not seeing her. "I didn't feel a thing. I got the call when I was on the road. Everyone kept acting like I should be devastated, walking on eggshells around me. All through the funeral, I heard the whispers, how brave I was being. You know, Kathy kept trying to get me to open up, talk about how I was feeling. I wasn't feeling anything."

Rosalind was silent, knowing that he wasn't done.

"For two months, it was like I had a block of ice in my chest. It didn't happen to me. I just wanted to get back to work. It started to annoy me that people would get all choked up and ask me how I was. There wasn't anything wrong with me. Couldn't they see that? It got to be September. Kathy started hinting around about a birthday party for me, but I guess I just missed the signals. My head was down. So I walk into my house after a day at work. It's dark. I snap the lights on, and everyone yells, 'Surprise!'

"There was everyone, Mom, my cousins, Uncle Phil and his new wife, you remember her. Everyone I hadn't seen since the funeral. I just stood there looking at them, at the hole in the center of the circle where my father would have been. It finally hit me. He wasn't there. He wasn't coming back. I was thirty-four, and I'd woken up in some other man's life. How did I ever get here? I looked at Kathy, and all of them, and I panicked. My mind went white and empty. Dad was dead. The light in the world had gone out. I tried to remember the last time I felt good, the last time I knew who I was." He blinked. His eyes swam into focus. Rosalind could feel it coming, like the charge in the air before a thunderstorm. She wanted to tell him to stop, not to say it, but she was too late.

"It was when I was with you. So here I am."

Rosalind was very careful in answering, her words falling like drops of blood. "I'm so sorry about Arthur. I know he meant the world to you."

Paul held up his hand. His voice was hearty, full of self-aware humor, but the gesture mixed a beckoning in with the words, making them a plea. "I know how this must sound. I'm not a fool, Ros. I know that someone answered your phone the other afternoon. Someone who said they were your husband."

"Someone did," Rosalind said.

A twitch of pain danced across his face. "Of course. You said you weren't remarried."

"I'm not." Rosalind felt the words gathering, the words that would tell the truth about what had happened to her. *I'm not remarried, but I fell in love with a beautiful boy with a bull dagger tattooed on her back. When I am in her arms, I know who I am.* She couldn't say any of this to Paul without cruelty, and so she kept silent. There would be another time to speak of Taryn.

"I'm not here to make trouble for you. I just need to be around you for a while. I wish I could explain it, but…Please. I feel like I'm losing my mind. Like the end of the rope has already started to fray. Just let me spend some time with you."

CHAPTER FIVE

Joe watched Taryn hang up the phone, slump down the hall, and kick the front door. He followed at a safe distance, watching the storm clouds gather in the girl's wake. The air was tinged with lightning when she came to rest on the porch, staring moodily at the wreckage of the autumn garden. He sat down next to her, resting against the peeling lavender paint.

The days had started to get dark around six. Mariner Street was lit in patchwork by street lamps. Across from the house, at an angle, the lamp in front of 41 Mariner made a loud pop and went out. Joe glanced sideways and saw the brooding eyes of Taryn fixed in that direction. If the force of her emotion hadn't burned the lamp out, it certainly could have. Joe sighed and shifted his shoulders against the wall.

"The worst thing is being left alone in your head. You start out wondering, what's he look like, this guy she married? Pretty soon it's, I wonder what he did when he walked in. Did he try and kiss her? Is she glad to see him?" Joe said.

Taryn's dark head rested back against the wall next to him, eyes shut. "Does he remind her of something she doesn't have, something I can't give?"

Joe's hand landed on Taryn's knee. "You'll make yourself crazy like this. He's probably bald."

"Short," Taryn said with a curl to her lip that might have been humor.

"Boring as dirt," Joe said amiably.

"Old. At least thirty."

"Watch it, boy. I can still kick your ass."

"Boy," Taryn said in an echo, opening her eyes. "You've known me a few years, right?"

"A few."

"And you've seen me change?"

"I've seen you turn around. I've seen you blossom," Joe said with great warmth.

Taryn slumped forward, resting her arms on her knees. Her hands hung loose, and her head bent forward on her neck, as if too heavy to hold up. A handful of hair swung down, hiding her eyes. "The first time a woman called me a boy, I got this catch in my gut. Like a fire had been lit. Something just woke up with that word. Part of it was how she was looking at me. Like I was sexy and dangerous and trouble, and she couldn't wait to find out for herself. I loved it. First night we were together, I could tell that Rosalind loved that part of me. She had a place in her heart all furnished for me, just waiting for me to move in. And I wanted to." Taryn raised her head, staring at the street as the darkness came on.

"Part of you got recognized. It changes everything when that happens. When you meet a woman who recognizes you, who sees you and loves you for it, you'd do anything for them. After all the years of not being seen, to have someone look right at you changes the world," Joe said, his voice deep and burring.

"I know she loves me, Joe. I want to be better than myself when I'm around her. I'm changing. I won't be a boy forever. And I don't know what I'm going to grow up and be. There aren't any role models, you know? My mind just stops." Taryn leaned back against the wall, looking at the man sitting next to her. "I envy you sometimes, you know? You got everything handled. You know who you are, and nobody can tell you different. You sure didn't have any role models."

"T, I don't have everything handled. It's never finished, becoming who you are. You don't get to say, 'I'm thirty-five. This is it. I'm done changing until I'm dead.' I never saw myself where I am now. Goblin's a teenager. She'll be dating before I turn around. Which means she might make me a grandpa one of these days. Think I'm ready for that?" Joe said with a sigh.

"What was it like for you when you were a teenager? When you looked like a girl?" Taryn asked.

The expression on Joe's face was a mix of pleasure and surprise. "You've never asked me that before."

"I don't know. You just seem like such a guy, I never think of you as having lived as a woman," Taryn said and shrugged.

"I take that as a supreme compliment. You know, I've always treasured that about you. From the moment I met you, you treated me like one of the guys."

"Shit, you're The Guy. If I was a man, I'd be you. You know?"

"T, my teenage years were one long horror movie. My body didn't match me, who I saw, and the split between them freaked me out. I was even harder to live with than you are," Joe said with a quirk of his lips.

"Bite me. When did it change?"

"I thought doing normal woman things would help. All my female relatives and friends were getting married. That was the script I followed. Meet a nice guy and settle down. Ray was the nicest of guys. I got married. I got pregnant. I have to say, I will never regret having Goblin. But after Goblin was born, it got much harder. I went into a depression that didn't lift. I'd done everything I could to stop feeling like I did. If having a baby didn't work—the most solid outward example of being a woman I could imagine—what hope was there for me? But the conviction that I was a man didn't go away. It got to the point where I had to do something, or stay in the hole and never come out." Joe glanced at Taryn.

"How old were you?"

Joe scratched at his beard. "Twenty-four. I started hormones just as Goblin was starting school. Ray and I had divorced. He'd come out. It was time to dance with needles and surgery."

Taryn snorted. "You hate needles. You still have me help with your injections."

"That part was hard. Sticking myself in the thigh every two weeks was nothing compared to the changes. I started going through puberty all over again. Acne, growth spurts, mood swings that you couldn't hold a candle to. Testosterone is wild stuff," Joe said.

"But when did you get so, you know. Cool?" Taryn asked.

Joe laughed, a short, sharp bark of mirth. "Cool. Hah! That took a while. My body didn't start changing right away. My voice took a couple of months to lower. My beard took forever to come in. I had top surgery right away, but the rest was slow in catching up. I was living full time as a man. At first I was terrified of not passing. I had to work myself up to leave the house. That gave me a lot of time alone, sitting on my ass, thinking. Was it only the exterior that made me a man? What was I waiting for to be complete?"

"Sounds familiar," Taryn said.

"One day, I read this thing online. A memoir of a Nubian who'd been at a pharaoh's court in Egypt. He was a dwarf, an acrobat. He wrote that he had to decide that he was a man, no matter what people saw. Once he knew it, they knew it," Joe said.

"So that's what you did?" Taryn asked, her eyebrows pulling down.

"I said, I am a man. And decided that it was up to me to show the world what kind of man I was."

"I like that."

Joe reached out and ruffled Taryn's hair. His hand slowed, his fingers digging into her mane.

"You'll be okay," he said softly.

"You've heard that clothes make the man. That ain't so, but they do help make the king. You all got your gear?" Taryn asked. Her stance, leaning one arm on the smooth gray marble of the mantel, was deceptively casual. She was aware of the energy in her audience, of the eagerness she could feel in the air. They tried to hide it, tried to look cool in front of her, but each in her own way was burning. Sam had been early. Wolf had been late. Laurel was still hugging Joe, but Robbie was on the couch, attentive, focused, professional. Taryn flashed her a quick grin. Robbie wouldn't have any trouble passing with her height, her confidence, and her athletic frame.

Taryn had asked each of them to bring clothing appropriate for their male persona, keeping in mind their age and body type. "It might be fun to have five guys in suits and ties, but we're going to a dive. Bikers and frat boys, folks from Allen Street. Not guys in suits. We wouldn't get in the front door."

Robbie had done her homework. She'd come dressed in loose khakis and an Oxford button-down shirt under a leather jacket. Her hair was freshly cut close to the scalp, a high and tight that showed off the bones of her handsome face. She'd found a pair of black plastic frame glasses that squared her features off and made her look like a college guy out on the town.

Taryn had to admit that Wolf had done her homework as well. The skate punk look worked with her youth and mannerisms. She'd bleached her hair from purple to a cold ivory like a frozen flame. Her eyes were bright, and she kept fidgeting with her cigarette pack.

Grace would be a problem. Taryn could see that right away. The clothing she'd picked was good, a little upscale, but workable. The charcoal slacks draped a little too loosely on her, showing off the curve of her hips rather than camouflaging. The way she sat on the couch was pure girl. Legs crossed, hands folded. Taryn almost sighed. Grace had her copper hair bound back in a ponytail and tucked into the collar of her shirt. Grace had great presence onstage, but reverted to a self-conscious femininity offstage.

Sam was sitting forward on the couch, her elbows balanced on her knees, her shoulders rounded. Too conscious of hiding her breasts, Taryn thought. Binding would help Sam remember to keep her upper body stiff. She'd found a gray sports coat at a thrift shop and wore that over a white shirt and a pair of jeans. She'd gotten her hair cut as well, tighter on the sides, but with length on the top. It fell curling into her face, giving her a sweet, young boy's look. Sam's eyes were wide under heavy brows. Her smile was always halfway there.

"Okay. We start with binding. Joe, would you help me out?" Taryn asked. She turned and smoothly peeled off her T-shirt, enjoying the gasps from her audience.

"Nice ink," Wolf said, looking at Taryn's back. Sam blushed and looked away when Taryn turned around.

"Don't get shy. Everybody has to do this. You start with the Ace bandage. Hold it high under your left armpit. Push down and out on your chest as you bind. If you squeeze your breasts together, it gives you away. Down and out looks more barrel chested. Have your partner walk around you with the bandage. Just like wrapping a package. Don't pull so tight that you can't breathe. You'll be wearing this all night."

Taryn held up her arms and let Joe walk around her, binding her down. She took two safety pins off the mantel and handed them to Joe.

"Just like that. Nice and tight. Use safety pins, not the little metal things that come with the bandages. They come loose and claw into your skin, and that sucks." Joe stepped away. Taryn stood, hands in her pockets. "There you go. Step one. Now you."

Wolf was first to tear off her shirt with a carelessness that matched Taryn's. "Robbie, help me out here." She held the Ace bandage high under her left arm and handed the end to Robbie.

"You're too short. I have to walk around you," Robbie said.

"You're a basketball player. Everybody's short to you," Wolf said.

"Ain't like you got much to bind," Robbie said, pulling on the end of the wrap.

"You flirting with me?" Wolf grinned.

"Yeah. I want Laurel to break up with me so I can chase your skinny ass."

Grace unbuttoned her shirt and smiled at Sam, who promptly ducked her head. Sam tried to look everywhere but at Grace's body as she helped her bind. Sam held the end of the wrap and looked around for safety pins. "Sam, it's a little loose. Could you tighten it?" Grace asked. Sam swallowed.

Taryn had slipped into a boiled white shirt, so bright it made the eye hurt, and was buttoning it with her left hand. "You see how the binding helps? It gives a nice smooth look to your shirt or jacket. And it'll remind you to hold your upper body stiff, help with your stance. You don't want to get done up all handsome and come off like a drag queen."

"Grace, help Sam out with binding. Listen up. I've got something special for you boys. We're gonna talk about packing."

Taryn sat down on the couch, balancing her elbows on her knees. She leaned forward, a handsome young man in elegant disarray, shirt opened at the collar, well-polished boots under black trousers. The face under the shining hair was still and beautiful, the face of an altar boy touched by the divine. Silence came into the room, a hush that the whisper of a bandage being tightened barely disturbed.

"Wearing some rolled-up socks?" Wolf asked, dropping down into a crouch.

"That's part of it. There's a lot of reasons to pack. It makes your costume complete, if people look closely. It reminds you, when you stand, or sit, or walk, of how you are presenting yourself," Taryn said, her voice easing down into a lower register as she spoke.

"So you don't cross your legs like a girl?" Grace asked.

"Yeah. Believability. But there is something more to it. If you are a boy, and you want to develop a relationship with your cock, you gotta know what it's for." Taryn paused, waiting for an interruption, but there was only the quiet. "You wear your cock like a promise. You are there to bring pleasure. When you put it on, you're telling the world that you are ready to use it."

"A man does not go around thinking about how his cock brings women pleasure. He's thinking about how it brings him pleasure." Wolf snorted.

"We're not talking about being men. We're talking about being drag kings," Sam said.

"What the hell is the difference?"

"Drag kings perform. We make an act out of masculinity. When you get offstage, not everybody is male," Taryn said.

"I want to know how to use my cock as a woman," Wolf said.

"If it will help you focus on getting into character, fine." Taryn stood up and walked swiftly to the end of the room. She turned on her heel slowly and looked the audience over. "When you see a woman, you have to tell her it's all about her. The way you walk, any glance in her direction. It's all about her. You have to communicate that you know what you are doing. Give her a look. You know what she needs. You can swagger. You can be cocky, a punk. But under all of it, they have to know that you are in love with pleasing them."

Taryn stepped out of the living room, through the archway into the middle room. She stepped back in, her walk slowed to a stroll, a prowl. She was conscious of the eyes on her, but didn't give too much away. Her head turned casually, sweeping the room. She stopped by the mantel, and as if it were the most natural thing in the world, glanced over at Grace. Just a side glance, a flicker of a moment, but Grace shifted and crossed her legs.

Taryn leaned on the mantel like a bar, turning her back to the watching crowd. Her head was bent down, absorbed in thought, drawing the eye like a magnet. Like a flash of lightning Taryn's head raised, looking into the mirror above the mantel. Her eyes found Grace unerringly, caught her looking back, and held. Taryn eased her shoulders back, turned her hips, and smiled. That smile was more demon than altar boy, profane, knowing. One hand, seemingly by chance, hooked into the front pocket of her black trousers, a minute shift of her hips presented the bulge that the cloth concealed.

Taryn held Grace with her eyes until Grace blushed. Then her smile shifted, became the soul of charm. "You see what I mean?" Taryn asked, laughter in her voice.

"I do," Grace said, her hand absently fixing the collar of her shirt.

Taryn rubbed her chin thoughtfully. "Okay, Wolf. Come in the room and present yourself to Robbie."

Wolf's thin, angular body whipped around, her face wreathed in disbelief. "*Robbie*? You want me to come on to Robbie?"

"You got a problem with that?" Robbie asked, crossing her legs and folding her hands in her lap.

"Fine. It's all make-believe. I got it." Wolf gave a half shrug, indicating that she was too good for this foolishness, but would suffer through it. She ran her hands through her cold ivory hair, erasing any semblance of order that it might have fallen into. Wolf took a breath, then she seemed to vanish like a light snapping. In her place was a sullen, bored boy staring off into the distance. He slouched into the room, ignoring everyone.

There was a bare spot of wall next to the fireplace. Wolf leaned her back into it. A glance was thrown over the room, the inhabitants dismissed. A cigarette pack came out from one of the dozen pockets in the paint-stained pants and tapped rhythmically against a narrow wrist. Wolf flipped a cigarette out and caught it negligently between thin lips. Another bored sweep of the room with half-lidded eyes. Wolf slouched over to Robbie, cigarette hanging on her lip. Without ever quite looking at her, Wolf mumbled, "Got a light?"

Robbie sat staring at her. "That's it? That's the big seduction?"

"You don't want to come on looking too interested. Women love this aloof shit," Wolf protested.

"When was the last time you had a date?" Robbie asked.

Taryn reached out and plucked the cigarette off Wolf's lip, stalling her retort. "I hate to say it, but what Wolf did made sense. That is how her guy would act. No skate punk is gonna slide up with a dozen roses and ask to buy you a glass of champagne. It was believable."

"That's just how Wolf acts anyway!" Robbie said, standing up.

"She took it a step further, made it an act. She based it on her own personality, but it worked," Taryn said.

Wolf smirked at Robbie over Taryn's shoulder. "What'd I tell you?"

Taryn flipped the cigarette over and slid it behind her ear. "You don't know half of what you think you do about women, but the drag worked."

"Have you ever done that, T? Approached a woman while you were in drag?" Sam asked.

"A time or two. Lots of women already saw me in the show, so they know what's going on," Taryn said.

"Do women like that? Knowing it's you, I mean."

"Depends. Some don't get it. They can't stand the idea. Some like it, like it's interesting."

"Can't stand it? I can see not being interested, but—" Sam said, getting indignant.

"I'll tell you boys a hard truth and a sweet truth. Hard truth: some women don't get drag, don't like it at all. It's just too queer. Like when people started to hate the stereotypes about dykes and reacted to anything butch. Sometimes when you throw out a stereotype, you go overboard and throw out people who remind you of it. But the sweet truth: there have always been some women who love it. So we celebrate and do it for them."

Taryn strolled out of the room and returned, hauling Joe by the arm. "For this last bit we need a model. This is Joe, who tried to duck me but will be our facial hair model for the evening. Joe, this is Grace, Wolf, and Sam. Robbie you know."

Joe held up his hand. "Good evening, gentlemen. Robbie, how nice of you to bring Laurel back to us. I was just about to rent her room out."

"You've got the scissors and the spirit gum. If you took my

advice, you've shaved. If not, you will after tonight, I guarantee it. Pick a mirror. Brush the gum all over the area you want to have hair and let it get tacky. I'll be right back."

As she headed up the stairs, Taryn heard Joe addressing the group.

"Taryn's wrong. Clothes do make the man. Naked people have little or no influence in society."

"Don't be too impressed with him. He's quoting Mark Twain," Taryn leaned over the rail and called out.

When Taryn came back down the stairs, Joe was seated in the middle of the floor, with the group ringed around him. There was a bemused expression on his face, not unlike a lion being scrutinized by grade-school students.

"I tend to keep my beard tight. I look a little too much like Grizzly Adams otherwise," he said to Wolf, who was peering at his chin.

"Is it too full for a kid my age?" Wolf asked, her face grown serious in contemplation.

"Scruffy punk like you would have something more wispy," Joe said cheerfully.

Wolf nodded, then stopped. "Punk?"

"Sorry, you reminded me of another swaggering thug I know."

"Hey!" Wolf glared at him, letting the threat go unvoiced.

"How high up my cheek should I bring my beard?" Sam asked, moving closer to Joe.

"Give it a good clean line from about here down." Joe reached out and touched Sam's jaw.

"You guys look like you're in good hands," Taryn said. She dropped down next to Robbie, who was sitting apart from the circle, mirror in hand. She'd applied the hair to the spirit gum and was now trimming her goatee with a professional touch.

"You handsome devil," Taryn said, hitting her on the shoulder.

"Look out Denzel." Robbie set the mirror down and smiled brilliantly.

"Better not let Laurel see you like this or I'll never get you out of the house tonight."

Grace was brushing spirit gum onto her chin. Taryn tossed a pile of folded clothes into her lap.

"One pair of well-worn jeans with requisite holes. One black

T-shirt, nearly gray with age, Carpe Diem lettered on the back. Your sullen poet threads."

"You've been raiding my laundry again. Between you and Misha, I won't have anything to wear. Of course, Goblin's now at the age when she steals all my shirts and socks," Joe said, shaking his head.

"Is it all right?" Grace asked, glancing from Taryn to Joe.

"It's fine. Evidently Taryn knows best."

"They'll be big on you, but that will work better with denim. We want you to look like you haven't worked a full day in five years. You live on cigarettes and coffee, and never get out of bed before noon. Can you look soulful, aggrieved, and worried about the rainforest?" Taryn asked, ignoring Joe.

Grace thought for a moment. "I can try."

"Go slip these on. It'll help."

Dinner was finished. The waiter was hovering nearby with intimations of dessert and coffee. She might have been chewing on cardboard and sawdust for all she remembered what she was eating, Rosalind thought. There hadn't been much to say to Paul after his request, and he'd taken her silence as a comfort or a reassurance of place.

He'd asked to be around her. What in the world was she to do with him now? She wanted to ask where he was staying but was halfway convinced he hadn't made plans. Then she would have to offer him the use of her house, and she knew trouble when she headed for it. For a moment, Rosalind pictured Taryn's face while she explained that her ex-husband would be staying with her. For an uncertain amount of time. *How was your evening, dear?*

Paul was never one to linger after a meal. He usually had the check paid and was putting on his coat before she'd put down her fork. Rosalind tried to picture Paul sitting down to a meal with Joe in the kitchen of 34 Mariner, enduring the rough but joyous celebration each meal was meant to be. She saw, briefly, before her mind rejected the image, Paul sniffing at a glass of hot wine, brows wrinkled in distrust.

Rosalind glanced up at Paul, shaking the pictures from her head. What she saw made her freeze. There was a cloud, solid and metallic, roiling gray and burnt umber around Paul, emerging from his chest. She blinked, but the cloud didn't vanish.

"Are you all right? You have something in your eye?" Paul asked, looking at her.

"Yes. Yes, that's exactly it. I'm going to run off to the restroom and try to get this out of my eye," Rosalind said, pushing away from the table.

The restrooms were around a sharp corner, hidden behind anemic-looking ferns. Rosalind ducked around the corner, then poked her head back out, hoping the fronds gave her some cover. Paul's back was to her. He was tapping his fingers on the table, glancing at his watch. The cloud was still there. She was seeing things, but they weren't going away. Mighty Aphrodite.

Rosalind dug in her pocket for change and picked up the phone. She breathed a quick prayer to anyone who might be listening that Rhea would answer the phone.

"Yes." It was Rhea's voice. Rosalind almost cried out.

"Rhea, it's Rosalind. I need to talk to you. Something odd is going on." Part of her mind had time to recognize how she sounded and how crazy she would appear calling any other house.

"You found the third," Rhea said calmly.

"Third?"

"In need of healing. Well, bring him by. I was expecting him to show up tonight." Rhea hung up, leaving Rosalind staring at the phone.

"So you're going to show me your house?" Paul asked as Rosalind started the car.

"Yes. And have you meet a…neighbor of mine. But there's a conversation we need to have first," Rosalind said, looking sideways at Paul.

"You're driving. Talk away." He settled into the seat and seemed to relax. *Taryn's seat,* Rosalind thought. He had no idea of what was coming. He seemed glad to relinquish all control to Rosalind. It filled some need in him, just having shown up in Buffalo and made contact with her. She could see the exhaustion start to work its way to the surface. All the things he hadn't felt in the past two months weren't buried far. There was a slightly puzzled look on his face, as if he wasn't sure where he was, but that wasn't unpleasant.

The Saturn started moving through the dark, making the loop toward the Niagara River and downtown Buffalo. There was no easy way to begin. Rosalind gripped the wheel, wishing that Taryn were with her. Taryn's headlong emotional style would make short work of this conversation. There would be no hiding, no overly careful phrasing, just a naked explosion, declarations of love and passion with no thought to the consequences. *You'd think I'd have learned how to do that, after loving Hurricane Taryn.* But the conversation would not come.

"You're sighing," Paul said, his head tilted back against the seat.

"Am I? I was just thinking of...someone."

"Someone. The same someone who answered your phone yesterday afternoon?" Paul asked. There was no mistaking the edge to his voice, the faint whiff of petulance.

"Yes," Rosalind admitted.

"You might as well tell me about him, then. Is he an academic? Teaches at UB?" Paul asked.

Is this what they call biting the bullet? Rosalind wondered. "No. He's a she." It was oddly appropriate phrasing, and it felt very good to plunge in and say it. She glanced over at Paul to see how he was reacting.

The skin around his mouth had gone pale, yellowish. His eyes were very wide, unblinking. "You're dating a woman?" he asked with a flatness that wasn't reassuring.

"Yes, I am."

"My. You have been enjoying your freedom."

It was a blow. He was striking out in pain. Rosalind counseled herself to remember that and not take it to heart. But it hurt. "I don't think that was called for," Rosalind said, trying to keep her tone level.

Paul rolled his eyes. "Called for? I didn't say anything wrong. How would you like me to receive this information? What's the politically correct way of responding when you find out the woman you married is chasing women?"

"I'm not chasing women. I'm involved with one," Rosalind said. *And we are divorced*, she added silently.

"Involved. So is this a one-time thing, like an experiment? Bit of the old liberal curiosity? No, really. I'd like to know. Is this a full-time conversion?"

She managed to keep the car on the road, to follow the curve of blue gray pavement past the black water of the river. Was there any easy way to do this? "I'm gay, if that's what you are asking."

"If that's what I'm asking. You've gotten cold, Ros. Is that new, too, or is my memory failing me?" Paul said bitterly.

"Paul, I know this isn't easy. Can we try to be civil about it?"

He gave no sign that he'd heard her. His eyes were lit by oncoming headlights. He was silent a long time. When he spoke it was almost a whisper. "Tell me something. Is that what went wrong between us, this gay thing? Is that why we crashed and burned?"

Such pain, blind to anything but its own existence. Rosalind wasn't sure that she could reach him beyond it. The words she couldn't say clogged her throat. *I came into the world for one person, and I found her.* Maybe it would be easier for him to be angry, to have something to blame, like her being gay. Maybe it was the least she could offer him. He had always been her friend. Perhaps she owed him this. "I think that's a part of it."

He nodded, hearing what he wanted to. He was silent until she reached the corner of Allen and Elmwood, a block from her house. Rosalind drove down Elmwood, past A Pound of Flesh. Paul twitched as they passed the shop, as if he'd sat on a needle. "A pound of flesh, closest to the heart. Shylock, wasn't it?" he asked her.

"Yes." She turned on Mariner. "This is my street."

Paul looked around in disbelief. "This? But this neighborhood is so run down. I expected you to live in a more upscale spot, maybe near the university. What do you see in this place?"

"It's an interesting place to live. Very alive. And the people are remarkable." Rosalind parked in front of her house. "Do you want a quick tour?"

"Why quick?" he asked.

"I wanted you to meet Rhea," Rosalind said.

"Your neighbor. Is she the one you're...involved with?"

"Rhea? Good God, no." Rosalind choked back a laugh at the thought.

"So why do you want me to meet her." Paul said it flatly, making it a statement.

BURNING DREAMS

"I think she can help you. You have to meet her, or nothing I say will make any sense at all."

Paul seemed more pleased by the interior of her house than he had been by the neighborhood. He stood in the living room, commenting on the wood floors and the fireplace, the scrollwork on the banister.

He headed right for the stairs, leaving Rosalind to jog after him, hoping to barricade the bedroom. He was diverted by the window at the end of the hall and walked to it with interest. While he was craning his neck to peer out, Rosalind glanced into her bedroom and saw the lingering chaos of recent and hearty use. Pillows were still heaped on the window seat, under the bed. One was on the dresser. There was a pack of cigarettes next to the pillow, crushed and empty. Rosalind grabbed up the pack and stuffed it into her pocket.

"You don't keep the quilt on the bed anymore?"

The voice made her jump sideways into the door. Paul had left the window. "Oh, well, no. It's in the closet. I thought I'd bring it out when it got cold," Rosalind said, pushing him away from the room.

"It's already October in Buffalo," Paul said, looking over her shoulder.

She could tell that he'd seen something from the way his eyes squinted, then flared. The thought that danced across her mind was irreverent. He looked exactly like a horse that had seen a rattlesnake. He clenched his jaw in a kind of grimace and turned away.

Rosalind followed the sight line and saw it—a silver condom wrapper on the floor under her bed. She wanted to say something to him, but he had gone downstairs. She found him sitting on the couch, his hands knotted in his lap. He looked so tightly wound a breeze might blast him apart. "All rawhide and whalebone," his father used to say, gently mocking his son's temperament. "He's as tight as a Puritan. Thank God you came along to lighten him up, Ros."

"Hey," Rosalind said, sitting down on the couch next to him. Though she didn't recognize it, her voice had taken on the exact tone Taryn used when speaking to her.

Paul sat looking straight ahead, dry eyed and barren. "Nothing is the same, is it?"

"A lot has changed. But a lot is still the same," Rosalind said gently.

"Like what? My father is dead. My life isn't something I recognize.

And the person I thought who knew me best—my wife—has changed so much I can't keep up with it," he said with a bitter laugh.

Rosalind wanted to correct him on the title wife, but he seemed so lost, she let it go. It would push him further into himself, when what she wanted was to reach him. "I'm still the person you grew up with. I'm still the person who was always your best friend," she said, nudging him.

"Sure."

"I'm the person who knows the real story of how you got caught shoplifting in seventh grade. It wasn't comic books. It was *Playboy*," Rosalind said.

Paul laughed, more of a dry coughing scraping through his throat. "Shit," he said at last.

"Come on. We need a cup of tea with Rhea."

"Let me get this straight," Misha said, pulling the pillow off his face. "We—that would include me—are going to chaperone a bunch of Taryn's friends to a bar. While they are dressed like men. I am right, yes?"

"That about sums it up," Joe said.

Misha groaned and pulled the pillow back over his head. "What time is it?" he mumbled through several layers of cloth.

"Nearly eight."

"In the evening?" Misha sat up and tossed the pillow aside.

"In the evening," Joe said with the patience of a parent.

"Well, that's respectable, then." Misha swung his legs to the floor. He reached for the pack of cigarettes on the windowsill. He held the pack out to Joe, who declined with a small motion of his hand.

"They are finishing up now, so you'd better get ready," Joe said.

Misha stood up, clad only in his jeans. He picked up a T-shirt from a pile on the top of the desk and pulled it on. "Very well. I am ready. You've been working out, Joe. Your shirts are getting bigger through the shoulders." He wondered why Joe grumbled something about his clothing being raided.

"Tell me something, Joe. This dressing as men, this masquerade. Do you approve of it?" Misha asked while pulling on his boots.

"Approve? Sure. Taryn's very good at it. Some of her boys need work, but it's their first time out," Joe said.

"No, no. Not artistically. I thought it might trouble you, as a man. Taryn was just starting this when I…left the city. You were helping her with her walk, how she looked. This surprised me." Misha exhaled a cloud of smoke. He took up a rubber band and pulled his hair back into a ponytail.

"Taryn is family. Why would it surprise you?" Joe asked, leaning on the desk.

"It could be said to make a mockery of manhood, this act," Misha said, his eyes glinting like obsidian, catching a spark from his cigarette.

Joe titled his head thoughtfully. "You like Egyptia, right?"

"Of course. She is wonderful. A doll. She was always close with…my brother," Misha said, his tongue betraying him on his brother's name. Joe appeared not to notice.

"Misha, Egyptia's a drag queen."

"I know this," Misha said, irritated.

"She dresses up in women's clothing, puts on makeup. You think she walks like that in her day job? You think she goes by *she?*" Joe asked.

"Of course not. Don't make me out to be a fool, Joseph. It is not the same thing. Egyptia is gorgeous. She is more herself this way. It mocks no one," Misha said.

"I don't think masculinity is so fragile that a few girls dressing up as men will shatter it. Maybe masculinity isn't only the province of genetic men. Hell, Misha, you were a boy once. You had to learn to be a man."

"I was born knowing," Misha said, smiling to take the edge off his words as he shrugged into his leather jacket.

"Then you'll be a good role model. Come on. Egyptia's meeting us there. That should make you happy. And a few others," Joe said, turning toward the door.

"Who are these others?" Misha asked, following him.

Joe started walking down the stairs. "Oh, the women running the drag show. Linda and Ellie."

"Ellie," Misha said, with no particular emphasis.

"Sure, Ros's friend. You remember her."

"Perhaps."

In the living room he saw Taryn, her back to the stairs, adjusting the tie on a short, somewhat thickset young man. A car salesman, Misha thought, with that earnest expression and secondhand sports coat. It wasn't until she spoke that Misha recognized the young woman behind the full beard.

"How does this look?" Sam asked.

Taryn pulled down the points on her collar. "Like a million bucks." Taryn turned, glancing over her shoulder. Misha saw a goatee, parted in a devil's grin. "Good morning, Misha."

He walked into the living room, eyebrows climbing up. Taryn had a black jacket on over a white shirt and stood with her hands in her pockets, watching him.

"You look very convincing, Taryn," he said after a moment.

"Thanks, Misha. So do you."

CHAPTER SIX

Rosalind thought that the very air of 34 Mariner would draw comment from Paul, the hum like electricity or hives of bees, the perpetual sunbursts of creativity and decay. He passed through the purple and green door without a word, as if he'd lost a fight, and lapsed into a defeated silence. Joe's red convertible was gone from its spot in front of the house, and the living room was empty. They'd missed the drag kings.

Rosalind could see signs of them everywhere: hand mirrors, scissors, and spirit gum set out in a rough circle on the floor, pages torn out of magazines, showing handsome young men pouting in clothing ads. A shiver ran from her fingertips up her arm as her hand brushed the couch. Taryn had been here not long ago.

Rosalind's mind threw together an image of Taryn in drag: glossy black hair, brooding eyes, sullen pout so like the pretty boys in the magazine ads. Yet there was something else in Taryn's presentation, a glimmer of danger, an undercurrent of humor, a knowing smile that let the audience in on the masquerade. Soul became image became soul, until the very performance became more real than the object. All life became performance and all performance became real, the trickster's knowledge, the power of passing through the restricted realms. Rosalind had seen it in action, been drunk on it, fallen in love with the trickster herself. The image brought with it an immediate stab of longing that made it hard to concentrate. She was here to introduce Paul to Rhea, Rosalind reminded herself, not to pine for her boy. If things were different, she'd be with Taryn tonight. But there was Paul, who needed her help.

Rhea was in the kitchen. How could she not be? Rosalind thought. The meeting had taken on a ceremonial air, from Paul's conspicuous silence to the witch sitting in the vast kitchen like a spider in her web. Rosalind wondered how to prepare Paul, what she should say to him about Rhea, or the house, or Taryn before the meeting happened. They were in the doorway, and there was Rhea sitting at the table. The moment of preparation had passed.

Paul walked into the kitchen, looking so out of place Rosalind felt it like a knife on her nerve endings. She felt, wildly, that this was too much, her past walking into the center of her current life. The leap of faith was too great. How could everything that she loved be explained to the man in whom it aroused such pain? He didn't belong here with his careworn face, blank from shock, the distant, flat look in his eyes, his blue suit rumpled, his tie undone an inch but no more. Some animals are born unable to see, and they manage quite well. Some humans are born able to see, but they never adapt to what their eyes tell them. Paul's eyes had always been open, but she doubted his vision.

Rhea stood up. Rosalind remembered her own first meeting with Rhea, the palpable hostility that had taken so long to cool into friendship. Rhea was many things, as she'd learned, but instantly empathic was not one of them. She left that to Joe, letting him embody the characteristics she had cut off or never learned. So it was a pure surprise to see Rhea's eyes grow glassy, like black stones under a moving brook. Rhea looked at Paul and she wept. Soundless tears slid down her still face, heedless of her expression or her control. It was as natural as rain. Rhea seemed to be less the author of her tears than their recipient. She walked toward Paul, this small, thin woman with her serpentine hair, tears gilding a face that betrayed no sorrow. She walked right up to Paul, who stood frozen, and touched his cheek.

"You cannot cry, and so I must," Rhea said to him, as if she didn't really expect him to understand.

"Rhea, this is Paul, my old friend. Paul, this is Rhea, the owner of the house," Rosalind said formally.

Paul shook himself, as if remembering who he was. "I'm—"

"I know who you are," Rhea said, taking her hand away. She motioned to a chair. Paul sat.

"Rosalind, would you make him a cup of tea?" Rhea asked, courteous as a queen.

"Not hot wine?" Rosalind asked, only half kidding.

Rhea seemed to take it seriously. "He's not ready. Misha could manage it because he'd acquired the taste long ago. This one will need time."

"I'm not sure of what's going on here, but could you please not discuss me like a German shepherd?" Paul asked, annoyed, as if annoyance could help him regain part of himself.

"Very well. I will be specific. You are in dire need of healing. Rosalind saw that and brought you to me," Rhea said.

"What are you, some kind of faith healer?" Paul asked.

"No. You need to heal your own faith. I work on the spirit. The body often benefits as well," Rhea said calmly.

Paul pushed away from the table. "Jesus, Ros. What is this sideshow? You going to have the gypsy read my tea leaves next?" Rosalind opened her mouth, but Rhea was already speaking.

"It's terrible, isn't it?" Her eyes roamed over Paul's face familiarly.

"What is?" he snapped.

"Finding what you think will complete you and being wrong. Loving someone so much you would lay down your life without thought, but not being their chosen. Knowing that you would do, or be, anything for them. Having them give you their love, in measure, but never their heart. And having to know the difference."

The blood drained from Paul's face, leaving it chalky. "How did you—"

"I've been there. Over and over again. I have given my heart away, to the same girl, in every lifetime. But I am never the one for her." Rhea spoke in a measured tone, as if she were discussing the weather. It seemed to mesmerize Paul. He leaned forward on the table, his eyes wide.

"Did you have to know who was the one?" Paul asked, ignoring the gender Rhea had used.

"Oh yes. That is my particular gift from Fate. I had to know who

replaced me. And until I could accept her, I died. Again and again."
Rhea smiled.

"And did you have to see the one you loved? Be around?"

"Oh yes. I always live with her." Rhea's tone was lighter. She
sounded almost amused.

"I don't know if I could do that," Paul said, shaking his head.

"You'll have to find a way. You need to live here, in this house,
until I say you can leave. Or you will never survive. It will be the
cornerstone of your healing," Rhea said.

Rosalind had expected Paul to react harshly, even violently, to
Rhea's words. He was fresh from the outside world, unused to how
things worked in the house, completely without frame of reference. He
didn't. He simply sat looking at Rhea, trying to comprehend. "Am I a
prisoner?" he asked, looking around the kitchen.

"You are. But if you stay here, I can help you learn to be free.
It won't be easy. Giving up pain never is. You grow so attached to it,"
Rhea said.

There was an intimacy to their conversation that made Rosalind
feel like she was eavesdropping. There had to be something to focus on,
to keep her from interrupting. How in the world could Rhea ask Paul
to stay in the house? She knew how Taryn felt. Rosalind turned her
back and searched the cupboards for tea. She faced a myriad of glass
jars, some corked, some covered with skins, some open. All unlabeled.
Cooking was Joe's domain, and he seemed to do it by instinct, never
looking at a recipe or label. It was like watching a dance performance,
the fluid way he had of reaching out his hand and taking what he needed.
A step, a great swooping stride, and the right glass jar would be open,
the right herb raining down over his creation. There were many jars
that only Rhea touched. These were likewise unlabeled. How was she
supposed to find the right one? But Rhea had asked her to make tea,
and Rhea had never asked anyone to do what they were not capable
of doing. So Rosalind closed her eyes and reached out, taking the first
jar her hand felt drawn to. The kettle was on the stove. She turned the
flame up and waited.

"How did you let go of your pain?" Paul asked Rhea. He was
fascinated with the witch, ignoring even Rosalind as she moved around
the kitchen.

"I had help. I fought against it, but the same love that tears you apart also gives you room to build again. But that's not what you want to ask me. You want to know how you can let go of your pain. Even though you don't believe me, even though this very conversation is something you are standing apart from, watching, an observer. The idea of being free is so seductive you will suffer through something you don't believe, in case it might be true. Poor, wounded, lost man. You have a heart that longs to believe and a head that is too well trained to let you," Rhea said.

"I think I'm being a very good sport here," Paul said with a small laugh.

"And that is so very important, being a good sport. You've made that your life, being reasonable, being calm. To the point where passion is a stranger, and life herself is at arm's length. You need some unreasonableness. You need things not to make sense for a while. Which is why you will do what I say. I think Laurel's room would do for you. She's staying with her girlfriend anyway. Joe's study already has Misha. I can hardly put you on the third floor with Taryn."

"How long am I expected to stay?" Paul asked, seeming to accept the absurdity of it all.

Rhea looked fixedly at him, squinting her eyes. "Until Halloween, I'd say. Beyond that, it's up to you."

"That's nearly a whole month from now! This has been fun, but I have a life. I can't just—" Paul exploded.

"Go ahead," Rhea said calmly.

"You expect me to pack up and run off to Buffalo for an entire month? Just put my life on hold? That's ridiculous."

"You already did. The water is boiling, Rosalind," Rhea said.

Rosalind shook herself out of her trance and poured the tea. She brought a cup to Paul, setting it in front of him without meeting his eyes. She set one out for Rhea and poured herself one on a whim.

"Jasmine, a good choice. We'll need the calmness," Rhea said, sniffing at the tea.

"What do you think of all this?" Paul demanded, seeking Rosalind's attention.

"She's already stuck in the middle of a conversation, trying to explain this to Taryn. Don't mind her," Rhea said, smiling at Rosalind in a way that wasn't exactly comforting.

"Paul, this sounds crazy, but if anyone can help you, Rhea can.

And you need help. You came asking to spend some time with me. This would certainly let you do that," Rosalind said.

"So who is this Taryn that everyone is worried about? Your husband?" Paul asked Rhea.

The smile on Rhea's face grew, deepened, a smile of remembered pleasure and unalloyed affection. It was a look of love that Rosalind had seen before, when Rhea would watch Taryn—in the shop, working with Joe. There had been one morning when she'd been curled up in Taryn's arms on the couch after a night spent talking. She'd opened her eyes and seen Rhea standing in the middle of the room, watching the two of them. It was the first time she'd ever seen that look directed at Taryn while she was there. It took Rosalind a moment to recognize that Rhea was including her, that her approval and delight were bestowed on seeing the two of them together. In that moment, she got a glimpse into the expansiveness of the love Rhea bore Taryn, a love great enough to rejoice in Taryn's own happiness. If that was what she was offering to teach Paul, how could Rosalind refuse it?

"When I marry, it won't be to wildfire, thank you. My lover's name is Joe. Taryn is…a resident of the house. And also Rosalind's lover."

The cat was out of the bag and darting across the floor, Rosalind thought.

Misha balanced his pool cue against the table and reached behind his ear for the cigarette he had stashed. He lit it with a flick of his wrist, snapping the match head off with thumb and forefinger when he was done. "You are going to break sometime before the next Ice Age?" he asked Joe, who was bent over his cue.

"In good time. True pool approaches Zen. When the moment is right, all things flow together," Joe said.

"Shoot the damn thing, and stop with the philosophy," Misha said. Restless, he surveyed the bar.

It was a low-ceilinged, smoky room, dark as the devil's heart. The bathroom was a swampland, covered in obscene graffiti. The main room looked as if a riot had destroyed it and no one had rebuilt. Misha sighed in satisfaction. It was good to be back. He loved the Old Pink. He'd have been perfectly happy to bring his bike and park it out front on the sidewalk with the Harleys, but Joe had insisted that they walk. It was to keep him from driving drunk, and Misha knew it. No one had given a damn if he lived or died since…his mind balked at the thought. He reached for his beer.

Taryn was sitting at one of the tables in the back, surrounded by her boys. Holding court, Misha thought. Taryn looked good, a little too pretty and slick to his eye, like a gay man. He'd found that if a man was stunningly good looking and well dressed, he was probably gay. He'd asked his brother why once. "So they can date me," had been his brother's smiling answer. His mind kept dancing around things he didn't want to think about. It was making him angry. Misha killed his beer and looked back to the kings. The tall one, Robbie, was handsome. He could admit that. Misha felt a stab of pain under his ribs, the old envy of his brother. He'd been so handsome it was a sin. It was a good thing he wasn't gay as well, Misha thought. He'd never get a date with Stephan around.

Taryn left the table and strolled to the bar. Misha choked back a smile. Most of them were too young to drink, so Taryn returned with a handful of sodas. As if Taryn had any ground to stand on. She was still shy of twenty-one. She was turning into Joe. The thought of Taryn transforming into Joe sent Misha into laughter, and he started to choke.

"Are you trying to keep me from breaking?" Joe asked, holding his stance.

"No. I was thinking of Taryn turning into you."

"You have it backward. I want to be Taryn when I grow up," Joe said, and made his break.

Taryn was deep in conversation with the red-haired one, the king wearing Joe's clothing. It had been Taryn's whim, but it suited her, or him. Misha couldn't keep up with the pronouns. The red-haired one now sported muttonchop sideburns and a soul patch, with properly unkempt hair hanging down to his shoulders. He looked remarkably like the kind of boy Misha would have beaten up in high school. At the red-haired one's elbow was the used-car salesman, the fellow with the cheap sport coat and the full beard, looking raptly at the red-haired guy as he spoke to Taryn. The white-haired punk was watching television with the tall, handsome black girl in the goatee. It was funny to watch them. The bar was nearly empty. It was early in the evening. They clustered together like a pack of adolescents in the back, under the television monitors, hunched over their drinks, throwing sidelong glances out at the bar, over to the pool table, watching him and Joe. *Want to see how a man acts in public?* Misha thought. The used-car salesman was looking at him. Misha grinned at them and spit on the floor.

He would give Taryn some credit. As the initial unease thawed, they loosened up. They slouched respectably in their bar chairs. They began to look more and more like young men out early, having a drink, not hunted felons. It was Taryn's impossible self-confidence that did it, leading them to relax in turn. Misha's lip turned up. Pretty boy, he thought, going back to his pool game. Stephan had told him about the night he'd met Taryn at a Halloween party Rhea was throwing. Stephan had gone out on the porch to fetch Joe and found him talking to a youth in silver armor, whose sweet-faced beauty was more than half-demonic under a crop of black hair. Though Stephan was happily involved with Ray, Joe's ex-husband, he'd felt his heart start hammering. He introduced himself with all his charm, only to find out rather abruptly that this heavenly youth was Taryn, Rhea's new girlfriend. Ah, the vagaries of life, Stephan had said to him.

Taryn had that effect on people. Either they got so besotted looking at her they couldn't think, or they took one look at her and felt pure animosity. With Misha it had been the latter. He'd found the teenager arrogant, insufferable, without the resources to back up the boasts her very walk made. It was a good two years later, when Rhea and Taryn had ended, when Joe and Rhea had begun, that Misha had to start revising his opinion. Taryn welcomed Joe into the house with genuine warmth, something Misha frankly doubted at first. Who wanted to live with their ex-lover and her new boyfriend? But the bizarre arraignment worked, and a family coalesced at 34 Mariner. It was something in the air in that house, a joy and a sense of peace. Stephan and Ray loved it there. They spent a great deal of time visiting. Where Stephan went, Misha went, so the odd family extended him a cousin's welcome, and at last, a brother's. For a man who knew from childhood that the only being who would ever love him was his twin brother, it had been unnerving.

Misha was a nomad, scion of a long line of nomads, dating back to his ancestors in the Caucasus. His mother had attributed it to his Cossack roots, and even further back, to the Scythians. As in most things, he and Stephan were opposites. Where Misha was restless, apt to disappear for months on end, Stephan loved belonging to a single place. When they had lived in Toronto, Misha spent most of his time with a touring company, and Stephan had built a life for them. When his brother, handsome as Adonis, had chosen to settle down with an American, of all things, Misha had been devastated. Stephan was leaving him. And to move to Buffalo? He couldn't have picked a more backwater, dead-end, relentlessly American small town. When Stephan seemed genuinely happy with Ray, enjoying helping to raise Ray's daughter, joining in the odd community, Misha had given in. He kept touring with production companies, working as a master electrician, but he came back to Buffalo between trips.

He had to learn how to be around a family, even such an unexpected one. He was sarcastic with the teenaged thug, grudgingly admiring her hardness and resiliency. He was used to the vagaries of modern gender, after exposure to Joe, but Taryn annoyed him. She was a girl, she looked like a boy, and it didn't bother her. He wanted to grab her by the scruff of her neck and demand she pick a gender and stay with it. It didn't help that women found her fascinating, and she dated more than he did. And the women who were attracted to Taryn didn't all seem like gay women. Life was resolutely unfair.

Misha thought about the new woman Taryn was dating. Rosalind. Another woman who didn't look at all like she'd be interested in a cross-dressing punk. She was attractive, more his age. She dressed like she had a good job. Yet she was mad for Taryn. What was it with them? She was not Taryn's type. Taryn had always displayed a sense of true democracy in her amorous habits, but the ones that lasted more than a night had a certain similarity that he'd come to notice. After Rhea, she never dated for more than a weekend a woman who was older than she was.

The women who came to stay at 34 Mariner for a week or so were uniformly young. They all had that look of entitlement after the first night, and they all lost it by the end of the week, when Taryn's indifference drove them out. Taryn had been cruel in her dismissal, and final. It was strange to watch. She'd last a few days, but the bored look would appear on her face, the mask of sullen distance. In a few more days, whatever new friend had been keeping company at 34 Mariner would be gone and Taryn would be going out every night. There was a relentless searching in the way Taryn went after women, a desperation to find something that never appeared. He doubted that she could even name what she'd been seeking. In this one, she seemed to have found it. Misha's beer was empty. He held up the bottle to Joe, who shrugged, then gave a half grin. Misha walked to the bar to order two more.

Rosalind sat on the couch facing the fireplace. It was late, between the time when all the cats went out to prowl and the hour when they dragged themselves home. Rhea had set six fat white candles burning on colored glass dishes in place of the dried flowers she usually kept in the hearth. The flames made weird shadows on the burnt orange tiles, hypnotic storytelling. Tales of love and death. Old stories. There was a mug in her hands. Rhea had poured her something and told her to sit.

The warmth in her cupped hands, the persistent burning of the new tattoo were all that registered. She felt curiously empty, bled out, light as smoke. Paul had exhausted her with his questions, his needs. She'd told him the story of Taryn, counterpointed at times with Rhea's observations. His disbelief was solid, a wall she couldn't breach, no matter how slowly she spoke, no matter how many times she repeated herself. Yes, she had a lover. Yes, Taryn lived here. Yes, Taryn was young. None of these things said what she wanted to say, the words he couldn't bring himself to hear. *Yes, I love her.* Rosalind couldn't capture Taryn's essence, couldn't get Paul to see past the fact of her existence.

Finally, Rhea had asked for some time alone with Paul. She had implied that it was to begin his healing, but Rosalind suspected, once she'd been installed on the couch, that it was also for her to escape. So she sat with the weight of the past, sipping whatever concoction Rhea had given her, wishing she were drinking hot wine. It wouldn't get any better when he met her. If the story of Taryn was unpalatable for him, he would be unprepared for the reality. It was one thing to hear rumors of a leopard and another to bed down with one in the house.

There was the small matter of introducing Taryn to Paul. As a new roommate. Rosalind raised the mug to her lips, its unfamiliar muddy gray rim giving her pause. She felt a moment of irritation. Why hadn't Rhea given her Taryn's blue glass mug? It was her mark of status, and she felt attuned to its lack. The memory came back with force—Taryn hurling the mug across the kitchen. The fight. About Paul. Rosalind pushed the tears away with the back of her hand, hearing the soft brush of Rhea's feet coming down the hall.

"How is he?" Rosalind asked, pushing up from the couch.

"Sit. He's sleeping. The first round does that to them. I put him up in Laurel's room." Rhea sat down next to her on the couch, tucking her feet to the side.

"Does it make you tired?" Rosalind asked her, slipping a glance at her sharp profile.

"Not anymore. I'm used to it. You will get some distance from it. It won't drain you as harshly as it did tonight," Rhea said.

"I didn't do anything tonight," Rosalind protested.

"You decided to help an old friend, no matter what it cost you. You call that nothing?" Rhea patted her on the knee, a gesture so unexpected that Rosalind teared up again.

"I just hope she understands."

Rhea looked into the dancing flames. "When I met Taryn, she was sixteen. She'd been thrown out by her family, after…Dean. I expect she told you."

"Yes," Rosalind said, teeth clenching on the memory.

"She had no reason to trust anyone. It was like bringing a wild animal into the house. The starving young lion who will grow sleek by feeding from your hand, but never tame. I gave her love. I don't say this to boast, but she gave everything she had in return." Rhea paused and smiled.

"She'd die for you, Rhea. You know that," Rosalind said fiercely.

"What she couldn't give to me was her heart. That was waiting for you. If she has given me a lifetime of loyalty for what I have been to her, do you really expect less? It is time for her to understand and to stretch herself."

There was a noise coming down the street, and it sounded to Rosalind's ear like a badly slurred Russian folk song. Her grandmother used to sing it to her in Polish, warning her about roguish Russian sailors. She recognized the cadence—"Dark Eyes"—bellowed in an enthusiastic, drunken male voice. Misha, in full thrall to Dionysus.

"The neighbors are going to love this," Rhea said, standing up.

"I'm one of the neighbors, and I don't mind. It's kind of funny," Rosalind said.

"Let me go out and have a word with him. Them, from the sound of it. That's Joe supplying harmony."

Rhea walked out on the porch. There they were, staggering up the sidewalk from Virginia, enjoying their night of male bonding. Taryn looked exalted by the night. Her skin glowed like dawn. Her eyes were dreaming, sliding half closed under heavy lids. There was a smile she wasn't aware of on her lips. Joe looked on the verge of sober, bearing up Misha's weight. Misha was wrecked, his hair spilled down over his shoulders. He hung between Joe and Taryn, giving only a half-hearted attempt at walking. As they carried him, a wounded man being dragged to safety by his buddies, he sang the folk song with relish. Rhea wondered if he thought he was in Toronto or Odessa. Misha rolled his head to the side on the last line and rested against Taryn's neck, oddly like a lover.

"Be quiet, *chelovyek*. Rhea will wake up and put a spell on us," he said in heavily accented English.

When they staggered one house closer, Rhea saw that Taryn had removed her goatee, leaving her skin with a reddish cast. She looked to be brimming with joy, drunk on it as much as Misha was drunk on alcohol. Doing drag brought this out in her, eased the fear. Creativity is a powerful healer.

"She is awake, bonehead," Taryn said to Misha.

Rhea folded her arms and waited. Joe looked apologetic immediately. Misha closed his eyes. Taryn grinned, the smile of a devilish boy who knows he's too charming to be punished.

"Is Rosalind here?" Taryn asked.

Rhea put out her hand, stopping all three as surely as Medusa. She walked down the steps to Taryn and leaned close to her face, whispering, "You have a woman in there eating her own heart for fear of your reaction. You have a chance to show her how you feel when she truly needs you. Don't waste it."

Ice formed in the chambers of Taryn's heart. Rhea could see it happening.

"Is she all right?" Taryn asked, her voice harsh from escaping emotion.

Rhea touched her cheek, as she first had when they met. "Go on."

Taryn dropped Misha's arm and bolted up the stairs. The living room was dark, spattered with light coming from six candles dangerously close to gutting out. Taryn's eye passed over the room on her headlong way toward the stairs. It wasn't until she was on the second step that the form on the couch registered as a person sitting in the dark. She paused, pivoted, and stepped back down, all her momentum gone. There was silence coming like a breeze from the living room, even after the person on the couch had to be aware of her, of her boots announcing themselves on the wooden floors. Taryn walked into the room, her stride abbreviated, checked, uncertain at the lack of response she was getting.

It was Rosalind on the couch. There was no mistaking that. The fickle candlelight gilded the edge on her cheek, the curve of her forehead, lost itself in kinship with Rosalind's hair, barley and snow and dull gold. But the silence was awful to Taryn's ears, the lack of a loving greeting seemed like punishment. She saw Rosalind's eyelids flicker, saw her eyes move away. It clenched like a fist in Taryn's gut, that small movement, that tiny avoidance. She was causing Rosalind pain, and Rosalind wanted to get away from it, from her. Taryn set her jaw. She would not be avoided.

She stood directly in front of the fireplace, blocking the light, unknowingly giving herself an aura of fire. Once there, she didn't know what to do. Rosalind hadn't spoken to her or jumped up to kiss her. It made no sense. Rhea had said something was wrong. It must be very wrong for Rosalind to be acting like this. "Hey," Taryn said, making it a greeting and statement of concern. The silence was gnawing on her. She couldn't leave it alone.

She heard a sob escape Rosalind's lips and saw her shoulders coil forward. In complete bafflement, Taryn crouched in front of the couch and put her hands on Rosalind's folded arms. "No, angel, don't cry. What ever it is, I'll fix it." The sound of her voice had an effect on Rosalind, but opposite of the one she wanted. Rosalind started to cry harder. Taryn tried again. "I'll stop doing it, or I'll start doing it. If anybody hurt you, I'll kill them. Please don't cry. You're killing me."

Rosalind pulled away, sitting back against the couch. She wiped her tears away with the back of her hand.

"Am I making you sad? Did I do something?" Taryn asked, afraid to move.

Rosalind shook her head.

An awful thought slammed into Taryn's skull. "You still love me, right?" Taryn asked.

Rosalind nodded.

"Not having second thoughts?"

Rosalind shook her head. Taryn felt her heart start to beat again.

"Then it doesn't matter what it is. If we have that, we can deal with anything else."

She saw Rosalind start to cry again, not as hard, just the slow track of tears down her face.

"Please tell me what's going on," Taryn said.

"Come sit here with me. We have to talk. Rhea will scold you for getting your boots on the couch," Rosalind said, watching as Taryn stepped onto the couch like a cat. Taryn sat down on the wide arm, feet planted on the cushions, facing Rosalind.

Taryn shrugged. "Let her. You never scold me."

"I guess I don't. Did you have a good time tonight?" Rosalind asked, clearly stalling.

"It was great. One of those nights that everything feels... important, I guess. You keep looking around for the movie camera, it's that good. If you had been there it would have been perfect."

"I have a few things I need to tell you, baby," Rosalind said.

Taryn nodded, deliberately keeping her arms relaxed, her body loose.

"Paul came to Buffalo to talk to me. He's not well. I saw that when we went to dinner tonight. He lost his father a few months ago, and he isn't handling it."

"Shit, if my father died I wouldn't lose any sleep," Taryn said, her mouth twisting at the thought.

"Paul and his father were very close. I barely recognized him when he came in. He's changed, and not for the better. He needs help. I saw something hovering around him, like a cloud. Something like what I saw around Misha. I don't know of any good way to say this." Rosalind looked down at her hands

"Just say it."

"Paul's still here."

"In Buffalo?" Taryn asked.

"In the house." Rosalind sat back, unconsciously recoiling from the expected reaction.

Taryn cocked her head, not comprehending. "*This* house?" She looked around the room, as if expecting him to pop up from behind the furniture.

"I brought him here. I thought Rhea could help him."

It took a colossal effort of will not to jump off the couch as if she'd been branded. As it was, Taryn half rose, forgetting her vows to remain calm. Her hands opened, as if seeking something to throw. Her breath came hard into her lungs, tinged with copper. "You brought him here. Rhea did a healing."

The way Taryn said it sounded obscene, as if this stranger had violated something sacred, the boundaries of her home. Rosalind had the clear impression that Taryn was choking down a black rage, that if she looked, she could see the red film before Taryn's eyes. She sensed that part of the anger was directed at Rhea, for healing him. Rosalind watched Taryn master herself, watched the moment when Taryn made the choice to exhale and sit back down. "Healings never take one evening. How long?" Taryn asked in a voice close to normal.

"Rhea mentioned something about Halloween."

Anger walked into the room and sat down between them, red eyes rolling back in joy. Rosalind could almost see it, solid, cleaving the connection that they created by being near one another. She felt it, the cold blowing in, the winter touch. Taryn was very young and very impulsive. She was going to blow up, say things that she might regret later. It was the later Rosalind kept her eye on, already planning for the time when Taryn had calmed down enough to talk to her again. It would be ugly, but she thought they could make it. She was forming that conversation in her head, so she almost missed what Taryn was saying in a voice soft as a whisper.

"Samhain. That long. I hate that he's here. I think I'd rather have anything else than that." Taryn turned her head to the side, clenching the muscles along the column of her neck.

Rosalind thought they might tear through Taryn's pale skin. Taryn was silent a long time. Too long when measured in heartbeats. She wasn't ready when Taryn looked full at her. The impact of Taryn's eyes was enough to make her gasp.

"I bet, five years from now, we'll have a dog with three legs you saved from a car wreck, a house full of mangy stray cats you can't help but feed. Any woman fool enough to love me has a heart too soft for the world. It makes sense you couldn't cut him loose."

It was a moment handed to her like a gift, another chance to be stunned at what life had given her. She didn't know how to answer, how to meet the look that singed her skin. She thought she might cry again, but her eyes were dry, fixed on Taryn. At last, she held out her hand. "Come home with me."

CHAPTER SEVEN

Paul dreamed. In his dreams he walked through a strange house, opening doors that led deceptively to other doors. Rooms that emptied into other rooms, all a cool gray like autumn rain. He felt no urgency, just a tiny annoyance that all the doors led nowhere, that the light never got beyond that twilight glow. It wasn't dark enough for fear, or bright enough for joy. Paul woke in a strange bed, sheets scented with a perfume he didn't recognize. For a moment he wondered if he'd gotten drunk and met someone. He looked under the covers. He was still wearing his shirt and trousers. His jacket was folded at the foot of the bed. His tie was in the jacket pocket, the end hanging out like a tongue. He didn't recognize the room. Great swaths of bright cloth draped the walls, disguising plaster spotted with ancient paint. The ceiling was fifteen feet high, painted tin. The floors were polished hardwood cushioned with throw rugs of scarlet and gold. He had to still be in that odd house with that odd neighbor of Rosalind's.

He remembered talking to her in the kitchen, a woman who reminded him of a snake with her shiny opaque eyes, the hypnotic motions of her thin hands. Had she drugged him? He had no memory beyond her chasing Rosalind out of the kitchen after—yes. After she explained about her new girlfriend. He must have been drugged. Rosalind had been acting drugged. Maybe this odd house was full of cult members. The one he'd met so far didn't seem normal, and the others sounded just as bad.

And this girlfriend…A child. Just twenty. A total punk, from all reports. When Rosalind spoke about her, Paul knew she was trying to be careful with his feelings, but she lit up every time she said her name. There had to be some kind of mind control going on. Rosalind was famous for attracting dangerous people. They sensed her generous nature and took full advantage of her. She was too sweet to tell them to take a hike. Maybe that was what was happening here. Rosalind had gotten mixed up with some weirdness and was too polite to escape.

There was a staircase at the end of the hall, narrow and steep with no railing. Noise drifted up the well. Conversation, the banging of pans. The cult members were home. He could go confront them and see about getting Rosalind deprogrammed.

The cult members were having breakfast. Paul took one look in the kitchen and steeled himself. Hippies, anarchists, pagans, maybe even vegetarians. Seven of them sat around the stained wooden table that might underneath all that use be a handsome antique. Paul recognized Rhea. Next to her was a bearded man spearing pancakes onto the plate of a young girl. He was well built. He kept his hair military short, but Paul could see extensive tattooing where the sleeves of his T-shirt stretched around his arms. The girl couldn't be much more than fourteen, thin as a rail with her brown hair braided with beads. The man beside her had his hair likewise braided and looked like an escapee from a biker movie.

Was one of the others Rosalind's girlfriend? There was a girl about the right age, but she had white blond hair halfway down her back and one arm around the African American man sitting next to her. Only it wasn't a man. It was a girl. A tall, handsome girl with an athlete's build. So that meant that the pretty woman with the flawless chocolate skin and obvious blond wig was probably not a pretty woman at all. Paul had trouble wrapping his mind around it. There they were like a Norman Rockwell painting gone bad, having a pancake breakfast.

"There's a guy in the doorway," the girl with the braid said, pointing to him. All eyes turned on him in a suspicious fascination, as if he were the oddity in his slept-in blue suit. Paul had buttoned up his shirt and carried his jacket over his arm.

"That's Paul. He'll be staying here for a while," Rhea said.

The explanation seemed to satisfy them. They went back to

eating. "You've been sleeping in my bed," the woman with the white blond hair said to him. A feeling of unreality hit him. *Am I in a fairy tale?* Paul thought.

The woman, Rhea, looked right at him. "You have no idea," she said, not unkind.

The cellar door banged open. Up out of the earth came a figure out of a fairy tale, a boy whose face belonged on a statue of Apollo. Paul caught a handful of impressions all at once: a thatch of black hair that looked as if it had been cut with a butcher knife, eyes that reminded him of stained glass. He wouldn't have been surprised to see the boy wearing a tunic with a sword belted over it, but he saw a white T-shirt and a pair of jeans that sagged dangerously low over unlaced boots. There was a tattoo of a man's head on his right arm. Paul got a good look at it as the arm crossed in front of the boy's body and grabbed the hand of the woman who was yanking at the jeans.

"If these get any lower, you won't be able to walk." It was Rosalind, speaking in a tone he'd never heard before, a mix of smug pleasure and reproach.

Paul thought of the table and its gender confusion, the deliberate misleading of the eye. Intellectually, his mind was prepared for the leap. He knew that the boy had to be Rosalind's new girlfriend. Rosalind had tried to prepare him in her careful way for this moment. There was no cushion for the blow, no way to block out the sight of Rosalind's hand on the small of her girlfriend's back, no way to steel himself against the slashing of the girl's arrogant smile. He'd expected her to be young. Rosalind had mentioned that. He hadn't expected this—the hatred he felt, how it made his teeth ache, how his bones felt loose in their sockets—all a complete surprise. For the first time in his life, Paul had the urge to strike another human being. It didn't help that Rhea cleared her throat, that Rosalind's eyes found him and instantly filled with pity. It didn't help that her girlfriend's face hardened, the playful smile vanished like a trap snapping shut.

"Paul," Rosalind said. There was concern in her voice, but it was nothing like the tone she'd used a minute before. It was almost too much for him. She stepped around the girl, moving her hands away conspicuously.

"Good morning," Paul said, feeling the bite of hate on his tongue.

"Taryn, this is Paul." Rosalind turned to Taryn first almost by instinct, her body angling toward Taryn even as she approached Paul.

For a moment, there was silence, the silence of water freezing on metal. Then Taryn held out her hand. He wasn't much to look at, this man Rosalind had married. It wasn't that he was unattractive, he just didn't have any spark to him. Joe was average looking, but when he smiled, the world fell in love with him. This guy was bland as caulk. He looked nervous, with his eyes darting around the room. He held his hand out and shook hers, briefly, never meeting her eyes. It irritated her. She had to choke her ire down. During the night she'd made vows to Rosalind and to herself to bear this with grace. If Rosalind had thrown her support behind this guy, she could stand by Rosalind. So she kept her peace and didn't slug the guy for the way he looked at her from the corner of his eye.

"Have you eaten?" Rosalind asked Paul.

"No. I just came down. I...look, I don't know about all this. It was amusing yesterday, but I have a life." Paul took Rosalind's arm and tried to steer her away from the table, but somehow the towering girl got in the way. He tried to head for the counter. His path was blocked. Finally, in exasperation, he leaned down and whispered to Rosalind. "I don't think this is a good idea. I think some people might have a problem with it," he said, indicating Taryn with a small motion of his head.

"Door's that way," Taryn said, pointing down the hall.

"Taryn," Rosalind said.

"Tell him not to talk about me like I'm not here."

"You can't possibly think this is a good idea," Paul said to Rosalind.

"It doesn't matter what I think. You should only stay if you think you can be helped here. I can't do that for you."

A ceramic plate was pushed into Paul's stomach. He had to grab it with both hands. "Pancakes," the man with his hair in braids said helpfully when Paul stared at it.

"You can eat standing up if you care to. Taryn often does," Rhea said from the table.

Paul looked down at the plate, then over at Rosalind. He saw Taryn perch on a bar stool, her boots hooked in the rung. Rosalind leaned awkwardly on the counter. Something about their posture told Paul this wasn't how they normally ate. He had a suspicion that Rosalind customarily stood between Taryn's splayed legs.

He took his plate and sat down at the table. The bearded man introduced everyone with an ironic sense of propriety. He was Joe. The biker was Misha. The girl in braids was Goblin. The one whose room he'd taken was Laurel. Her friend was Robbie. The pretty woman who was really a man was called Egyptia. It was a collection of names, nothing to tell him what relation any of them were to the other. The names were absurd, like a roomful of actors giving their stage names.

He'd joined a fantasy role-playing group while in college, trying to keep up with Rosalind's mad infatuation with acting. He thought it would make him more flexible, more creative. All the participants insisted on going by their character names all the time.

He finally gave up when one of them met him on the quad and yelled out, "Brule the Spear Slayer!"

So here he was now having breakfast with the cult members, feeling more lost than he'd ever imagined himself feeling. He didn't have an exotic name. He didn't even have a snappy nickname. How was he supposed to find his way here?

"I heard something upstairs last night. Were you home, T?" Goblin asked.

"No," Taryn said. She could feel Paul's hurt look. She wasn't trying to make this hard on him, but the jackass had to know that she and Rosalind slept together. Was she supposed to pretend that they didn't until Halloween?

"Oh. That's odd. We have extra company, then. Samhain is coming. Have you seen anything?" Goblin asked Joe.

"Not yet. I don't think he's here for me," Joe said.

"Don't worry, Goblin. He's a good houseguest. He's waiting until I can see him. Followed me down from Toronto, yes, Rhea? International ghost," Misha said, the slight tremor in his hand spilling his coffee onto the table. Goblin saw it and immediately changed the subject.

"T, I've got a report due in history. Help me out?" Goblin asked.

"I can't write for shit. You're already Hemingway. You don't need my help," Taryn said.

"It's about Alexander."

"That's different."

Paul sat in a stupefied silence as the cult members started eating again, as if this sort of thing happened all the time. What would it take to shock these people? Armed guards kicking the door down?

"Rosalind, if you have some time this afternoon, I could use your help," Rhea said while pouring syrup from a stoneware jug.

"Sure. I teach at six, but I'm free until then," Rosalind said, glad for the distraction.

"Good. Meet me at the shop at one. Taryn will be designing Misha's new tattoo," Rhea said.

"Misha, you trust T enough to tell you what to wear on your body?" Robbie asked, smiling.

Misha took his name as a cue and took off his shirt. He turned around in the chair, showing his back. With his recent weight loss, the muscles showed like snakes under paper-thin skin. Across the width of his shoulders stretched a horizon with the sun setting on a sea of grass. A Cossack horseman rode full out, wind whipping back the mane of his mount, the flare of his trousers and long coat like the wings of a mythic bird. His right fist was raised in a salute, his mouth opened in a shout that Rosalind could almost hear, a paean to the masculine freedom of the nomad's life. "Taryn designed this one. How long ago, two years? Yes. And she disliked me then. But she understands." Misha pulled his shirt back down.

"Rhea did the work?" Robbie asked.

"Taryn doesn't design for anyone else. You must not have been coming to the house long," Misha said, looking at her.

"Just started seeing Laurel and hanging with T. I was thinking of getting one done," Robbie said, glancing at Laurel to see her reaction.

Laurel laughed. "Rhea did mine."

"And I remember where it is. You are not whipping it out to show, either. Say…you didn't go and design that one, did you, T?" Robbie asked, putting her arm around Laurel.

"Don't ask a question you don't want answered," Taryn said, her voice dropping down into a growl. Her eyes flamed dangerously. She leaned forward and fixed them on Robbie. Robbie backed down.

"I want to hear the answer to that. Did you?" Rosalind said.

Taryn's look changed in an instant. Her eyebrows shot up. Her eyes went wide. "Uh…well…see, it was a long time ago."

"Nothing in this house happened a long time ago. It's all within the last three years. You must have been awfully busy," Rosalind said, her tone more subtle than Taryn's but just as dangerous.

Misha laughed out loud, a braying laugh that cut right through the room. "I now know that I have lived long enough. God may take me when he will. I have seen Taryn cower at a simple question. The swaggering punk has become a whipping boy."

"Funny. After last night, I didn't think I'd hear you using the word *whipped,* Misha," Taryn said lightly.

Misha's face darkened. He sat back and scowled. "That was a mistake of fortune. A mere fluke."

"Ellie kicked his ass at pool. Humiliated him," Taryn said to Rosalind.

"One game! The second was a draw," Misha said.

"Only because she was nice enough to stop whipping you," Taryn said.

"You haven't told me how last night went," Rosalind said.

Misha growled something in Russian and stabbed at his pancakes. Taryn smirked at him. "I think it went well. The kings learned a few things."

"And nobody got killed. I had my doubts about Wolf when she—*he*—started hitting on that big guy's girlfriend," Joe said.

"You don't tell it right," Misha said. "I am off playing pool with Joe, beating him two games out of three, and out of the corner of my eye I see this girl all but crawling into Robbie's lap."

Taryn held out her hand, stopping Misha. "Whoa. We don't want to rupture any domestic bliss."

Misha's eyebrows pushed up, forming ridges into his hairline. "But Robbie pushed her away. Ignored her completely," he said in self-defense.

"Hey, when you got what I got at home…" Robbie said expansively, unleashing a killer smile on Laurel.

"You're lucky you already told me about that. I can see it now. I'll be up against the butch code of silence every time you guys go out together," Laurel said.

"I got your back," Taryn said to Robbie.

"Nah, it's cool. I gave her the rundown," Robbie said.

"Enough. This isn't a remake of *The Outsiders*," Rhea said.

"As I said, I was beating Joe at pool. This girl, attractive enough in an American college-girl way, had taken a fancy to Robbie. I looked over to the table now and again. It was amusing. This girl clearly was drunk and seemed to think they were all males. As I said, she was drunk. Though the lights were very low, and they were sitting down, so you couldn't see how short most of them are." Misha was enjoying the sound of his own voice and had wandered off with it for company.

Goblin interrupted him. "Robbie's nowhere near short. Neither is T."

"That isn't the point. The others are. It might look odd if they all stood up. Like it was a short man's convention. It would injure their illusion, even in a dim bar," Misha said.

"I saw Misha staring at the table and looked over. Robbie was politely pushing this girl off. I saw Robbie get up and go to the bar. The drunk girl sat down in Robbie's chair," Joe said.

Misha took up the narrative from Joe. "The thug, the white-haired Wolf, leaned on the table, very close, and was talking to this girl. This was now more interesting than beating Joe again, so we stopped to watch. Joe watched to spring in like a panther at the first sign of trouble. I tell you, you are becoming an old man, Joe. You barely drank. You kept a worried eye on the table all night—"

"You're going off on a tangent, Misha," Rhea said.

"Were you there? The story must be told in its own time. You people have no patience," Misha chided.

"I talked him into finishing the game. We saw T get up and walk away from the table, going up to the bar with Robbie. Wolf was leaning over the drunk girl and had an arm around her. It was loud, so I guessed she was just talking to her. I was making my last shot when I heard the crash," Joe said.

Egyptia waved her hand, cutting Joe off. "Men just cannot tell a story. Step back before you hurt yourselves. Let a lady do it justice. What these beer-drinking, pool-crazy men left out is the real story. During the time between Robbie going to the bar and the little Lobo getting knocked down, I entered the bar. Without my usual flair, true, but it was a leather and Levi's night, you know what I mean? So butch it straightened the hair in my wig. All those Harleys and leather jackets and boots and, stop me, I feel flushed. So I went toned down, more Martha Stewart than the Divine Miss M. And was there anyone there to tell a girl how fine she looked? No, there was not. Made me feel nostalgic for the old days when a queen didn't go to the market without her face on and a full escort.

"So who do I run into outside the door but Miss Actress Herself, our Rosalind's friend Ellie. She at least knew how to greet royalty. She yoo-hooed all across the parking lot and came running over to kiss my hand. She introduced me to this femme sister in dreads with all this silver all over her hands. More rings than Tiffany's. She's the director of the boys' show. They got all dressed for the night and they were excited about it, showing me the cute little leather jackets with the nipped waist and the jeans. Now I feel better 'cause I got some girls with me, so we go in.

"We're kind of hanging back, watching the men play pool. Linda, the director, says she doesn't want to let the kings know that she's there, not right away. She wants to see them in action. Honey, she did get to see them in action. We were down at the other end of the room, around the end of the bar, like we were on a safari stalking tigers and shit. Linda's got her eyes on that table and is talking to herself. Actors must be crazy, I figure, and leave her alone. Ellie seems like real good company, so I go to talk to her, and she's watching the men play pool. In specific she's watching Misha play pool. Miss Ellie goes, 'He thinks he's so good. I could take him.' I guess she was talking about pool.

"So I see Robbie up at the bar. I go say hi. Hell with all this state secret shit. Hand to Jesus, when I saw Robbie I just about died. I thought I'd found my perfect man. Tall, handsome as Denzel, dressed like a Gap ad, looks over at me and smiles. And it's Robbie. What does T think she's doing, making it hard for a girl to know who to be attracted to? Taryn's off getting a beer. I give that boy a piece of my mind when he comes back. So Robbie's telling me about this girl who was hitting on him. Imagine that. I tell Robbie to peep at the table. Now Wolf's got an arm around the drunk girl. Sam and Grace are sitting there wide-eyed as kittens. Taryn turns to look, and Wolf is kissing this girl. And this great big slab-of-beef boyfriend just came in the door.'"

It took Paul several minutes before he could follow the conversation. The rampant misuse of pronouns, the gleeful reassignment of gender left him as confused as the foreignness of the participants. He gathered that there had been an outing to a bar last night and many of the people at the table had been there. Paul hated to look stupid. It was a source of pride to him to be just a little bit smarter than everyone around him, a little more culturally sensitive, better read, more urbane. He fit beautifully into the rarefied atmosphere of a university campus. It was his one true vanity, his intelligence, his education. Now he was dropped down into a group of people that ignored those very qualities that gave him status. He couldn't quite figure out who in the hell everyone was, let alone what they all did for a living. Wasn't that the first thing out of a new person's mouth, after what's your name? What do you do? It gave an invitation to talk about your work, your studies, all the things tied up with your identity. How could he categorize this colorful mob if he had no idea what they did? Like an ethnologist, he set to work analyzing the tribe.

This was some sort of a clan or extended family unit, based physically around this house, 34 Mariner. The head of the family, the patriarch, seemed to be the bearded man called Joe. He was referred to by the other people as a father figure, either teasingly or genuinely, and he exuded a parental calm Paul associated with fathers. This was an old-school man, pretty normal looking, dropped down into this odd clan. The others showed him deference even though he never raised his voice, never lost his sense of humor. He didn't appear to be a drag queen, a witch, or a biker. Just a regular Joe. He did have his group markings, though. Paul could see that he had extensive tattoos on his arms. Probably on his back as well. Everyone at the table had so far admitted to tattoos, visible or not.

Goblin, the girl with the braids, was Joe's daughter. He could see it in their faces, the resemblance. Joe seemed to treat Goblin as more of an equal, though she couldn't have been older than fourteen or fifteen.

The matriarch was Rhea. She spoke little but saw everything. She was treated with a great reverence but less warmth than Joe, as if she were in possession of knowledge that made her stand apart. Only the thug seemed to ignore her status and treated her with the same rough affection she showed to Joe. Where the others gave Rhea careful physical deference, the thug would swagger over and kiss her on the cheek. Rhea was the real Alpha, the power behind the throne. He'd noticed that she rarely asked questions. She made statements with the assurance of a leader. She had the look of a woman who could keep a secret.

Laurel and Robbie were romantic partners. He could see that. Egyptia was a family friend, or a nonresident of the house, but seemed well beloved. Misha, the biker with the Russian accent, seemed a little too forced, too jovial, as if he was unsure of his place. Paul couldn't make out what he was doing here.

Which brought Paul to Taryn. He felt a flush of anger when he glanced at her. She was sprawled out on the bar stool with one arm across the countertop. She couldn't have taken up more space if she tried. It was pure teenager, the casual slouch, the look of self-absorbed distance, but her eyes were old. They punched holes in the air, imparting energy whenever they rested on the person speaking. He could feel the resentment coming off the girl in waves, the way she refused to look at him, the way her oversized hand flexed on the counter, twitching toward Rosalind. All the charm of a serial killer in a teenage boy's body. What in hell was wrong with Rosalind?

He looked at last at Rosalind, who seemed absorbed in the drag queen's story. She smiled at Egyptia's descriptions of the people in the bar, nodded encouragement to continue. Paul had grown up with Rosalind. He knew that she'd always had the gift for making friends. As a toddler she'd been in love with people, able to run right up to strangers and charm the life out of them. There was no armor around her. Her interest in you was genuine, direct, wholehearted. He'd never met anyone who could make people feel at ease the way Rosalind could. So it wasn't surprising that she'd be able to charm these people. But it was more than that. She seemed at home here. The edge of tension he'd sometimes seen in her, the knowledge that she had to be pleasing to everyone, was gone. She wasn't trying to be charming. She was happy, and that happiness was very attractive. People could feel the joy in her and liked to be around it. She looked like a woman at home in herself. It made him want to die.

He turned his attention back to Egyptia's story to keep from thinking about it. A brawl had broken out, instigated by some guy named Wolf. The drunk girl's boyfriend had stormed over and shoved Wolf back, knocking over his chair. From what Paul could determine from Misha, Joe, and Egyptia's alternating telling of the tale, Wolf had bounced up from the floor, snarling and spitting. It looked like a bloodbath until Joe stepped between the combatants with Taryn beside him. Paul could see Joe doing that. He had a quiet air about him, but the way the muscles moved under his shirt, the way he carried himself, Paul was willing to bet he'd been in the service. He imagined that Joe could handle a bar fight.

The story was abruptly over, the chairs scraping on the floor as people rushed away from the table. Paul sat in disbelief, looking at the wreckage of breakfast. His imagination had been able to carry him to this point, but now he hit a wall, a stretching gray expanse opaque as death. Joe, clearing plates, patted him on the shoulder.

"It's a big family. You'll get used to it," he said, moving toward the sink.

CHAPTER EIGHT

Rosalind stood behind the glass counter with Rhea, watching Taryn work. Taryn sat with her sketchbook propped on her knee, looking at Misha through narrowed eyes. Her hand started to move, lazily scribbling. Her eyes never left Misha. In a few minutes, she held the book up to him.

"This will have two parts to it," she said.

Misha looked the page over. It took his eye a moment to decipher the pencil drawing. It was a tomb, an open-air temple with a catafalque. The sarcophagus, even in pencil, had the sheen of white marble. There was a faded wreath of olive laid atop the chest. A man sprawled next to the sarcophagus as if grief had clubbed him down. One arm was flung across it in a futile embrace; the other hid his face. All that could be seen was his long hair, disheveled, as if he'd been tearing at it. Misha shivered. "And the other part?" he asked, his voice small.

"Rhea will tell you when you are ready for the second," Taryn said.

"Where?" Misha asked.

"Lower back. Above the seat of the spine, where the energy coils," Taryn said.

"Rhea, must it be this?" Misha asked, turning to her.

"It's what Taryn sees. You are able to sleep now, yes?" Rhea asked.

Misha nodded slowly. "Yes."

"And you are eating," Rhea said.

"Yes."

"Then the healing is proceeding along the right path. It's up to you. You can always go back to Toronto," Rhea said.

"No." Misha peeled off his shirt. "Begin."

Taryn kissed Rosalind good-bye and slipped out the door. Rhea sat down behind Misha and started drawing the lines on his skin. Rosalind came and sat next to her, pulling a chair from behind the counter.

"Taryn left quickly. Off to rehearsal?" Rhea asked, as if Misha were deaf. He gave no sign that he could hear anything, staring ahead as if he were made of stone.

"So she said. I think she just wanted to go. It's a little tense right now."

"Mmm. First day is hard. I told Joe to have Paul help him with clearing out the backyard, getting the garden ready for winter. It will be better if he's physically exhausted tonight." Rhea finished the outline of the tomb and started sketching the man.

"Is there anything I can do?" Rosalind asked.

"Tell me what you see as I'm drawing," Rhea said calmly.

Rosalind looked at Misha's back. At first all she saw was skin, lines of ink. Gradually, the lines turned red, a hot angry color, burning and coiling. "It's like his lower back is on fire."

"Mmm. He resents the image. That's a good sign. Taryn picked the right one," Rhea said.

Misha continued to stare straight ahead.

"It looks so…ravaged. Bereaved," Rosalind said. It looked excessive to her, the grief the man in the drawing was displaying. How could that be good for a man who was already haunted with grief?

"Taryn understands. The only way around certain emotions is right through them, an excess. That is Misha's way," Rhea said.

Rosalind laughed, then covered her mouth. "Sorry. I just caught this image of Paul trying to manufacture an excess of anything. I don't think he has it in him to be that dramatic."

"Did he ever?" Rhea asked.

"Not that I saw, no. He never told me about it if he did."

"Men have fewer ways to talk about emotion. They can hit, or they can rage. Not all people are meant to rage with grief. Or love," Rhea said.

Rosalind laughed again. "Sorry. Another funny image just popped into my head."

"What was it?" Rhea asked.

"Paul and Misha with a bottle of wine, talking."

"What about?" Rhea asked.

"I don't know. It was just a picture in my head."

"What about?" Rhea asked patiently.

"Love. It's too soon for grief."

"I think you are exactly right. We'll have a symposium. A dinner party. We will eat, we will drink Joe's homemade wine, and we shall talk about love."

Paul heaved a shovelful of compost onto the heap, the muscles in his back complaining. He couldn't remember when he'd worked this physically hard. When Joe had said gardening, he'd pictured seed packets. This was manual labor. Paul glanced at Joe, who was cheerfully swinging a pickaxe against a cluster of roots. The man was incredible, working without pause, without seeming to tire. He'd taken his jacket off, and through the thin cotton of his T-shirt, Paul could see his shoulders, round as cannonballs. This guy had to be military. He had the build. You just weren't born with a body like that.

"Never knew gardening was so much like work," Paul said, leaning on the handle of his shovel.

"In the old days, it was the women who did all the real work. We'd be sitting around in the sun, waiting for a moose to hunt," Joe said without breaking his swing.

"Darn that Industrial Revolution." Paul wiped his wrist across his forehead.

"Funny. I thought all academics were Marxists."

"I'm old fashioned, I believe in capitalism. How'd you know I was an academic?" Paul asked. This was the first normal conversation he'd had in this house. It was comforting.

"Ros told me you teach in Poughkeepsie."

"I thought you were going to tell me I just looked like an academic." Paul examined the blisters forming on his hands.

Joe stopped swinging the pickaxe. "I try not to make up my mind about people on how they look. Why don't we knock off for a bit? I bet I have some cider left in the house."

Paul dropped the shovel. "Sounds good. Joe, can I ask you something?"

Joe stopped walking and looked at him. "Sure."

"This place. This house, and Rhea, and…well, you seem like a normal guy," Paul said.

"Thank you," Joe said and grinned.

"I don't get it. The whole thing." Paul sat down on the back steps.

"I'll help if I can. What do you want to know?" Joe said.

"The house, for one. Who really lives here? And why?"

"Rhea owns the house. She's lived here for a lot of years. Goblin and I live here, for a little over two years now. Goblin's my daughter. We moved in after Rhea and I became lovers. Laurel has a room. She got hooked up with Rhea through the Women's Studies department out at UB. She was a grad student looking for a place to stay. She's been here over a year. You are staying in her room. She's staying with Robbie. Wren and Isis had a room, but they moved out after Isis decided to get pregnant. They are old friends of Rhea's from her anti-nuke days," Joe said.

"And Misha?" Paul asked.

"Misha's a guest, like you. He's my brother-in-law. He lives up in Toronto mostly. He'll be staying for a few weeks."

"Does this happen often? Strangers living with you? You seem to take it all in stride. I could be anybody, but you give me a room. You've fed me. I'm even wearing your clothing. For no reason other than Rhea saying I need it. It's bizarre," Paul said.

"You agreed to stay with a bunch of strangers because Rhea said you needed it. That's pretty odd, too. I like to keep an open house. And everybody seems to be wearing my clothing these days," Joe said amiably.

"What does Rhea do?" Paul asked.

"She has her own shop. Tattoos, piercings, some books and special items. Over on Elmwood. You know where that is? That way. We're on Mariner. It ends in Allen. Half a block up is Elmwood."

"Think I've seen it. So she doesn't do this mystic thing for a living?" Paul asked.

"Nah. She doesn't take money for that. People find her when they need her."

"And what do you do?"

"I work from home. I subcontract to a subcontractor to write computer manuals for Qatar. I was doing Burkina Faso, but we got outbid. Lets me set my own hours, and I'm always home when Goblin gets in from school."

"That's interesting. How'd you end up doing that?" Paul asked. Things were starting to make some sense, people were becoming distinct individuals. The background wash of color became a pattern.

"Fell into it. A couple years back I was having some surgery done, and I wanted to be able to work from home while I adjusted. It ended up working out great. Life's like that, you often fall into what you need when you aren't looking," Joe said. He knew that Paul had stopped listening from the distant look that came over him.

"How long has…the other one lived here?" Paul said, hesitating.

"Taryn's lived here for over three years."

"Taryn," Paul said, making the name into a sound fraught with menace. He sat with his face gone opaque, with questions catching in his throat.

"You want that cider now?"

"Tell me how they met. How Ros came here."

"Sure you want to hear that? It's late. We've been busting our backs all day. We could wash up, get your room set up more to your liking."

"No. Tell me. I'd rather know."

"All right. This will take a while. We'll talk as we cook."

The windows to 34 Mariner were bravely open, daring the chill of October to cut at the skin. It was going on dark, the five-minute window between the sky as the inside of a shell and the sky as a lead pipe spotted with rust. In the warmth of the kitchen, two men, dressed alike in jeans and button-down shirts, prepared food with a manic energy.

"Damn. You should do this for a living. Where'd you learn to cook?" Paul said as he chopped cilantro. He watched Joe in frank admiration. The man never once looked at a recipe.

"Necessity. You have a kid. You're a vegetarian. You learn to cook," Joe said, setting the lid back on the saucepan.

"Necessity is living on macaroni and cheese and peanut butter all through grad school."

"I have nightmares like that. I made sure Goblin knows how to cook. When she leaves, I know at least she'll eat."

"That's a good attitude for a parent. Most people don't get that at home. I've managed to become workmanlike in the kitchen, but Ros is a disaster. All she ever made were reservations." Paul faltered, on the name or the memory. Joe kindly let the moment pass. Paul cleared his throat and changed the subject.

"Let me see if I have this right. Rosalind met Taryn at a show and has been coming here ever since?"

"That's right," Joe said.

"It doesn't make any sense. This isn't like her at all," Paul said, clearly struggling.

"People don't always act the way we think they should."

"You seem so casual about it. What if your daughter started dating someone like Taryn?"

"As long as they treat her well, she can date anyone she likes. I think she's headed for boys. She went through her requisite crush on T, but it passed."

"What happened to Goblin's mom? You get divorced?" Paul asked.

Joe nearly dropped the pan. "Ah…well. I did get divorced, yes."

"Sore topic? Sorry."

"Not at all. It was a relief, and I'm still good friends with my ex."

"Divorce is ghastly. We make it seem almost normal in conversation. Divorce. We should have a word that calls it what it is, a murder. Death of a bond between two people that was never meant to die. You hear the statistics about half of all marriages ending in divorce, but it'll never happen to you. Then it does. There are people who get married three, four times. How the hell do they do that? How do you forget the pain long enough to try that again?" Paul looked down at the knife in his hand abstractly. He looked back up at Joe. "Would you do it again?"

"Sure. I believe in love," Joe said.

"I don't think I could. It would make the first one seem less. How can you pledge eternal devotion to more than one person in your lifetime?"

Joe was at the sink, so Paul couldn't see his face. "Marriage is a funny thing. I've had friends get handfasted for a year and a day, and then dissolve the relationship with no bitterness. I've seen people get married and divorced in nine months. And I've seen people pledge eternal devotion the moment they met and never doubt it." He turned back from the sink, his smile in place. "I think we are ready, except for the wine."

Paul watched as Joe took a huge pot down off its hook and set it on the stove. "Is that the infamous hot wine Ros told me about?"

"She told you about the wine?" Joe asked, seeming both surprised and pleased.

"Only that she'd been drinking hot wine lately. I couldn't believe she'd developed a taste for a thing like that. I can't understand how her tastes have changed."

"I have to run down to the cellar and get the wine."

"What wine do you use?" Paul asked, following him.

"My own. Red wine with the taste of apples and smoke to summon the fall, a strong red with a lusty heart to strengthen the blood for winter. It has been said, and I'm not just boasting here, that my wine can make you want to live through February, even when your socks get wet because the bus was late and you walked from downtown in a blizzard. But don't take my word for it. Help me prepare it, and judge for yourself." Joe vanished into the darkness of the cellar.

Paul hesitated on the steps, stayed by a qualm he couldn't identify. He wasn't afraid of the dark. He was an educated man, an adult, but his feet refused to pass the yawning mouth of the open door. Joe descended easily into the pit, but he was unable to follow. He waited, fretfully, for Joe to reappear. There were scratching sounds coming from the darkness, a faint breath of wet, cold air. This house had cats. That had to be the scratching.

Paul disliked cats. He disliked pets in general. They took up excessive amounts of time and energy and money, then, just when you'd gotten so emotionally dependent on them you couldn't function, they died. A house with cats was a suspect house. He wasn't surprised. It belonged to Rhea, who was his idea of a woman who'd have cats. Many cats. But Joe, he didn't seem like a cat guy. Dogs. Joe'd have dogs. He must be putting up with the whole cat thing because of Rhea and Goblin. Teenage girls liked cats.

Paul wondered about the dinner they were preparing. It was enough food to feed an army, a vegetarian army with a taste for Mediterranean and Indian food. The house had been empty all day except for him and Joe, and he found that he was enjoying that. It gave him a chance to get used to the culture shock, but it was more than that. Joe was an easy guy to talk to. It had been years since he'd had a close male friend. A lot of years. He'd always been intimidated by male company while in college, not quite feeling at home, not sure if he shared the same world. It was marginally better in grad school when the topics turned to things he excelled at naturally. But there was always the feeling of one-upmanship, competing for grant funding and assistantship. Nobody really gave a damn what his dissertation was about except his advisors, and they were known to wander.

The oddest thing he'd noticed, next to the people who lived there, was that there was no television in the house. He'd asked Joe about it, and Joe had only shrugged.

"We do other things for entertainment."

Other things, like this dinner party tonight? Joe had gotten a phone call from Rhea and set off immediately cleaning the house. He'd told Paul that they were going to have a dinner party. A symposium. Now what could this collection of oddballs mean by that?

Paul was enjoying the preparations, the constant motion, the attention to detail, without having to think beyond the moment. After watching Joe stir the wine as if he had all the time in the world, Paul felt himself falling into a trance-like state. He was lulled by the sight of that sinewy hand moving in an endless round. He felt a moment of fear that he'd lose all contact with the solid ground if he surrendered to that motion, that there would be nothing to anchor him ever again. The fear settled into his chest, fanning out its wings like ribs of ice. Paul couldn't tear his eyes away from the pot of wine, even as the fear blossomed into a panic.

Then Joe looked at him and smiled. There was such reassurance in that smile. It was like hearing a joke and only realizing how hilarious it is while repeating it to another person. Of course it was funny. Of course it was all right. Weren't they getting ready for a dinner party? Joe handed him the ladle. "Stir this while I clear out the living room," he said.

"Anything I need to add?" Paul asked.

"Nope. Just go in circles, big lazy ones. It can't stand still right now."

Paul concentrated on moving his hand as Joe had. The motion was deceptive. There was more involved in keeping the motion slow and measured than he thought.

Paul heard a lot of scraping and banging from the front of the house. When Joe walked back into the kitchen, he looked over the wine and smiled. "Great. I got all the furniture out of the room, and the pillows and quilts are all set out."

"Theme evening, right? I'm surprised you don't have supper couches," Paul said.

"You priced ancient Greek furniture lately? I'm lucky I have enough pillows. But you live with Rhea, you end up with lots of pillows. She had the whole house furnished in them and bolts of Indian cloth before I moved in. No, everyone can recline while they eat and bloody well use their imaginations."

CHAPTER NINE

Joe had the perfect host's sense of when the guests would actually begin arriving. He never said a word, but when Misha and Egyptia came up the steps he and Paul were there to hand them wineglasses. Egyptia glanced down at Paul, smiled, and took the glass on her way to the living room. She immediately staked out her territory in the crimson silk pillows opposite the fireplace and reclined like Cleopatra on her barge. She'd worn a midnight blue dress that flowed around her long legs, looking like a bruise at the heart of a rose. Misha took a moment to haul off his boots and drop them in the hallway. He took the glass from Joe, raised an eyebrow at Paul, and dropped into a crouch next to Egyptia.

"Yes, honey, come sit by me. A queen needs attendants."

"I'll be your bodyguard. I'm not good at serving anyone," Misha said.

"You just sit there and look mad and evil, like one of them stone things on churches. What do you call those things?" Egyptia asked Paul, who was standing in the archway.

"Gargoyles," Paul said.

"Them. Your nose isn't long enough, but it'll do. You have been busy! Look at this," Egyptia said as Joe started bringing in platters.

"You know me, Egyptia. Stick me in a kitchen and I'm happy," Joe said.

Egyptia sighed. "I just love it when men wait on me."

"As do I," Rhea said from the doorway. If Egyptia had the splendor and pomp of royalty, Rhea had its stern moral authority.

"You are not the type to suffer anyone serving you, Rhea," Misha said.

"Depends on who's doing it," Taryn said. She swaggered in the door, her face brushed with red from the walk up Elmwood. Taryn stepped out of her boots and left them next to Misha's. Rhea sat gracefully to the left of the fireplace, where her high-backed chair normally sat. Her eyes followed Taryn as she sauntered across the floor.

"Where's your jacket?" Joe asked. Taryn was wearing a black T-shirt and a pair of black pants that he didn't recognize from the laundry.

"Left it somewhere," Taryn said and shrugged. Her face was a mask as she chose the left of the fireplace, dropping down at Rhea's feet. She crossed her legs and leaned her head on her fist, not looking at anyone. Certainly not at Paul, who was torn between staring at Taryn and looking away, his eyes dancing like water drops on a skillet.

"You are missing an appendage," Misha said to Taryn. One eyebrow rose in response.

"Paul, would you help me get the rest of the food?" Joe asked.

"Where is Rosalind?" Misha asked. Taryn raised her head a fraction and gave Misha a look he couldn't miss. The air hissed with it.

"Rosalind is teaching. She will be here shortly with Ellie," Rhea said.

Misha turned to Egyptia, a look of studied indifference on his face. He waited a moment, his brows drawing down as if trying to remember the name. "The one with the hair like a dandelion?" Misha asked.

"The one who kicked your ass at pool," Taryn said in a clipped tone, sneering at Misha. Only Joe and Paul returning with trays of bread kept them from escalating the moment.

Joe sat down to Misha's right, diagonally facing Rhea across the length of the room. He seemed not to mind Taryn sitting at Rhea's feet, taking up the space Paul thought would belong to a partner. Paul stood, awkward, not wanting to choose a space, not wanting to look lost. Joe rescued him by indicating the pillows at his right.

That left him facing Rhea obliquely, and with Rhea, the black-haired thug. It hurt him in a dull, persistent way having her in the room. He couldn't help looking at her. She didn't seem to notice anyone else in the room. The strange eyes were lowered to the floor and only flickered up when Rhea handed her food. She looked, Paul thought, like she was in pain.

Taryn absently took whatever Rhea handed her, eating without interest. The glass of wine Joe handed her sat untouched on the floor. Paul expected conversation, but they were oddly quiet for the meal itself. Perhaps the conversation was meant for later. He was glad to be sitting next to Joe. Misha offered a foul joke, and Egyptia hit him on the shoulder, laughing in encouragement. Misha grinned around a hunk of bread, tearing it in his teeth. He was chewing copiously when a voice called out, trilling into the room.

"Yoo-hoo! Two to come aboard!"

Misha swallowed. The front door opened and Ellie came in like a whirlwind. "No, no, don't get up." She blew kisses all around, stopping to kiss the air next to Egyptia's cheek.

"Have we missed much?" Rosalind asked with a smile that looked rehearsed.

Her eyes went around the room, stopping on Taryn. Taryn looked up. Paul couldn't see any change in her face, but Rosalind seemed to read volumes there. The silence between them was so intimate it affected Misha, who coughed and rubbed the back of his neck. "Not so much. There's food," he said to Ellie.

"I hope so. I was promised dinner. How's the old pool game?" she asked him, smiling brilliantly.

He found his meal very interesting.

"Where should we sit?" Ellie asked, turning around in the center of the room. She saw the empty space to the right of the fireplace, large enough for two. Her eyes sought out Rosalind, who was still locked with Taryn. Taryn made no sign that she was moving. Ellie took the cue, grabbing Rosalind's elbow. "I'm claiming you for the evening. I don't have a date."

They sat down in the plum pillows to the right of the fireplace, Taryn and Rosalind sitting in profile to one another. Even when they didn't look at one another, there seemed to be no one else in the room. They ate in silence. Rhea offered the blessings at the doors and windows of the room after the meal, then tossed the knot of sage into the small fire. Joe cleared the dishes and brought out the pot of wine. He set it down on the hearth to the right of the fireplace, seated on a ceramic trivet. He handed out the mismatched glasses and mugs, reserving a red glass goblet for Rhea.

She accepted it graciously with a languid move of her hand. Taryn stayed coiled at her feet, her head bent down. Rosalind looked at Rhea, letting her pain show for a moment. Rhea shook her head, a small, crisp motion. "We have guests with us tonight. We should offer an explanation. Taryn, would you do it?" Rhea asked.

Taryn looked over her shoulder, saw something in Rhea's face, and agreed. Taryn stood up, naturally taking the center of the room. "Yeah. All right. Tonight's a symposium, named after the Greek custom of holding a dinner party, getting drunk, and talking all night. They made it fancy sometimes by choosing a lofty subject like the nature of the soul, or how to best seduce the beautiful boy they'd seen that afternoon at the marketplace. Plato wrote about a dinner party full of actors and poets and comic writers, all getting drunk and talking about love. This used to be called philosophy." She strolled back to her place on the floor and lounged into the pillows.

"Tonight's theme is Love. We'll begin this the way Phaedrus began the symposium that night with Socrates. I paraphrase Plato speaking as Phaedrus, but the gist was this. If a state or an army could be made up solely of pairs of lovers, they would be the very best and bravest, seeking to outdo one another in honor. The divine inspiration of love would make heroes of them all. I know you've heard it said a million times, an army of lovers cannot fail." Joe raised his wineglass in a toast.

"Whoa. This is unfair to the romantically challenged among us. I'm not enough of an expert to hold forth on Love," Ellie said.

"You're an actor. Fake it," Misha grumbled.

"Thank you, Dr. Zhivago."

"You'll start, Misha, and set a good example," Joe said, raising his glass. He nodded at Misha. The Russian was rolling his wineglass between his open palms, smiling to himself. He seemed able to taste the wine. He was drinking it more slowly tonight, not just tossing it back. Misha took a sip from the glass and rolled it over his tongue. His accent was more pronounced when he drank. It deepened now.

"That tender name, that young girls and matrons alike feel in their trembling hearts, when I walk near them. Love."

He winked broadly at Ellie. Rosalind saw something interesting happen to Ellie, a quickening. A challenge had been presented. Misha nodded at Egyptia, who fanned herself. "Mercy. What was I saying? Yes, yes. Love. The first magical moment when the condom breaks, and he doesn't run." Egyptia lowered her eyelids and batted them at Misha.

Rhea sat up, her posture the envy of dancers. Rosalind had long wondered what it would take to see Rhea lose some of that iron control. As she spent more time around 34 Mariner, she'd begun to see the degrees of Rhea's affection, the small ways she expressed emotion. Subtle things, like the way Rhea sat with her leg just close enough to touch Taryn's back. The restraint of the gesture amazed Rosalind. How did Rhea manage it, that removal? It was all Rosalind could do to keep from crossing the room and taking Taryn in her arms. If she were sitting any closer, she'd have pulled Taryn into her lap by now. She had abandoned any restraint in the face of Taryn's open need. Rhea might never have, Rosalind thought, even when she'd been Taryn's lover. The wall around her was ancient, mortared with blood, unmoved by time or trial.

Taryn projected an air of studied indifference, but her core of melancholy tore holes in it big enough to leak daylight. How had she ever gotten what she needed when she was with Rhea? The security of a home, the comfort of a ritualized relationship, those had been what Rhea offered. Maybe, Rosalind thought for the first time, that was all Taryn could accept when she was younger. A chance to have a relationship with limits. A place no one else held in her life. Was that still enough? Rosalind was looking at Taryn when Rhea started to speak. Her voice was like sand being poured over marble, a voice of movement without liquidity.

"I've grown strong enough to feel it and survive, after six hundred years. Love," Rhea said, looking across at Joe. It was a rare moment of open affection between them. Joe's smile warmed the room. In that smile Rosalind saw the surrender of commitment. Joe had given himself to Rhea and seemed surprised that she kept accepting the gift. Rhea leaned forward and picked up the wineglass. She laid her hand on Taryn's shoulder and offered her the glass. Taryn raised her head, her eyes opaque. She took the glass reflexively, but did not drink.

"The Romans thought Love was a goddess. We name venereal diseases after her." Taryn spoke softly, looking across at Egyptia and Misha.

Rosalind took a deep draft from her glass to keep from crying. She let the wine hit the back of her tongue and held it. Taryn thought she could get away with that?

"Love steps in front of an arrow and accepts its own death, to let the loved one live," Rosalind said, not looking Taryn's way.

"Love never lets a friend run into danger without the proper accessories. Serves you people right for subjecting the rest of us to such a topic," Ellie said with a smirk.

"The topic picks itself. We just bring the wine," Joe said.

Paul looked down at the glass of wine in his hand. It smelled exotic, like he imagined India would smell, night-blooming flowers and the bite of pepper. The color was intoxicating, the garnet burning at the center of the glass from the fire's reflected light, a honeyed heart in a scarlet cloak. The color snagged on his memory, familiar but unplaceable. Everyone was looking at him. He had to speak. He was starting to understand these people, but this evening seemed plain cruel. How civilized did he need to be? He brought the glass to his lips but couldn't bear to drink. At the last second some qualm stayed him. He moved the glass away. Someone was speaking in a voice of dust. He realized it was him.

"Love is a fool's game. A fairy tale, only you are never told that the big bad wolf not only eats Red Riding Hood, he goes into business selling picnic baskets and little woodland cottages."

Paul looked back into the wineglass, trying to remember where he'd seen that color before. He didn't see Rosalind looking at him with grief. Taryn, however, did. Joe cleared his throat. "The first round is done. The glasses aren't empty yet. That's a poor showing for Dionysus. I propose another round."

Misha tapped Joe on the knee and held out his empty glass. His smile was loose, easy. The wineglass was full and back in his hand before he had time to chide Joe for being a poor host. Misha tipped out a few blood-bright drops onto the floor in a libation to his favorite god. He was well built for excess, relaxing under the spell of the wine, smiling more easily. His skin was reddened, warmed by the internal fire, his eyes bright and unguarded. The god was with him, lifting him up. Dionysus was the god of the theater as well as the god of wine, a fact that Joe remembered as Misha saluted Ellie.

"Love came looking for me, to ask my advice on matters of the heart."

Ellie took up the gauntlet and saluted him back. "Too bad you were unable to help out, being only a master of the bedsheets. Lord of linens."

Everyone else in the circle leaned forward, their eyes darting back to Misha as if it were a tennis match, or a duel. The Russian grinned hugely and tossed back his entire glass, holding out his free hand for another. Joe complied, handing over his own.

"Don't be cruel, Lady, I pour out my life's blood from your wounding."

Ellie pursed her lips as if in thought. She leaned over and whispered in Rosalind's ear. Rosalind sat back and shook her head. Ellie laughed.

"Blood? That's grape juice. You gonna piss on me and tell me it's raining? Try telling a woman the truth for once," she said.

Egyptia sat up and pushed at Misha's shoulder. "Ooh, she got you."

Misha shook his head. One sinewy hand reached back and undid the band that held his hair; the other cradled the wineglass. Brown hair spilled down over his shoulders, Samson unleashing his strength. "I'll tell you all the truth you're willing to hear, American woman."

"It's like that, is it? All right." Ellie put her wineglass down. "I'll need your jacket, buddy."

Ellie snapped the collar of the jacket up and undid three buttons on her shirt. She then grinned at Rosalind and strutted around the room. She planted her feet in front of Misha and let the jacket slide down her shoulders. Ellie bent forward and leaned into Misha, giving him an unobstructed view down her shirt. Misha leaned forward. Ellie snapped back up. "I rest my case."

The room collapsed in laughter. Ellie strutted back to her pillows, accepting Joe's high five as she passed. Misha reached for his leather jacket as she passed. Ellie evaded his outstretched hand and sat down with it draped like a victory flag across her shoulders. Egyptia sashayed back to her own spot. The queen looked down at Misha and batted her eyes. "Sorry, honey. You know I adore you, but girls have to back each other up."

"Ellie, that was fabulous! Look at him, he's speechless," Joe said.

Misha smiled sarcastically at Joe, then stood up. He tossed back his head, unconsciously giving the impression of a stallion scenting danger. He took in a deep breath, ignoring everyone in the room. He began to sing, his voice deep and brown, the voice of a man who'd grown up singing but never been trained. He sang first in Russian, his eyes half closed in the recall of pleasure. Rosalind recognized the song at once. It was the folk song Misha had been singing when Joe and Taryn carried him up the street. "Dark Eyes." His voice was full of wine tonight, but it was a softer tone, a yearning. He finished the song, tipped his head to the side, and opened his eyes, watching Ellie. He sang it again, the Russian blending into English.

He finished with a dance step he'd learned from his mother, a sharp snapping down of the heels, arms curved out as if holding sword and shield. He didn't look at Ellie, but he didn't need to. He sat back down with a satisfied smile.

"All right, you've got some of your own back. Stop your smirking. Why is it that the worst men can make any language sound so damn sexy?" Egyptia asked.

"Well done, Misha. I think we're finished with the second round. Anyone for more wine before we continue with the philosophy?" Joe asked.

"Plato's symposium spent time defining the nature of Love, so we don't have to," Joe said, sipping his wine. "I think they were arguing whether it was a god, or a spirit between men and gods. I won't bore you with that. We're modern folks. We can talk about what love is for us. For me, it's easy. Love is what makes a community strong. It's what lets us find pride in ourselves, no matter what lies the world tells about us. It makes us care about the world the young ones are inheriting." He nodded to Misha.

"Joe is a reasonable adult," Misha said. "He is, in his way, quite wrong. Love is not the affection that springs up randomly between people. Love can only happen when someone knows you. That only happens if you share blood."

Egyptia looked at him with arch disdain. "Remind me not to let you talk again. You just sit there and be all rugged and quiet. Love is like a hot fudge sundae. Sometimes you know it'll be bad for you, but you just can't help yourself, you get such cravings. Sometimes it stays with you; sometimes it's gone when you blink your eyes, but it's always sooo sweet."

Rhea drank slowly from her glass of wine. "Love is what rebuilds the house after pride has torn it down." The witch smiled at Joe and ran her hand through Taryn's hair.

"Love makes everything else worth it," Taryn said. She cast a sidelong glance at Rosalind.

"Love gives you back your soul when you've forgotten you have one," Rosalind said.

"Love is a great spectator sport," Ellie said.

It was Paul's turn to speak. The conversation had been running around the room with a speed beyond his readiness. He hadn't tasted the magical wine as everyone seemed to and now he felt its lack. The sobriety that weighed him down was the weight of gravity in a room of cheer he couldn't share. It was a knife he held in his hand, not a wineglass, a knife that he could draw along his tongue until it bled. He felt that the hot wine would burn his mouth, that the strength of the mysterious spices would scald him. But he wanted to belong. He wanted to be a part of this odd circle and these odd people, to join in the rituals they devised. It made little sense, but he liked Joe. The kindness of the man had seen him through a day that would have been plain torture.

Paul's hand shook on the wineglass. He wanted the red haze to seep into his blood. He wanted to feel the sharp-edged joy that everyone else was feeling. The wine was softening the evening. He could see it in Misha's cocky grin, in the flirtation he and Ellie tossed back and forth. Everyone seemed ready to laugh at a joke he wasn't getting. Rosalind was right there with them. Even sitting next to Ellie, smiling with delight at Misha's performance. He could see her eyes slip over to the brooding girl with a look he could only call longing. And he knew with a certainty pure as hatred that if he were not in the room, she would be sitting with Taryn in her arms. The Rosalind he knew had never been big on displays of affection, though her warmth was given easily in small gestures, a touch of her hand when you spoke to her, a look of sympathy that melted the coldest heart. She was restraining herself now.

Paul took the glass and tossed it back, draining it in one motion. The wine burned his throat, but it was that or crushing the glass in his fist. It hit him like a shot of ninety-year-old scotch, moving him from sobriety to drunkenness in a heartbeat. He'd missed the taste, but the potency was enough. He turned to Joe, amazed. "This is good," Paul said, feeling his words begin to slur.

"It's strong. Be careful," Joe said, always the parent.

Paul laughed. "I didn't think anybody in this house would say that. Doesn't seem like a careful place." He held out his glass. Joe looked at it for a moment. Misha jumped up and grabbed it, refilling it from the pot by the fire.

"I will play host. Joe is distracted. Here."

The wine was a live coal in the glass. It savaged his mouth when he drank. He felt it galloping along his limbs. There was a loosening in his chest. The pain seemed to retreat. It took him two gulps to empty his second glass. "Love," Paul said, gesturing with his free hand. He felt wise suddenly. Who knew more about this than he did? "Love is the beast with teeth. Love eats your heart and grins at you through the blood. But everyone goes hunting it just the same. Love is the only madness that you can practice and not be locked up, because there wouldn't be any room left in the world or anybody left to guard the jail." He held out the glass again, and Misha took it from him.

"At last, a man with some sense! You haven't been infected with the sentimental nonsense these people spout." Misha filled both their glasses and returned to sit near Paul. Joe moved over by Egyptia, giving him room.

"Here we go," Egyptia said, frowning at them.

"Sentimental? No. Not that," Paul said.

"I have a theory," Misha said. "There are people who are born fools about love, and people who are not susceptible. The fools outnumber the rest of us and go around thinking they have the world all sewn up. While it is possible to be woken from this romantic sleepwalking and join us, it is impossible to go from being awake to being a romantic." He looked at Paul for confirmation. Paul looked befuddled.

"I don't know…"

Misha looked at him with the steady gaze of a priest in communion with his god. "Think about it. Love isn't a choice. It's a sickness that comes on us unawares, like the flu. But do we wish our friends a speedy recovery when they fall? We do not. We listen to the conflation of lust and idiocy as if it were a rational person's choice. We allow them their madness, even if we see its eventual destruction. A man may lose his well-being, his home, all his possessions, his good name, and his friends, if he loses his heart. He will do things that are against his judgment and sense. He will ignore what he knows to be right. He will make a mockery of his reputation, to gain the favor of his romantic longing. Far better if we call the inflammation of lust by its rightful name. Let a man have his lust sated and not be roped down by chains of sentimentality. Would you be owned by something just because you desire it? That makes a man little better than a slave."

Paul drank his wine more slowly, as if trying to focus. "But that makes love out to be nothing but lust. A bestial drive."

"And what else might it be? We are programmed for billions of years to propagate the species. We dress it up in fancy modern terms, but love is a drive of biology," Misha said.

Taryn shook her head. "Now really, Misha. If it's all reproduction, explain me. Explain Egyptia, and Joe. Explain Stephan."

Paul saw Misha's face go gray, as if a ghost had walked into the room and stood right in front of him. It was the list of names that did it, but he wasn't sure which one had made Misha blanch. Misha's eyelids slid closed. He exhaled as if he'd been punched. "There is no accounting. It is only a theory," Misha said at last, not looking at Taryn.

"A theory more people hold than you know. If you follow it, there are two ways it can go. In one, homosexuals are just a natural variant, occurring in many animal species and most human societies. In the other, reproduction is the only natural biological urge. That would make all us queer folk perverse accidents. Contrary to nature. And if you follow that thinking to its end, nothing against nature has the right to exist," Joe said.

Misha shook his head, angry. "Stop it. You know full well I don't believe that rot. I always stood by my brother. Always. He had more reason to exist than most people walking this stinking planet."

"It pays to be aware of what people do with ideas," Taryn said.

"I thought we were talking about love," Misha said crossly.

"We are. It's been said that love is only a name for lust. Anyone?" Joe asked.

A cool, dry voice reached out from the corner of the room. "Misha has a point," Rhea said.

"I do?" Misha asked, surprised.

"Yes. Not the one you think. Lust can be the drive that spurs humans toward one another. Or rather, desire. And desire is a frightening thing. Certainly a kind of madness. Being out of control is terrifying, and the strength of desire can make it feel like you are at the mercy of your own hunger." Rhea scratched idly at the back of Taryn's neck with her nails.

"Amen," Rosalind said and promptly blushed. "I mean, I've read that. But desire for beauty is the first wakening of the soul. Desire for the beloved, for example. From that beauty we are drawn upward to the beauty of honor and excellence, our soul is reminded of the love of truth behind that beauty and rises toward the eternal. From the good to the best, drawn on by Eros. If we believe that, then desire isn't an animal drive, it's the first sign of the soul waking. Proof of our immortality, if you will."

"Now you're talking! We should be throwing a parade when we start drooling over a new lust object! It's the soul waking up," Ellie said.

"It's a persuasive theory," Rosalind said. This time she looked over at Taryn and caught her breath. Taryn's eyes were on her, burning. Her soul woke and responded, moving out toward her skin in a wave of heat.

"I have another one," Joe said, standing up. He brushed his hands on his jeans as if his palms were sweating. "Without love, the house is empty. With love, emptiness is a home."

Joe broke off, embarrassed. He looked at Rhea and smiled. "I'm an old-fashioned guy. I only know one way to approach love, and that's to give it a place to live." He reached into his pocket and drew forth a small leather bag. Rhea's eyes got very round as he went down on one knee in front of her and drew a circle of silver out of the bag. "Rhea, will you marry me?"

Rosalind remembered Rhea in the kitchen of the house, the

morning after the ritual that freed her from her eternal sacrifice, saying that she hadn't been surprised in six hundred years. From the look on her face, that had changed. She recovered with grace, standing and taking the ring from Joe with solemn dignity. "It has always been yes between us."

There was no room left for Taryn as they came together. Taryn backed away toward the fire with an awkward half step, clearly wanting to get out of the way and clearly wanting to keep her place at Rhea's feet. The confusion broke Rosalind's heart. Despite any remaining tension between them, she stepped over and took Taryn's hand, giving her a place to rest. The look Taryn gave her was one of uncovered gratitude, as if Taryn couldn't remember to be sullen.

Paul watched as the room reacted like a handful of confetti tossed up. Rhea and Joe stood, hand in hand, in the center of the whirlwind of congratulations and backslapping. They were a couple he'd never picture on a wedding cake, pagan and strange, but they looked good together. Joe's carefully symmetrical, muscular body was contrasted with the thin woman with the wild hair, a thinness that spoke of steel or bone. Paul knew Rhea to be short, Rosalind's height at best, but next to Joe, she seemed taller.

He had a vicious, splintered moment of memory, standing next to Rosalind in front of the altar. The sweating, fumbling happiness had been layered with worry. He'd looked at his bride and felt it, the fear he couldn't shake. She was smiling. She always smiled. She was saying and doing everything right, but she wasn't there. Not the center, not the hidden portion he'd always known was secreted away in a locked room of her heart. Paul had hoped that the marriage ceremony itself might change that, that magically, he'd be admitted into Rosalind's inner world. So he'd held on to his one hope, until he placed the ring on her finger, until she smiled for him with affection, his oldest friend.

There was no burning, no opening. Whatever was sealed inside her would forever be a mystery to him. Perhaps it was this way with all men and women, and he'd allowed boyish fantasy to cloud him with hope. The gnawing worm of fear was explicit—that there was indeed such union, but he would never know it.

There was something in his eye. He looked away from Rhea and Joe. The frenzied sheen of joy was beyond him. Even the bombastic

Misha seemed delighted, as if marriage was a good thing when practiced by these two people. Paul choked down the block of grief in his throat and looked for Rosalind.

It was a mistake. She was standing with her arm entwined with the thug, her face shining with happiness too strong to hide. It ate him raw. He saw the pleasure and associated it not only with the news of the wedding, but Taryn, who she was holding. The hate was soothing. The balm spread when he saw Taryn step forward and shake Joe's hand manfully, an affectation Paul instantly loathed. There was a grandiosity to the girl's gestures he associated with bombast. Mannerisms too studied to be natural. It gave him a hook on which to hang his rage. The wine soured in his stomach.

"Hey, everybody. Quiet down a minute. I know I'm a relative newcomer here, and I know I don't have the right to this that Rhea does. But if she will indulge me, I'll ask," Joe said.

Rhea put her hand on the man's arm. "What I have is yours."

"T, I'd be honored if you'd be my best man," Joe said.

Taryn threw her free arm around Joe. "I'd be second best man to you any day."

"It was bound to happen. I have lost both of you to your male bonding. Then I assume some freedom in my choice. Rosalind, would you stand up for me?" Rhea asked.

"I'd love to," Rosalind said, blinking back tears. She held out her arm as if to offer Rhea an embrace. Rhea hesitated, dropped Joe's hand, and leaned forward. Supple strength, the resistance of whalebone. It was like embracing a basilisk. Rhea gave only the upper portion of her body to the hug.

"This is gonna get ugly, but I'm ready. Y'all go on. Fight over who gets me." Egyptia struck a waiting pose, hand on her hip.

"You must stand for me, Egyptia, and lend my side your elegance," Rhea said.

"If you get the royalty, I get the surly Canadian?" Joe asked.

Misha threw back his head, sending his hair flying over his shoulders. "Russian. Canadian. I feel so welcome."

The symposium wandered off into talk of plans. Someone suggested having the ceremony at the house, another with an outdoor ceremony. The idea seemed to grow organically that it would happen on the beach at the cabin in Canada, where Rhea's parents had property.

Halloween was the only day anyone considered. The question of who would perform the wedding came up. Names were bandied that sounded like animals or constellations. There was a round of wine like heated plums.

Paul felt exhaustion fall on him. His eyes drifted half closed. He leaned his head back against the wall. His last sight was of Rosalind, now sitting next to the thug, talking intimately to Rhea. The two women leaned across Taryn's body, both casually resting on her thighs as if she were a shared possession. Taryn looked amused and smug at being used for furniture. She lounged back against the wall, siphoning all the heat from the fire as if there were no finer spot in all the world. Her eyes hadn't cut his way once all night. It was as if he didn't exist for her. "You will never have it either," he said, and sleep took him.

Misha and Joe had carried Paul up to what was now called his room. "Don't worry about him. It's his first time with the wine and everything. He'll be fine," Joe said to Rosalind when they came back down. Misha made a disparaging noise, sat down, and poured more wine. He picked up the argument he'd been having with Ellie mid-sentence.

"…completely wrong for the part. Impossibly so."

"And your judgment is based on what? The phases of the moon? It can't be based on any actual standards of artistry."

Egyptia and Joe started cleaning up. Rosalind jumped up to help them. "You know what you're gonna wear for the wedding, Joe?" Egyptia asked, balancing plates with her long fingers.

"A pair of jeans and a work shirt?" Joe asked wistfully.

"You're joking. He's joking. I swear you are impossible to get dressed up. We'll have to send you out with Taryn to go shopping. That boy can dress."

They piled the dishes in the sink. Joe separated out the compost and the trash. The back door was open, letting in a cold rush of air. "Do you see Astarte?" Joe asked Rosalind.

"The calico? No, I don't." Rosalind looked around the room at the cat's normal sleeping spots—the counter under the coffee mugs, the back side of the table, under the sink. The cat rarely left the kitchen.

"Damn, she might've gotten out back. Rhea wants to keep her inside. It's getting cold at night. And in her condition—"

"Starry's not sick?"

"She's in a family way," Egyptia said.

"I'll go look for her." Rosalind opened the screen door and trotted down the steps.

Even in the dark Rosalind could tell that major renovation had happened in the yard. Paul and Joe had been busy. The garden was cleared and ready for the snow. The compost heap had been moved back. A new section of fence patched the gap that had existed in the back wall. Plenty of places for a cat to hide, from the woodpile along the side of the house, to the maze of shingles and tar buckets from the roof repair two seasons ago, the crawl space under the back stairs, and a maze of tunnels that seemed to run into eternity underneath the house itself.

Rosalind stood in the yard and looked back at the house for a moment. The light in the kitchen spilled out, inviting, pale gold and warm as a hearth fire. This was a place where things began and ended, a place to go forth from into the world, a place to return to always. Even, she thought, after death. Misha's brother must have been called by the fire tonight. Rosalind had the feeling that he was here, watching, waiting to speak. There was an eagerness she felt when she thought of Stephan, though she'd never known him. The thought of being watched by a ghost would have sent a chill up her spine a few months ago, but now it seemed as normal as any other guest dropping in. They were people looking for a warm place to spend a few hours.

Rosalind heard a noise by the back wall, a crunching of something moving through the leaves. She moved toward it, calling out, "Kitty! Astarte! Hey, Star. Hey, Starry. Starry, starry night." She was aware that she'd never let a human hear her babble like this, but animals were different. The immense calico would never roll her eyes at any endearments Rosalind managed to dream up. There was an abbreviated yowl from the pile of leaves. Rosalind fished the cat out. "No more happy wandering for you, lady."

The cat didn't object to being carried back toward the house and lay boneless in Rosalind's arms. She was at the foot of the steps, trying not to chide the calico for her weight, when she heard voices in the kitchen. Taryn's voice, dark and heavy as smoke, hung in the air.

"How long did you know?"

"Clever man. He carried the ring in his pocket for weeks, waiting for impulse to strike so I wouldn't be prepared," Rhea said, a smile in her voice.

Rosalind hesitated on the first step. The cat was quiet in her arms as she waited. She wasn't sure why she paused, something in Taryn's tone. She wanted to hear what Taryn next said to Rhea.

"So you're leaving me," Taryn said. Rosalind knew the look that went along with that tone, the sullen glare of gem-hard eyes under drawn brows. A look meant to be anger that spoke of hurt.

Rhea was silent for so long, Rosalind had to curb the urge to march into the kitchen and interrupt. Something was being played out that predated her. When Rhea spoke, her voice was blunted, as if she spoke through layers of cloth.

"You have learned to be cruel."

"No," Taryn said, her voice dropping down to match Rhea's.

"You made your choice long ago. I have endured it. I thought you approved of Joe," Rhea said a bit stronger.

"I love Papa."

Rosalind thought there might have been amusement like flecks of mica in the granite of Rhea's voice. "But you must come first, always."

"Nobody else ever did," Taryn said.

"Remember the night we met Joe?" Rhea asked.

"Samhain. Yeah."

"You liked him then. But he made you sad," Rhea said softer still, as if she were moving closer to Taryn. "So fierce and so sad. Even now."

"I saw him coming. You and him. I'm not stupid," Taryn said.

"You fear that you are. You never were. Now you know how it felt when I saw Rosalind coming."

"That's not—" Taryn broke off, swallowing the end of the sentence. "That was after. You already had Joe."

"Yet you still came first. You have always known that. It cannot be that way forever."

"Why do things have to change?" Taryn asked, and her voice was full of tears.

"My beautiful boy." Rhea's voice was tender, more intimate than Rosalind could have imagined. "For anything new to be born, space must be made. Old things pass away. Your Rosalind reminded me of that. You have your happiness. Let me have mine."

Astarte chose that moment to let out a yowl, perhaps responding to Rhea's voice. Rosalind sighed and walked up the steps. Taryn was leaning against the counter, staring at Rhea with a look that made a mockery of gravity. Rhea was inches away, the distance that only lovers and intimates may assume. They weren't embracing, but the way their bodies related to one another in the domestic space of the kitchen, they should have been. Rosalind opened the screen door with a tap of her foot and released the calico onto the floor. Astarte sauntered over to Rhea and wound around her ankles, happily banging her skull into the witch's calf.

Rhea let the cat's attention be her excuse to move away from Taryn. It was subtle, a twist of her body as if to pet the joy-maddened cat, a step toward the door as if lost in thought, a glance back at Rosalind as if just noticing her for the first time.

"She was out in the backyard," Rosalind said.

Rhea scratched her fingers over the cat's round head as the calico squinted and danced. "You feed them, and you love them, but look out. No matter how domesticated you think they are, if you leave the door open even a crack, they vanish," Rhea said.

"She never goes far," Taryn said.

"No matter. It is the longing to escape that never fades. Good night." Rhea scooped up the cat, who hung over her arm like a folded blanket, blinking as they headed for the stairs.

"She only bolts when it gets too noisy or crowded in here. If it's quiet and she gets to keep her favorite spot, she'd never move," Taryn said, folding her arms across her chest. Taryn hated to lose an argument. But Rhea had left the kitchen.

There were things Rosalind wanted to ask, words that came tripping over one another, eager to offer advice, to soothe and comfort. She had to restrain herself. A glance at Taryn showed her that Taryn wasn't ready for any comfort. She stood in her stubborn pose, staring after Rhea with a look of confusion. There was something hard and obstinate in her inability to understand what had happened, a willful emotional ignorance. It wasn't the time to draw her out, Rosalind decided. The moment between Taryn and Rhea would have to find its conclusion first.

So Rosalind made her choice, breathed a quick prayer for patience, and held out her hand, offering what she knew her beloved would not refuse. It wasn't difficult to lure Taryn away for the night. Taryn seemed to breathe a sigh of relief as they left 34 Mariner, as if the air had gotten very thick. She held Rosalind's hand and crossed the street, not looking back.

Chapter Ten

The invasion began with a dinner party. The war started over coffee. Walking down the narrow staircase at the back of the house, Paul tripped. A sliver of wood pierced his big toe, sending jewel-like drops of blood arcing into the air. It likewise pierced the sense of unreality he'd been suspended in. Like a blanket torn off on a cold morning, the sensation left Paul holding his foot and cursing, utterly aware of where he was. He was standing on the back staircase of some pagan house in Buffalo, playing sleep-away camp with his ex-wife's bizarre friends. More precisely, the friends of her new girlfriend.

Paul's lips twisted, and not from the physical pain. *Girlfriend* might be the technically correct term, but he'd met the thug. She wasn't a girl. He wasn't sure what she was. The words didn't fit. And the cheerful misuse of pronouns last night…had that been the wine? He had a vague recollection of Egyptia being referred to constantly as *she*. Not once in his hearing had anyone called the drag queen by a male pronoun or used a name other than Egyptia. But the thug had been referred to by name, by nickname, by a variety of pronouns indicating a fluctuation of gender he couldn't track.

It had made some sense as the wine hit him. The masculine pronouns were used by women, primarily Rhea and Rosalind, and were spoken in honeyed tones. There was some special quality being recognized or assigned to her at those moments, some quality that brought out caressing tones of voice, looks of melting affection. At those moments there was something well beloved about *Taryn*. He had to force himself to think the name.

He tried to pry the sliver out with his nails but only succeeded in sending fresh gouts of blood out of the torn flesh. Paul bled and hobbled his way down the staircase and into the kitchen. Joe was cooking. He'd already learned to expect that. It was nice that such a masculine guy seemed so at home in the kitchen. It gave credence to his secure sense of self. For a moment Paul had a glimpse of his father, standing at the stove on Sunday mornings making pancakes for the family. Arthur turned and smiled over his shoulder, and it was Joe.

Joe's smile broke when he saw the wound. In an instant Paul was seated. The blood was being dabbed by a gentle hand. The edges of the savaged skin were examined. It was ridiculous, he thought, how good it felt to be on the receiving end of that attention, how parental Joe became in the blink of an eye. Paul clamped his teeth on the well of gratitude he felt, knowing it to be misplaced, out of proportion, but as real as the sun. Fortunately Joe was away at the sink, sterilizing a pair of tweezers, and missed the struggle.

Joe took Paul's foot in his hands and turned it with a touch like a surgeon's. "This will hurt," he said calmly, as if pain were only a minor fact, one to be acknowledged and borne with courage.

"Will you give me a lollipop if I don't cry?" Paul heard his own voice grate out and was angry at the way it sounded, the need in it. He meant it to be a joke, but the humor eluded him.

Joe was sitting on his haunches, looking up into his face. "There. Not so bad, right?"

Paul looked at the splinter of wood, five inches long and slimy with his blood, pointed like a javelin. "When did you take that out?" Paul asked, amazed.

"Just now. You didn't feel it?"

"No. My nerve endings must be a little dead after last night. All the wine. Christ, I'll look like I have stigmata," Paul said.

Joe stood up. "Holy wounds never seemed like a good idea, if you ask me. Suffering isn't one of my virtues. You want to keep this?" He held out the shard of wood.

It was like being in a movie. His buddy had dug a bullet out of his flesh. Now he could grimace manfully and laugh, keep the bullet as a good luck charm. But Joe was already turned away, unsentimental about the object that caused pain. So Paul bit down on his answer and kept silent. There was a handful of bandages on the table. He tore one open and slapped it on his foot, roughly. "Is that coffee I see?" Paul asked.

Joe was at the sink. He tossed an affirmative over his shoulder. "It's half chicory, fair warning. Milk's on the table if you're partial. Honey and sugar on the counter. Grab a cup. Let me finish peeling these potatoes and I'll join you."

The wall of coffee mugs loomed. On the counter there was a glass mug set apart on a trivet. It glowed a deep cobalt blue in the morning light, the color of angel's blood. It was closer. He didn't have to hobble as far, so Paul picked it up and poured himself a cup of coffee. It was a handsome mug, he thought, big enough for an adult. He sat back down at the table, admiring it.

"Oh, just don't grab the mug on the counter. Rhea just bought that for—" Joe stopped midsentence, looking at Paul. "Oy."

The screen door was open. Intellectually, Paul supposed that this youth had to have another range of expression, but all he had observed were shadings of rage. She seemed designed for anger, primed for it, the planes of her face taking on a hardness that added years. She was still wearing the same black clothing from the symposium last night, artfully rumpled; her hair had been combed only with fingers. He knew the look. He'd been young once. She'd been awake all night. He fancied he could almost smell the sex on her. And it was no mystery who she'd been keeping company with. Like a cat coming home by daylight, he thought. She didn't have to fling it in his face.

Taryn had had a beautiful morning. Rosalind had managed to soothe the knot in her left from the encounter with Rhea. She had rehearsal today and looked forward to it. There was still time to catch Joe for coffee. Maybe talk about the wedding. She'd come in the door in high spirits, feeling the welcome that was hers by right. This was her home. Her territory. Nothing would ever change that. Joe was at the sink. She could see his head and shoulders from the back window. Paul was seated at the table. All the pleasant fantasies of homecoming evaporated. The thorn in her flesh was still there. And he had her mug.

"Put it down," she said.

"What? Is something wrong with this mug?" Paul asked, looking suspiciously at it.

"There is now." The voice was one of controlled fury.

He didn't resist when she took it from his fingers. She didn't spill the coffee on his lap, though the tension in her forearm might have told him how close she'd come. The mug was examined with eyes as blue as the glass. "Did your lips touch it?" Taryn asked mildly.

"Of course," Paul said irritably. He knew something was happening. He wasn't sure what.

Taryn nodded, to herself it seemed, and walked to the back door. She tapped the screen door open with her foot, and hurled the mug the length of the yard. Paul heard the glass shatter against the back wall.

"What is wrong with you?" Paul said, stunned by the impulsive violence. He was used to controlled, civilized people. This display of emotion was unnecessarily dramatic. It had to be false. He looked at Joe, expecting support. Joe was looking at the thug with compassion, as if this outburst were understandable.

Taryn hitched one shoulder, like a horse flicking off a fly. Her eyes were inflamed, wide and deadly. Paul felt the cobalt stare like the edge of a knife. It was with effort that Taryn mastered herself. She stood up a little straighter, breathing deeply. The fire in her gaze cooled. She walked right past him and poured herself a cup of coffee.

She ignored him. Even after that explosion, that burst of emotion, she cooled like hot iron plunged into water. It was as if he no longer existed. He flickered and went out. It was that abnegation, that loss of self, that Paul could not stand. He rather liked it that he was important enough to send the thug into a rage. When she drew herself back inside that indifferent shell, it stung him as her anger could not. "You don't mind handling other things my lips have touched," he mumbled loud enough for her to hear.

The fist caught him on the side of the jaw, backed by a beautiful hip pivot. Someone had taught her how to hit, he thought, as he fell back against the table. He met the edge of the table and it gave under his weight, overturning. There was a crash of ceramic, the bright splintering of glass as a vase of flowers Rhea had picked ended their life against the floor. One elbow struck the floor. The pain was greater from that than the blow across his jaw. Paul grabbed at his elbow and swore, his feet kicking bruised flowers aside in their scramble for purchase. He felt like a crab on its back.

He'd never been hit. It was frighteningly real, explicitly physical. No metaphor about her dislike, no snide comments or cynical asides. Taryn had hauled off and decked him. Paul got back to his feet in a protective crouch. Boxing movies always said to keep your hands up, but his damn elbow hurt too much to let it go. He ended up with his shoulders hunched, watching for the next explosion. It never came.

Joe had moved almost as fast as Taryn and now held her by the arms, dragging her away from Paul. From the effort it took to hold her back, she was still in the grip of her rage. Paul had never imagined a person with eyes like that. It scared him far more than the physical violence. She was lunging against the restraint. She was strong. He could see the muscles stand out in Joe's arms as he swung her away. "Taryn, knock it off!" Joe roared. He pushed her back up against the sink and pinned her. Paul thought of a man trying to restrain a tiger.

Paul could see the flash of her eyes. Her lips were set in a snarl. She wasn't looking at Joe. All that anger was concentrated on him.

"He's here for healing!" Joe yelled, but Taryn ignored him. Something had broken in her. She fought her way forward. Joe pressed her back against the sink. It wasn't easy. His shirt tore. "God damn it, Taryn! You know better. You never strike a guest in my house."

All motion ceased. Joe froze, aware of what he'd said. Taryn went quiet in his hands, still as death. For the first time, she looked at him. There was intelligence behind her eyes, but it was uglier than the rage. Joe dropped his hands and stepped back, looking sick.

Taryn stalked to the back door, the swing of her stride murderous. Paul flinched, but he knew he wasn't the issue anymore.

"Taryn, wait. Wait," Joe said, pleading. He held out his hands.

She kicked the door open. She spoke without looking back. "You tell Rhea I'm gone."

"More coffee?"

Taryn pushed the cup forward on the table with a lazy motion of her wrist, as if the matter were too inconsequential to command her attention. Her eyes were hooded, fixed on the middle distance, as if she expected the wall of the coffee shop to open suddenly on a magnificent vista.

The girl serving her coffee lingered by the table, hoping to catch her eye, but Taryn was spectacular in her indifference. Taryn was unaware that to her audience she looked like a painting of a sullen prince, jaded and world-weary.

Taryn's eyes flickered to the right, saw someone still standing there. The girl offered her a nervous smile. Taryn's eyes stilled as she saw her for the first time. She shifted under the weight of that contemplation.

"Is there anything I can do—get for you?"

One brow rose sardonically. It would be easy. All she'd have to do was grin, nod her head toward the seat next to her. The girl would blush, but she'd sit down quickly. A few questions to put her at ease, a few answers to throw her guard down, and Taryn knew she could collect on what that shy smile was really offering her. The steps were so familiar. They never really changed. And from the way she was looking at Taryn, it was still the one thing Taryn knew she could do without effort. The one thing she had left and couldn't screw up by being just who people expected her to be.

"What's your name?" Taryn asked, dropping her voice automatically into a lower register.

The girl blushed. "Michelle."

"I'm Taryn."

"I know." There was a hint of boldness, of spirit, under that shyness. Taryn usually liked that.

"Sit down."

Michelle did, just as quickly as Taryn imagined she would. No hesitation here, she just needed a little push, an excuse. She was looking at Taryn to provide it. "You're new here," Taryn said, looking her over thoroughly.

Michelle nodded, one hand touching her throat. Taryn knew that look. It would feel so good to get her power back. So easy to get the affirmation she craved. "So you know my name. What else do you know about me?" Taryn asked, hearing her own voice like a rewound movie, falling back into a teasing tone. Had it always sounded like that?

The image slipped into her head of Rosalind on that first night, how she'd broken right through the walls. *Tell me what you love.* It hurt too much. She pressed the memory down. That was over. She'd ruined it all.

"I've heard things. I know you perform," Michelle said, bolder now.

"I'm always performing." Taryn's grin was evil, but it was reflex, the drained husk of a grin. Michelle laughed appropriately, not knowing the difference. It brought dust into Taryn's mouth. The world had ended. She was performing. Like a trained monkey. The voice in her head spoke, clear as the note from a bronze bell. She was supposed to be asking the girl some questions about herself, show some interest. That was always good. Taryn couldn't think of a question to save her life.

Michelle was pretty enough, with fawn-colored hair curled like spiderwebs down to her shoulders and big blue eyes that ached to know more. She had a Catholic schoolgirl's face, innocent and hungry. Taryn felt the familiar stream of thoughts rise. *I am the knowledge she seeks, profane and earthly. I am a good time waiting to happen. I am the magic fuck you've been dreaming about. I am your revenge against your mother. I am a trained monkey.*

The resentment choked her. Michelle was still looking at her, interpreting her silence as a romantic ploy, filling her sullen withdrawal with sexual meaning. It would be so easy to complete the spiral of destruction, finish out with a bang. She'd already savaged her entire life, lost her home, her family. And though her mind balked at it, surely lost Rosalind. That one unstoppable moment of anger when she'd hit Paul, she'd managed to destroy everything she'd tried to build. Nothing ever really changed. How long had it taken her to run true to form? Why not make the break clean?

"You want to come home with me, right?" Taryn asked abruptly.

Michelle blinked in surprise. But she nodded after a moment and smiled shyly. "Yes, I do."

Taryn looked at the wall. "I don't have a home." She felt the tears sting at the back of her eyes, and closed them. There was nothing she could bear seeing.

"Pardon me?"

"You seem nice. I'm an asshole. I'm just wasting your time. You should take off," Taryn said in a voice as old as the world.

Michelle looked her over very carefully. "You're not wasting my time. I don't know you, but you look like you could use some cheering up."

"I know what I need. But I can't have her."

Michelle's face fell. She pushed back from the table, crossing her arms. "Oh."

"Yeah." Taryn stood up and tossed a few bills on the table. "I'll see you around, Michelle."

There had to be another way to feed the ache in her. With a kind of desperation, Taryn headed for rehearsal.

"Hey, Joe. Is there any—what the hell happened here?" Rosalind stopped short in the doorway, looking at the wreckage of the kitchen. Paul was turning the table back onto its legs. Joe was on his knees mopping up water and glass shards from the broken vase. Rosalind grabbed a dish towel and knelt down to help him. "Did a hurricane come through?"

"In a manner of speaking," Paul said tightly. When he turned, Rosalind could see the bruise on his jaw, flowering red and indigo like a tropical plant.

Rosalind sucked in a breath. "Good Lord." And she knew. The air was full of hard energy, jangled and sore. Paul radiated the wounded resentment of the victim. The ax had fallen. Rosalind squared her shoulders and set about picking up the pieces. "Tell me."

"She hit me." He said it with such satisfaction he smiled through the words, though he wasn't aware of it.

"I can see that. But what happened, Paul?"

"You're not the least bit surprised that your paramour assaulted me? You've been away from home for too long, Ros. Your perspective is gone."

Rosalind turned away from him. It was then that she noticed that Joe was crying. "Honey, what is it?" Rosalind said, sitting down in front of him in the wreckage of flowers. She took his face in her hands, stunned. His brown eyes were hazed, circled in red. Tears ran down into his beard.

"I did the one thing I swore I'd never do. I took somebody's home away from them. And I did it to Taryn."

It was easy to read the room, the overturned table, the spreading bruise on Paul's face, Joe's frightening guilt. She'd thought it would work out, having Paul in the house. Rhea had been so calm about it, so certain. Rhea was always certain. Taryn had bitten down and accepted it. The symposium had gone as well as could be expected. There had been no uprising. It had lulled her into a sense of security. From the evidence in the room, the explosion had happened, triggered by a wrong gesture, a misplaced word. It didn't matter. The only thing that mattered was cleaning it up. "Where is she?"

"She's gone. Because of what I said. She won't be back, Ros. I've never seen her like that."

"What did she say?" Rosalind asked gently.

"She told me to tell Rhea she was gone."

"Listen, we know how Taryn gets. She'll blow up, but it will pass. Give her some time. Let me go find her. She's tightly wrapped right now. She just needs reassurance, with the wedding, and Paul—"

"If I'd kept my head, I could have seen that. But instead of reassurance, I took sides. And it wasn't her side I took. I don't think she'll forgive me," Joe said.

"I don't want to hear any more of that. Of course she will. She loves you, Joe. And I'm sure she didn't make it easy on you," Rosalind said, lifting the torn half of Joe's shirt.

That brought a rueful smile to Joe's lips. "Easy, no. I don't know how you do it."

"My own fault. Rhea warned me she'd be a handful." Rosalind stood up and pushed a hand through her hair. "I don't want you to worry. I'm going to find her and kick some sense into her."

"You'd be the first. Rhea used to let her rage."

Rosalind cast him a long look, her eyes cool as stones.

"I'm not Rhea. And Taryn isn't seventeen anymore."

❖

Linda Alejandros paced back and forth in front of the stage with restless energy Taryn recognized as kinship. Linda seemed to be able to summon and harness that energy, where she still felt it like lightning strikes. "I want Sam to step forward after Grace, then Wolf. Wolf, when you finish your monologue, pick a woman from the audience, take her hand, and lead her up the aisle and out. You got it?"

"Exit through the house?" Wolf said, hooking her thumbs in the pockets of her torn jeans.

"Yes," Linda said with exaggerated patience.

"That's a little weird."

"Trust me. Try it. If it doesn't work, we scrap it. I want you to take it from 'Cool, tough and lonely,' and run to the end. It's not quite there yet."

Wolf started the monologue, swinging around the stage with the exaggerated swagger of a pirate film. Taryn sighed and leaned back against the wall. Rehearsal was working as she'd hoped, letting her set her emotions aside for a few hours. They'd be waiting at the door like jackals when rehearsal was done.

"Almost. There's still something missing. You have the toughness down, but the vulnerability isn't there. Let's try something. Taryn, come down here and do Wolf's monologue. Wolf, I want you to watch this, and see what she does differently." Linda motioned to Taryn.

Taryn stood up and rolled her shoulders. She strolled to the edge of the stage and on impulse, sat down, one leg hanging down, one drawn up. She rested her arm on her knee and stared out into the house, letting the silence fall down on her. In the silence was pain, like flashes of heat lightning. She dropped her head then raised it slowly. Taryn flipped up the collar of her denim jacket, reached into the pocket, and took out her cigarettes. She thumbed the pack open, drew one out with her lips, but didn't light it. She looked up at the house, suddenly, her eyebrows wrinkled up in an expression of anguish. It lingered as she took the cigarette in her hand, a nervous gesture trying to pass as tough.

"I'm sitting on the steps of the high school smoking a cigarette, cool, tough, and lonely."

Taryn ran her hand down the sleeve of the dark denim lovingly, smiling. "I've got my James Dean jacket on, protecting my skin."

The cigarette was flipped behind one ear, in a fluid motion Taryn was standing, hands in the back pockets of her jeans.

The pain was gone, now a cocky grin lit the angular face. "Can you get inside?" It was spoken as a challenge. Taryn started swaggering up the front of the stage, a parody of arrogant young masculinity, the myth of the boy-god. Linda was standing to the left of the house. Taryn paused in front of her.

"If I saw you out one night and told you with my look that I know what you need…would you trust me?" Taryn dropped down into a crouch, smiling seductively into Linda's eyes. "I can take you home and show you what it feels like to touch the rim of heaven. I've got the walk. I've got the look. I'm the boy of your dreams. Do you believe me?" Taryn held Linda with her eyes, the seductive smile softening, the vulnerability slipping back into her expression. The brows wrinkled. The fine lips were slightly open. When she was sure that Linda was about to answer her, she was up and away.

"When you take me home and find out who I am under my clothes, what would you do? The armor has its purpose. I keep the jacket. I keep my skin. Can you get me to unzip my heart?" Taryn stopped, center stage, her hand holding the jacket closed. "Pass it on."

Linda started pacing again, talking to Wolf. "Tough and vulnerable. You see what I mean? Play with the audience a little bit. Pick a woman out of the front row and direct the seduction to her. Move away once she falls for it. Try it out. Thanks, T."

Linda called from the front of the house. "Sam! I want to try your monologue."

Taryn's eyes drifted closed as Sam started talking, her soft voice dropping down as she spoke.

It was easy to feel the pull of emotion like the force of gravity, binding her down. She was already bleeding; the inside of her skull was slick with the blood. *I can't,* Taryn thought, without articulating what she was unable to do. She kept her eyes shut, wanting only to sleep. Even rehearsal had lost its healing magic.

"Taryn?"

If she kept still, the voice might go away.

"T?"

It was gentle, but kept repeating her name.

"You okay?"

Taryn shook her head. Of course not. The world had ended, and it was exhausting trying to pretend otherwise. She opened her eyes, feeling the pressure of people looking at her. Linda was standing over her with Sam and Robbie behind her.

"I'm just tired."

"You want to call it a night?" Linda asked, watching the horror bloom in Taryn's expression.

"No, I'm okay. Did you call me? Is it time?" Taryn said standing up.

"I'm still working with Sam. Why don't you take five, then I'll be ready. Okay?"

Taryn ran a hand across her jaw and mumbled. "Yeah. I'm gonna grab a smoke."

The concrete stairs at the back of the warehouse had a window that overlooked the parking lot. Taryn propped it open and sat down on the landing. The cigarette was in her hand, but she hadn't lit it. She wanted to rest, but there seemed no place to land. Her eyes fell closed.

"You have to light it for it to burn."

Taryn's eyes snapped open. From where she was standing, Rosalind's face was on a level with hers. It was easy to read the mixture of anger and relief there. The anger she'd expected, the relief she had not.

"Oh yeah?" Taryn said, examining the cigarette. It was hard to know what to expect. Taryn steeled herself for the yelling.

"So I've heard." Rosalind seemed not to know what to do with her hands. She folded her arms and unfolded them. "Linda told me you were out here. I started in the usual places, coffee shops and diners. They told me you'd been at Spot. It's getting to be a habit, chasing after you."

This must be the prelude to the fight, but it seemed too quiet. "You're getting good at tracking me down."

"It's a skill I'd rather not have, Taryn." It was said seriously. Taryn could only interpret it one way. It was going to be a slow death. She couldn't stand that.

"So I guess there's nothing else to say." Taryn hurled the cigarette at the wall.

Rosalind exploded. Her hands flew up in a sharp gesture, driving

Taryn back. "It's like talking to a brick wall! Honestly, you are the most exasperating, boneheaded, fatalistic— Have you got any idea how insulting this whole indifferent act is? I love you, you fucking moron. I'm not breaking up with you. I just spent the afternoon tracking your ass down. What is it going to take to convince you that I mean it when I tell you I love you? I always will, Taryn. I know about Paul. I get mad with you, and frustrated sometimes. It doesn't matter. I love you. Don't you dare interrupt me."

Taryn sat back and closed her mouth.

"I'm done with the testing. You tell me right now what it's going to take to have you believe me. I love you. I know how you feel right now, baby. I do." Rosalind's voice softened, she saw the tears start in Taryn's eyes. Taryn didn't bother to wipe them away. "You feel like you lost your home."

Taryn clamped her teeth down, to keep from sobbing. Rosalind took Taryn's head in her hands, to keep her from bolting.

"You haven't. You haven't lost Joe, or Rhea, or anyone at that house. You have to know this. I am your home. You are never going to lose that. It's time to let that fear go. No matter what else happens, I'm your home."

Taryn's jaw worked, clenching with the rhythm of a pulse, the knot of muscle standing in relief under her skin. She looked like she wanted to speak but had reached the end of her words. Having no language, Taryn returned to the body. She pushed up from the concrete steps and captured Rosalind.

Rosalind felt the hard muscles of Taryn's arms tremble as if under great strain, Atlas heaving the world on his shoulders. Even so, it was an embrace, a conversation between their bodies, a surrender to the need to touch. For a moment, Rosalind closed her eyes. *If we could just stand like this forever there would be no need for anything else.* She found herself held gently, with restraint, as if Taryn were afraid to unleash her own reaction. Abandon was possible after reunion, so it was enough. A beginning. Taryn had risen to meet her. They could take it from there.

Rosalind moved closer to Taryn, encouraging her to hold on. She thought about telling Taryn that she wasn't breakable, but Taryn read her body and pulled her closer. When Taryn spoke, her voice was cut to ribbons, bled dry. "I wish there was someplace we could go."

Rosalind kissed Taryn's neck. "I know, baby."

"Buffalo can be so damn small sometimes. I feel trapped."

"It's not a small town; it's a big room," Rosalind said, deadpan. The relief she felt when Taryn laughed was enough to bring tears to her eyes. How could anyone hear that laugh and not spend their life bringing it about?

"You're only supposed to say that when your ex-girlfriend is now dating another ex-girlfriend," Taryn said.

"You're my only girlfriend, so you take what you can get."

Taryn's head turned down, one eye fixed Rosalind with a baleful stare. "I'm all you could get?"

Rosalind sighed. "Conversationally you take what you can get." She brushed at the front of Taryn's hair where the spikes had started marching off to the left. Typically, it refused to be remolded. "With you, I just got lucky."

"I wish I could prove that to you. That you got lucky with me," Taryn said.

"Then prove it to me. Come running to me, not from me. A girl could get a complex if her boy hightails it at the drop of a hat. Don't you trust me?" Rosalind asked, as simply as she could manage.

Taryn stiffened, her body falling into military lines. "With my life," she said fiercely.

"Trust me with your heart, baby. It's all I'll ever ask of you."

They sat holding hands like teenagers in the darkness, occasionally glancing up at the house. Neither moved toward the car door. Taryn lay boneless in the front seat, drained. The lights were off in the living room and in Joe's study on the second floor, but the house was never empty. Rosalind imagined that if she went around the path to the back of the house, everyone would be gathered in the kitchen. For the first time, that seemed daunting rather than welcoming. Taryn seemed to feel the same. Taryn stubbornly refused to look at the house. There was much to get settled, but Rosalind could see the exhaustion in every line of Taryn's body. She needed time and she needed care.

"Wait here. I'll go get some things. You can stay with me tonight," Rosalind said, accepting Taryn's melting look. The maternal instinct she'd never been sure she had lit and glowed. *God, I'll have to be careful. I could get used to this…*

Rosalind made it up the stairs without a creak, knowing to hit the outside of the third step and avoid the seventh. There was no point in announcing her arrival. If luck was with her, she could slip in and out like a phantom.

Taryn's room was dark, but she knew her way around. It was only after selecting a random black T-shirt and pair of jeans that she noticed the woman on the windowsill. Rhea was outlined by the streetlight, her profile a cameo against the buttery aura. She was looking down at the car and the figure slumped there. "How is she?"

"Worn out, but she'll be okay. How's Joe?" Rosalind asked, acclimating to the strangeness easily. Nothing was ever routine with Rhea.

"The same. Heartbroken, but he'll be all right. They are so alike, but they come to anger in opposite ways. He's drinking brandy and pretending to read Nietzsche."

"Ouch. Could you tell him that she loves him and she's sorry? I thought taking a little time would be better." Rosalind held up the clothing.

"Her boots are by the front door. She'll want them," Rhea said.

Rosalind nodded. There wasn't much left to say. Rhea allowed no openings for comfort. The silence pushed her toward the door. At the bottom of the stairs Rosalind looked casually to the right, into the living room. The pictures in their antique frames were on the mantel. On the end was the shot of Taryn at eighteen, sitting on a picnic table in profile. Rosalind had seen that picture dozens of times. It was one of her favorites of Taryn. Taryn was looking out over the water with an expression of such peace and absorption. Her face was white under the shock of hair, stirred by a late-fall wind. It seemed to capture the moment of transition between the rage-filled Taryn who had been Rhea's lover and the Taryn who was starting to pull away at eighteen. Taryn, on the brink of growing up, preserved in the pale gray light of the lakeshore. The decision was made as soon as it occurred to her. Rosalind wheeled around and dashed back up the stairs.

The gym bag was tossed into the backseat with a flourish. "Wake up, baby. We're going on a trip."

Taryn sat up. "Where?"

"Waverly Beach," Rosalind said, unable to control her smile of triumph. She adored surprises, adored being able to give them. It was one of the things she'd discovered about herself, in becoming a lover, the amount of joy she took in bringing pleasure to her beloved. *Good thing I don't have more money. I'd be buying her a motorcycle about now.*

"The beach house? How did you get Rhea to give you the key?"

"I asked," Rosalind said with a note of smugness in her voice.

"What in the world made you think of this?" Taryn tilted her head, her lips curving upward just at the corners.

"Hey, my boy needed some time away. I provided it," Rosalind said, shrugging. The look Taryn gave her was enough to make her stop and catch her breath. "You keep on looking at me like that and I won't be able to walk."

"Then I'll carry you," Taryn said with the sensual thrum to her words that Rosalind hadn't heard in days.

Rosalind sagged against the steering wheel and fanned herself. "My my my. You are a wicked, wicked boy."

"I'll be anything you want."

"Wicked is just fine. Now you put those eyes away and let me drive."

CHAPTER ELEVEN

They crossed the Niagara River by way of the Peace Bridge. The road was slick and empty save for a few tractor trailers making the night run into Canada. From the house on Mariner, it took five minutes to be suspended between countries on the arc of steel over the moving water. Rosalind thought back to Rhea talking about Buffalo as the perfect place for transitions of all kinds. She'd interpreted that as mystic, but the physical nature of it was revealing itself to her. Buffalo was a place of borders. It would have border magic. She'd have to ask Joe about his transition, how the city had been for that crossing over.

It was an impulse that had moved her to ask Rhea for the key to the beach house, an impulse sparked by the picture of Taryn. Her impulses were getting easier and easier to trust, more like listening to a new source of information, a voice she hadn't been trained to hear. Wasn't it impulse that made her follow Taryn across the bar on the first night they met? She'd always wanted to be the kind of woman who heeded her impulses, who had adventures, who listened with respect to the voice of her desire. That had come true. Rosalind looked at her lover, the handsome boy who was watching the country pass away beneath them. She wondered who Taryn had wanted to be, what kind of person. And if that had come true for her.

"We're at the border," Taryn said, breaking Rosalind's reverie.

"Right. Is this where we declare ourselves? I've got a few things I'd love to declare," Rosalind said.

Taryn shifted in the seat. "Just tell them we're going to visit friends. The less said the better."

Taryn seemed uncomfortable. It didn't make any sense.

"So I don't tell them I'm going to cross the border to have wild sex with my girlfriend?" Rosalind said and waited for Taryn's laugh. It didn't come.

"Sure. Then wait and see how long it takes them to haul me out and beat me," Taryn said, looking forward.

Rosalind wanted to ask if she was kidding, but the light had changed. She pulled up to the booth and rolled down her window, smiling just as helpfully and innocently as she could. The officer in the booth was a thickset, fair-haired young man with a child's pudgy face. He looked down at his computer screen as he spoke.

"Citizenship?"

"United States," Rosalind said dutifully.

He glanced up at Taryn. "And him?"

Taryn leaned forward and spoke in her lowest register. "United States."

"What is your purpose in Canada?" he asked, looking at Rosalind.

"Visiting friends at Waverly Beach."

He stopped and looked back over at Taryn. "What about you?"

"Same."

"Where do these friends live?" he asked.

"Waverly Beach," Rosalind repeated, wondering if he were slow.

"I was asking him."

"Waverly Beach," Taryn said, her voice like distant thunder.

The officer stepped out of the door of his booth and looked into the car, squinting at Taryn. "How long are you going to be staying?"

"Just for the night."

"May I see your identification?" he said, holding out his hand.

Taryn reached back into her pocket and pulled out her wallet. Stone-faced, she handed the license to the man. He held it up to his face and stepped back into the booth.

"Shit," Taryn said softly.

"What's wrong? You have I.D.," Rosalind whispered.

"That says I'm female. Sometimes that sets them off."

The officer approached the driver's side of the car. There was a difference in his stance. Rosalind could read it immediately. His shoulders were held back. His hands were coiled halfway into fists. He looked like a dog that had just caught the scent of a rival on his yard.

"Please pull the car over to the building." There wasn't a trace of request in his voice.

The parking spots in front of the building were all vacant. Rosalind turned the wheel for the nearest one.

"Not there!"

There were two guards waiting in front of the building, one male and one female. The shout came from the man. He was built like a man who lived on doughnuts and beer, with thin legs made thinner by brown uniform trousers and a belly that hung over his belt. He motioned impatiently at Rosalind, making her move one space over, for no reason she could discern. The woman was of medium height, with a hard, plain face and thinning dark brown hair twisted back in a bun. When they got out of the car, the man met Taryn and the woman met Rosalind. It reminded her too much of a wild animal documentary she had seen on how jackals work together on the hunt.

The man stood at Taryn's elbow. Rosalind thought she saw Taryn's shoulders twitch. Taryn was dressed in dark jeans and a black T-shirt under her denim jacket. Her breasts, Rosalind remembered, were still bound from rehearsal. The jacket hung unbuttoned from her broad shoulders. She'd slipped her unlaced boots onto her feet. Her expression was sullen. She looked exactly like a boy, and for the first time Rosalind felt a stab of fear at that recognition.

"Please bring your personal belongings and follow me," the woman said.

"May I ask what is going on?" Rosalind used her polite but slightly puzzled voice. It usually worked well with supercilious waiters and rude store clerks. It tended to lull them into a sense of security. If necessary, it could transform in a heartbeat into righteous indignation, but it was best to start at a softer place.

"Just routine. We are going to search your car. And we have a few questions for you."

They were escorted into the building. It happened so quickly that it took Rosalind a full minute to catch what was going on. The female guard opened a door on the left and stood holding it. Rosalind went into the room. Taryn moved automatically to follow. The male guard grabbed her arm, jerking her back. "Not you. In here." He pointed at another door down the hall.

When the female guard shut the door behind them, Rosalind turned around and looked for Taryn. "What's going on?" she asked.

"We just have a few questions for you." The guard stood in front of the door, preventing her from bolting immediately.

"No. Why isn't Taryn here?" Rosalind moved closer to the guard.

"There were some inconsistencies with your companion's identification. We need to have a male guard handle the examination."

A cold wind blew through Rosalind. It slowed down the reaction of her eyes, formed ice crystals on time. She was able to see the grain of wood in the door, the spot of oil on the guard's collar. She was able to watch her own reaction from a distant place, her emotions carefully held back. She took a single long breath, like a diver about to go under, and experienced that breath as half an hour long. When she spoke, it was with the calmness and precision of a surgeon. "You cannot have a male guard examine her. Taryn is a girl. It says that right on her license."

The guard's lip curled up. She was used to people trying to deceive her, and this stank of it. She looked offended, as if Rosalind were lying to her in a manner too blatant to show any respect. Rosalind realized her tactical error a moment too late. The guard was already on the defense. It was death to make a stubborn person feel that you thought they were stupid. She might have been open to reason. Now she was going to be pure obstacle.

Rosalind tried to backpedal. "I know this looks funny, but I'm not trying to deceive you. She's just got a very masculine presentation."

The guard seemed to consider this for a moment. She looked Rosalind over from head to foot and back. She looked at Rosalind's face, the trace of makeup she wore, the small silver earrings showing through her long hair, the fingernails painted a rich plum. She seemed puzzled. It was possible to read the parade of thoughts in her face and see the exact moment the connection was made. The guard's face hardened. The look was now personal. The disgust was changing with the information. Rosalind felt naked under that look, and more than a little dirty. She'd made the guard feel better, but she'd now made herself suspect as well.

The guard retreated into a professional distance laced with a hint of superiority. "I'm sure this will all be cleared up shortly."

It was the sense of superiority, of moral smugness, that handed Rosalind back her rage. *You think you're a better person than I am? Fuck you*, Rosalind thought acidly.

Her eyes dropped down to the guard's name tag. "Listen, Jennifer, is there any question about my identification?" Rosalind asked sweetly.

The tone threw the guard off. She answered without thinking. "No."

"Good. Then I'm going to join my friend."

The guard had to jump in front of the door to keep Rosalind from opening it. "I can't let you do that."

Rosalind gave a measured look. This was wasting time. Taryn had been left alone with the male guard far too long. She was done arm wrestling with ignorance.

"Ever been in an international incident, Jennifer? You will be in a minute, if you let a male guard strip-search a twenty-year-old girl. Tort law is powerful stuff. It crosses borders. And sexual harassment settlements are getting bigger all the time. You read me, Jennifer?"

"We have reasonable suspicion—"

"Then be reasonable. Search my car. Comb it over with dogs. If you find anything—drugs, firearms, fireworks, illegal produce—come search us. That's how it's usually done, right?" Rosalind asked.

"Usually," the guard said slowly.

"I'm not going to leave her alone while you decide to do the right thing. If you need me, I'll be in the next room." Rosalind opened the door. The guard stepped out of the way.

At her best, Taryn was hardly a model of self-control and decorum, but today she was down to raw nerves, primed for violence. Taryn had a certain carelessness about her body, the ability to use it like an instrument, to abuse it with the despair of the young. Even so, there were limits.

Rosalind remembered Taryn's reluctance to get fully unclothed with her when they'd first been lovers. That reluctance went bone deep, and Rosalind was still learning how out of character it had been for Taryn to open up to her so quickly. To choose vulnerability with a lover, where the idea of the body as a part of identity was respected and desired was one thing. To be strip-searched by a male border guard was another. Nakedness was never just bare skin. It was perception, the self-perception of the individual, the external perception of the viewer. What might be honored and sought after in some circles could easily be a target for humiliation and violence in the larger world. In the clash of perception, the minority viewpoint is the first to be crushed.

"Go *fuck* yourself!"

It was Taryn's voice, anger pitching it upward into a shout.

The door was unlocked. In a snapshot of a look, Rosalind took in the room. On the table was a cigarette pack, open, with the contents strewn out and broken. The silver lighter had been pulled apart, the casing looked cut. *Not Rhea's gift*, Rosalind thought. A black leather wallet was open and turned upside down, like a tent. Taryn was backed up against the wall, her legs braced wide and her hands up in front of her body. Her eyes were wide and staring. The guard was in front of her, his back to Rosalind. "It's all right. I don't need any help," he said without turning around.

"Yes, you do."

The guard turned around at the sound of her voice, the expression on his face almost enough to make Rosalind laugh. Almost.

"Get away from her." Rosalind's voice was low and dangerous, a tone she'd never used before.

"Who the hell are you? What are you doing in here?" the guard asked.

"I'm stopping you from performing an illegal strip search." Rosalind stepped closer to Taryn, who had a frightening smile on her face. "You okay?" Rosalind asked softly.

"Motherfucker tried to feel me up," Taryn said, glaring at the guard.

"Illegal? Jennifer, get this woman out of here."

The female guard had entered behind Rosalind and seemed to be watching with interest. "She says this is a girl," Jennifer said, rolling her eyes.

"This? You have got to be joking. Who the hell is she? Look, Miss—" The male guard pointed at Rosalind.

"*Dr.* Olchawski."

The title worked. The guard's face twitched. "You're filing a complaint?" he asked.

"I'm filing a lawsuit if you don't back off right now," Rosalind said savagely. She stood like a shield between Taryn and the guard.

"I've got the authority to conduct a search." The guard took a few steps back, glancing down at his companion in puzzlement.

"Based on what? You didn't search our car or belongings first. You have no reasonable suspicion that we are carrying contraband or any illegal substances," Rosalind said.

"I have the authority to conduct a nonintrusive search based on the individual's appearance and demeanor. The identification provided was observed to be in error."

Rosalind took a glance at the guard's name tag. "You hauled a twenty-year-old girl off into a room to be strip-searched by a male guard, without witnesses. At the moment, all you are facing is a sexual harassment suit. Don't make it into a civil rights case as well, Martin."

"Are you threatening me?"

"No. I'm promising you legal action if you continue with this farce. If you think you're going to press for a strip search, I demand that a female guard be brought in and my lawyer be present."

"Your lawyer?"

"Sandhya Srinivasan. Shall I place the call?"

"You're bluffing," Martin said.

Rosalind smiled with unfeigned ease. The tension was gone now that she'd committed completely to a course of action. She would bring them down for what they'd done. If the world would not grant them justice, she would change the world. "Try me."

It was the smile that finally frightened Martin. He pulled Jennifer by the arm. They left the room abruptly.

Taryn ran her hands through her hair and exhaled. "Unbelievable," she said in admiration.

"What is?"

"You just scared the pants off a fascist. I've never seen a grown man scuttle backward like that."

Rosalind looked toward the door. "This may be a temporary reprieve."

There was a feral grin on Taryn's face. She was straightening out her clothing, pushing her T-shirt back into her jeans. She stalked to the table, rooting through the wreckage. A few cigarettes hadn't been broken. She shoved them back into the pack and pushed the broken ones aside with a sweep of her hand. The bulletproof attitude seemed too quick, too automatic. The jump of adrenaline was in Taryn's movements, the sudden pacing, the slashing gestures. The urge to fight had flooded her system. It would take hours to come down.

Rosalind took Taryn's hand, slowing her constant motion. "Are you okay, baby?"

Taryn stood very still. "I am now." She squeezed Rosalind's hand.

The silver lighter was a total loss. The casing had been bent back with pliers. The top edge had been cut. Taryn picked it up and put it carefully in her pocket. The door to the room opened. Rosalind saw how Taryn flinched. It was the female guard. Martin had vanished. "You're free to go," she said sullenly, holding the door.

"Just like that?" Rosalind asked.

"Nothing was turned up in the search of your vehicle."

"Wow, that sounded nothing at all like an apology," Rosalind said.

"Let's get out of here," Taryn said restlessly.

"Okay. Nice seeing you, Jennifer."

As they passed, Rosalind heard one word hurled after them, under the guard's breath. She could let it go. They had been lucky so far. Was it worth antagonizing the guards any further? Just one word, tossed after them like offal. It's what the guards would be calling them as soon as they were out of hearing range. *No sense in getting worked up about it,* Rosalind told herself. There were many people in the world who would call them exactly the same word, with the same hatred and contempt. She could let this one go. Rosalind looked over her shoulder at Jennifer. "That's Dr. Dyke to you." She took Taryn's hand and walked back out to the car.

It was a charcoal night in Canada, the streets nearly single-lane country roads that Rosalind followed on Taryn's direction. Two lefts, then a sharp right, and it might have been any small-town back road in the deep woods at night. The thick overhang gone loose with autumn, the air cold and sharp with no hint of water. There was a patch of grass off a small side road with no sign. Rosalind parked at Taryn's direction. A wooden gate arched over a path of cut stone, flanked by gardens gone down with the season. The path led up between pine trees to a set of steps that ended in blacktop. There was a small single-story house on the left, another off to the right.

"Rhea's place is on the left. The right belongs to a cousin. They never use it this late in the year. They come up and close it for the season by September," Taryn said, walking past Rosalind toward the house, shouldering her gym bag.

Rosalind walked toward the end of the blacktop, where it gave way to a sloping lawn. The grass ended at what looked like a short drop. Beyond that was the pale stretch of beach and the iron gray of Lake Erie. There was light from the beach, other houses crowding close, the orange light of the city off to the left, the faint hint of stars like the forewarning of snow. Now she could smell the water, the swampy, fishy smell mingled with a metallic tang. Industrial and natural, vying for space. Rosalind felt the bite of the wind starting up but resisted it, looking out over the water. It was ugly and somber and gorgeous at once. It stirred a feeling of profound loneliness in her that landscapes of manicured beauty never could. She had no idea of how long she stood there, transfixed, until she was surprised by Taryn's arms reaching around her.

Taryn leaned down and kissed the side of her face. "It's something, isn't it?"

"It's beautiful." Rosalind stroked Taryn's arms, watching the surface of the lake roll like molten lead.

"You find things beautiful nobody else would," Taryn said, her voice in Rosalind's ear.

Rosalind felt Taryn's arms loosen and protested. "Where are you going?"

"You're shivering," Taryn said.

"You walking away won't help that. Come back here and warm me up." Rosalind watched as Taryn's broad back vanished into the dark.

Her voice floated back up the lawn, disguising her location. "I'll make a fire. How about that?"

"Only if you put your arms back around me when you're done," Rosalind called out into the night.

The fire pit was down at the end of the lawn, off to the right. When Taryn got the driftwood started with whatever alchemical skill she possessed, Rosalind could see the border where the grass dropped off. There was a wooden staircase in the center, a picnic table at a right angle to the edge of the drop, and the fire pit. Taryn crouched like a gargoyle over the flame, seeming immensely pleased by her ability to bring fire to the darkness. There were sections of driftwood logs set in a semicircle around the pit. White granite blocks formed the outside ring. Limestone and shale lined the pit itself.

Rosalind sat down on a segment of log and watched as Taryn gradually built the fire up, hand-feeding it larger sawn logs. Taryn finally stood up and dusted her hands off on her jeans, smiling triumphantly at Rosalind. She half expected Taryn to sprint off into the night and kill a stag, in keeping with the way fairy tales always went.

"Come sit down," Rosalind said. Taryn sat between her knees, resting her back against the log and stretching her legs out toward the fire.

"What are you thinking about?" Rosalind asked.

"The show."

"Ah, the show," Rosalind said with exaggerated understanding.

"Whenever anything else hurts or tears me up, I go there."

"Why, baby?"

"Its like a drug. I've been onstage before. But this...this is different, you know? I'm not a prop in a drag queen's number. This is something I made. Me. It's incredible, and I had a hand in making it."

"Of course it makes you feel good. You should be very proud of it, from what I've seen."

"It's the most important thing I've ever done. Other than meeting you, it's the best I've ever felt. Most of the time I'm just me, you know? I don't think about it. This is how I dress normally. But onstage, you have to think about everything. You get to be a lot of people. You take on what they want to see. And everyone loves you for it." Taryn turned her head toward the lake. "I'd forgotten how much I missed it here."

Rosalind massaged Taryn's shoulders through her jacket. "This is wonderful. I can't believe we haven't been up here yet. I can't believe Rhea doesn't insist on coming up here every weekend," she said.

"Rhea's funny about this place. Her cousin has the other house and she doesn't like to see him. And there's the family thing." Taryn fell silent. Rosalind got the distinct impression she was weighing her next words. The fire spat out a handful of sparks. Taryn got up and adjusted the logs. She crouched by the fire as if mesmerized, then turned her head toward Rosalind, squinting from the heat. "Rhea's family has money. She came out to her family. They politely offered her this place and told her never to contact them again."

"How long ago was this?" Rosalind asked.

"Twenty-two years." Taryn moved back from the fire and settled back into her place. "Rhea bought the house on Mariner on her own. We used to come up here more when we first got together, but that ended pretty quick. She lets Joe's ex-husband Ray bring Goblin up here, but I think she hasn't been here in a couple of years. She doesn't talk about it, but I know it bugs her."

"That's awful."

Taryn shrugged. "They made the choice. I've met her cousin. If the rest of them are anything like him, it's not that big of a loss."

"I can't imagine losing my family like that," Rosalind said, unaware of how still Taryn had grown.

Taryn's voice rolled like the lake, metallic and smooth on the surface with the hint of unguessed depths beneath. "But what if you had to? If you came out to them and they offered you no other choice."

The stars cast down their distant snowy light into the silence that followed. The fire danced without sound, awaiting the answer as surely as the girl who sat like a statue between Rosalind's knees.

"I'd be heartbroken," Rosalind said honestly, even knowing how Taryn would hear those words. "But I wouldn't give up on them. That might be their reaction at first, but everybody needs time to adjust. Given time, I could bring them around."

Taryn had retreated within herself. Her posture hadn't changed, and Rosalind couldn't see her face, but she could feel Taryn withdrawing like the tide going out. "Given time, you could bring mountains down," Taryn said, her voice thin.

"I can feel you. Don't you know you pull at me like gravity?" Rosalind said, her hand on the back of Taryn's neck.

"If your family rejected you, I was wondering if I'd be enough. If it would be worth it to you."

Rosalind wrapped her arms around Taryn, pulling her in close. Taryn closed her eyes and leaned her head back against Rosalind's chest. "If my family did what Rhea's did, it would still be worth it. I'd be sad, but I wouldn't have any regrets. You are my home, baby."

Rosalind felt a wetness on her arm where Taryn's cheek was resting. "Are you crying?"

"I don't cry," Taryn growled. "I'll never know what I did to deserve you."

"It's not about deserving. Love just is. We have the choice to accept it or reject it. I'm glad you accepted it," Rosalind said, squeezing Taryn tighter.

"I'm uneducated, not stupid."

"You have an eclectic education, my beautiful boy. And a fierce intelligence that you try to mask, a hunger to know. You could hold your own with anyone."

"Even Paul?" Taryn said, her voice hesitating on the name.

"Even Paul."

They stared into the fire for a while, listening to the water.

"Tell me about him," Taryn said, at last.

"You know Eric and I were always close," Rosalind said, knowing that Taryn liked her brother. She felt Taryn nod and kissed the erratic part in the crisp hair. "Paul was my best friend, so he was almost an Olchawski himself. Our house is on Freedom Road at the very edge of the town of Poughkeepsie. Borders came up early in my life. I never looked at it like that before. Paul's family had the house next to us, but next to wasn't like in Buffalo. It's a good five-minute walk through the fields. We're on the lucky end. Nobody was interested in developing our corner of the town."

"What's his last name?" Taryn asked.

She seemed more willing to hear about him, Rosalind thought. "Bennett."

"So your married name was Bennett."

Rosalind hesitated. Taryn had asked. It was better to trust that she was able to talk about it. They couldn't avoid the topic of her marriage forever. "Yes."

"When did you go back to Olchawski?"

Rosalind sighed. "As soon as we separated. I didn't tell Paul until the divorce was final, but I finished my doctorate in my own name."

"When did you meet him?"

"Before kindergarten, actually. We were in the same class, same grade all through high school. And we hung out every day after school, at my house or at his house. There isn't much that happened to me between the ages of five and twenty-eight that Paul didn't know."

"You had other friends," Taryn said as if it were as inescapable as the lake stretching away into the infinite night sky.

Rosalind smiled. "Oh, sure. But Paul was always around. He knew that I hated square dancing in third grade, that I loved old movies. He went through my James Dean period, my Greta Garbo period. He was there when I first read *Hamlet*."

"You lose your virginity to him?" Taryn asked lightly.

"Nope. I lost my virginity to you," Rosalind said.

"You don't have to say that. I'm okay with hearing it. Tell me about it." The stubborn tone she recognized was back in Taryn's voice.

"It wasn't Paul. I didn't start dating him until grad school. I was seventeen and decided that it was high time I got it out of the way. Late bloomer and all that. I was dating a guy I liked. That seemed to be enough. He was on the track team. Paul made fun of him savagely. I thought it was intellectual scorn, but it must have been jealousy. I never saw that then. Poor man. I was so serious and earnest about the whole thing. I was old enough. I was emotionally mature. I liked the guy but wasn't about to give up my future for him. I understood about birth control. So we did it. It was a surprise for him. He was delighted with my resolve. April Fool's Day. That turned out to be prophetic! It was the middle of the afternoon at his parents' house. They were out bowling. We were down in the guest bedroom off the basement." Rosalind shook her head at the memory.

"Did you like it?" Taryn asked.

"He seemed pleased and I was glad to get it over with. But I didn't feel anything except a vague intellectual triumph. I was normal. I did what teenagers normally did. I went home by four in the afternoon, and there was Paul sitting on my front porch the way he always did after school. I told him what had happened, of course. I told him everything then. I wondered if something was wrong with me that I didn't feel swept away. He seemed relieved, actually, and told me that I just hadn't met the right guy. Poor man, the things I put him through."

"Must have been nice to have somebody to talk to," Taryn said neutrally.

"It was. You know something? I was never terribly comfortable with girls my own age. I felt like I was missing something. Two steps behind the joke, so to speak. I wasn't boy-crazy enough. I hadn't met the right boy yet." Rosalind slid her hand inside Taryn's T-shirt. It came to rest over Taryn's heart. The wave of energy that traveled up her arm was familiar, but it still made her gasp. "Like an alchemist's stone. I felt this, the first time you took my hand in the bar. Remember?"

"Always." Taryn's voice thrummed on the word, like the last chord struck on a song.

"The recognition I felt when you looked at me scared me. It was too strong to be real. That was before I knew all the connections, before I would have believed in reincarnation. I was so attracted to you when I saw you onstage I thought that must be what was happening, the surge of desire. But I looked into your eyes and I knew you. It was easier to think it was lust and save the mystical implications for later when my brain could accept what my heart already knew. But you lived with Rhea. You were in that environment already. What was it like for you?"

Taryn placed her hand over Rosalind's. "Rhea had warned me about you, so I was interested. I felt the recognition. You know I had a vision of you before we met?"

"When?" Rosalind asked. Taryn had never told her this.

"When I was seventeen. It was Halloween. The night Rhea and I met Joe. During the Samhain ritual, the voyage to the Isle of the Dead. I was in the circle and I got this flash. You were walking on a street. There was snow on the ground. You turned around and asked me if I was going to catch up to you. I felt it right then—the recognition—and it scared the hell out of me. It was a glimpse of something I'd never had. It made me furious, just that splinter of it."

"Why furious, baby?"

"Because I couldn't believe it was real. That a feeling like that was ever going to be mine. It's hard, when you don't think you're hungry, to have someone point out that you're starving to death," Taryn said, without particular emphasis.

"You had Rhea."

"And I loved her. More than I thought I could love anybody. It wasn't long after I came to Buffalo, after I'd been thrown out. I figured, no, I knew that I'd never have a home. Rhea came along and proved me wrong. You know I hate to be wrong. I could only believe it to a point. Past that, I was still alone. That was okay. I'd gotten stronger once I realized that. People just fuck you up. Rhea was perfect. She left me my defenses."

"It sounds sad. I'm sorry to say that. I know how you feel about Rhea. But she's always seemed a little distant, a little reserved," Rosalind said carefully.

"Cold. You can say it. It's okay. It's how she has to be. But I understood that. It was how I had to be too."

"Why did Rhea have to be?"

"You know how she sees things? That started early. Grade school. She was just a kid. She didn't have any defenses. People's energy would just bleed over into hers. She'd be swamped. And they would drain her constantly. It took her a long time to learn to defend against that, to be able to be around people without losing herself. And that was just the basics. You know how you meet somebody and they seem perfectly nice, but you can't stand them? It makes your skin crawl being near them. That's their energy. Or people will want to hang around you and take everything they can from you. It happened to Rhea all the time. It was just exhausting. She had to learn to be cold to protect herself. Now she can control it, give energy when she wants to. Like when she tattooed you."

"Did you feel this with Rhea?" Rosalind asked, aware of how vulnerable she sounded. She understood about Taryn's relationship with Rhea. She had been supportive of it from the start. But there was a part of her that still cried out, "Love me best. Let me be the only one you've ever loved." She managed not to give in to that part of herself. Taryn was good about offering her reassurance. There was no doubting that Taryn loved her. There was no doubting that Taryn loved Rhea. From what she'd overheard in the kitchen between them on the night Rhea and Joe announced their marriage, there was something left unfinished between them. *I am an adult,* Rosalind reminded herself. *I don't need her to tell me she loves me best. It can be enough that I'm her lover now.*

Taryn moved away from her hands. The breaking of the connection was sharp. It brought tears to Rosalind's eyes. How could she move away now? Rosalind blinked furiously and looked away, not wanting to admit that the loss of a response was killing her. Taryn didn't love her best. She hadn't even answered her. The log shifted as Taryn straddled it, facing her. Taryn leaned forward and kissed her, moving slowly enough that Rosalind had time to read her face, had time to anticipate the touch of her lips. When Taryn finally kissed her, Rosalind moaned into Taryn's mouth. She closed her eyes, knowing that she was unable to resist this, unable to stop herself. Whatever place she held in Taryn's heart, she would fight and die for it.

Taryn pulled back for a moment. It was like the weight of gravity receding. "Only you."

"Forever?" Rosalind asked, knowing that she was abandoning any pretense of mature distance.

"Forever. I belong to you."

Rosalind put her arms around Taryn's neck and leaned closer, demanding the kiss again. She felt Taryn's hands move down to her hips. The night didn't seem cold anymore.

"I think we should go inside," Rosalind gasped, managing to get the words out between kisses.

"Yeah?" Taryn asked, starting to unbutton Rosalind's shirt.

"Yeah. Before we can't walk."

The house was small, two bedrooms set off a single hallway, a kitchen narrow as a knife blade, a living room that held a worn couch and a wood stove. It was furnished like the sixties had never ended, smoky green faux-wood paneling, framed prints of duck hunting and noble Labradors. Rosalind took this all in a single sweeping look while Taryn doused the fire in the pit. Rhea hadn't touched the place since it was dropped on her as a final good-bye. It had the air of permanent melancholy. She could understand why Rhea didn't visit.

Taryn came galloping in the door with a familiar clomp of unlaced boots and the house became a palace, a gilded setting for the handsome girl. Taryn swung the screen door open and smiled at Rosalind, and there was no place on earth she'd have rather been.

"Fire's out," Taryn commented, kicking her boots off.

Rosalind wrapped her arms around Taryn, nearly knocking her over. "I love you," Rosalind breathed into her back. Taryn smelled of wood smoke and autumn. It was easy to close her eyes and drift away, holding on to her.

Taryn's voice was like honey being poured on a hot afternoon. "You'll get me into bed a lot sooner if you let me take my coat off."

Rosalind shook her head. "I don't want to let go."

"That could get complicated," Taryn said.

"I don't care. You're mine. You said so. I don't have to let go." Rosalind leaned her head against Taryn's back and held on tighter.

Taryn's voice was very soft. "No. You don't."

"I want you to live with me." She'd said it as soon as the thought crossed her mind.

Taryn managed to pull away enough to turn around and face her. "Are you serious?"

"Yes. I've had enough of being restrained. I want you with me where you belong."

There was danger in the invitation. Rosalind knew that very well. The volatility of the past few days was still sparking. A few calm moments she'd had with Taryn were only an oasis. Taryn was in the middle of a transition. Her household was changing into something new. She herself was changing. Was it fair to ask for more from her now? Would Taryn even accept? They hadn't been together all that long, a laughably short period of time for the commitment Rosalind was making. She looked into the eyes in front of her and had to smile. The physical details were slow in catching up. She'd already committed everything she had to this handsome youth. Leap of faith? *More like bungee jump*, Rosalind thought. But there was such a certainty that flowed out of her as soon as she'd asked, as if the question had been waiting impatiently to be asked. She couldn't help but follow her heart, now that she was so aware that she had one.

"Okay," Taryn said, returning Rosalind's smile.

"You're saying yes?" Rosalind asked, hope making it hard to believe.

"After the way you came to my rescue at the border? I was out of luck, and you came charging in the door like Joan of Arc. Nothing stops you. Of course I'll move in. I'd follow you anywhere." Taryn was gazing at her with adoration, as if she were a hero. It was hard to keep still under the power of that look.

Rosalind blushed. "I couldn't let them hurt you."

"That's just it. Not a lot of people believe I can be hurt, or know when I need backup. When that guy hauled me off, I wanted to slug him, but I couldn't after—"

"This morning. I know. Oh Taryn, I'm so sorry." Rosalind took Taryn's hand.

"Don't be. I got myself into it. Things like that happen to me all the time. If you can handle that and be pissed off at them, I know where I belong."

Rosalind felt Taryn's hands lift her hair, caress the back of her neck. The surety was gorgeous in Taryn's voice, the confidence was back. Taryn had found her magic again.

"Let me come live with you. Let me take care of you. You won't regret it."

"I'd never regret anything with you," Rosalind whispered, inviting Taryn's kiss.

The bed in the back room was as hard as railroad spikes in a burlap sack, but when Taryn laid her down Rosalind couldn't have cared less. Taryn stood by the bed and threw her coat on the floor. She stretched her arms over her head, peeling the smoke-stained T-shirt from her body with a rough grace. The tattoo of the bull dagger rippled under the Ace bandage.

"Let me help you with that," Rosalind said, sitting up. She took the pins out and unwound the bandage, feeling Taryn's ribs shift under her hands. It was deliciously intimate, the stages of bringing Taryn out of drag layer by layer, revealing the body that carried her own contradictions.

Taryn crawled onto the bed like a cat, the muscles in her shoulders moving like cables. This body was both a source of pleasure to her, and a catalyst for fear. It all rested in the viewing. When you come to something with love you seek to be encompassed by it, to understand it and make it a part of you. It was in that openness, that mystery, that Rosalind came to Taryn.

The first night she'd spent in Taryn's arms had felt like coming home. Their lovemaking often had an edge of passion that approached desperation in its sharpness, a fear of never getting enough, of never having that hunger sated. Rosalind recognized it as the echo of the past, the terror of losing the beloved, of having to live without her again. That fear was absent tonight.

With the part of her brain that could still form words, Rosalind thought, *We must have finished that cycle.* The grief was gone, leaving in its wake a joy that rolled out without boundary. Present tonight was not a homecoming but a sense of creation, of beginning anew. Like a wheel spinning. Rosalind pulled Taryn close, breathed a prayer of thanks, and gave up thinking for the night.

Chapter Twelve

It was the pain that woke her. The spectacularly hideous bed in the lake house had moved from merely uncomfortable to agonizing in the space of a scant few hours. They had made love with a will to make the night eternal. Rosalind had thought that they would see the glow of dawn coming through the thin ivory-stained shade, but the moon held sway over the cold night. Rosalind held sleep at bay as she moved against the body of her lover, too involved in the newness of the experience to rest. There was reassurance in the emotional connection, but the sating of her body's hunger was pure joy. It had never felt like this, this surety. She knew that Taryn would be gazing down at her with such a look of pride and pleasure in another five years. Another ten. There was no lingering fear of having to take her fill now, in the moment, because this joy was too pure to last. The future had started to take shape in her imagination.

Eventually Taryn had collapsed, exhausted from the emotional and physical strain of the day. Rosalind could see Taryn fighting to keep her eyes open as they drifted shut. "Rest, baby. I've got you," she whispered. Taryn murmured something unintelligible and rolled her head to the side, already gone.

The territory of the bed was made passable only by languor that followed hours of lovemaking. *Satiety. What a lovely word. I'll have to start using it in sentences*, Rosalind thought. She lazily traced the outline of Taryn's lips as she slept, until Taryn groaned in protest and moved her head. Rosalind had to be satisfied with wrapping her arm around Taryn's torso and fitting her body to her sleeping lover. It was too dark to make out the fine details of Taryn's face. She constructed them from memory, comparing the face of the Taryn she knew to the pictures she had seen of Taryn at seventeen and eighteen.

She'd been much thinner then. The flesh had been like a sheath over her bones. It took living with Rhea to start filling her out, giving the gauntness back a measure of life. At seventeen, she had looked savage, brimming with rage, in the few photographs that survived. At eighteen there was more of a sense of peace to her. She looked healthier, more often lost in thought. There were no photographs she had seen of Taryn at nineteen, the nebulous time between being Rhea's lover and being Rhea's friend. In that space of time Joe had moved in and Taryn had started working out with him as he transitioned. The weightlifting added the muscle that would be a part of the swaggering boy she knew. It wasn't until Taryn had turned twenty that a photograph was taken of her smiling.

Rosalind wondered what Taryn had looked like as a child, if any pictures of her survived. Taryn wouldn't have thought to bring any when she'd been thrown out of her home. From the bits and pieces Rosalind had managed to pry out of Rhea and Taryn, the girl hadn't brought anything with her but the clothes on her back. She hadn't owned anything when she moved into 34 Mariner. Moments of this nomadic instinct still showed in Taryn's carelessness with her possessions, as if she never expected to have anything for long.

Rosalind thought about the contents of Taryn's attic room. There was the bed and dresser, not too difficult to move. Beyond that, a stash of clothing, mostly jeans and T-shirts, three lovingly maintained suits, the boots that she wore whenever she was awake. Some books, many of them Rhea's, the drawings and designs, the contents of the altar. It wouldn't take an afternoon to move Taryn across the street to 41 Mariner. *Have to find a way to get her to feel at home, start to set down some roots,* Rosalind thought, as sleep reached out for her.

Rosalind woke with her back a Celtic knot of pain, alone. An hour had passed, perhaps two. It was just starting to leak daylight around the edges of the shade. Rosalind forced herself to grip the edge of the bed and swing her legs over, promising her back that the motion would help. And Taryn, if tracked down, might be persuaded into giving a back rub. Rosalind found her jeans and sweater, cursing the cold floor. It was only October. This did not bode well for her first Buffalo winter.

Taryn wasn't in the house. Her jacket was thrown over the back of the couch. Rosalind thought that Taryn might be surprising her with a fire. On a morning like this it would be a sweet surprise indeed. There was a wood stove in the house. Why hadn't she used that?

It was as cold as iron edged in ice out on the porch. The grass on the lawn was blue-green under a rime of frost. The fire pit had been stoked into life. Red-eyed coals showed through the layer of ash. It wasn't long past dawn. The light showed rose and pearl on the underside of the clouds over the metallic green water of Lake Erie. In the dawn light the beach was tawny as a fawn, spotted with a field of white shells above the tidemark. A rowboat with the hull stove in lay forlorn to the side, a drunk left at dawn in an alley to sleep it off. The beach curved around to the right until the land reached out to block the view.

The houses above the beach were replicas of Rhea's house, small and close together, bearded with sloping lawns. Many looked closed for the season. A few had plumes of white smoke drifting from tin stovepipes. To the left was the skyline of Buffalo. Rosalind could make out the downtown buildings, the harbor. It was marvelous and strange, how tidy and unimpressive the city looked from the shores of Canada. How different from the city she had come to know. Life rarely makes sense from an outline.

Set into the hillside was a set of stairs leading down to the beach. The railing looked new, blond wood nailed down on top of weathered gray posts. As she set her hand on the rail, a red-winged blackbird landed, inches from her fingers. The bird hopped in a circle, then flitted off. It took Rosalind a moment to see the bird feeder, set at the border of the lawn.

The steps ended in a dancing floor of dunes, quilted together by tufts of renegade grass. The grass gave way to sand proper, speckled with algae and smooth lake stones like bird's eggs. The small white shells cracked under her heels like popcorn as she walked. The swampy smell was less apparent with the morning, but the industrial, chemical tang was heavy in the air.

Taryn was down by the water's edge, hurling stones violently out into the lake's heart. Rosalind could see the sheen of sweat on her neck and arms, despite the cold. As she watched, Taryn drew her arm back like a panther gathering for a strike. In a blur of motion, it whipped forward. From a distance, she might have appeared to be skipping stones, but up close it was plain that she was locked into a contest. Her will and the strength of her arm were pitted against the expanse of distance. Her face was turned toward the American shore. Blue eyes were narrowed with concentration in a face as ghostly in color as the shells, Rosalind saw, when Taryn glanced back and found her.

A sickly green aura hung around her, the color of rotten things.

"Hey. Sleep well?" Taryn asked, cupping the egg-shaped stone in her hand.

"Mmm-hmm. Stiff waking up, though. I wondered where you were," Rosalind said. She wanted to say, "I missed waking up next to you." Something was wrong. It was easy to read. Taryn hadn't come to embrace her. Even the greeting lacked the volcanic warmth Taryn gave when feeling emotional. There was a wall up around her. It didn't seem set to exclude her lover. Taryn had looked at her and smiled as she walked closer. But the barrier to intimacy was there, protecting Taryn against something. It left Rosalind wondering what had put the wall there and how long it would take her to tear down.

"Aren't you cold out here?" Rosalind asked, risking a position near Taryn on the beach.

Taryn squinted off into the distance. "See that?"

Rosalind followed the extended arm. There was a cargo ship moving across the lake toward Buffalo. From their vantage point the rising sun lit the dull metal, making it glow an unearthly coral. The brightness was stunning against the water, a precious stone set in lead. The strength of color seemed out of place in the muted landscape.

"That's beautiful. Is that an oil tanker?" Rosalind asked, taking a step closer to Taryn.

"Nah. More likely a grain ship, headed for General Mills. Over there. Look at Buffalo. Now, where the city ends, under the Skyway. That's GM. That's why downtown smells like Cheerios sometimes."

"I see it." One more step. Now she was at Taryn's side, leaning close to her shoulder.

"Look south. Down the lake. See that?" Taryn asked.

There was an arm reaching out into the water, a peninsula of concrete and earth. On this strip of land Rosalind could see a factory complex. Smokestacks sent an occasional gout of flame into the sky.

"That's Bethlehem Steel. Past the border of Buffalo, that's Lackawanna." Taryn hurled the rock she was holding. "Behind the steel plant is a bunch of streets with houses. You wouldn't expect them to be there, between the power lines and the mill, but they are. On the corner of Lincoln and Pine there's a house that faces the plant. I mean looks right at it through a chain link fence. Right at Cold Mill Door Number 112 as a front yard. That end of the plant is mostly closed down since 1980. That's where I grew up."

"How long have you been out here?" Rosalind asked.

Taryn dropped into a crouch and selected another stone. Rosalind knew what she was throwing at, what Taryn hoped to strike. The past isn't a moving target, but it can still be very hard to hit. "'Bout an hour," Taryn said, rising from her crouch. She weighed the stone in her hand.

"Bed too hard?" Rosalind asked lightly.

"I had a nightmare. I haven't had this one in a couple of years," Taryn said. Her eyes locked on the outline of the steel mill.

"Tell me about it."

Taryn hurled the stone. "It starts in blackness. I can't see anything, but I can hear all this sawing and hammering and shit. Then it gets light, like the sun coming up. It's a meadow, surrounded by trees. I'm with my father. We're working on something together, building something. But it's laying down in the long grass. I can't see it all yet. I can see the wood we are using. It's burned and scarred, like what's left in a fire the next day. And we are constructing something out of this wood. I hear him tell me to slap a coat of paint on it. I do. Then we raise it up and I can see it. It's a cross. It looks huge and black against the sky. He tells me to climb up there. And I do. I know what's coming. I've seen it done. That's the terrible thing. I know, but I do it anyway. I hang on the cross. He throws gasoline all over me and lights it up. I burn."

Cold, blunt shock punched through Rosalind. It was a struggle not to let the horror she felt show on her face. Instinct told her that a reaction like that would shut Taryn down further. She wasn't looking for comfort, was probably far from the place where she could accept it. Taryn was in survival mode, her emotions shut down. Her tone was eerily calm as she described the sensation of being burned alive. Her detachment wasn't something Rosalind could match. The nightmare was ghastly, the reality behind it more ghastly still. Taryn had been betrayed and abandoned by her natural family. It wasn't surprising that she carried scars. The surprise was that she had learned to trust anyone. Rosalind felt a wave of gratitude for Rhea. If she couldn't have been there for Taryn, it was right that Rhea had been.

A shudder passed through her frame, the remembrance of older pain, or the cold October air cooling the sweat on her neck. Rosalind wanted to tear off her sweater and press it on Taryn, haul her back up to the fire pit. It took a colossal restraint not to do just that. Taryn was out of her body, unaware of the trembling. Her brow was knit; her weight was forward, balancing on the balls of her feet, ready to fight. There was no enemy within reach.

The blue eyes scanned the far shore, then cut back to Rosalind. She was struck by the question she saw there. It wasn't just the horror of the imagery in the dream. Taryn was struggling with why. There had to be a way she could help Taryn focus, bring her back. Dispel that putrescent cloud.

"When did you last have this dream?" Rosalind asked.

"Last time I was up here with Rhea, I think. I used to have it all the time when I first got to Buffalo. Rhea had to set some protections against it. I wasn't sleeping when I moved in." Her eyes flicked away from Rosalind's face.

"But you haven't had it since?" Rosalind said.

"It knocked off before Joe moved in. Didn't think I'd have it again. It's like a sign something awful will happen."

Rosalind felt the stab of fear start low and arc up. No talk of signs and symbols, portents and magic was ever idle around Taryn or the household. Her nerve endings were attuned to her lover. Taryn couldn't hurt without her aching in sympathy. Perhaps that was all this was, feeling the remembered fear along with Taryn, rather than a foretelling of doom.

"I'm not a psychologist, baby. Or Rhea. But this might just be a nightmare," Rosalind said and was gratified to see Taryn's eyes focus on her. She wanted to believe. How could Rosalind not offer her hope?

"You had this dream when things were changing in your household, when you and Rhea were moving from lovers to friends. It ended after Joe moved in and some stability was restored. I don't think it's a vision. There are reasons for you to have nightmares that are from the mundane world."

Taryn's lips twitched in the start of a smile or a grimace. "Yeah."

"Now everything is changing again. The wedding, Paul. A lot of changes around 34 Mariner. It might have triggered the emotional memory," Rosalind said and was gratified to see Taryn's trembling stop.

"Sometimes a bad dream is just a bad dream?" Taryn asked, smiling.

It was her knowledge of her lover, of how Taryn thought, that allowed Rosalind to give Taryn what she needed. "Tell me the story of Alexander and the Gordian Knot."

Taryn's eyebrow arched, but she was too attuned to the story not to accept. "When Alexander crossed into Asia with his army he heard that there was a prophecy. The man who untied the Gordian knot would be king of all Asia. The knot was an old-fashioned rope knot used to tie the yoke of a chariot or a wagon. It was like a mass of snakes, so intricate no man could unravel it. Alexander went to Gordium and had the chariot wheeled out. He took one look at the knot and saw that it couldn't be untied. The ends of the knot were hidden in the mass. It was impossible. His men saw it, too. But Alexander was never one to resist a challenge. He did what no one else had ever done. He drew his sword and slashed the knot in two with one stroke." Taryn's eyes glowed cerulean in the morning light. Her body had come to rest. She shook her head, looking at Rosalind. "You're unbelievable, you know that?"

"Me?" Rosalind asked innocently.

"You." Taryn wrapped her arms around Rosalind. Her flesh was chilled, but she was focused. Her natural energy had returned. "You know just how to get to me. Tell me about the Gordian knot. Make me lecture myself. I don't know how I ever made it before I met you." The putrid cloud had subsided, only the morning sky hung luminescent behind her. The hope Rosalind had offered had taken root.

"I'm glad I can be here from now on."

Taryn took her hand and strode toward the stairs. "Come on. I understand. We have a knot of our own at home to slash."

The return across the border was without incident. The woman in the customs booth gave a bored glance at the car, asked their business in Buffalo. Rosalind was surprised at how relieved she was to say *coming home.*

There was a perspective that the journey had given them, the chance to step outside the boundary and look back toward the earth like a spirit crossing the veil. The West Side looked beautiful in the morning light. The trees along the side streets were rust and bronze and full-on blood. The labyrinthine way back to 34 Mariner was the reentering of the mystery. Taryn came in like a beloved son come back from a vision quest, her eyes sparking with the secrets. She was rehearsing something in her head. An occasional word slipped out.

"You ready for this?" Rosalind asked, partly to hear the surging joy in Taryn's voice. The season of her mood had changed. When Taryn was happy there was no more charming thing in all the earth. The smile that answered Rosalind's question made her stop and catch her breath.

"I am because you are with me. I don't think I could get out of bed without you anymore," Taryn said, her voice the promise of music.

"I hope that means you wouldn't want to get out of bed with me," Rosalind said wryly, unable to fight off her answering smile of naked joy. This much happiness was scary. The smallest things set off a torrent of emotion. *If she just glances at me every now and then for the next fifty years or so...*

"You know what it means. You're everything. I put on flesh and got born so I could be near you."

This time Rosalind lost her breath. It was several moments before she could speak, and then only by taking Taryn's hand and anchoring herself to it. "We...haven't talked about that much, since the night of Rhea's ceremony. I haven't seen more pictures from the past."

"Rhea says that when a cycle is completed, the memories fade. It's the spirit's way of making room for the future. Might be just you and me from now on," Taryn said. Rosalind missed the catch in Taryn's voice.

"I think I could handle that."

"Even with the chilly reception I've earned? You might not want to be at my back when I go in," Taryn said, looking at the house.

"Then I'll be at your side."

❖

In 34 Mariner, darkness is a matter of perception. Even the heart of the night is lit from hidden candles, the stealthy glow of streetlights, the firefly tips of incense. The darkness is never a cover, for the Sight of the inhabitants extends beyond the senses. The intricate weaving of energy like sparks cast from the celestial fire of Shiva's dance can be read like a book. The witch who wandered the hall between the kitchen and the front door, pacing without the succor of rest, was haunted by the Sight. The emotional outburst that had happened a day before refused to fade.

The signature left was red and throbbing as a fresh wound, like a heart torn open. It was too sharp for her to stay in the room. Rhea had to keep walking away from the knife edge of pain. Inexorably, she was drawn back to it. The pain was familiar and had the scent of one well beloved. Back and forth she was pulled and repelled, like the tide. Joe had taken Paul away for the day to get his energy out of the house. Misha had stumbled along, bemused.

Rhea was left talking to the past, trying to reason with a girl who no longer existed. There had once been a rage-filled seventeen-year-old who roared through these halls. Rhea had learned this girl's seasons, as any careful gardener might, and knew the signs of a coming storm. She could predict the length and severity, and thus be ready to hold firm until it blew past. Then, with the calmness she was known for, go about tending the wreckage. There was a certain pride she took in her ability. She was the only person who knew how to handle Taryn. Rhea's pride was very dear, having been very costly.

That pride was now displaced. It was hard to face. She had managed to avoid doing so, with all the other distractions of Rosalind's entrance into their lives. Even in the crucial moment of rage when Taryn had discovered her illness and the cost, they had been left alone together. Joe and Rosalind hadn't returned until she was already tending Taryn's wounds. It was easy to be generous then. Her place secure, she could give approval to Rosalind's efforts to caretake. Why not? The impulse to protect and cherish Taryn was something she understood. But it had always been her impulse, to indulgently share with a select few. Joe had rights to Taryn now, but his bonding with Taryn was in the masculine realm and didn't interfere. Now, in the moment of profound tearing, it was Rosalind who went to Taryn. Rosalind who Taryn ached for, who she needed. It is hard when you've always known who you are to find out that you might be wrong.

Rhea paced and thought. *I am forty-four years old. Inanna knows I am hardly a Crone. Wisdom still eludes me. I haven't lived this long in…ever. I have reached the end of my experience, but fallen so into the habit of having no new experience, I am lost. Taryn is off binding herself ever closer to her lover. I am cast out of the only place I've always held. What now? I don't have the imagination for this. Am I getting too old to spend the night pacing for her?*

It wasn't just Paul that Taryn had to come to terms with. It was her, Rhea thought. *I am keeping her here, keeping her twenty forever. She can't heal until she makes peace with me. She can't make peace with me until I let her go, and see what she does with that freedom.*

In the kitchen the late-morning light was mellow and cool as amber, coming in diffused from the side windows. Rhea took a chance and looked into the kitchen, seeing the same angry red pulsing hang in the air. Left with the broken bones of emotion, again. That was familiar. It brought comfort. Something strange happened as she watched: the red glow flared outward, then dimmed to a dull maroon, compacting. *Shiva's fire, now what?* Rhea thought. The burning in the air was gutting out, running out of fuel. She'd never seen anything like it.

The color of the fire was irresistible suddenly. The heat it gave off even as it faded was seductive, a hearth on a winter night, an embrace at the edge of death. It made all other illumination seem pale and wan as twilight, all colors but a bled-out reminiscence without the strength of this shade. This was an altar fire. It called for sacrifice and immolation, but it was going out.

It was horrible, the urgency that consumed Rhea, the need to belong to it. She thrust her arm into the center to feel the heat, and felt only the dance of the flames over the surface of her skin, the image of fire without the burning heart. Rhea tried to give herself to the fire, but it was too late. It had gone out.

Taryn came striding in like a soldier returned from war, blood pulsing with its song of joy along her veins. Real or visitation, Rhea couldn't be sure yet. Strode like Taryn, but it might be an apparition walking into the emptiness of the kitchen, where the light had gone out. Rhea was sitting at the table, staring blankly at the back door.

"Where is everybody?" Taryn asked, confident that Rhea had

heard her boots drumming against the wood floors. When Rhea looked up at her and frowned, Taryn took it for annoyance, not puzzlement. When Rhea stared at her in silence, Taryn felt the weight of obligation to speak. "Look, I know I threw a fit and vanished. I'm sorry. I wanted to apologize to Joe. Is he here?"

"He's not here," Rhea said, uncertain if she was still talking to a memory. The fire had left her shaken. Her defenses were sanded away. Everything was abstracted, strange, including time.

The figure stomping around her kitchen in search of coffee might well be the rangy teenager she knew. The body language was the same. The restless energy and whiplash moods were the same. She saw the familiar hand reach out for a mug and settle on one the color of burnt sugar. The blue glass mug was gone. Taryn had shattered it after Paul's lips touched it. Time had passed. The boy who took a swig of coffee and raised his eyebrows at her was no longer the youth she had loved. The point was driven home when a woman walked into the kitchen and Taryn's face changed. Her eyes glowed. Her smile was a welcome that even Rhea had never seen. *That is the giving away of the soul,* Rhea thought, coming back to herself.

"Rhea's giving me the silent treatment. Nobody else is here," Taryn said to Rosalind.

"I'm not giving you anything. Joe, Paul, and Misha went out to breakfast with Ellie. I wanted some time to cleanse the house. After yesterday…" Rhea's words trailed off.

"After I went berserk. I've got some apologizing to do, to Joe and Paul. Don't look at me like that. I know I was a jackass," Taryn said.

Rhea had to work to close her jaw. Taryn was leaning against the counter with her usual slouch, draining the coffee mug with a will. There was no evidence that she felt displaced. The seething hostility Rhea expected was absent. Whatever Rosalind had done at the lake house was pure magic. Taryn was a different person.

"The emotion left here was staggering. I thought it best that I handle this alone," Rhea said. She couldn't identify the feeling of exhaustion that pressed on her. It grew stronger as she saw Rosalind slip her arm around Taryn's waist as if she had every right to do so.

"You look beat," Taryn said, putting the mug down.

"Imagine that you are wrestling with the devil and the devil gets up and leaves," Rhea said, her voice hollow.

Taryn tilted her head, her eyes raking the empty space in the center of the room. "I thought it was grappling with an angel."

It was too much, the familiar tilt of the head, the fine edge of sarcasm masking a desire to believe. Rhea had crossed the room before she knew it and was touching Taryn's face. "Both. Or neither."

"You don't believe in the devil," Taryn said and smiled. The smile made Rhea aware of what she was doing, of Rosalind's eyes following the exchange. She moved away from Taryn as if she'd been burned.

"I believe in joy, but I have the sense to fear it. Love is not the beast with teeth. Happiness is. I am not the sort of woman to be devoured," Rhea said.

"That's just it, Rhea. You are. You want to be devoured." Rosalind spoke without considering the words. It was so clear, the image of Rhea lost without something to stand firm against. Joe came without complications, a well-grounded man who knew himself, who had made the journey into adulthood on his own. It left Rhea without a place she knew.

"Psychology from the professor?" Rhea said, tasting the sharpness of the words.

"Just something I saw," Rosalind said.

"Keep your sight off me," Rhea snapped, backing away from the both of them. It hurt, the way Rosalind's arm stayed around Taryn's waist. How the woman's hand rested on Taryn's hip. It was too intimate a gesture. It betrayed them. They'd been making love recently, and their bodies were tied together by the force of their own gravity.

Rhea trembled. Those pathways in her heart were dead. This couldn't be hurting her. Taryn had left her bed long ago. This kind of jealousy wasn't hers anymore. Had it ever been? Oh, but it scalded, knowing that Taryn came fresh from this woman's bed, from her body. The scent of lovemaking was on Taryn like a perfume. That scent…

The renegade memory snapped at Rhea. She saw herself wrapped around the youth like a snake, her teeth sinking into Taryn's shoulder. That shoulder was thinner, less curved with muscle. The Alexander tattoo wasn't on the right arm yet. It would be months before they started it. The bull dagger had begun to take shape. Taryn was all of eighteen. *I do not want to remember this,* Rhea thought desperately. *This is no longer my memory. I am no longer that woman.*

"Rhea, hey now," Taryn said, her voice polished and caressing. She stepped forward with the smile Rhea knew well, a demon's grin, a boy who could not be refused anything. Oh, how she knew that smile, how often Taryn had melted her with it. When Taryn stepped forward with her hand extended, Rhea felt the desire to take that hand and forgive her. To pull her close and keep her. It was an old response, the emotional pull the youth had on her, the pull of the moon.

But to approach her Taryn had to move away from Rosalind. They had to break physical contact. It was a reminder that they were rarely apart. Rosalind's agate eyes followed Taryn when she moved, lingered on her face when she spoke, perfectly besotted. Such abandon, it scarred Rhea's vision like fishhooks. She hadn't felt this heat of jealousy in years. What in the world was going on? *You will not charm your way out of this*, Rhea thought violently.

"No. A smile and a shrug will not buy your way out. Save the seduction for your girlfriend. Do you have any idea what it is like to spend the night walking the floor for you? I thought you were gone for good. And you come sauntering in the next morning—Taryn's here, all is well!"

"You knew I was up at the cabin. You gave Rosalind the key," Taryn said.

"I gave *Rosalind* the key. *Rosalind* came and asked me for it. You didn't even come in the house. You left me alone with that in the kitchen with the splash pattern of your anger. You just walked out and went with her. You didn't even think about it, did you? Just went right to Rosalind. Perfect. You went right to the woman who had her arms out for you. Not caring who you leave behind, not caring what it's like to love you—"

Rhea was vaguely aware that she had started shouting, that her voice kept rising and would not stop. Her will had slipped its leash. She felt a giddiness in the release of her anger, coupled with a sickness like vertigo. But it was too late, too late to undo what had been done, too late to call back any of the words. She was crying, furious, split open like a ripened fruit, pouring a rage that was wounded love down on Taryn's head like hot oil. And she couldn't seem to stop.

The words themselves were indistinguishable, one long rant of rage and abandonment. In that stretch of language might have been Taryn's name, facts of the years she had lived in Rhea's house, suspended like flies in amber. As if facts could bind her. As if the recitation of facts like a chant could weave tighter the web. On a practitioner's level, Rhea knew that this was not so, a created binding could not stand against the binding of the heart. But she was beyond intellect now, reacting as purely as an animal to the stimulus of loss. She could no more be reasoned with than a mother tiger when her cubs were under the hunter's gun.

Rhea's pain took on a rhythm like contractions. *Yes,* she thought. *Yes, something is being born. Through resistance it will come into the world, crying and covered in blood.* But there would be no stopping it. The inevitability echoed in Rhea's heart with a recognizable gladness. She was used to hardness, to inevitability. It would hurt. She would suffer for it. That was good. The measure of her love would be the measure of the blood she shed. So mote it be.

She was shaking. She had ceased howling, and now there was only a thin, high keening that would not stop. Rhea grieved, even as she recognized that one life was passing into another. The new life might well be glorious and what she'd always sought, but she grieved for the loss of what she knew. For the self she'd always known. In doing so, she mourned with the power of a woman's heart the loss of the youth she had always loved.

How long she had waited. Half her lifetime, waiting, since the memory of who she was and who she protected revealed itself to her. It was ghastly, the waiting, knowing that she was supposed to be the mother of Taryn this time. That was what she'd arranged in their last time around. After her death she watched in horror as the youth she loved, grown now to a woman of steel, gave in to despair. Love had shattered her, this handsome woman. This was not new. The pattern always went this way. Love and betrayal, with Rhea left watching from the far side, the distant shore. Unable to intervene. But this time, everything had changed. This time, the woman could not shoulder the loss. She had taken her own life. Everything changed.

For the first time, Rhea was born not knowing where Taryn was. The anger and impulse had sealed her off. She didn't want to be found. Rhea had to trust that they would meet once in the flesh, that Taryn would have the sense to come back, to be born as she'd agreed to do. Early in her life, as her abilities manifested, Rhea realized that Taryn's soul was nowhere near. Stubborn as a child, refusing to be born. Refusing the pact they had made—*Be born to me. Let me take care of you always.* Even then, the missing lover had been what she yearned toward.

As her skills as a medium matured, Rhea searched everywhere. Nothing, not even an echo. So, not among the dead, not moved on. She'd been born. But where? There was a pool of silence at the center of Rhea's life, an emptiness she'd never felt. She was simply gone. Rhea did what she knew how to do: she endured. Her birth family severed their ties when she was twenty-two. She moved to Buffalo, eventually purchased the house on Mariner. There was work, different things, her practice. Companions. Lovers. But still, a pool of silence at the heart.

At length, she came to believe that she would come back to this region. The pull of her death would leave things unfinished. She'd be back, angry and young, unwilling to communicate. They would both come back here, the girl and the lover, but it was best not to think of such things. The pattern was tilted off its axle. Perhaps this time it didn't have to end in disaster. If only Rhea could find her and keep her safe.

In the years after she'd purchased the house on Mariner, it became a haven for women on their way to someplace else. Escaping abusive boyfriends, exploring sexuality, off to the Seneca Falls Peace Encampment, delving into witchcraft, politics, separatism—all manner of motion. It had once been a penultimate stop on the Underground Railroad, the last place escaping slaves would stay before they crossed into Canada. Echoes of those spirits remained. Anyone who stayed in the house would feel a yearning to be free. In the center of all this was Rhea, immobile, a Maypole others danced around, making a virtue of waiting. It was all she had.

In her forty-first year she felt it. It was like the scent of summer drifting past in the darkness of December, a memory of an emotion she'd felt once, long ago. That ephemeral. Rhea went looking. In the restaurant she'd finally seen her. Forty-one years was a long time to wait, a lifetime. She had watched through the window, transfixed. The heavens should open. White bulls should be sacrificed on altars of jade and porphyry. Incense should rain like falling stars. Instead, a grim-faced boy was bussing tables. She was thin as a blade. Her hair was shaved like a soldier's. There was a tint of blue to her skin, bruises dark as plums under her eyes. Hard to recognize as female. The hands were large on thin wrists. The motions she made with them were restless, blunt.

She grabbed plates, cleared silverware, swept debris into a bus pan. She was irritated, sullen, scowling at the distraction of a customer walking too close. Jealous of her personal space, touchy as a cat. A short, sharp tilt of her head, and Rhea saw her eyes. There was no mistaking them. A swing of her shoulders and she was gone into the kitchen.

It would be possible to wait until she finished her shift to meet her, but Rhea had waited too long. Sixteen years too long, from the look of her. She looked terrible, more than just the surface. Her aura was heartsick. She needed food, rest, a safe place. She needed a home and the protection of a loving heart. Things only Rhea knew how to give her properly. Rhea was inside the restaurant before she was aware she was moving. She was back on the floor, wrestling with a full bin of coffee mugs, headed toward the bar. She sensed someone in her path and looked up, annoyance already in place. Rhea stared. There was no helping that. If she were the kind of woman who cried, she would have cried right then.

She saw only an obstacle, a strange woman with unshed tears looking at her, wild eyed. "What?" she snapped, her eyes narrow, distracted.

Rhea had placed her hand against the girl's cheek. Taryn, this time. Taryn. She rested her hand against Taryn's cheek until she grew still, until a glimmer of recognition came into her eyes. The brows wrinkled, as if she were unable to accept what her heart now knew. That she had a home. That this strange woman would provide one for her. Years later, standing in the kitchen, all the anger bled out of her. She was facing that girl again. Yet, no. There was little of the youth she had loved in this handsome boy. Sleek as a panther, pampered with years of good attention and love, the gorgeous sheath of muscle over the sharp bones, the wealth of tattoos. This was Taryn now. Even her eyes were different. The agonizing blue held a sureness that could only be a true knowledge of love. So it was ending. Rhea felt that as clearly as she had felt the beginning. It was terrifying in its newness. She'd never lived long enough for this to happen. She was now, apparently, a woman who cried.

In a moment Taryn's arms were around her. Rhea trembled, unable to stop. She heard Taryn murmuring something, the deep timbre of Taryn's voice inherently soothing. The trembling stopped, but Rhea stayed in Taryn's arms. She felt lighter, fragile as spun glass. It was too soon to move away from Taryn's body.

"You're moving out, aren't you?" Rhea said, resting her head against Taryn's chest.

"Yeah."

"I could feel it. I think that helped set me off," Rhea said thoughtfully.

"Are you okay?" The voice was a rumble under Rhea's ear.

"Mmm-hmm. Yes, I do feel better. The spell passed. It was hard, but necessary. A clearing, burning away the underbrush."

"You had me worried," Taryn said.

"A good change. You always have me worried," Rhea said. She felt Taryn kiss the top of her head. Rosalind was about her height. Did Taryn show this softness with her? Rhea closed her eyes and held on tightly. For a moment they held like that, frozen. Then Rhea pushed away. "I believe I know what we need to do," she said calmly.

"What?" Taryn asked.

"You need to give me away."

Chapter Thirteen

The previous morning

"Souvlaki for breakfast?" Paul asked, looking askance at the menu.

"Only way to go. Why hit a Greek diner otherwise?" Joe asked reasonably.

"When in Rome," Misha said, reaching his arm across the back of the booth. Ellie, sitting next to him, pretended not to notice.

"When in Athens," Paul said, automatically correcting him. He was squinting at the menu, and so missed Misha's gesture. Ellie grabbed his hand and pressed it down to the table before Paul looked back up.

Joe was right about the breakfast. That made sense to Paul. Joe seemed to be right about everything. He made it look effortless, the managing of the menagerie around him, the collection of personalities that would make a sane man blanch. He seemed so solid. After the violent scene in the kitchen when the thug had assaulted him, Paul had watched in horror as Joe cried. Paul wasn't used to seeing men cry. His father had never cried, even with his liberal nature. It was not something that men did, a lesson no boy could miss, spoken or unspoken. Paul felt a welling anger against the thug, coupled with an anxiety at seeing such emotion from a man he'd come to admire.

When Rosalind had come in and found the wreckage, it was Joe's reaction that had seemed to trouble her more than the physical evidence of assault. Paul understood from this, and from Rhea's reaction when she'd come in minutes later, that a tragedy had occurred. The tragedy was not the violence unleashed by Taryn. It was her absence. What in the world was it about this girl that made the house revolve around her?

Joe had set to cleaning the kitchen, comforted by Rosalind's visit. Paul sat down in a chair with his back to the wall and watched, still stunned. His hand reached for the aching spot on his jaw where the fist had caught him. It was hard to believe he'd been hit. Not only hit, but knocked off his feet. Paul felt a cold breeze come into the room and looked up, wondering if someone had left the front door open. Rhea was in the doorway.

Joe saw her at the same time, and his face crumbled like a house with the foundation washed away. Rhea's expression was still, set, but all Paul could think when he looked at her was...heartbreak. He watched Joe cross the floor to her, wearing his grief openly.

"She's gone," Joe said, his voice replete with sorrow.

Rhea let Joe embrace her, more for his benefit. "Take Paul and go. I will clean this up alone," Rhea said.

Paul had the distinct sense she didn't mean the remains of the kitchen.

So they'd gone out to breakfast, hauling a blinking Misha out of bed. He'd insisted on calling Ellie, and to everyone's surprise, she'd agreed to meet them.

Joe's mood improved dramatically with distance from the house. He was his affable self by the time they sat down in the booth. Ellie had glanced at the spreading bruise on Paul's face, taken the emotional temperature of the group, and chosen not to notice. The blend of people worked well. The conversation was light and distracting. Paul felt himself relax into it.

Joe was smiling again at some joke from Misha. He didn't seem embarrassed by the emotion he'd shown. Paul would have been mortified to cry in front of virtual strangers, then have to face them for a meal. Paul attributed it to Joe's comfort in his masculinity, and derided himself for the corresponding lack. Why did everyone around him seem to know who they were and be at peace with that? It was like none of them had ever had to struggle with identity.

"So what's on your agenda for the rest of the day?" Ellie asked, glancing around the table.

"Drama, magic, parenting, dinner. The usual," Joe said and shrugged helplessly.

"So it won't blow your plans if I steal Misha away?"

Misha looked casually out the window, fascinated by the traffic on Elmwood.

"Steal away. It'd be good to get him out of the house. He sleeps all day," Joe said.

"Good. I was going to show him how to play pool," Ellie said.

Misha propped his chin on his fist and turned one dark eye on Ellie.

"That is, if you're up for it," Ellie said sweetly.

"It is good for a man to know his limits, or so it is said. I have yet to find mine. So, I am up for it." Misha smiled broadly at her.

After breakfast they left Ellie and Misha sitting in the booth. Joe glanced back in the window as they walked past, shaking his head. Misha was leaning on the table, nose to nose with Ellie, talking. She looked like she didn't believe a word, but she was smiling back at him.

"I don't know which one of them to feel sorry for. Misha can be such a mule."

"Don't you want to warn her?" Paul asked, his stride matching itself to Joe's.

Joe looked at him as if he'd said something strange. "Ellie's a full grown-up. She seems to know what she's getting herself into."

Paul thought about Taryn suddenly, about Rosalind. There was a strong sense of loyalty in the household, a loyalty that forgave all manner of behavior in residents. Joe would no more warn Ellie away from Misha than he would have warned Rosalind away from Taryn. And Paul knew in his bones that Taryn had been no angel when they'd started seeing one another. Rosalind had passed that loyalty barrier. She was now family to these people. An ugly thought presented itself to Paul. It would explain a lot about the behavior he'd seen but didn't understand. The fierce attachment, the emotional hold the thug seemed to have over her would suddenly make a grim kind of sense. And it would give him a lever to use against Taryn. "Has Taryn ever hit Rosalind?"

Joe stopped dead in his tracks. "What?"

"Has she ever done this to her?" Paul asked, touching the bruise on his own face.

"Great Goddess, no. She never would," Joe said with conviction.

"You understand why I'm asking the question. She's certainly capable of it. I never want to see Rosalind hurt. Particularly when I could prevent it."

The sounds of the traffic going by on Elmwood seemed very loud when Joe didn't respond. Paul looked over at him, puzzled and nervous. The man sighed and ran a hand across his face. "Listen. I like you, Paul. I get a feeling about you. And I know there's no love lost between you and T. But you can't be saying things like that about my family."

Paul's eyebrows shot up. "Your family? I thought she was just staying at the house. Renting a room."

"Taryn's my blood," Joe said simply. He saw the way Paul's face fell and sighed again. Joe reached his hand out and clapped Paul on the shoulder. Poor guy didn't know if he was coming or going. "Rosalind is, too. I'd never let anyone hurt either one of them."

That seemed to help. Paul looked less stricken. "I don't get it. Anyone would want Rosalind in their family. But that…" He hesitated on what to call Taryn, and finally let silence be description enough.

"Granted, you haven't seen Taryn's better side. But it is there. Let me ask you this, you think Rosalind would love someone who wasn't a good person?" Joe asked.

"I don't know how to answer that. Look at her. She's violent, and uneducated, and young, and…how can she know anything that Rosalind needs?"

Joe sighed and sat down on the curb. "Siddown. I have a feeling this might take a minute. You're still looking at it as an outsider. Taryn's a pretty powerful personality, sure. But she did have to come out, and that puts anyone through a cauldron of fire. When you have to fight to figure out who you are, then fight to have the space to live in the world, you learn certain things that can't come any other way."

"You speak about coming out like it's an initiatory rite. An enviable thing."

"It's not enviable that the world is hard enough to mandate coming out. But the process can be a revelation."

"Would you want your daughter to have to come out?" Paul asked, thinking he'd scored a hit. No matter what supportive things Joe said for the queerer aspects of his household, he was a normal guy with a normal daughter. And no parent wants more pain and danger for their child.

"Yes. I hope Goblin has to come out."

It flabbergasted Paul. "But we don't have to do that! Why put yourself through pain you don't need to go through?"

"I had to come out. It made me look at every aspect of my life and weigh them. It made me select, piece by piece, my body, how I carried myself, how I wanted other people to see me. Who I was at the core, and how I could do that justice in the world. It refined me, burned away all the dross. Pain can teach you things, if you listen. So yes, I hope my daughter has to come out. And I hope it makes her a better person, too, no matter who she is."

"Straight people do not have to come out."

"Paul, I'm a transman. I was born with a female body. I'm Goblin's mother."

"But—the beard, your build, you seem so normal!" Paul sputtered.

"Testosterone. And thanks."

"I thought you could tell. I mean, I thought I could tell. Like Egyptia. She's a guy, you can see it. She's pretty, but she's a guy."

"Okay."

"So you're Goblin's mother? Who's her dad?"

"My ex-husband, Ray. Ray's a great guy. After I came out as trans, he came out as gay. His lover for many years was Stephan, Misha's brother."

Paul hung his head. "This is all a little much for me."

"Give it time," Joe said.

"Why didn't you tell me the first day?" Paul asked suspiciously.

"It didn't seem appropriate. You weren't acclimated yet, and frankly, while it is important to me, sometimes I don't think about it."

"We worked together. I trusted you. You reminded me of my fa—" Paul cut himself off. He didn't want to continue that thought. "I have a lot to think about. I'll see you back at the house, okay? I'm going for a walk."

❖

Paul spent the rest of the afternoon mulling over what Joe had said. Rhea was still in the kitchen when they got in, burning shallow clay dishes full of bitter herbs and lighting candles. There was no need to be told to stay clear. Paul retreated to what was now his bedroom. He could hear faint sounds drifting up the stairs, a smattering of the arcane conversation between Joe and Rhea, what sounded like chanting.

Rhea and Joe, about to be married. Joe as a woman? He tried, but he couldn't picture it. Egyptia was one thing. He could accept that; she was pretty, but he could still tell what was going on. The world still made sense. But with Joe, you couldn't tell. Did it matter how he was born? He'd spent a lot of time with Joe, and he'd never seemed like anything but a nice guy.

It was too much. Since he'd first arrived he'd been the outsider, having to relearn everything. When did that end? When would he be done? When would the world start making sense again? When would he be at home?

He had to focus on something he could answer, a smaller question.

Paul lay on his back in Laurel's bed and stared up, where the Indian print cloth draped from the high ceiling onto plaster walls where the old wallpaper had been steamed away. This was an old, old house. Funny it was still so run down. *Rustic urban decay?* Paul thought, knowing he was avoiding. Joe had asked him a question. Could he answer it? Would Rosalind love someone who wasn't a good person?

He broke the question down carefully. The first part was asking for his evaluation of Rosalind's judgment. He thought about that. Since he'd met her, Rosalind had been the warmest, most openhearted person he'd ever known. She'd never turned away friendship or affection. She was kind to everyone. She never had a hard word ready. Kindergarten. His mother had brought him into the room, he reluctantly, holding on to her hand in a death grip. It was terrifying, facing all the shouting, pushing kids running past him, fighting for blocks and trucks. He would not stay. Would not.

His mother tried to push him forward. He hung back behind her leg. The teacher tried to lure him into the room. He turned his face away. There was a little girl who saw all this and took action. She marched across the room, ignoring the adults, and held out her hand. Her hair was blond like barley, pulled back in barrettes with Minnie Mouse on them. She smiled so sweetly at him that he forgot to pout, and smiled back. She took his hand. He followed her across the room. He'd never stopped following her. Somewhere along the line she'd dropped his hand, but she would still smile for him. Still offer him her friendship, just as she always had. *Friendship.* The word hung suspended in Paul's mind. He looked at it from several angles, like an architect. Warmth, compassion, loyalty, affiliation. Always there.

His mind moved on to the second portion of the question, where he had to evaluate Rosalind's ability to love. He went to the word and stopped. The gears broke down in his reasoning. Love. Romeo and Juliet, ninth grade. English class, Ms. Barone. They'd read the play for the first time. Fourth period. The bell sounded. Lunch was next. Paul's mind had already moved on to that, where he and Rosalind always sat together.

She was quiet walking in the hall, her books clutched to her chest. Almost like she was in a trance. He'd been saying something and became aware that she wasn't listening.

"Then a horse landed on the roof," Paul said, looking at Rosalind's downcast face.

"Sure," Rosalind had said.

"When exactly did you stop listening?" Paul asked.

"Oh, I'm sorry. I was just thinking about the play."

"Sucks that they both die," he'd said, fishing for the cause of her sadness. It was like Rosalind to be taken with melancholy at other people's misfortune, even fictional people.

"Before they died, they knew a love that made everything else in their lives inconsequential. Their families' fighting, the banishment, the killings. None of that mattered. Passion burned all that away," she had said, her eyes unfocussed. "And they were our age."

"That should cheer you up. We're not dead yet. I can still be your Romeo."

"No, it's just that I don't think…" She'd stopped, as if aware of where she was. Who she was with. "Never mind. What's for lunch?"

She had never finished that sentence. He wondered about it now, what she'd been thinking. She tried to tell him something then, and he'd been afraid to hear it. Would Rosalind love someone who wasn't a good person? Paul stared up, feeling the coldness seep along his limbs. It was not a question he could answer. He'd never seen Rosalind in love before.

Lethargy fell down on him. His body turned to lead. Paul slept, restless, aggrieved, his mind flashing images that made his flesh shrink. He saw himself as a teenager outfitted in doublet and hose, dagger at his waist. Romeo for a school play. Here was the stage, the painted backdrop. The balcony. He looked up, knowing she would be there, the girl meant for the role. Rosalind as Juliet, leaning on the balcony. She was as young as he was, her pale hair touched with artificial moonlight, her face sweet and sad. He stepped forward and delivered his lines with all the awkward ardor of youth, professed his love and his devotion. Now it was her turn to speak. He knew the lines she was supposed to say in reply.

It was as if she hadn't heard his declaration. Rosalind, on the balcony, aged before his eyes, the fresh youth that Juliet had thrown away blossomed into womanhood. The look of sweet sadness never left. Now a woman in her thirties leaned on the balcony, still wearing the costume, though it fit awkwardly now. He had stayed the same, the boy in his fanciful getup, gazing up at her, just beyond his reach. The woman whose sadness he could not touch.

She turned away from the balcony and smiled. With that smile she changed. Welcome and passion mingled. A woman's ardor was naked on her face. It was a Juliet such as he'd never seen, a woman grown into the knowledge of her heart. She spoke, and he had never heard such a tone, love that was part longing and madness. He knew the lines, from the morning after the wedding night. But they were meant to be spoken to him.

"Art thou gone? Love, lord, ay, husband, friend! I must hear from thee every day in the hour, for in a minute there are many days." The woman turned as she spoke, winding her arms around the neck of a beautiful boy.

Paul woke, sweating, tangled in the sheets.

They went out that night, Joe and he, Misha and Ellie. Rhea was, by common consent, left alone in the house, working whatever magic she could. She had to have been up all night. She was still pacing in the morning when they left again for breakfast. This time, Misha and Ellie met them at the diner, having spent their own time together. They sat in the same booth, but this time Ellie acknowledged Misha's arm across the back of the seat, even took his hand now and again. Joe seemed weary, distracted as much as Rhea by the absence of the thug. Just as well, he wasn't able to muster up the courage to spend a lot of time with Joe. He was grateful for the buffer of Misha and Ellie.

Despite himself Paul thought about Rosalind. If the absence of the thug was casting such a pall over the rest of the household, what would it do to her? He shied away from the idea. It didn't sit well with him. There was too much importance put on an element he didn't yet like. It was too soon for such thoughts.

They were walking back up Allen Street toward Mariner. He marveled at how crisp the fall days were. It was mid-October. He had good cause to be grateful for the jacket Joe had loaned him. Paul cast a glance sideways into the plate glass window of a storefront and stopped dead. Looking back at him was a man he didn't recognize. The clothing was that of a mechanic, jeans and denim shirt, a tan Carhart jacket, work boots. All Joe's clothing. His face was pale, mottled gray, like the inside of a shell, unshaven, brow wrinkled, eyes nervous. It was a face that didn't match the body, dressed head to toe in the clothing of another man. He couldn't remember what had happened to the blue suit he'd been wearing when he arrived in Buffalo. It couldn't have been all that long ago. Misha and Ellie were walking together. He saw Ellie reach out and take Misha's arm. Joe had his head down, lost in thought. Rhea would be cleansing the house again.

They turned the corner from Allen down Mariner, and Joe's head came up. He paused for a moment, as if he'd heard something. "Hot damn!" Joe shouted, before sprinting down the street.

"What's gotten into him?" Ellie asked.

Misha shrugged. "He is like Rhea, listening half the time to things we cannot hear. You learn not to ask."

"Okay. Looks like fun." Ellie took off after Joe.

Paul had to run to catch up. Joe was bounding up the stairs like a gazelle, showing a wild energy Paul had never seen. He was down the hallway and in the kitchen with Misha and Ellie close behind.

"It's gone," Joe said, his voice full of wonder.

Paul wondered what he was referring to, then he entered the

kitchen. He could feel it immediately, the lightness in the air. Gravity had halved. There was a crisp breeze from the back door. It smelled faintly of apples and new-cut hay. A faint tang of incense and bitter herbs lingered in the corners of the room, in pockets up under the beams, but the heaviness was gone. Rhea was holding an antique-looking broom, the kind of thing he'd seen in paintings, in Amish houses, in documentaries. The handle was a dark stained wood, twisted and gnarled under a faint sheen of lacquer. The bristles were straw, mingled with what appeared to be locks of hair. Odd decoration for a broom. Paul let himself be caught by the broom, because it kept his eyes from wandering to the person standing next to Rhea.

"Taryn…" Joe started to speak, his deep voice breaking on the name. Paul looked up, unable to stop himself. She moved right past him, embracing Joe. Taryn pulled back and grabbed Joe by the shoulders. Paul watched her head bend close to Joe's. There was an exchange of words, too low to hear. Joe smiled suddenly, the first genuine smile since the fight.

"We'll work it out. All right?" Taryn asked.

Joe nodded. "All right."

She was moving. He flinched automatically. He saw her hand, open. They were face to face. He'd never seen the color of her eyes unclouded by rage. It was too much, the undiluted weight of her regard. He wished there was a place to hide. If she kept looking at him, there would be nothing of him left. Her indifference had stung. This was far worse.

"I'm sorry I hit you," Taryn said frankly. "I don't like you, and you have no reason to give a damn for me. But you're here. Way I see it, we can kill each other or we can agree to be civilized."

"Civilized," Paul repeated, surprised to hear that word from a barbarian. Here was no hint of civilization, not in the pagan face of this boy. The veneer of calm could crack at any moment. He'd seen the tiger beneath. She took the word as his answer and held out her hand. There was no escaping it. He'd have to take it. Everyone in the kitchen was watching them. Paul took the hand. The focus shifted away from him. He could breathe again.

"We were up at the lake house. That place is stuck in a time warp. Salvation Army 1960s. The place needs some work. Rhea, I know you don't want to touch it," Taryn said, standing in front of the witch.

"I sense that has little to do with what you are about to propose," Rhea said, shooing Taryn away with the broom. Taryn grinned.

"Rosalind said something to me that got me thinking. We have two problems. Joe and Rhea are getting married up at the lake, but the house is a dive. Paul and Misha are here for healing, but so far there hasn't been a lot of peace around the house for that to happen. So here's the deal. Misha, Paul, Joe, and I will fix up the house. We can work in shifts, leave Paul and Misha time with Rhea, leave me time for rehearsals, Joe time to get ready for the ceremony. We're more likely to get along if we are working on something together. And there can be peace at the house."

The proposition had seemed half ridiculous to Paul, but it was accepted without question. So the next morning he found himself packed into the back of Joe's monstrous red convertible next to Misha, crossing the Peace Bridge into Canada. Taryn sat up front with Joe, sprawled across the front seat with an ease he envied. She tensed up when they approached the border, coiling her long limbs in and watching the customs booth with a wariness that seemed out of place. Had to be paranoia. The border guard barely glanced at the car, asked Joe a few bored questions, and waved them through. *When you're that hostile, the world must look hostile to you,* Paul thought smugly.

He was surprised by the size of the house. It was more of a cabin, really, but not a romantic hunting lodge. It struck him as the kind of place that might be full of draft dodgers on their way from Buffalo into the wilds of Canada, eluding the specter of war. They'd started by hauling most of the furniture out of the living room. There was no place to put it but the driveway. Joe handed out hammers and told them to start tearing the paneling down. He didn't seem to notice that Paul was avoiding him. Taryn seized a crowbar from Joe's toolbox and went at the wall with an enthusiasm that Paul was afraid to stand next to.

Paul held up a piece of the smoky green paneling. "You might want to save some of this," he said to Joe, who was hauling an armload out the door.

Taryn paused in ripping away the face of the wall. She hadn't yet looked directly at him, but she was starting to acknowledge him when he spoke. The sound of her voice was foreign to him. He jumped every time he heard it. The growl was gone from her tone, but there was a lingering rumble underneath. Did she always sound like that? How in the world did Rosalind manage to hear anything spoken in that tone? It was dangerous, but Paul tried to picture Taryn beneath Juliet's window. It came out more like Stanley Kowalski.

"This? This is crap. Even Rhea isn't this Gothic," Taryn said.

"I was thinking white for the walls," Joe said, tossing the debris out the door.

"It has been confirmed. Joe is so straight it hurts. No sense of design at all," Misha said from his perch on the edge of the wood stove.

"What would you put up?" Joe asked him.

Misha looked at the living room. "In a box this size? A box planted on the shore of a gray lake in a land of perpetual twilight? Nothing so painful as more blandness. Can you imagine white walls when the snow comes and the lake is a greasy mass of ice and slush, stretching away to a gray horizon? No. Some color, I beg of you. Something to lighten the mood of even the witch woman."

"You have the soul of a poet, Misha," Joe said.

"Thought you didn't have a soul," Taryn said.

"That would be vampires. Enough from you, or I will have Rhea teach me to return after death, and I will show you how much of a soul I do have."

Paul watched very carefully as Joe walked over by Taryn, casually draping an arm across Taryn's shoulders. It was his first chance to see them together as friends. The image was surprising. "What do you think of red?"

Taryn looked at him. "Red?"

"Yeah. Like the color of that dress of Rhea's. You know the one," Joe said.

"The one you got her for Solstice last year. That would work," Taryn said thoughtfully.

"You know what that means."

Taryn grinned. "Joe and I have to make a run to the hardware store. You guys need anything?"

"A sense of purpose. And more beer," Misha said.

"Beer's in the fridge. Take a break till we get back," Joe suggested.

"Exactly. You'd fit right in on my crew, Joe," Misha said, pushing off the stove.

"I get to drive!" Taryn called, sprinting out the door.

"Not after the last time you drove."

Misha strolled back from the kitchen and handed Paul a beer. The gesture pleased him. He smiled. "Thanks."

"You will learn. It is never too cold to drink beer on the border of Buffalo and Ontario." Misha walked out onto the porch. Paul followed him.

"You're from Canada?" Paul asked. He'd heard something along those lines at the dinner party, the symposium. The rest of the night was a red blur in his memory, but he recalled that.

"More or less. Toronto mostly these days. Now that is a city. None of this provincial American steel town nonsense. Have you been?" Misha asked him.

"No, never have. I've never spent time in this end of New York state before."

Misha glanced at the lake. "Well, you must make the drive to Toronto. If not now, on one of your trips."

"Trips?" Paul asked. It was the first time anyone had broached the topic of his leaving, of his having a life beyond the moment and the immediacy of Rhea's house. It felt strange to remember that he had come from somewhere else.

"Oh, yes. Now that you have ties here. You have visited Buffalo. You will return. Trust me. I know this. It is like a sickness. You try to stay away and you cannot."

Paul grimaced. "I can't see that happening. I'm hardly…I mean, I don't exactly have ties here."

Misha looked at him patiently. "Rosalind is here."

"Oh, that. Well, it is her first job. She'll probably move around some before she settles down, finds a department where she wants to stay. She's an excellent teacher. I don't expect she'll have any trouble. But the job market can be tight. Maybe the West Coast," Paul said. The air was cold. The beer was like ice in his throat.

"You are joking with me?" Misha asked.

"Of course not. She's a wonderful teacher," Paul said.

"Not about that. You really can't see it?"

Paul frowned. Misha was staring at him inquisitively. It was annoying. "See what?"

"She is home."

Paul laughed. "Oh, I didn't mean to imply that she doesn't like it here. I know she has friends here. I wouldn't expect anything less. She has friends everywhere she goes. I'll bet she keeps in better contact with the people we knew in Ithaca than I do."

Misha shook his head. "You are an idiot."

"Excuse me?"

"I don't know you well enough to spare your feelings. You seem like a fine enough fellow, and Joe likes you. But you are wearing blinders that would do a draft horse proud," Misha said.

"Now see here—"

"No. You see. Until you do, I don't expect you'll be able to leave. Oh, don't get puffed up against me because I am the one to tell you the truth. It is the same for me. Until I learn to see, I will not be able to leave," Misha said.

"And what is it that you have to learn to see?" Paul asked, sarcasm tingeing his words.

"My brother."

"Oh, really? That seems easy enough. And where is your brother?"

"Back at the house waiting for me, I'd imagine. I haven't been able to tell, but Rhea tells me he comes into the room when she heals me." Misha's voice was calm.

"That doesn't make any sense," Paul said.

"He's dead." Misha looked out at the lake, blinking back tears.

The silence was thick, cold, and distant as the far gray shore.

"I'm sorry. I didn't know," Paul said miserably.

"That is the second time I have been able to say that. So. The first was just last night. Ellie asked me about him. American women, so forward. A good heart, that one, and spirit. I was able to say, Stephan died. That would be the third time right there, sealing the charm. I should be able to say it as naturally as breathing now. No strangeness to it at all. My brother is dead. Stephan is dead."

Misha's face was wet. He cried at every word, stunning Paul. He went from crying to gulping air, sobbing. He'd forgotten Paul entirely. It was as if some wall within him had been breached. He was helpless before the emotion. Misha's body convulsed with it. Grief came on like the strike of an illness. The man folded down onto the porch and stretched one arm out, his other covering his eyes. There was no mask over his despair. The paroxysm of sobbing wracked his body. He lay sprawled on the porch as if on a grave. His face was pressed into the wood. He was crying out words between the gulps of air, but Paul couldn't understand them.

The excess emotion paralyzed Paul, robbed him of speech. First Taryn in her scintillating anger, now Misha in his welter of grief. All the emotional outpouring, savage and hot, that seemed to burst upon them and carry them away. If he stood still, would it swallow him up like a rain-soaked river? He should be grieving the same way. His father was dead. There was only silence inside him, unbroken. Somewhere in that silence was grief and perhaps even love. Somewhere there was understanding. But what road would lead him there? What would be his healing?

Misha lay, spent. Paul looked around, desperate, hoping Joe and Taryn would return magically. He felt his own inadequacy. He knew that even the thug would be better at this than he would. She understood the nature of extremes, lived in it. He'd read somewhere about crimes of passion, to love was to be able to kill. Taryn looked like she could do both.

A man, a near stranger, had cried himself limp before Paul's eyes. They were comrades of necessity, living and working together by the vagaries of fate. Christ, was he starting to think like these people? He had to do something. What would Joe do? Paul crouched by Misha's exhausted form. He reached out to touch him, his hands wavering, extending and retreating. Finally he clasped Misha's shoulder.

"I'm sorry, Misha. I know it's hard. My father just died. But your brother must have known how much you loved him."

There was movement from the prostrate man. Misha pushed himself up to a sitting position, his head resting in one hand. "He knew. It was not so much of a thing. Everyone who knew him loved him. I cry not for him, who continues. Nor for Ray, deprived of his husband, nor

Goblin, deprived of her stepfather. I cry for myself, deprived of him. I am a fool, a coward, and a bastard."

"I don't think…" Paul said, losing the words.

Misha held up his hand. "I am telling the truth. Do not argue with me. There are some who are born for love, no? They are surrounded in it everywhere they go, always at the center. Rosalind seems to be one. Goblin will be. Stephan was. There are some who love rarely, and only with their whole heart. Rhea. Taryn. I am this way. Only once have I known love, and that was my brother. My twin. He shared my soul. It is fanciful to say such things, you think? That does not make them less true. The words exist because the truth exists for them to describe. Taryn would not argue with me. It is fanciful only if you have not lived it. Imagine this. There is one person below heaven that knows you to the bones and sinew. Knows your mind before you speak, has only love for you. Now imagine that the light in the world goes out. They are gone."

"I don't know if I could imagine that," Paul said.

Misha shook his head. "Believe that, if you must."

"You called yourself a coward."

Misha waved his finger in Paul's face. "And a bastard, don't forget. When I found out that Stephan was sick, truly so, with his body wearing out, my imagination failed. I tried facing the idea that he might not always be here. I could not. So I fled, on the road with a show. I could not be contacted. Joe and Ray cared for Stephan. Even when he died, I felt it. But I would not call, would not come down. Joe knew I was in Toronto by then. I expect he mentioned that."

"He never said a word," Paul said.

"It is beyond him to be unkind, even with this? He is a good man. A better man than I am, birth or no," Misha said.

"Birth or no," Paul repeated. He stood up, restless suddenly. He walked to the door, then looked back. Misha hadn't moved. "When my father died, I didn't react. I handled the details of the funeral. I was there for my mom and the family. I put on a suit, said the right things. It wasn't out of strength. Hell, I didn't even call Ros because I couldn't bear the thought of telling her. That would make it real. When something in me finally snapped, all I could think about was my ex-wife. She was the only one I wanted to see. I thought I could get something back, some moment when I'd been happy, I guess," Paul said. "Then I got here, and nothing made sense. The one real person I could relate to, this solid, stand-up guy, tried to help me find a way through the mess."

Misha seemed interested. His face lost the blankness of grief. "Did you know that Rosalind had taken up with Taryn?"

"No, she didn't mention that. I didn't give her a chance." Paul looked at Misha, considering. "You knew about Joe, right?"

"What about him? Oh. Well, yes, of course."

"Did you know him before he was a man?"

"He was always a man. He just made a few adjustments externally."

Paul decided to switch tracks. "What about Taryn?"

"On and off since she was seventeen and first Rhea's lover," Misha said.

"What kind of person is she?"

Misha looked at him, amusement creeping into his dark eyes. "Good company in a bar fight. Poor company in a church. A demon, a dog. Enough to bring stony Rhea to her knees, to win Joe's admiration. But you are not asking me a question I can answer."

"Why not?" Paul asked.

"You want to know why. Watch and judge for yourself."

Taryn and Joe pulled up in the red convertible, and the conversation dropped. The work resumed. Misha seemed better. He went back to his old self without further drama. Paul felt like he was left with his questions unanswered. It sat with him the rest of the day.

It was difficult for Paul to take Misha's advice and watch Taryn, but he tried gamely. Her energy was manic. She bounded from room to room, threw punches at Joe as he tried to work, tore down paneling with a will. At one point she was standing with one boot up on the wood stove, peeling off her T-shirt. Paul stared. Her back was a map of muscle, covered in tattoos. Under the tank top she wore, he could see the lines of ink, like a mosaic, the dagger that stretched from her right shoulder diagonally down to her left hip, the snake in the tree on the left shoulder, a black bird in a circle on the back of her neck. Then she turned and caught him looking. For a moment he expected the fires of hell to blaze up in her eyes. The skin at the corner of her eye tightened. A smile twitched on her lips.

"We'll get the walls done before we start on the floor. Misha, I want you to look at the wiring in the bedroom. It's a mess," Joe said.

"I will rewire the lot. It is a miracle this place hasn't burned down."

"Paul, you have a session with Rhea tomorrow morning, and T, you have rehearsal tomorrow afternoon. So that leaves you guys on shift for Thursday."

CHAPTER FOURTEEN

Paul's sessions with Rhea were never completely predictable, but they had taken on a rhythm. For the first few she had him lie down on the floor or the couch. He wasn't sure what she did. His eyes slid closed and he fell asleep solidly. He would open his eyes to find cats sleeping, packed tightly against his body. There were four or five of them, including a big calico that liked to nest in the crook of his neck. Once he'd woken to find the cat squarely in the small of his back.

Rosalind had started coming to the sessions, helping Rhea in whatever magic she performed. He was uneasy with this at first, but the intimacy of it grew comforting. Her attention, for those minutes or hours, was focused solely on him and his well-being. He liked the thought of her keeping guard over his untenanted body.

This morning, he wandered down the front stairs to find Rhea in the middle room, sprinkling sea salt in a circle. Rosalind stood at Rhea's right, holding a stick of red chalk like a child would use to draw on a sidewalk.

"Draw it in the north or the south?" Rosalind asked.

"South today. The direction of fire. Good morning, Paul. Lie down in the center of the circle, please. On your back," Rhea said, not looking at him.

"Should I close my eyes?"

Rhea put the salt down next to her cauldron. "If you like."

Paul did so. It was easier than looking up at Rhea and Rosalind as they walked in a circle around him. He felt the pleasant sleepiness gather. In that state he listened to the women's voices singing, spiraling around him. He couldn't tell Rosalind's voice from Rhea's, so entwined were they. She was sounding like one of them now; her crossing over had been complete. What was Rosalind, the daughter of an atheist and a Catholic, doing practicing magic? Rhea had told him that Rosalind was gifted in her sight.

"What do you see?" Rhea's dry voice separated out from the chant.

Rosalind was down by his feet. "Tiny cracks. A web of them, branching out, leaking red."

"Yes. Random or patterned?" Rhea asked.

"It looks random. No, wait. There. See that? It's spreading. There is a pattern. The surface is being worn away, revealing it." Rosalind's voice was near his head, floating above him.

"Should we stanch the cracks?" Rhea asked with a deference Paul didn't believe.

There was a hesitation. At first he thought he'd fallen asleep. "I don't know," Rosalind said.

"Tell me your first impression," Rhea said firmly.

"No. They have to spread. The surface has to shatter." There was sadness in Rosalind's voice. He couldn't imagine why.

"We'll cast a protection around the whole. Please hand me the broom and take up the athame."

Paul heard singing. Was that Rosalind's voice? Funny, he'd always known she couldn't sing. Why was she proving him wrong?

"That will do for today," Rhea said. Paul found himself blinking awake. Time couldn't have passed, but there were the cats tucked into his sides, the calico and the gray tom. The circle of salt was gone, swept away. Rosalind was in the living room, reading the paper. Rhea was making a few passes with the broom in the northwest corner of the room.

"Much easier," she said with tight satisfaction. "Once she puts her mind to something, it happens. It's like spring in here."

"How's the time on the repair crew going?" Rosalind held out her hand to help him up.

"Good," Paul said, meaning it. "We got a lot done yesterday. It felt important to be doing work, any work. I had some time to talk with Misha. Taryn and I are starting the floor tomorrow."

Rosalind nodded, her expression doing an interesting dance between smiling and trying to look neutral. "You know, I have some time today. We could get lunch, maybe catch a movie."

"You and I?" Paul asked.

"Sure. Spend some time, something a little more, ah, normal. There's a Greta Garbo festival at the North Park. We could catch a matinee. You in?" Rosalind asked.

"What would she think?" Paul didn't have to place any special emphasis on the pronoun.

"She has rehearsal." Rosalind rolled the newspaper into a tube and tossed it on the couch.

The whole day, a portion of it at least, alone with Rosalind. It was unbelievable, a stroke of such unexpected good fortune that Paul couldn't believe it. "*Grand Hotel*?" he asked.

"*Ninotchka,* I think," Rosalind said, rustling through the paper.

Paul shrugged. "Good enough."

"Great. I have a few things to do at home. I'll meet you back here in half an hour."

It's a sad thing when all your dishes consist of coffee cups, Rosalind thought. She used to like to cook. It had been comforting, during writing her dissertation, to prepare her own meals. It was a way to assert her own domesticity after. Rosalind put the dish towel down. After she and Paul separated. Now she rarely cooked. All Taryn wanted in the morning was coffee. She'd become a regular in every Greek diner in town, thanks to Taryn's desire for breakfast after sex. Four in the morning they would wander into the Towne, laughing and elated, careless with who saw them and knew. The phone rang. Rosalind plucked it deftly and balanced it on her shoulder. "Hello?"

"Hey." The voice rolled out, dark and liquid.

"I love when you do that. You make me melt," Rosalind said.

Taryn's tone was perfectly smug. "I know. That's why I do it."

Rosalind smiled. "So why aren't you here? This new schedule

of yours is killing me. I get to see you late at night and before dawn. The darn lake house has your days; rehearsal has your afternoons and evenings. And it's going to get worse with the wedding and the show. I haven't had you long enough to share you."

"You woke up on top of me this morning," Taryn said.

"And that's supposed to be enough?" Rosalind let a note of petulance creep into her voice. She had to bite her lip to keep from laughing.

"I had to say something. Spending the rest of my life with you wouldn't be enough," Taryn said.

"I'd call that a good start." Rosalind's heart lurched. She knew it was Taryn flirting, but the possibility of truth behind the words made her blood race. She had to fight her own impulse to demand that Taryn make good on her vows. All in good time. Taryn was moving in with her. There had to be a respectable pace to the relationship. She couldn't risk scaring Taryn off. Even if she was half convinced that Taryn wouldn't be scared. "How's the work on the house going?"

"Not bad. We settled on a color for the living room. I have something special in mind for the bedroom."

Rosalind felt her pulse jump again. "I love it when you say that."

Taryn laughed. "It's going to be a surprise for Rhea."

Rosalind bit her tongue and pictured what kind of surprise Rhea used to get in that bedroom. "You can't tell me? I can keep a secret."

"You work with her every morning. She could just read your mind," Taryn said.

Taryn's refusal piqued her interest now Rosalind had to know. "Be serious. Tell me what it is."

"No."

"I seem to recall a certain boy who swore she'd do anything for me. Must have been just bedroom promises," Rosalind said thoughtfully.

Taryn didn't hesitate. "It's a mural. I'm going to do the wall with the return of Persephone to her mother Demeter. The spring legend. I'll have the Underworld in the lower right, gaping open. Black rocks, red shadows from the flame. Persephone will ascend to the field where her mother waits. As she walks, spring arrives. The earth comes back to life. Flowers will bloom in Persephone's wake, asphodel and hyacinths. Rhea likes those."

"That's gorgeous," Rosalind said, entranced.

"You haven't seen it yet."

Rosalind cradled the phone. The distance between them was sharp. "You tell a beautiful painting."

Taryn's voice betrayed her excitement. "We need a return-to-life theme for that place. I got the idea the night we spent there. It's my bride gift."

"For giving her away. It's perfect." Rosalind saw Taryn walking Rhea down the aisle. It brought tears to her eyes. " Hey, don't I get a dowry or something for you moving in with me?"

"Nah. When a young man leaves his maternal household and moves in with his wife he doesn't bring gifts. But hey, if you abduct me I might work some ransom out," Taryn said.

Rosalind sighed. "No. I'll settle for you walking willingly across my threshold."

"I'll do that tonight. I don't know how much more than walking I'll be up for. We start rehearsing the dance numbers tonight."

"Will Ellie be there?" Rosalind asked.

"Nah. She's hanging with Misha. That is weird, let me say. But Linda will be there directing."

"Listen, I have something to ask you," Rosalind said. "I want you to tell me the truth. I asked Paul to spend the afternoon with me. Have lunch and see a movie. Will that bother you?"

There was a pause, then a sound like a sigh through clenched teeth. "Yeah. But I want you to do it anyway."

"Oh, sweetheart."

"It'll give me a chance to practice being a grown-up." There was noise in the background. "Joe's calling me. Come see me at rehearsal?"

Rosalind smiled. "I'll be there."

Taryn's voice dropped down to a throaty growl. "If he touches you, I'm decking him again. I love you."

"Say it again," Rosalind demanded.

"I love you." Taryn's voice was a caress, a promise of paradise.

"That worked. I have goose bumps. Go on."

❖

The morning had been lovely. They had gone out for coffee, some place downtown that seemed special to Rosalind. It was a place full of languid young men drinking lattes, intense young women with short hair writing in journals. She seemed to relax here, as if the place unleashed a feeling of joy for her. They talked for an hour, effortlessly, like old friends. It was intoxicating. Paul felt young, felt the weight of the past three years fall away. They might have been back in graduate school, drinking coffee, talking about movies and books, existing in a world of their own. This was the Rosalind he remembered, and more. It was the self he remembered. He was light again.

He looked over at Rosalind. Her head was tilted to the side as she listened; her eyes were focused on him in their melting loveliness. It was a look that would bring out a storyteller in the most taciturn soul, the offer of a perfect audience.

"This place is great. I feel like a kid in here."

Rosalind laughed. "A lot of my students come here. It can get pretty funny, crossing the social boundaries."

"I bet you don't have any trouble with that," Paul said.

Rosalind's eyes flickered to the counter, where a young woman with fire engine red hair was taking orders. "You'd be surprised."

They drove to Delaware Park at Paul's request. Rosalind had gently tried to dissuade him, but when he met her resistance he couldn't understand, and it threatened his mood. She'd sighed and backed down. It was more trouble than it was worth, explaining the connection she had to the park, how she would forever associate it with her first date. The location had been claimed by Taryn, even the air was imprinted with her. The rush of desire that Rosalind felt when they walked past the casino made her weak. Paul was looking at the lake. He missed the expression of longing that Rosalind couldn't mask. The surroundings were pure emotional triggers.

I may never be rational about this city, Rosalind thought. *It will always be the place I fell in love. Right there Taryn first demanded that I love her. I first felt what it was to be the center of her attention, to be beloved. This will forever be a city that was the setting for that. The streets will carry the echo.*

Paul glanced back and saw Rosalind standing by the stone bench, transfixed. One hand was touching her own cheek, the expression full of light. *She loves it here,* he thought. "Penny for your thoughts?" Paul asked, charmed by her look. The hand dropped away immediately, the look vanished with a speed that made Paul feel sick. He had seen something that wasn't meant for him to see. It was one thing to know he'd never seen certain emotions in Rosalind, it was quite another to watch her hide them from him.

"I was looking at David," she said, pointing across the lake. It was a bronze reproduction of Michelangelo's masterwork, silhouetted against the sky. From where they stood, Paul could see the tapering back, the hand resting on the broad shoulder. It was the paragon of a young man, an ideal of masculine beauty.

"I didn't know you were a Michelangelo fan," Paul said, not wanting to delve too deeply into the moment. It might tell him too much.

"I've developed a taste for it," Rosalind said, blushing. She started walking down the path, and so missed Paul's muttering.

"Like hot wine."

The theater wasn't far from the park. The mood had changed as soon as they left. The sense of distance Paul felt between himself and Rosalind vanished. She was his again, attentive to his thoughts, responsive to his jokes, agreeably remembering the shared past. There was enough connection that he could stop imagining the ghost of a black-haired boy walking between them. No one else could match his history with Rosalind. It was his strongest weapon, and he played it to the hilt, drawing her out with moments she might have forgotten, handing over the gift of perfect recall of nearly her entire life.

They started talking about graduate school and the movie house in Ithaca. The warm feeling of nostalgia carried Paul along. Every story he related had the same message: See how well matched we are intellectually? He asked about books he thought she might have read. Recommended a few she should try. For a moment, when Rosalind smiled at him, everything made sense. All the anxiety was gone. He was twenty-five again. He knew who he was, where he was going, who he loved. He felt the pleasure of her affection, and it was sweet.

The movie house was perfect. The posters of Garbo floated him along in remembrance. How many Garbo films had they seen together? Surely it must be affecting Rosalind the same way. He couldn't have designed a better contrast to that house, those people. Paul was smiling, feeling his youth and triumph. He looked at the poster, automatically checking the movie times. *Ninotchka*…

Rosalind held up a flier. "There's been a change in the program. They're showing *Queen Christina* this afternoon." She glanced at his face, then at the door to the theater. "Listen, let's go get some baklava. There's a Greek diner down the street. It's a pleasant afternoon for a walk. We could—"

Paul felt the fragile bubble of his mood burst. Such a small thing, to deflate him. But wasn't that the way? Life hinged on a slender thread. Happiness was so fragile that it could be shattered forever by a single word. Rosalind guessed that it might be a disaster and sought to shield him from it. But a Greek diner wasn't something they had always done. It was a new thing, a product of her time here. It would be rife with reminders of her new life. He couldn't hope to hold her attention. No, he had to keep the afternoon going on as it was. Hope to rebuild the mood. Stay in the past.

"No, it's fine. Let's go see the film."

"Are you sure?" Rosalind asked.

"It's Garbo. How could I not be sure?" he said, flippant.

They sat in the dark. Paul munched popcorn by the fistful. It was intimately familiar, this moment. They had always gone to movies together. They had years of built-in signals. He went for popcorn as she bought the tickets. There was no need to speak. They'd done it a thousand times. He knew she had to watch all the previews. It was one of her favorite things. She absorbed them like short stories. He couldn't have cared less. For him it was extra time to get to the theater, but he knew her preferences. He smiled, picking the perfect seats. She liked to be near the front of the theater, to be swallowed up by the experience. He hoped she noticed the gesture. *No one else will ever know you this well,* he thought. He couldn't picture Rosalind sharing a film with the thug.

He'd thought that the movie would be fine. They'd seen it together years before. As soon as Garbo appeared as Queen Christina, he knew how wrong he'd been. Paul watched as she strode across the screen with her long legs, a regal, loping stride. She was dressed for hunting. Her councilor chided her. She laughed him off. She was the ruler of the country, beloved of the people. She had no intention of marrying. When he asked if she was going to die an old maid, her supernatural eyes flashed. She would die a bachelor. Paul watched, sinking in the chair. There was no place he could look. If he glanced away from the screen, he might see Rosalind's expression as she watched the tall and handsome Garbo with her man's clothing and the free swinging stride of a king. He didn't know if he could survive that. So he watched the screen as the queen's favorite, Countess Ebba, rushed in to greet her. He watched as Garbo strode to her, taking her head tenderly in hands meant to wield a blade or drive a team of horses. Watched, as Garbo kissed her. The king and her favorite.

"Let's go," Rosalind whispered.

Out on the street Paul started walking, hands jammed into his pockets. Rosalind was silent, but he could see that she was sparing his feelings. It made him more miserable. She had changed—he couldn't be sure of what she saw anymore, how she felt. He could only be sure that now, seeing that, her reaction was different. That a tall, handsome woman dressed as a king kissing another woman would affect her as it never had.

"We can't avoid it forever," Paul said, surprised to hear his own voice.

"I know."

Paul clenched his teeth, his jaw working like a grindstone. "Do you love her?"

"Yes," Rosalind answered softly.

"Didn't even need to think about that one. How much?" he grated. The pretense of adult remove was gone. The nostalgia was beyond his reach, maybe forever. It was good to feel something hot, even something ugly. He experienced a moment of gratitude to Taryn for bearing his hate.

"Paul," Rosalind said in a tone meant to put him off. He didn't let it.

"We've been avoiding it since I showed up in Buffalo. I've had time to adjust to the idea. You're not the person I married. You have new friends. You're gay and dating a twenty-year-old punk. Nobody is sparing my feelings but you. Answer me. What is this little relationship you're in? What can you possibly expect from this disturbed, violent, lecherous behavioral cartoon? Tell me the truth!"

"I would marry her tomorrow if she asked me," Rosalind said.

Paul stopped as if he'd been hit in the forehead with a broad ax.

"You…you can't." He sat down on the curb, mouth open. "Would she ask?"

"I don't know. Probably not yet. But I think someday she will," Rosalind said, sitting down next to him.

"You'd already say yes," Paul repeated.

"With all my heart."

"This…this isn't what I thought. How long has it been?" Paul asked, looking down at the street between his shoes.

"Less than a month," Rosalind said quietly.

Paul shook his head. "God. God."

"Paul, I know this has to be horrible for you." Rosalind put her hand on his arm. He kept shaking his head.

"You never were in love with me."

"I loved you. You were my best friend."

"It took you five years to say yes to me," Paul said, still shaking his head.

"It's not the same. Don't ask me to compare. It's not fair."

This brought a bitter laugh up from his chest. He choked on it. "Fair? So calm, so forgiving. And sweet. And fair. You never once were unfair to me when I told you about Kathy. So gracious when I offered to divorce you. So fair to me I wanted to kill myself for what I'd done, even though I knew you wouldn't sleep with me again. You were just too fair to tell me to fuck off." He started to cry.

"I'm so sorry. I had no idea what was going on with me. I just couldn't be who you wanted, and it was killing me. I had to let you go," Rosalind said, starting to cry, too.

Paul, anguished, looked up and saw this. He reached out abruptly and kissed her. Rosalind stayed perfectly still. He pulled away. "You wouldn't come back even if I asked you?"

Rosalind shook her head. "Don't."

"Come back to me."

Rosalind stood against the pale blue October sky, nearly blinding

Paul. She was still crying, tears mixed and joined on her cheeks with strands of hair, disturbed by the wind. The pain was alive. If he reached out his hand Paul knew he could touch it. She was torn. That had to be it. He pressed his advantage, using her silence as an admission of doubt. Maybe there was still time, no matter how romantic she waxed about her adventure.

"I know all this seems overwhelming, and new, and exciting. So does a train wreck in the first few minutes. I'm telling you this for your own good, Ros. Even if you think you want this to last, you are fooling yourself to think she does. I got to spend time with Misha. I asked him about her. This girl makes serial monogamy look weak. She collects trophies, Ros. Straight women in particular. You know she used to boast she could land any woman for a night? When she tires of you, and she will, she will drop you like you never existed. You sure you want your heart broken?"

"If she's the one doing it," Rosalind said, losing her grip on her anger.

"You're not thinking clearly. You ever talk to one of her ex-girlfriends, not just the people she lives with? I bet they'd give you a different picture of your inamorata. She's violent. She flies into rages. She hit me. She could easily hit you. You're an educated woman. How much do you have in common with a high-school dropout? And have you looked at her? There have to be chapters in the DSM-IV devoted to her identity disorders. No job, no future. She's trash. Let it go."

Rosalind watched him, her expression a brick wall. He kept talking, rapidly, feeling his last chance bleeding away.

"Does she know what happened to you on the first day of third grade? Can she ever offer you a home, a normal life? Even normal friendships? Will she take care of you when you get sick? Will she ever be able to buy a house? What about how you will be together? Right now, it's all very bohemian and exciting. In five years, it will get very old, the poverty, the violence, the isolation. Never having a normal conversation. Talking about books, or your work, or the world. You might think right now that you don't care what people think, but I know you, Ros. You do care, and it will come up. I'll bet she's looking forward to meeting your family. Thanksgiving should be a splendid time. Your mom always goes all out. Bet you can't wait for your paramour to swagger in and put her boots up on the table. 'Hi, Mom! This is my little dyke boyfriend.'" The coldness of her look finally halted him. He had never seen a look like that from Rosalind. It shook him to the core.

"Say anything like that to me ever again, and I will cut off all contact with you."

"I'm only trying to help you," Paul stammered.

"You don't have to like my choices, or her. But if you want to be in my life you will respect them both. I plan on spending my life with her. Granted, the deck is stacked against it. You think I don't know that? It's not a matter of reason, Paul. I love her. You'd better get used to it, now." It was said calmly, with a core of flexible steel.

Paul started to cry, feeling his last hope cut off. This wasn't the woman he knew. She didn't bend under his assault. Rather, she stared him down like an enemy. "It's like you died," he said, gulping air.

"I'm right here. It's only an idea about me that died. Hey…" She stroked the hair back from his face. "Remember what you told me in ninth grade?"

Paul looked at her, unable to speak.

"You said friendship is the most important thing. If we are always friends, we can never be sorry."

Paul bit back a sob. "I was in love with you then."

"But it's still true. We have a chance to really know one another. I can't ever be your wife again. But I'd like to be your friend." Rosalind held out her hand.

A tremor went through Paul. He looked at her, helplessly, his eyes wet. He lunged at her, hugging her as a drowning man grasps at hope. Rosalind felt his arms tighten, felt his breath come out in a shuddering gasp. At last he took her shoulders in his hands and pushed himself away. He looked at her. His breathing slowed. "I wanted to be the one. My whole life. I thought if I just waited, you'd wake up one day and see it. But you were looking for something else."

"I didn't know I was looking."

Paul grimaced. "I can't pretend to be thrilled about your new life."

"I know," Rosalind said sadly.

"But I want you in my life. If it has to be as friends, so be it."

In the noise and confusion of the kings exiting, two people slipped into the theater. Ellie jumped over the row of seats and landed next to Linda, scattering her papers.

"Hey, girlfriend!"

"Hello. Thought I gave you the night off," Linda drawled, making a notation in her book.

"Just can't get enough of the theater. It's in my blood. I wanted to show the house to Misha. He'll be doing the light hang," Ellie said, gesturing at the man standing with folded arms behind her.

His hair was brown, pulled back in a ponytail. He was looking around the house, eyes narrow in concentration or superiority. There was a roughness to his features that wasn't unpleasant. Linda looked at the spread of his shoulders. It was suddenly possible to place the leather jacket Ellie was wearing.

"Linda Alejandros. I'm the director." Linda held out her hand.

The palm of his hand was a hard as wood. "Misha Vlas," he said, his accent a mosaic of a well-traveled life.

"Misha's a juicer out of Toronto," Ellie said smiling, ignoring Linda's pointed look.

"We don't get techies wandering out of the woodwork to volunteer. What possessed you?" Linda said with a laugh.

He shrugged. "I was bored. Rhea suggested that I help out."

Linda nodded. Another one out of that house. She was going to have to get invited over there one of these days. Ellie certainly seemed to be enjoying her adventures, and Rosalind had met Taryn. Linda's thought of Taryn was only slightly wistful.

"Good to have your help, Misha. I was just roughing out a light plot." Linda handed the paper to him. He peered at it and frowned.

"Primitive," he muttered. Ellie handed him a pencil. He folded himself into a chair and started to work.

Ellie turned around and caught the number being rehearsed onstage.

Linda looked at her and smiled. "I was thinking of charging admission to rehearsals. Cheap thrills."

"You'd make a killing. How long have they been doing that?" Ellie asked.

"Few minutes. It was 'Jailhouse Rock' before. It just started getting good when they began the soldier scene. Now, the lap dances. Actually quite a beautiful number from a tech perspective, minimal props, just some chairs, and some rope," Linda said.

"Rope?"

"You'll see, night of the show. You like it?"

"Sis, it's making me sweat watching. I think you've got a hit on your hands." The door to the house opened. Rosalind stood in the doorway, paused in the most exquisite moment of shock and desire.

Onstage the dance continued. It took a few moments to remember how to breathe. Rosalind was grateful for the loud music. It gave her cover as she made her way to the front row. Misha was slouching in a chair working on something. Ellie and Linda smiled at her with too many teeth.

"How's it going?" Ellie asked, leaning close.

"Lovely," Rosalind said, watching the stage.

Linda tapped a pencil on the arm of the seat, looking at the stage with detachment. Rosalind was an academic. She'd understand. "I think they're making remarkable progress with the bar scene, considering. I had to beat Taryn over the head to get her to do it, but it is historical. We have to remember our culture. In the fifties many women didn't have anywhere else to go but the bars. The dance floor served as courtship, flirting, even, um…"

"Sex," Rosalind said, clipped.

"Well, yes."

"Good to know that all the grinding is historically accurate. I hate to think it was gratuitous," Rosalind said, raising an eyebrow at Linda.

"For ten bucks a ticket, we do like to give some cheap thrills. For a good cause," Linda said hastily.

"Artistic vision. I admire that." Rosalind sighed.

Ellie looked back at the stage "Yep. We're all fine."

"Remember the night you took me to Marcella's?" Rosalind asked.

"Sure. My first successful play at matchmaker. Not the target I intended, but hey, can't fault the results." Ellie grinned.

Rosalind nodded. "Picture Taryn, the first moment she appeared onstage."

Ellie's face grew dreamy, then she blushed. "Oh."

"Exactly. I knew what I was getting myself in for. You can't date that boy and expect quiet nights at home knitting."

Chapter Fifteen

Misha rolled onto his stomach, pushing the pillow out of the way. Ellie sat back against the wall, combing his hair through her fingers. The bed was small for two people, set into an alcove in Joe's office. The room used to be Taryn's. Ellie remembered it from Rosalind's description of her first night at 34 Mariner. Ellie liked the way the streetlight gilded the rough plaster walls, the way the touch of the air came cool as a hand just cupping new snow. It was a place for adventure. She was having hers. There was no denying that she'd sized Misha up as good recreational fun. His accent was delicious to listen to, even if she could only believe one word out of three. He was in theater, he had the nomad's blood, and they understood one another. She wasn't expecting to start to soften toward him. He'd started to talk about his brother, just a bit at first, and everything changed. He looked less like a strutting man, and more like a brokenhearted boy.

"Quite a mane you got there, Secretariat."

"My mother used to comb my hair this way," Misha said, turning his head in profile on the pillow.

"Did Stephan have long hair?" Ellie asked. As she expected, he tensed under her hand. He forced himself to relax again.

"No. He was too fashionable. He called me Samson. His haircut was new every week. You know such men? As soon as something becomes the fashion, they have moved on already."

"That'd make me Delilah. I like it. Was his hair the same color as yours?" Ellie asked.

Misha laughed. "No. Like corn silk, that fair. Flaxen. Pretty as a girl when he was young. Women cooed when they saw him. If we did not come from the same womb, he would be taken for a Scandinavian."

Ellie pulled the sheet down to the base of his spine. The skin was still red from the new tattoo. "It looks almost finished. Rhea works fast."

The color had been added to the figure. Rhea had captured the shade of Misha's hair, given his clothing the muted palate of gray and brown. She added subtly to the strength of Taryn's lines, making a whole image. The marble had the faint rosy tint of dawn, as if the man wept over the sepulcher at first light. The second part of the tattoo had just been outlined. It was an angel, standing behind and above the weeping man with a look of profound compassion. He had the body of an Apollo, perfectly balanced, heroically naked. He might have been a pagan god come down to offer solace to a mortal favorite. The way his wings were starting to emerge looked to Ellie as if they were reaching to embrace the weeping man. But the man was beaten down by his grief, unable to feel the angel's presence.

"Do you know where he is buried?"

"No. No. I don't," Misha said in the voice of a man bleeding to death in the snow. There was a hint of comfort in the numbness.

Ellie had to curb her natural reaction. She hadn't expected it to come this soon, the moment when the effervescent flirtation of a new entanglement became simply an entanglement. The bridge between recreational fun and something more. With a guy she was sleeping with, hanging out with, having a generally very entertaining but not serious time with, it was too soon. That moment was a death knell. Ellie knew herself, and cheerfully had few illusions about her own emotional makeup. Serious was not her nature. She adored being adored, and she was a brilliant hand at a whirlwind affair. When the entanglement threatened to get dull or common, her mood caught the flu and she was gone. The problem was, this was almost before the flirtation had even begun, this note of mortality. Misha was a haunted man, and from everything she knew about this house, they meant that word in the unromantic literal sense. He carried the ghost of his brother with him and was here to heal. They'd avoided that topic artfully. He was as gifted at avoidance as she.

Here it was the gravestone in the bed. She'd asked, prompted by the image of Taryn's design, the haunted man weeping on the grave. Damn that boy anyway. *Where does she get off having the talent to tell a story with her hands?* Ellie thought. A roguish answer supplied itself immediately. She filed it away to amuse Rosalind with another time. There it was, the choice. She could heed her instinct and keep up her end of the bargain. A cheap and tawdry affair of some fun and no import. She could keep the romantic illusion that she and Misha had worked rather well to create, decorate the façade with some aside and let the matter go. Or, the stubborn voice in her head reminded her, she could talk to him as a friend. She could ignore the fact that he was a man she was sleeping with, and tell him the truth, exactly as she'd tell a friend. As she would for Rosalind, be direct and honest no matter the cost. Ellie sighed and stroked the smooth skin of Misha's back. She liked him. It was a shame to lose that this rapidly.

"That sucks," Ellie said.

"What?" Misha asked, pushing up from the pillow.

"I probably shouldn't do this, but I'm no good at doing what I should. It's a crime that you don't know where he's buried. For God's sake, you're moping around in a wallow of grief that'd make DeMille faint. People who loved him surround you. They care for you, by all signs. All you have to do is walk down the hall and ask Joe, and you haven't done it. You're feeling sorry for yourself. You're not mourning," Ellie said.

The sheet fell away from Misha's body as he sat up, leaving him exposed. He stared at Ellie wide eyed, his jaw working. He frowned. His brows drew down over the night sea of his eyes, painted with fury and wounded pride.

He said something in his polished bronze voice, growling out the Russian syllables as if he couldn't be bothered with English.

"Let me guess. That means kiss my ass," Ellie said, wondering if her ears should blister.

He rolled his shoulders like an oarsman and pushed his hair impatiently behind his ears. He snarled a few words in Russian, then switched abruptly to English. "No one has talked to me this way in years."

"Yeah, well, emotional whiplash is my specialty," Ellie said and shrugged.

Misha raised an eyebrow at her. She smiled brilliantly. *Shirley Temple, eat your heart out,* she thought.

Abruptly, he exploded into laughter, terrifying the cat that had been sleeping under the desk. "He would have liked you," Misha said when his breathing calmed.

"I hope so. He had taste. Listen, all you have to do is ask. You know the hand is there to help," Ellie said.

Misha looked at her for a long moment. "That simple?"

"Why make it tough? Just ask Joe. Then go talk to Stephan."

"There is so much to say." Misha vaulted out of bed, draping the sheet like a toga. "Come on," he said, holding out his hand.

"I didn't mean right now—" Ellie protested.

"You are right. We do it now. It is my turn to wake Joe up from his bed. You are coming along," Misha said. Ellie grabbed for her clothing.

It wasn't his dreams that woke Paul for once. It was the noise. There was a barn dance being held in Joe and Rhea's room, that or a marathon, from the sounds of thudding feet and slamming doors. He belted on the robe he'd been given. It was a soft slate blue, faded with years of use. Paul assumed it was Joe's.

A scent of cinnamon arrested him on the way to Joe's room. It wafted up the back stairs, hooking his attention. His mind was full of holes, leaking. The scent wound its way in. He was fragile as an egg after his day with Rosalind. *After dreams die, how do you get any sleep?* Paul wondered with a recognizable twinge of self-pity.

The scent of cinnamon was layered with an undernote of orange. Someone was in the kitchen. Paul glanced at the half-closed door to Joe's room. Misha's voice spilled out, loud but hard to decipher. He headed down the stairs.

Rhea was at the stove with her back to the door. "Have a seat, Paul. I'm making your tea."

Paul sat at the table as if it had always been so. "How did you know I was up?"

Rhea smiled at him. It was the first spontaneous smile he'd ever seen on her austere face. It stunned him. For a moment her somber dignity was split. The glimpse of a lively humor showed through. He saw a different woman, one that wasn't ageless and stern, one that might have been young once. One that might fall under the spell of love. "Come now. You've been here long enough. Must you ask?" Rhea said.

"I guess not," Paul admitted. He took the teacup.

Rhea sat down opposite him at the table. He'd noticed that no matter how many people sat around the table, no one ever took Rhea's chair. Her claim of place was that thorough. "It's a three-part night. Three matters on the cusp. Such business calls for a cup of tea."

Paul found comfort in the warmth of the cup in his hands, in the scent of tea, in Rhea's arcane presence. She seemed in such a good mood, he was intrigued.

"Having a good night?"

Again the smile came, of such sensual import that Paul blushed. "Oh yes. But I think Joe was going to brain Misha when he burst in. He's so shy about some things." Rhea watched Paul fidget and glance away. She smiled again. "Paul," she said. He looked back at her. "How was your day with Rosalind?"

"We had coffee. We walked in the park. We tried to see a movie. She told me she'd never be my wife again," Paul said, feeling the bile rise in his throat.

Rhea was watching him, her eyebrow raised. "Was this a surprise?"

Paul let his annoyance show, but Rhea's expression didn't change. He sighed and folded his arms on the table. "Honestly? No."

"Why not?" Rhea asked.

"She tried to tell me, a dozen ways. It didn't sink in until this afternoon. I think it was the look on her face. She wasn't saying anything. She wasn't paying any attention to me. I knew she was thinking of her."

They sat in silence and drank their tea. Paul felt light. It was like a fire had burned down in him, only the smoke drifting as evidence the burning had ever been.

"What's it all about, Rhea?" Paul asked, moved by a whim.

She looked at him and suddenly he thought of a snake about to shed its skin, eyes sparkling like black diamonds. "Love and loss. And love again."

The immediacy of her answer and the surety of it impressed him. He let the strange mood carry him off. Of course a witch would have an answer to that question. It was a serious answer, and not what he'd expected. A closer answer to the whole of things. Maybe that was the key, the immediacy. The details made up the infinite. "Makes me think of *The Worm Ouroboros*," Paul said.

"You know the sign?" Rhea asked, smiling.

"I know the novel. A high-fantasy novel written in Elizabethan English. I had a professor in college who made us chop through it. The snake with his tail in his mouth."

"Yes." Rhea had taken on the air of the Mona Lisa.

Paul felt like he was being left out of the joke. He hated to feel stupid. It left him inserting literary references into conversations where they didn't fit. It was important that people knew how smart he was. This had only become more persistent since coming here, once he saw the contrast between himself and Taryn. The thug had high-school dropout written all over her. It had been the perfect area to highlight, to get Rosalind to see the light. Intelligence was important to her, possibly the only thing she took as natural aristocracy, though she'd never say so. But all the signs were there. The people she surrounded herself with tended to be very bright.

Paul thought about Rosalind's current circle. Joe seemed like a smart guy, not a lot of formal education, but a wealth of good sense and practical knowledge. Paul had the feeling that Joe had learned his computer skills hands-on, maybe in the military. Ellie was exactly what he'd expect in a close friend of Rosalind's, bright and sharp as a cut gem, intelligent, flamboyant, a teacher and an actor, all things that charmed Rosalind.

Rhea was more of a surprise. There was little to suggest common ground between the two women, but the bond of mutual respect was impossible to miss. Rhea's knowledge came from other sources. Mysticism had never interested Rosalind. On a few occasions he'd witnessed an actual hostility toward fortune telling, a reaction that Rosalind didn't seem to understand any better than he did. She'd managed to overcome that antipathy. Now she was closely tied to a witch, even assisting her in ritual. Paul was glad for this. He liked Rhea. All aspects of her personality spoke of control. It was comforting to be around such surety and steadiness.

The piece that didn't fit was Taryn. Paul found Rhea looking at him with the same gleam of humor. "I'm not an idiot, you know. I understand the symbolism, the snake with its tail in its mouth, the endless circle, the seasons, birth and death. I get it. It's not a hard concept."

"I've no doubt that you can analyze the symbolism. I bet you can even trace it back to the various cultures that used it. You can give a thorough anthropological presentation on its origins. You are a very educated fellow. That's what's getting in your way," Rhea said calmly.

"Right. I have to *feel* it in my heart, not *know* it with my head. I've heard it before. Anti-intellectual crap. There's nothing wrong with knowledge," Paul said.

Rhea raised an eyebrow. "I agree. But there is more than one way of knowing."

Paul shook his head. "Rhea, I don't want to argue with you. I'll grant that you seem to know things, and I won't hazard a guess as to how."

"Certainly you want to argue with me. It makes you feel strong. Nothing wrong with that. We all use it. But you need to be clear on your own motivations before you can fathom anyone else's."

"Now we're getting into pop psychology. I thought you magic people were above that," Paul said sarcastically.

"Ever the Western Man. Child of reason. Very well, we'll use that." Rhea stared into Paul's eyes. He felt naked. He felt her looking straight through to the back of his skull. "You cannot fathom Taryn's place in Rosalind's affection. It is the one matter you hold on to, unable to be free. What I say will not be able to answer that for you. Magic will not. So be a scientist. Observe your subject with perfect detachment. Record all evidence. Convince yourself."

Paul started to sweat. Had she just done what he thought she had?

"Yes, I did. I prefer not to. It's a tangled, messy way to work. But when you live with people the barriers get thinner. You get used to it. It's what you need. That's the final step in your healing. I'm telling you to do it. You have the justification you need."

"What?"

Rhea stood up. "It sounds like Misha is done. I can have Joe back. Good night, Paul."

"Wait. You have these cryptic half conversations. What do you expect me to make of them? What am I supposed to do?"

"You already know that."

"I just don't know," Paul said miserably.

Rhea reached out and touched his hand. He was surprised out of his mood at the cool feel of her fingers. She looked at him with what could only be kindness. "Don't fall so in love with being hungry that you forget what it's like to eat. Good night."

Rosalind sat on the edge of the couch pressed up against Taryn's thigh. She had her arms wrapped around Taryn's neck and was kissing her with all the semblance of passion. It was a calculated kiss, the form of desire without the substance, the empty skin of abandon. Rosalind wanted badly to feel the madness she had always felt in her boy's arms, the energy that jumped whenever they were skin to skin. It would not come, though she called to it. Desire was a strange beast, skittish to the extended hand, willful. Instead of drowning, she felt the old silence in her flesh and it chilled her. It was like being packed in clay, the removal from her flesh. The wall was back between her body and mind, the wall she thought was torn down forever. She could not stop the endless loop of her mind. Paul had said horrible things, but she didn't have to let them affect her. Just words. What did it matter what other people really thought about her and her lover? The outside world had no power over them. Except, it did. Maybe it would be better if she tried harder.

Rosalind stuck her tongue into Taryn's mouth. Did she usually do it this way? It was hard to think when she kissed Taryn. Left or right? Did she pull on the lower lip with her teeth, or was that later? Rosalind was busy with the checklist in her head and so was surprised when Taryn pulled away. "Wait," Taryn said inches from Rosalind's lips.

"Wha—?" She didn't register the word. It was one that didn't make any sense in the situation. Rosalind leaned back in.

"Wait," Taryn said firmly, setting her hands on Rosalind's shoulders.

"What's wrong?" Rosalind asked, feeling the coldness seep into her chest.

Eyes like the edge of a knife stared her down. "You're not here," Taryn said, her voice a warning rumble.

Rosalind pushed the hair back behind her ears. "Of course I am," she said, trying to sound steady.

"Bullshit. I know about going away. Don't lie to me. If you don't want me touching you all you have to do is say so. Don't wait for me to figure it out." Taryn sat back on the couch, her body closing off.

"Honey, no, that's not…"

There was candor in the level gaze that was frightening to face. Taryn could tell the difference when she was shamming passion and would not settle for it. What they shared had no room for a counterfeit. "Then tell me the truth."

"It's me. It's like I'm back in high school. There's this wall up between what I know and what I want to feel. It's never happened with you. I actually thought it'd never happen to me again once I met you. Passion has never been a problem with us, you know?" Rosalind laughed slightly.

The blue eyes softened immediately. "Yeah. I know."

"Like there was this special dispensation I received, once I came out. Never have any sexual hang-ups again," Rosalind said.

Taryn's mouth curled, half grimace, half smile. "Doesn't work that way. If it did, you can bet it'd be on the recruiting posters."

"I missed the posters, too? I never get to see anything," Rosalind said. She felt some of the ice in her chest start to melt. Just talking to Taryn was helping.

"When did it start?" Taryn asked.

"Today. When I was out with Paul."

Taryn nodded. "Oh."

"I hate this! I don't want to be this way. I don't want to be unable to feel you. It's ghastly. What if I never snap out of it? What if you're stuck with me, but I'm this block of ice? God, I don't know what I'd do if—"

Taryn reached out and pulled Rosalind down. "Come here."

Rosalind settled in against Taryn's chest. She closed her eyes, feeling the steady drum of Taryn's heart.

"What did you and Paul talk about that got you upset?"

Rosalind was surprised that Taryn used his name. She'd been getting better about hearing about him, but this was the first time she'd prompted for information.

"You. He warned me against you." Rosalind said.

The muscles along Taryn's jaw clenched, but she stayed still. "Okay. What did he say?"

"You're too young for me. We're from different backgrounds. It will never work. That sort of thing," Rosalind said wearily.

"It makes sense to ask. Really, looking at it from outside, from his perspective, how can he think anything else?"

"Now I know you're trying too hard. Who'd you rehearse that line with?" Rosalind asked.

"Linda."

"At least she's good. Care to tell me what you're really thinking?"

"I think I'd still like to hit him, sometimes. He keeps looking at me when we're working and it makes me nervous. But I'm sick of hating him. I don't care if he's a rat bastard. It's harder to hate him, after meeting him. I feel bad for the guy, you know? I took his place. He's got to be eaten up inside from that."

"I know."

Taryn pushed away and sat up. Rosalind could see the cloud roiling around her again, darker in color this time, blocking out more light. It made paying attention to her words harder. "He's the guy you... loved, before me."

"He was always my best friend. He knew me better than anyone else when we were growing up."

"Yeah, well, there you go. Part of why I haven't wanted to be buddy-buddy with him."

"You know you have nothing to be worried about. I left him before I met you. We settled worse than this from the past already with Rhea. If you could stop her death, you can do anything. We can do anything."

"Would you leave me for him? This time. Would you?" Taryn asked.

"Have you forgotten that there are other women in the world?" Rosalind asked at last.

"Of course not," Taryn said, sounding puzzled.

"Paul will always be around, in one way or another. He's always been in my life. But I would no more leave you for him than I would leave you at all. He's not a threat to you, baby. The outside world exists. We just have to take it on faith that we are both in this together."

"The day I hit Paul, there was this girl at the coffee shop. I could have had her for the asking. She was cute and interested. I thought I'd already blown it with you. But I didn't go for it." Taryn's voice came dark and brooding.

"Why not?" Rosalind asked, wanting to hear the answer.

"She didn't have what I need," Taryn said, her lips pressing into Rosalind's hair. "Only you. I don't care what we go through. Only you."

Rosalind had slept well in the circle of Taryn's arms. Her mind had grown quiet with Taryn's confident silence. She'd let herself relax into it, let her body revel in the warmth of Taryn's without any further thought. Simple, animal pleasure, the comfort of another body pressed up against hers on a cold night. When she woke, Taryn's arm was still draped across her waist, the large hand resting in the hollow of her belly. A squint-eyed look confirmed what Rosalind thought—the cloud was gone. Might have just subsided for the moment, but there was a faint glow around Taryn. Could be the early-morning light, the light of new beginnings.

Winter was coming. Frost carved fans in the corners of the bay window, reaching out tendrils along the leading of the glass. The light of dawn was tentative, silver and gossamer, precognitive of the distant winter sun. Rosalind could feel the air, greedy for the body heat hidden under the piled blankets on the bed.

Fall was such a short season here. If she hadn't been falling in love as the leaves were changing, would she have missed the colors? It was easy to imagine herself buried in work, glancing up in mid-October to find the sky gone a sullen gray, the trees bare and black. Beauty was short-lived in this environment.

Rosalind felt the warm hand stroking lazily along her thigh and rethought. Not short-lived, just changeable, capable of hibernating through the harshest cold. As if in confirmation, her nerve endings woke to a slow burn under Taryn's trailing fingers. Rosalind smiled with the discovery. When you weren't looking, life triumphed. She rolled over and kissed Taryn.

Chapter Sixteen

Paul's hand skimmed with precision across the surface of the plaster like an expert skier on a favorite mountain. He took a step back, surveying his work with satisfaction. It was a joy to be doing something well. He'd discovered he was good at the plasterwork, good enough for Joe to assign the job to him and leave him alone with it. Joe and Misha were trying to finish the floors in the living room. Misha had come late to the house, roaring up on his motorcycle with Ellie on the back. They both looked like they hadn't slept, but they were dancing with energy, the riotous happiness of all-night celebration. Ellie was wearing Misha's leather jacket. She had kissed him soundly before she let him get off the bike, the first display of affection Paul had seen between them. Misha had thrown back his dark head and laughed. He'd tossed the keys to Ellie, bowing like a squire to his knight. "The road is yours." Joe hugged Misha when he saw him, nearly making Paul faint. They set to work without a word, grinning at one another like schoolboys.

Taryn was at the kitchen table, bent over her sketchbook. She'd been late in getting to the house as well, with a similarly joyous spring in her step. Paul had retreated into the bedroom, glad of a task to occupy his hands and free his mind. Everyone had been to Mardi Gras last night, and he hadn't been invited. Paul glanced around the corner. He could, if he craned his neck, see her back and right arm.

He was used to seeing her in constant motion, brimming with

the restless teenage energy he envied and feared. The best word he had for her was *explosive*, in movement and emotion. The contemplative nature of her pose now mesmerized him. He wondered what she was working on.

The plaster was drying. It was as smooth as the inside of an egg. He cast a proud glance at it. Now was a perfectly natural time for him to take a break, maybe walk to the kitchen and get a drink. A beer, Paul reminded himself. A man on a break from working around the house drank beer. So it was ten o'clock in the morning. It was never too cold or too early for beer on the border of Buffalo and southern Ontario. The way the house was set up he'd have to squeeze past the table to get into the kitchen. This brought him into range of Taryn, and not coincidentally, her sketchbook.

Rhea's words had haunted Paul all night. He had his excuse now. He knew what to do. Or so she'd said. He doubted it. The witch had never stated what it was he was supposed to do. Paul had responded to the sessions with Rhea, even come to enjoy the healing, but it had all been passive. He lay where he was told, drank the teas she prepared, and breathed the bitter smoke of strange, burning herbs. He nodded as she made cryptic comments to Rosalind about his energy and his aura. None of it required him to think or to act. He was still safe in his distance from the weird rites of these people, an accidental anthropologist blundered into the lost tribes of the modern pagans. None of it would stay with him after he left.

But if she was proposing what he imagined…if she had looked into his head, she might have seen it. The one desire Paul hesitated to admit even to himself, the oldest longing he had ever possessed. The desire to belong, to put down the trappings of civilization and superiority and join in the ritual. To abandon all sense of distance and surrender himself to a group of people, to be one of them.

No one had answered his question: Why did Rosalind love Taryn? He knew now that it was a question that could only be answered from the inside. He knew that Rosalind had crossed that barrier, that she was as at home here as she had ever been anywhere. More, she had always been seeking a home that she seemed to have found in the skin-painted, sociopathic, bull dagger pretty boy who was her lover. The unstable combination of violence and sullen, seething anger stretched like the head of a drum across some unfathomable well of charisma. If he wanted the knowledge he would have to descend into the underworld after it, like Orpheus, like Gilgamesh. He would have to admit that he wanted to belong, to know them, all of them. Even Taryn.

She sat straddling the chair as if it might rear up and gallop off. Her black T-shirt had the sleeves ripped off. Paul found himself staring at the tattoo on her bicep, into the leonine gaze of the immortal boy king. He hadn't really noticed it before, not enough to recognize who it was. The far-seeing eyes looked right through him as he passed. Her right arm was shielding the sketchbook. Paul knew that she designed tattoos. The household attested to her prolific output. He'd seen Misha's work and Joe's, as well as the graphic novel she'd made of her own skin. Perhaps that was what she was working on now.

He pulled a beer out of the refrigerator. Curiosity bit at him. He wasn't sure. Maybe Rhea meant something else. Maybe it was going to be a disaster. Paul strolled back to the table. "Want a beer?" he asked, clearing his throat.

Taryn looked up as if puzzled. Misha and Joe had gone out on the porch. He had to be addressing her.

Paul watched the spark of suspicion flare in her eyes, then die. She nodded slowly, as if making a decision of grave import. She took the bottle he extended. Then, almost as an afterthought, she smiled at him. Paul felt it like a silver arrow piercing his chest. He remembered vividly one summer he'd spent at a camp in the Catskills, he'd seen a dragonfly appear over a mountain lake. It had hung there before his startled and grateful eyes, iridescent and incandescent in the last spears of afternoon sun. He felt that exact emotion again, captured by the unexpected pleasure of Taryn's smile. He felt generous and proud, basking in Taryn's recognition. On impulse he sat down at the table.

They sat looking gingerly at one another across the table, testing the truce. Paul felt the weight of the silence. He glanced down at the bottle, observed the pattern in the wood-grain paneling just over Taryn's left shoulder, feeling as awkward as a naked man in church.

"How's the plasterwork going?" Taryn asked.

Paul looked up, startled and grateful. "Good. I, uh, finished the wall. Like Joe wanted."

"Is it dry?" Taryn asked.

He wasn't sure if she was feigning interest, but it was the first conversation they'd had that didn't involve a third party or violence, or both. She seemed to be making an effort. That alone was worth gold. "Drying, I think," he said.

She folded the sketchbook. "I should get to work. I can lay down the color as it dries."

She pushed back from the table, tilting the chair up on two legs. Paul mastered the urge to tell her to keep all four legs on the floor.

"What are you painting?" he asked on impulse. She seemed to be in a very good mood. It was worth the risk. His standard of measurement was fairly low. If she wasn't hitting him or breaking things, she was in a good mood.

Taryn's head tilted. "A mural for the bedroom. My bride gift."

He could tell that she didn't expect him to understand. This must be some custom of the household, either an ancient one revived or a new one cobbled together. Paul had read about bride gifts in the Old World. He thought they were along the lines of a dowry, given to the husband to be as part of the marriage contract. The way Taryn said it, the gift seemed intended for Rhea. He couldn't imagine Taryn providing a dowry, paying Joe to marry Rhea. In the upending of roles that these people indulged in, Taryn was taking on the giving away of the bride, the father's place. This must be a part of that. She was also standing as Joe's best man, a topic Paul did not feel ready to tackle just yet. "Oh, right. For giving Rhea away," Paul said casually. He enjoyed the way Taryn's eyes narrowed. "Are you doing a decorative border? Texture? Sponge work?"

Taryn pushed the sketchbook toward him. He opened it. When his eyes took in the image, Paul had to admit that he'd been expecting something else entirely. Based on the tattoos he had seen he thought perhaps a geometric design, perhaps a gaudy, cartoonish picture. This was the framework of a true painting. It was roughed out in charcoal, vast slabs of darkness pierced with riotous white flame spilling out of the gaping maw of the underworld in the lower right corner. The eye was drawn to it, down and away from a field of asphodel and hyacinths.

A woman sat in the field, surrounded by flowers bent down, in homage or shared longing. She looked austere and composed over a core of profound sadness, a woman who had experienced the depths of love and loss. Even in the sketch, she had Rhea's face.

On a level below speech, he felt the story in the pit of his stomach. He knew the myth of Demeter and Persephone, the explanation of how spring and winter came to be. It was before his mind could form the words, make the right footnote to his encyclopedic knowledge that the heart of the story hit him in the animal center of his brain. He felt it flood his veins. Loss and anguish and vain seeking over the whole earth for the beloved girl stolen away by death. This painting took the impact one moment further, right to the brink of reunion. For out of the open mouth of the underworld walked the daughter of the Goddess, bringing the celebration of all living things in her wake. In her footsteps the grass sprang to life. The hyacinths bloomed round their bloodstained hearts, blazoned with Apollo's mournful cry. Death and life and death again, spinning. The painting showed an ending and promised a beginning. He knew he was crying before the tears spilled.

"This is wonderful," Paul said thickly.

"Thanks. For Rhea it had to be," Taryn said. In a show of tact he didn't expect, she pretended not to notice his tears. It was a gesture he found comforting. It was as if this girl had a sense that it was difficult for a man to be seen crying. The delicacy of her response was completely out of character for the teenage sociopath he imagined. Perhaps it was just the instinct to shy away from emotion, but that didn't seem to be the case. In most of the moments he had witnessed, Taryn was like a drunken man, lurching headlong into emotion with abandon. Violent, he could attest to, and explosive. Even brooding or coldly indifferent. Delicate, he would never have credited.

"It's missing something," Paul said.

The hard, wary look came into her eyes like the flicking open of a switchblade.

"It's a wedding gift, right? It's perfect for Rhea. But I don't see Joe in it."

Taryn gaped at the picture. "But…"

"I know it's for Rhea. And for that I think it's perfect. I've only been around for a short time, but this feels like an old image. You're going to put this on the west wall, right?" Paul asked, tapping the sketchbook.

"Yeah," Taryn said.

"If you look at the image it looks like Demeter is gazing off to the east. Paint something for Joe on the east wall. She can be looking at him," Paul said.

Taryn went still as a stag catching wind of a hunter. Abruptly she shoved away from the table, so swiftly that her chair banged into the wall. Paul flinched.

She stormed down the hall. "Come on. We have to look at the space."

Egyptia pushed the hair of her modest daytime wig back behind her ears. "Okay. Checklist. We got sweet rolls and cinnamon buns, coffee, cigarettes for Taryn, you for Taryn, and evil notes for Misha from that devil doll Ellie."

"Are you sure it won't look too suspicious?" Rosalind asked her.

Egyptia patted her on the knee. "Honey, we are just a couple of girls bringing coffee and sugar to our hardworking men. What could be less suspicious than that?"

Rosalind looked at the porch where Joe and Misha were lounging. "Twelve ninjas dancing on the lawn? Oh, all right. We're checking up on them and they'll know it. Let's get it over with."

"Yoo-hoo!" Egyptia called, waving her arm. She sashayed toward the porch carrying a covered basket on her arm.

"Is this Little Red Riding Hood I see?" Misha asked.

Rosalind looked at Misha and nearly dropped what she was carrying. The air around him was clear. The last time she'd seen him, he was covered in a cloud, wearing his grief like a blanket. Now, overnight, he was a window catching the light. Lucent. Paul still showed signs of his cloud, and Taryn's seemed to come and go, but Misha had lost his. She would have to ask Ellie.

"Only if you be my big bad wolf. But I hear you're showing your sharp pointy teeth to Miss Ellie nowadays. So nice to leave a girl out on the real juicy gossip. Move your big old boots, I am walking here." Egyptia stepped delicately over Misha's legs.

Joe stood up, smiling and holding out his arms. "Rosalind! An unexpected pleasure. What brings you up to Canada?"

Rosalind hugged him. "I thought you guys could use some pampering. You've all been working so hard."

"She came to see if Taryn was varnishing the floor with Paul's brain," Misha said, taking the basket from Egyptia. "Are those sweet rolls?"

Egyptia smacked his hand. "Get out of there. You got to save some for the rest of the men. Come to think of it, why are you just lazing around on the porch? Where are the other worker bees?"

"Paul and Taryn are in the bedroom," Misha said.

"You left them alone?" Rosalind asked, incredulous.

"They were getting along. Taryn was in a remarkably good mood this morning. It didn't seem dangerous," Joe said.

"It has been quiet for a long while. Perhaps we shall find Taryn painting the walls with blood," Misha said cheerfully. He tried to steal a roll from the basket.

"That's enough out of you. I'm not having you scare my girl Rosalind. Ignore the savage, honey. Why don't you bring the coffee in to your boy?" Egyptia handed the thermos to a grateful Rosalind.

"Thanks, I will."

The hallway was unnaturally quiet, giving Rosalind's apprehension a feast to gnaw. She saw, in a moment's horrible flight of fancy, Misha's suggestion. She was brought to the edge of riot by her own imagination, that gleeful part of her that indulged in the worst-case scenario. When she opened the door and saw Taryn, arm crimson to the elbow, hovering above Paul, she jumped.

"Lay down the blue next, Taryn?" Paul asked, standing up. He was facing the west wall, painting in a careful, tentative motion.

"No. Hit the black around the edges of the flame." Taryn was standing next to him, her black shirt speckled with red drops, rivulets running from the brush in her right hand. She was painting in furious arcs, the energy of the strokes making the painted flames dance and hiss. She stood before the mouth to the underworld, framed by coal and scarlet. "I'll lay down the fire. You do the sky. The flowers can wait."

"Good morning," Rosalind said, her voice rich with delight. Paul didn't look beaten. Taryn didn't look enraged. Nothing was inflamed in the air around them. They looked for all the world as if they were working together. Somewhere clocks were running backward, it was snowing out of sunny skies, and dogs were giving birth to kittens.

Taryn looked over her shoulder and broke into the most marvelous smile. "Hey."

"Rosalind! Didn't expect to see you here," Paul said. He sounded good. The tone was so unusual for him that it took Rosalind a moment to place. It was enthusiasm she heard in his voice, an excitement she hadn't heard in years.

"Egpytia and I thought coffee and sweets might be appreciated." Rosalind held up the thermos. She spied the beer bottles on the floor and looked accusingly at Taryn.

"It was his idea," Taryn said.

"You guys have been busy. What are you working on?" Rosalind asked, looking at the brightly splashed wall.

Taryn picked up a rag and dabbed awkwardly at the red river covering her hands. Rosalind set the thermos down and reached automatically for the cloth, taking Taryn's large hands between hers. She efficiently toweled the paint from Taryn's fingers as if it were the most natural thing in the world that she would take intimate control of Taryn's body.

Paul cleared his throat. "Coffee sounds like just the thing. You have cups?"

Rosalind handed the cloth back to Taryn. "No, I don't. I'll go get some."

"I'll go." He scooped up the beer bottles and spirited them away.

Rosalind reclaimed Taryn's hands. "Here. You have some left. You're as bad as a six-year-old. Paint everywhere."

"You won't retrain me if I get you to clean me up," Taryn said with a carnivore's smile.

The motion of the cloth slowed and became a caress. "I don't want to retrain you. I like you the way you are."

"Looking like I got dipped in blood?" Taryn asked, her eyebrows rising.

"Looking like you'd do anything for me. You were working with

Paul. I never expected that," Rosalind said. She pulled Taryn closer. "You amaze me."

"Got to hand it to Gordy. It was his idea," Taryn said. The traces of scarlet were still on her fingers. She stroked Rosalind's neck with the back of her hand.

"Gordy? Oh, Taryn. Tell me you haven't named him for the Gordian knot."

"He doesn't know. It won't hurt him. Take a look at this. It was his idea. He said Joe was missing from the painting. So we added to it." Taryn nodded at the east wall. Faintly, like a spider's web tracing on the fresh plaster was an outline. Rosalind walked closer.

She had to be in intimate space to see it. It was a man with stag's horns on his head, wearing an open-ended collar of thick metal. His bare chest was covered in tattoos of interwoven snakes. Breeches held up by a broad leather belt cased his legs. A cloak designed with spiral patterns was thrown across one broad shoulder. In his right hand he held out a wine goblet of beaten silver. His left hand rested on the head of a wild boar. His face was wreathed in a welcoming smile, the lord of the revels, the wild man of the woods. A hearty, powerfully built man, known alike to farmers and soldiers.

"If you look at Demeter, she's looking this way. So I put him in. I thought about Dionysus, but Joe's not really like that," Taryn said.

No, Rosalind thought. *Dionysus is a dreamer driven to ecstasy and madness, the sullen, beautiful young man beloved of the goddess. Not Joe.*

"Joe's the Green Man, the father of the world, the lord of animals and growing things. Cernunnos was perfect. I think Gordy was flat-out stunned that an illiterate like me knew anything about mythology. You don't come of age in a witch's house without learning," Taryn said.

Taryn had turned to look at the outline, her eyes shining as if she could see the finished painting already. "He was right. Joe needed to be there. And I'd never get this done without help. We're going into tech week with the show. I'm not saying I don't have the urge to slug him anymore. Just not as much." Taryn shook her head at the wall, amused by her own mood.

"Do you have any idea of the effect you have?" Rosalind asked.

"On what?" Taryn asked, tilting her head.

"On everyone around you. On me."

Paul returned from the kitchen, three cups swinging from his knuckles. The selection of coffee mugs took time. The memory of Taryn's rage and the explosion triggered by the blue glass mug was still fresh. He hesitated over choosing a mug for Taryn, even though the mugs up at the lake house were ceramic odds and ends without any personal claimants. There was one of a dusty gray glaze speckled with slate blue points that reminded him of twilight over the lake. That was the one for Taryn. For himself it was easy, a warm brown mug like burnt sugar; for Rosalind, a heavy white mug obviously stolen from a diner on some drunken night. On the bottom was a handful of Greek letters in minute script. It fit her new life. He imagined that she would like it.

Taryn was standing by the east wall framed by the drawing of Cernunnos. The towel had left a faint ruddy hue along her arms, outlining the long muscles. She looked like a Minoan prince standing before a fresco at the Palace of Knossos. The impression she gave of royalty was enhanced by the woman who pressed against her, arms entwined around Taryn's neck. In a gesture of melting tenderness, one red-stained hand lifted the hair away from Rosalind's face. The color of blood showed through the electrum strands, concealing nothing. Rosalind gazed on Taryn with adoration.

It was the first time he'd caught them together, unguarded. It hurt exactly as much as he thought it would, bludgeoning the air from his chest, splintering his ribs. He stood and let the pain wash over him. It was too late to flinch away. He was tired of running. The worst had happened. Paul was tired of feeling exhausted and brutalized. Inside, a fundamental stubbornness he'd all but forgotten woke. It dug in its heels and refused to move. So he stood his ground and stared into the room, letting the pain come like waves. And in the pain was release, and in the pain was redemption. His scarred emotions reeled under the onslaught, but he'd had more pain from imagining what this would be like, over the years. All the times when Rosalind had turned him gently away, unable to offer any explanation as to why she didn't feel what he felt, had hurt more than this. Now, just on the other side of the pain, was the explanation. There was nothing abstract about it. She loved the girl who was also her boy. It hurt his eyes to look, but it didn't blind him. He found that as he breathed and looked on, it became easier. The pain receded. Maybe, just maybe, the look of answering love in Taryn's eyes was a balm to him. It did assuage one of his fears, that Rosalind would throw away the treasure of her heart on a thug unable to keep or value it. Stanley Kowalski this girl might be, but there was a hint of Romeo there, too. Maybe he would never truly understand. But he could acknowledge that it existed, the bond between them.

After the pain was a moment of calm, the cessation of hurt enough to make him dizzy. Paul gratefully took the peace it offered, like a sick man reaching for medicine. *Enough,* he thought. *Let something else begin now.* "I brought three cups, but there was no milk in the fridge. Just beer," Paul said walking into the room.

Rosalind reacted to the sound of his voice. She didn't jump away from Taryn, but she did unwind her arms and pick up the thermos. "Not to worry. Taryn takes it black, I'm learning to adjust."

Paul feigned a shudder. "Ugh. It might take me a while to catch up with all these new tastes you're developing."

Rosalind held out the coffee, pausing over his mug. "Can you manage for now?"

Paul glanced at Taryn, who stood behind Rosalind with her thumbs hooked in her pockets. The Minoan prince was gone, subsumed in the very modern teenage slouch of her long body. Yet the look on her face, for all its youth, was alert and knowing. Her eyes were ancient, blue as the cobalt-glazed tiles of the Ishtar Gate in Babylon. Not a friend, exactly. Perhaps, not exactly an enemy.

"Yeah. Yeah, I think I can manage," Paul said, taking the mug.

CHAPTER SEVENTEEN

T he painting of the mural launched a week of furious activity on both sides of the border. With the show and the wedding both set for the same night, the thirty-first, it was decided that the ceremony would take place at midnight after the show. It was also decided that it would take place on the beach before a great bonfire, befitting the holiday. "Let the dead know where they are welcome," Rhea had said. Paul's distorted sense of time was confirmed when he found that comment easy to accept, literally and ritualistically. It was Samhain. Of course the dead would be attending the wedding.

The men worked to put the finishing touches on the house. He had been assigned, by his own desire, to finishing the murals with Taryn. They worked with energy, she laying down the patterns, he following with color. Every day by midafternoon she had to leave to make it to rehearsal.

Paul felt a deep sense of pride that he was trusted to continue the work with Taryn gone. A rough camaraderie had evolved between them. He felt safe in talking about the work, in handing her a beer, but not in pushing beyond those limits. Rosalind was a topic avoided mutually. But his curiosity about Taryn, now released from the cage of hate, was ravenous. Every moment he spent working with her revealed new contradictions. An incisive mind but no formal education, a violent temper given to moments of great tenderness, a sullen teenager with a confounding charisma. He knew nothing about her beyond the fragmented, mythic history of her place in the household. Where did she grow up? What events had formed her frightening attitude, her ironclad sense of self? His own sense of who he was seemed so permeable in comparison. Paul felt attracted and intimidated by her powerful sense of identity.

He tried, the day after Rosalind's visit, to engage her in conversation. They had finished the bower in which Cernunnos stood and were putting the tips on the boar's bristles. Taryn handed him a small brush for the detail work.

"The green branches look great behind his cloak. You never think of Buffalo as green. Reminds me of Poughkeepsie, actually. Did you grow up around here?" he asked, deciding on a casual approach.

She was working on the highlight along the boar's tusk. The brush moved slowly, delicate in her large hand. There were scars on her knuckles that extended onto the back of the hand like fine white drops of rain. He wondered how she'd gotten them. "Most people would say I never grew up," Taryn said when her hand paused.

He tried a different tack. "Where did you learn to paint?"

"By painting."

Paul laughed, a short, nervous chuckle. She wasn't making this easy. "No, I mean, did you study it in school, did you take lessons...?" He trailed off when he felt the weight of her eyes. She was looking at him the way a warrior might look at an anthropologist who asked her to explain the significance of the ax she wore.

"No," Taryn said, returning to the boar.

"You have a gift. I've always envied artists. I think a lot of academics do. We spend so much time in criticism that we miss creating," Paul said. If getting her to talk about herself was impossible, he found it easy to start talking to Taryn about himself. Her silence could be taken as welcoming. It wasn't the silence of a statue or an animal, uncomprehending, it was a fulsome silence of varied depths, and he sank into it. The occasional sidelong glances she gave him held the force of meaning. He could see how Rosalind could have been mesmerized by them, if Taryn ever unleashed the force of her personality.

"What do you teach?" Taryn asked. The sound of her voice was a surprise.

"English. Like Rosalind." He couldn't help adding the last piece of information.

Taryn stopped painting. The brush balanced between her fingers, tapping on her knuckles. "She's not a critic."

"Pardon me?"

"She teaches. She creates. You have the same education," Taryn said. "Maybe you're just a critic."

Paul felt the blood rise in his face from this unexpected attack. He turned away, furious. Here he was, making an effort, and all this thug could do was slap him down. He thought they'd been getting along. It had all been an act, a sham. To think he'd found something interesting about this brute—

Taryn's laughter rang in his ears. "You should see your face. It's purple." He turned to look at her. She laughed louder. "You are so easy to get. Like a grumpy old bear, poked with sticks till it wakes up and roars." She slapped him on the back. He ducked his head. "You're all right, Gordy. Relax. I won't go rough on you."

He smiled ruefully at his own hair-trigger reflexes. "Yeah. Heh."

"Finish this up, will you? I've got to fly. Linda's doing the dance numbers before tech tonight." She stood up and stretched extravagantly. She'd mentioned the show in passing. Joe and Misha had as well, but no one had told him anything about it. He felt like he was finally finding a place here. Being left out was irksome.

"So what's this big show you're doing?" Paul asked.

Taryn tilted her head and smiled in a way both lazy and seductive, like a drowsy panther casting an eye at a deer. "It's a fundraiser."

He felt put off. It wasn't information enough. This show was important enough for Taryn to abscond from the work on the house every afternoon, for Joe and Rhea to schedule their wedding for midnight. And Rosalind, though she would never mention it, seemed transported when it turned up in conversation. The whole household and the assorted visitors were all involved in one fashion or another. He felt that, if he were ever going to truly belong here, he'd have to be a part of this, too. "What kind of show is it?" Paul asked stubbornly.

"A drag show," Taryn said, watching him.

"Sounds like fun. Do I get to go?"

Taryn looked at him as if he'd sprouted horns. "You're kidding," Taryn said, her tone making it half a question.

"I'm not. Every single human being attached to the house is going. I'd like to come." He hadn't expected this. Taryn seemed baffled.

"It's not your scene." Taryn shrugged into her jacket, apparently considering the conversation finished.

She was walking away. It brought the humiliation in him back to a boil. "My scene? Jesus Christ! Not a single thing in this misbegotten town was my scene, but I moved in. I put up with it. Now that it's starting to make sense you're going to tell me I can't come along?" He acted without thinking. He grabbed her arm.

It was like grabbing the tail of a tiger. Taryn moved like a whirlwind. Paul was left holding an empty sleeve. The unholy light was back in her eyes, the easily sparked rage. He could see her tremble with it, and he backed away, clutching the jacket. "What the fuck is the matter with you?" Taryn snarled.

"I just—"

She tore the jacket back out of his hands. "Finish the painting. Don't mess with things that don't concern you." She walked away without a backward look.

❖

Having an open-door policy is a wonderful thing, Rosalind mused, *until you need to close your door.* She'd been trying frenziedly to get through the stack of essays before her office hours started. She could have finished them if she'd come in that morning, but somehow, she ended up taking coffee and cinnamon buns to Canada. After finding Taryn and Paul working together, getting along, she couldn't leave. Work seemed much less important than witnessing a miracle.

It was hard to tear herself away. It was always hard to leave Taryn. She let a portion of her mind wonder about that as she worked like a demon. It wasn't getting any easier as time went on. Even knowing that Taryn all but officially lived with her at 41 Mariner wasn't helping. They'd decided to make the official date for her moving out after the wedding. It had a nice symmetry to it. She did have Taryn's boots under her bed every night. That should sustain her. "I think I'm past the point where sustaining is enough. I want it all," Rosalind said to the paper in her hand.

"I don't know if an essay can give it to you," Ellie said.

"It could have the decency to try. That's all I ask," Rosalind said, smiling. "What are you doing here? I thought you were tearing up the open road on Misha's bike."

"I wanted to come back to earth for a minute." Ellie sighed. She moved a stack of papers and sat down in the chair next to Rosalind's desk.

"Just as well. I need to ask you something. What in the world did you and Misha do the other night? I went up to the lake house, to see how the work was going, and he was clear. No cloud."

"We saw his brother. It was a little bit my fault. He was moping, so I called him on it. I may have called him a Slavic Norma Desmond. I don't exactly recall. I told him I didn't think it had to be such a big deal. Find out where your brother is buried and go talk to him. It's the kind of conversation that nobody else can have for you."

"So he did?"

"We did. We went down and woke up Joe, who has to be the best-natured person ever. He didn't throw things at us, he rubbed his eyes and told us where Stephan was buried. So we hopped on Misha's bike and tore out there."

"Where is he buried?"

"South of the city, on a hill overlooking the lakeshore. Rhea had the land. Beautiful spot, really. Joe and Ray paid to put up a nice stone."

"Did Misha talk to his brother?"

"Oh, he did. He approached the grave on his knees, he wept, he prostrated himself on it. I don't know enough Russian to know what he said, but I got the gist. It was all forms of I'm sorry, and you're a bastard to have left me. It sounded like that to me, from the cadence. When he was done, he pushed back up and sat for a long time, then we went back to 34 Mariner."

"So Stephan didn't talk back to him."

"Not at the gravesite. Really, I suggested that because it was symbolic, and Misha seemed to need a symbol. No, it was just him talking at the grave. I know it made him feel better to finally say those things. He even looks lighter to me."

"Well, good for him. Maybe that's all we can expect, a one-sided conversation with the dead. Doesn't mean we stop needing to talk."

"What about you? Been keeping busy?"

"The show, the wedding. I'm trying to get everything done so I can be free all weekend. What possessed me to assign so many papers?" Rosalind asked helplessly.

"You should teach acting. We rarely have to correct papers. Can't you play hooky with me? We never get to see one another." Ellie gave Rosalind her best plaintive, wide-eyed look.

Rosalind shook her head. "I refuse to fall for that. We never see one another because you're off at rehearsal every night, because you're at the house with Misha. Shall I go on?"

"No need, I get your thrust. You have office hours soon?"

"Any minute. And I get to start off with a problem, just to make the day special." Rosalind frowned at the paper in her hand, then shoved it back into the stack.

"So I should enact the better part of valor and bug off? Not until you tell me what the problem is," Ellie said.

"I could use your perspective. I have a student who hasn't handed in a single assignment since the first week of class," Rosalind said.

"Ouch. It's already mid-term. Naturally you asked why. What was the response? Illness, family trouble, stress, or aliens?" Ellie asked.

"That's just it. I got no response. Hostile silence would describe it best."

"Give them an F and move on. It's sad, but some do earn it. If they won't communicate, you don't have any other choice."

Rosalind rubbed her eyes. "It's a little complicated. I think the problem she's having is me."

"Oh, honey, they can't all like you. I had this guy last year who just—"

Rosalind interrupted her. "It's Colleen. The girl who was keeping company with Taryn when she and I met."

"Ah. I see the reason for your hesitation. Social and educational worlds collide; trouble ensues."

"Maybe. I don't want to strike up any trouble. I don't want to be unfair to her, either. I can understand how she might feel. But at this point, she's failing the class. I have to do something."

"Sweetie, you have the best people skills I've ever seen. Trust your instinct," Ellie said. There was a tentative knock at the door. Ellie rolled her eyes. "My cue to turn into a pumpkin. Listen, the workmen are all meeting at Buddies after rehearsal. Meet us there. Heck, meet us at rehearsal." Ellie opened the door. A sullen young woman with bright metallic red hair stood in the hall. "See you tonight."

"Come in, Colleen," Rosalind said as warmly as she could. Colleen did, slouching in the chair Ellie had cleared. She lowered her eyes and played with one of the bracelets on her wrist, daring Rosalind to speak. *You think you can sulk? I get to deal with the master,* Rosalind thought.

"Colleen," Rosalind said and waited. As she had hoped, Colleen raised her head. Her skin was as fair as a natural redhead's, darkening to purple shadows around her eyes. She had taken some of her earrings out. The remaining ones hung like ragged teeth between empty spaces. "You know why I asked you to meet me?" Rosalind asked.

Colleen stared at Rosalind, keeping her face blank. The impression she gave was one of aggressive stupidity, willful ignorance. Rosalind tried not to react to it.

"You haven't handed any work in all semester," Rosalind said, hating the sound of her own voice. She sounded like a teacher, but in the worst way. Deadly serious, shielded by professional distance, disapproving. In a moment of impulse, Rosalind threw away the speech she had prepared. "But that's not what I want to talk to you about," she said and was rewarded with a look of surprise from Colleen. "Buffalo's not a very big place, and the community we both move in is even smaller. I'd like to think that won't affect our relationship in the classroom, but it already does. I'd like for that to stop."

Colleen looked at her sharply.

"So I'm not talking about class or grades. I'm talking about Taryn."

"You want to talk about Taryn?" Colleen asked, abandoning her sullen pose. She sat up in the chair, surprised out of her hostile body language.

"I do. Back in September you saw Taryn and me out at a coffee shop in an…intimate moment," Rosalind said delicately. "You and I haven't gotten along very well since. Normally, it wouldn't be any concern of my students who I am involved with. This isn't a normal circumstance."

Rosalind looked into Colleen's face and saw skepticism. She saw also youth and hunger. In Colleen's searching eyes was a need to be validated, to have the emotion she had given acknowledged. She had fallen for Taryn when seduction meant nothing lasting to Taryn. Rosalind felt a stab of remembered pain at her own morning after, when Taryn had kissed her good-bye with no indication they would ever see one another again. She'd been crushed, devastated that the handsome girl could take a night like the one they'd shared and put no lasting value on it, no emotional connection like the overwhelming one she felt. It was only the mysteries of fate and love that rescued the night for Rosalind, when Taryn eventually returned her affection. But how many women had had a night like that, a morning with the surgical separation Taryn mastered, and never knew anything more? Rosalind knew what Taryn's reputation had been, and it wasn't pretty. In the first flush of love and madness it hadn't mattered. Nothing mattered except the moment. Taryn loved her. Compared with that miracle, what was a little thing like Taryn's past? It was her nature to forgive, and she forgave grandly, expansively, everything she knew and everything she didn't, motivated by the expansiveness of her love. There was nothing about Taryn that she couldn't accept. She might have breathed a prayer of thanks that she wasn't one of the women who Taryn had ensorcelled before, but she didn't cast them much thought. Rhea was the only woman Taryn loved. Rhea was the one to be dealt with, rivaled, and in the end, understood. Why worry about a horde of faceless women that meant nothing to Taryn?

Now things were different. Now, in the certainty of Taryn's love, in the growing complexity of their life together, new things seemed important. They were building something. That creation demanded roots. In the reaching of their connection, the past became territory to be mapped and reclaimed. All things come through love. All understanding is possible only through love.

So Rosalind found herself allying in sympathy with the wounded girl sitting in front of her. Colleen couldn't be more than nineteen. She was pretty in the luxurious way of youth, despite her attempts to harden her appearance. Her makeup was applied to shock. Black spider legs of mascara threatened to run with the wetness gathering in her eyes. The pain was fresh. Taryn had just betrayed her with indifference only a moment ago. Time behaved differently at nineteen. No, Rosalind thought, that wasn't it exactly. Time behaved differently for lovers. For her, it had been an eternity since September, since the night she first saw the drag king onstage. Since Taryn asked her out for coffee and took her home. Time had folded on itself. Eternity had opened up with the opening of her heart. Desire won out. Life came in the form of a handsome girl. The world began that night. But where had Taryn been the night before? "Colleen. Why don't you tell me what happened between you and Taryn."

Rosalind didn't think she'd make it to rehearsal. There were more papers to correct. It was already Thursday. The show and the wedding were set for Saturday. Rosalind felt the madness that infected every member of the household, the growing excitement, the coiling of energy that burned in the belly, the desire for constant motion, action, anything to make the time go. Her skin itched. She couldn't wait for the show. She could only imagine how it felt for the other performers.

For Taryn, she knew. This was the most important thing she'd ever done. The first chance to be celebrated for who she was, to take elements of herself and project them, larger than life. For the first time in her life, she was cheered for being. That unreserved, unconditional love that she'd never had, writ large upon a space of her own creating. Not only was she Taryn, she was Taryn amplified—the boy, the man, the king.

Ellie had pulled her aside at the beginning of the week and given her a light-hearted but serious discussion on how to be the partner of a performer going into tech.

"You know I love you. We love you. Taryn loves you," Ellie said. Her smile was accompanied by a gymnastic set of eyebrows, comically moving from concern to reassurance.

"Of course."

"Good. Well, this week it may not seem like it. You've never had a lover in theater, or been in a show yourself, so it's up to me to give you the explanation. Actually, I was hired by Linda to give the talk to all the partners of our performers. I get to hit up Laurel next. Beside the point. Tech week is the culmination of all the collective work of a bunch of very creative and high-strung people. It's when the rubber meets the road. Art smacks face first into the limits of time, lighting, personality, and preparation. It's messy. The crew gets stressed, the performers get high strung, and the director wants to kill everyone she sees. And that's not even dress rehearsal. The axiom is, the worse the dress rehearsal, the better the opening night. So don't expect Taryn to come home early. Expect her to come home surly. And stressed out. And inside out. I won't be a lot of help, I'm afraid. I'm working on the show, too. But we all love you. I just wanted to warn you. More divorces happen during tech week than at any other time. And I'd never want to see that happen to you guys. Not that it would. Not that I could spare Taryn, even if it happened. The show must go on."

After the talk with Colleen, Rosalind had tried to work, but it wouldn't come. Colleen's tear-stained face, washed with cheap mascara, haunted her. It seemed to help. Colleen was much warmer toward her at the end of the session, agreeing to Rosalind's liberal new deadlines. But Colleen's story stayed with her like a pit of lead in her stomach. Rosalind thought about Taryn, pictured the loving expression in Taryn's eyes replaced with a hard distance. The perfect boy could be a perfect asshole. And had been, to Colleen.

It was like hearing about a different person, a handsome butch who ran cavalierly through weekend lovers. There wasn't a promise of more, but who ever believed that intense emotion could be one-sided? Taryn had taken Colleen to bed, not knowing or caring that Colleen, who tried to look hard, bent like pure gold in her hands. She had given Colleen a few nights, spaced over three weeks' time, but hadn't given her anything else. Rosalind thought about 34 Mariner, about Joe and Rhea, about Egyptia, Goblin, and Laurel. She couldn't imagine not knowing them, not being welcomed into the family. She couldn't imagine not knowing Taryn.

Rosalind was caught up in her brooding, not ready for company just yet. She slipped into the back of the theater. The tech run hadn't started. Linda was still rehearsing the dance numbers. Rosalind sighed. This wasn't the display to be watching in the state she was in. Taryn, looking Satanic in full black, working the chair and the rope.

Paul's last desperate attempt to win her had hit its mark, but not in the way he'd hoped. He'd thrown all the artillery he'd gathered against Taryn, tossing up her history as a Lothario, implying the hardened soul she must have. He had sought to prove the baseness of her nature. That had been the argument's downfall. Rosalind had already taken her measure of Taryn's soul and found it good. But the history couldn't be argued away. It had happened as Paul had said. Taryn was trouble, and no woman in her right mind would seek out an emotional maelstrom. Or so Paul believed.

The problem is, Rosalind thought while gazing at the stage from the back row, *I knew she was trouble.* Taryn, with a swing of her right arm, slapped the rope against her thigh. *But, oh Lord, if that's trouble, then give me some.*

Rosalind thought of Colleen's tear-stained face, of the dancing she had seen, of Taryn's naked back moving under her hands, of nails spiking down into tattoos. Of blue glass mugs filled with black coffee, walking on the edge of a leaden lake on a frozen night. Maybe she had been with a lot of people before. Okay, yes, she had. Did that mean she was incapable of loving one?

It wasn't Taryn's interest in other people she feared, Rosalind saw suddenly, like a teardrop flash-frozen. It was fear of having to justify herself as a choice, weighed against the whole world. Faced with that, there was no rational way to make a case for a relationship: one cannot be many, and scarcity becomes glaring under that light. But the choice had been both of theirs. Taryn had also made that choice. It would be hers to defend or reject.

❖

"Okay, people, enough, I'll have the fire department out here because you're burning the house down. Save some of that for the show. Okay, boys onstage in five for the monologues," Linda said.

The kings scrambled backstage, some to prepare, some to grab a quick smoke before their call. Linda left the house lights down. Rosalind found the darkness comforting. Taryn had strolled off with Robbie.

Linda called out, "Send Sam out here! We have a minute. Let's finish teching the second number. Misha, you with me?"

"Against all sense and judgment." Misha's voice came from the booth behind Rosalind's head, rich and bored.

"Good. Give me the lights for it."

Ellie burst onto the stage wearing a headset and waving a tuxedo shirt, blue as a robin's egg and drowning in a froth of frills. "We have a problem. Sam's jacket has split at the vents. We can't do the second number."

"Do you have a sewing kit?" Linda asked with exaggerated patience.

"I'm the stage manager. Of course I have a sewing kit," Ellie said.

"Then fix it. Cancel the lights and give me the monologues, Misha."

CHAPTER EIGHTEEN

Grief was thick on his tongue, unmoved by the watery amber of the beer. Paul looked down into his glass, tilted it, and watched the foam crawl back down. The working men had gone out for a beer late at night to accommodate the rehearsal schedule. Taryn was as much of a member of that group as himself, or Misha, or Joe. No distinction was made for her gender—or rather, as he was beginning to see, the lack of distinction revealed more about her gender. She was one of the guys, with an ease he envied now with greater sharpness. They were a group he worked with, ate with, lived with, yet there was a glass wall up between them. He could look in on their fellowship, but when the time came for backslapping, for the proposing of a toast, he was made conscious of being Joe's guest, of being the little brother tagging along, of being the outsider they had to remind themselves to entertain. It was subtler now that he had been here for…How long had he been here? Time had no normal relation to the house, or anyone who lived in it.

It was Taryn, Paul decided. She was the moving heart of things, linking together all the people who moved around her, a king with her court. The hub of the wheel. If she accepted him, he would be in. But he bruised himself against her walls, was left bloody and battered when he sought entry to her inner life. There had been some progress. The mural was the key. But this afternoon had set back anything he thought they had gained, had proved the end of the cease-fire. Tonight Taryn roundly ignored him. She sat at the far end of the bar, telling war stories from tech rehearsal to a delighted Joe and an indulgent Misha.

The drag queen, Egyptia, swept into the bar. He gasped. He'd only seen her in her more modest everyday clothes. Her nightwear was a revelation. She was gorgeous, over the top, full on cinematic glamour that made a mock of restraint, a broad wink and a hip sway that proclaimed womanhood as an art form to be worshipped.

"You look incredible," Paul said in admiration.

The queen paused in her promenade. "Why thank you, honey. I knew you had to have some taste somewhere." She blew a kiss at his cheek and sashayed toward the circle of men at the end of the bar.

Paul watched her closely. There were subtle clues as to her biological sex, the size of her hands, the strength of her jaw, but in the sum of appearance, Paul couldn't see any hint of maleness. She was an attractive woman; his own attraction to her came as only mildly surprising. Egyptia, in the largess of her presentation, inhabited all the recognizable traits of femininity. He was trained from birth to respond to such clues, to find them arousing and intriguing. Paul cast a quick look at the end of the bar, at the boy sitting there. Taryn swung a beer bottle by the neck like a truck driver and elbowed Misha in the ribs. Not a clue as to his biological sex in his presentation. Paul finished his glass of beer. It was like being lost in a Shakespeare play, all crossdressing and mistaken identity.

"Paul! Come on down here. We're doing shots."

So it was in this light that Paul turned toward Joe, in the merry escape of an actor in a Shakespearean comedy, in the gleeful complicity of seeing the boy beneath the maiden's skirts, the handsome young woman in the youth's raiment. All was not as it seemed. All was exactly as it seemed. The image became more real than nature. The artifice was beyond God's own art. His fascination came from the choice implied in it, the act of will: I am what I desire to be. I am what you desire.

Paul took the glass from Joe and smiled at Egyptia as he would at any stunning woman sitting at a bar. He felt the moorings of his life slip. They'd been slipping since he arrived, broken and desperate in this cold city. This was the first moment he was aware of the change as it was happening. He could feel it beginning. For the first time, Paul opened himself to it. He took the shot glass from Misha, the weight an anchor in his hand, a scepter and a brand.

"Na zdorovye!" Misha called out in his ringing voice.

Paul drank down the molten gold, the fluid heat of the sun. He was already spinning like a child's toy.

"We need a game," Misha said.

"You men and your games. Always hitting things, or each other, or playing at it," Egyptia said. Her disapproval was arch, calculated. It brought a roguish smile to Misha's face. Egyptia seemed to enjoy this. Her shimmering eyelids lowered slowly, like butterfly's wings; her smile was somnambulant. "You see what happens when you don't have womenfolk around you?"

"With Ellie and Rosalind abandoning us to go off with each other, we're lost," Joe said.

"Now why in the world did they do that? They spend all day pining away for you when you're up in Canada," Egyptia said.

"It's my fault," Taryn growled. She frowned at the shot glass before dropping it back on to the bar.

"That's not hard to believe," Misha said.

Taryn didn't react to him. Something had been primed in her at Egyptia's question. She leaned on the bar, looking intently at Egyptia, seeking advice or absolution. "Let me ask you this. What do you do if your lover comes to you and tells you to apologize to some chick you slept with before you even met?"

"This isn't one of them hypocritical situations, is it?" Egyptia asked.

"Hypothetical," Paul said automatically.

He winced when Egyptia turned to look at him. She raised her eyebrow. "I know."

Egyptia took Taryn's face in her hands and examined her like a gemstone under a jeweler's glass. "Ooh, I see. What we have here is a failure to comprehend. You need translation from femme to butch." She patted Taryn's cheek.

"Yeah. I don't get it. Why would Rosalind give a shit about this chick? It's not like we were seeing each other or anything. It was just sex," Taryn said.

Egyptia shook her head. "What did Miss Rosalind say to you?"

"She collared me after rehearsal and told me I owed Colleen an apology."

Egyptia sat up and folded her hands in her lap. "Refresh my memory. Colleen was who?"

"We slept together a few times in early September. You know, red hair? Pierced tongue? She works at Spot."

"Oh, right. And how does Miss Rosalind know her?"

"She's her student," Taryn said.

Egyptia stopped and gave Taryn a withering look. "Tell me you didn't sleep with the student and graduate to the teacher. Tell me you did not do that."

"Well…"

"Please. We know our Rosalind has a feeling heart. This girl is her student. She's gonna care. And as I recall, this was in your dog days. You did this girl wrong." Egyptia held up her hand when Taryn tried to protest. "Please do not interrupt. Let me provide the femme subtitles. Rosalind heard the story from Colleen of your houndish ways. She, with her sweet heart, identified with this poor girl. So you are in the doghouse, where you belong. She cares because she knows how it would feel."

"But I wouldn't—" Taryn said, spitting the words out. Egyptia patted her coiled hand until it relaxed. It was a light-bending facet of a moment, a woman tending to a wounded boy as he was confronted with his own thoughtlessness.

"But you did, baby. And Rosalind has heard about it. For all she knows, if she'd come along a week earlier, it might have been her. Don't get riled up. I'm just giving you the subtitles. If a woman knows you did wrong, she'll wonder when you're going to do it to her. Nobody can hurt you like the one you love."

"It's not that way between us. She's my girl. She knows that," Taryn said stubbornly.

"A woman can know something and still need to hear it. She told you that you owed this girl an apology. Now, I'm talking out of church here, but deep down she wants to see that you've changed. The punk you used to be wouldn't dream of apologizing. If you do it, it's because you are someone else now," Egyptia said.

"She doubts me?" Taryn asked as if the words alone made her bleed.

The queen smiled at the tortured king. "Sweet boy. We're talking about a woman's heart. You ever try to reason with a heart?"

"*Reason* would not be her strong point," Misha said.

Taryn bared her teeth at him.

"No fighting. Let's have that game you called for, Misha, before you get any more unruly on me," Egyptia said. She touched Taryn's arm. "We understand one another, little boy?"

"Yeah. Thanks, Egyptia."

"Don't let Misha choose. He's in a brawling mood," Joe said.

"Fine, I'll pick. We'll play You Don't Know," Egyptia said.

"That's hardly fair to Paul. He hasn't been with us long enough," Joe said.

Egyptia smiled at Paul. "We'll start the first round with Rosalind. He's surely known her long enough. Bartender! Bring a bottle and another glass."

"Rules are simple. You face off with your enemy. Using a person both of you know fairly well, the attacker asks a question about that person. If the defender doesn't know the answer, he drinks." Misha set the bottle down between Paul and Taryn. "Since we are using Rosalind, you go first."

Paul looked into the hooded eyes of the boy sitting opposite him and thought that such eyes should be met above crossed steel. Misha had proposed a game. It was more bullfighting than backgammon, but he would play. This was his territory, knowledge of Rosalind. The thug would never match him. That he was already getting drunk briefly intruded into his thought flow, that the boy seemed coldly sober wasn't a concern. He'd had decades when he'd been the closest person alive to Rosalind. He'd start with a jab, feel his opponent out.

"What's Rosalind's middle name?" Paul asked. He watched the tight smirk pull Taryn's lips into a blade line.

"Sophia."

She knew that one. He'd have to up the ante. "What does it mean, and who was she named for?" Paul asked.

Taryn hesitated. "It means *wisdom*. It's Greek. But I don't know who she was named for."

"Judges?" Egyptia asked.

"You only answered half. Drink!" Misha said.

Taryn shrugged and poured out the shot.

"She was named for her grandmother, who died in the war. Sophia Wollantynowicz. Her mother's mother," Paul said. The rules might not allow for elaboration, but he couldn't help it. He watched with satisfaction as Taryn killed the shot

"What is Rosalind's favorite kind of sushi?" Taryn asked.

"She doesn't eat sushi," Paul said.

"Wrong." Taryn slid the bottle toward him. "Drink."

"Judges?" Egyptia asked.

"I'm afraid I'll have to back T up here. Rosalind has gone out for sushi with Rhea and me, and she seems to like it," Joe said.

It was a minor matter. Tastes change. He'd simply missed this new fad. It would be better to stick to the areas he knew solid as bedrock.

"What's Rosalind's favorite play?" Paul asked.

He watched Taryn's eyebrows draw together. "*Romeo and Juliet?*" Taryn guessed.

Paul shook his head. "No. *Midsummer Night's Dream.*" He slid the bottle back to Taryn.

The duel began in earnest. Paul hit his strong points relentlessly. Taryn drank. She didn't have his encyclopedic knowledge of Rosalind's past. He reveled in it, asking things only someone who had known her for years might know, things that only came up in conversation gradually. The intensity of the relationship was on her side. The length was on his. Paul noticed, as Taryn drank more, that she concentrated her questions more on how Rosalind thought, what she liked, what she felt. It was a glimpse into Rosalind's internal life that he hadn't seen. He started drinking, one shot for Taryn's two.

"How old was Rosalind when she had her first kiss?" Paul asked.

Taryn stared at him, then reached for the bottle. She wiped her mouth with the back of her hand. The steel glint was gone, the eyes a little unfocussed. Paul watched a fire rise in them. Taryn pointed the bottle at him and smiled demonically. "What makes Rosalind—" She stopped midsentence, stayed by some qualm or glimmer of compassion. The bottle landed back on the table. "What does Rosalind like for breakfast?" Taryn asked indifferently.

She was being kind to him. Even drunk, with him goading her, she was being kind. And she was no good at masking it. The anger in her rose to the challenge; he could see the effort it took to set it aside. Still she responded to something else, a stimulus stronger than the impulse to fight.

It took all the joy out of beating her. "Eggs. Coffee. Toast with marmalade or jelly. Or so I still assume," Paul said.

Taryn knocked the shot glass onto its side like a bored cat redecorating a mantel. "Yeah, sometimes. Souvlaki, if she's been up all night."

"Judges?" Misha asked.

"Sounds like a draw to me. Look at the bottle. The tide has gone out. You and Joe play now and give them a rest," Egyptia said.

Misha took the bar stool from Paul with enthusiasm and mounted it like a charger. "I'm in the mood for a challenge. I say we use Rhea."

Joe sat down opposite him. "It's your funeral, Mikhail Malinin Vlas. But you know that when you use a witch's name, you might summon her."

"She could use to get out more. Summon the witch," Misha said.

Joe shrugged. "Okay. Pick up your glass. You'll need it. When did Rhea buy 34 Mariner?"

Misha laughed. "After she got out of prison. You'll have to try harder than that."

Paul and Taryn, their place at the bar usurped, wandered off to a table. By an unspoken compact the game ended in a draw, leaving a feeling of incompleteness between them. It had started as a duel and ended without heat, leaving them vaguely unsatisfied and adrift. The mood at the bar had passed them by. They both seemed relieved to wander away from its pull.

"Misha is in trouble. Rhea doesn't seem like she gives away anything about her past. Even living with her doesn't help. There are some people you can only learn about obliquely, gathering bits and pieces from the people around them," Paul said.

Taryn shrugged. "Rhea gives you what she thinks you need to know."

They were having a conversation, Paul realized with quiet delight. The thug prince was talking to him again. After the blowup over the painting, he wasn't sure if she ever would. That seemed to be a facet of life in the household, the storm and subsiding of emotion. It was frightening to him, who had been raised without shouting or drama, to endure the level of chaos they accepted as natural. An outburst happened, like a crack of thunder, then it passed. The communion of these people allowed for the messiness of human emotion. He'd never been in an environment that was forgiving of the volatile landscape of the heart. It was a relief to be allowed room to be imperfect. Strange to learn such a quiet, compassionate lesson from the impulsive kindness of a drunken boy. He had a fair idea where the lesson had come down to her. "You've known Rhea for a long time?" Paul asked.

"Since I was sixteen." The note of pride in her voice was unmistakable. There was tenderness beneath the armor. The mention of Rhea's name evoked such warmth from Taryn. What would Rosalind evoke?

"You know I couldn't stand you when we met," Paul found himself saying.

Taryn laughed explosively. "Yeah. Me too."

"And it didn't help that Rhea told me I had to stay in your house," Paul said, finding himself smiling.

"I wanted you dead when I heard that," Taryn said cheerfully.

"I thought you were going to kill me in the kitchen that morning. You were so violent." The humor had subsided. This was dangerous territory they were marching toward. "I did what I could to convince Rosalind that her relationship with you was a mistake. I asked her to come back to me."

He could see from the stillness of her face that Rosalind hadn't told her that. He expected fury, a physical reaction, particularly now that they were both drunk. What he saw was vulnerability she couldn't mask, an arrow that reached to an open wound. She was afraid of Rosalind leaving. He felt the matching emotion in the pit of his stomach. That had been his fear and it had come true. He'd lost her. But the deeper fear, the root of it, was the terror that he would never truly know her.

"When Rosalind and I got married, I was pretty sure that she loved me. Just like she had always loved me, growing up. But deep down I was afraid that something was missing. That she wouldn't go mad for me, wouldn't die without me, that she wouldn't be the Juliet to my Romeo. I was right," Paul said quietly. "All things show up through contrast. I can see it now only because I've seen her with someone she would go mad for. Her Romeo." He watched Taryn's face, saw the alert intelligence that belied her youth. "You don't have anything to worry about."

He didn't know how she would respond to him. He'd said it because it needed to be said. It lifted the millstone off his throat. He could breathe again. Whatever her reaction, the speaking had done him good. Was this what Rhea meant by choosing to heal himself?

Taryn got up and walked away. No preamble, no word, just turned her back to him and walked to the bar. She even walked like a boy, all shoulders and boots, Paul thought. Just as callous as one, as well. *Hell with it,* he thought. *I'm done wallowing in the trough of my pain.*

He was surprised when she sat back down at the table. She had a black marker and a cocktail napkin in her hands and proceeded to slash out a few furious lines. Taryn glanced up at him and he was hit with the force of it.

"Here," she said, pushing the napkin toward him.

It was the mouth of a cave opening out of living rock. The lines had torn the thin paper with their strength. Coming out of the cave was a bear, primeval in size. From the tilt of the bear's skull, with one warning eye opened at the viewer, he knew that he had just been roused from a long sleep. There was a hint of danger in the curve of the bear's right paw, a suggestive display of natural armament. The bear might just be walking out of the cave, or it might be roused to a protective charge. It was a mountain of muscle hidden under a thick coat.

It went through him like a silver knife. "Is this me?"

"Your tattoo. Center of the back, I think. Rhea would know," Taryn said.

"How did you?"

"It just came to me while you were talking," Taryn said and shrugged.

Paul looked down at the image, entranced. "Unbelievable."

"It'll remind you of your power once it's done."

"I never thought about getting a tattoo before. My students would laugh their heads off. I have a midlife crisis, rush off to be with my ex-wife, and end up living in a witch's commune and getting a tattoo." Paul started to laugh. "I've got to be drunk. This is hysterical."

"Sounds normal to me," Taryn said.

"No offense, but it would," He continued laughing, knocking over his beer bottle. "The funniest thing is, it makes perfect sense to me now that I'm here."

"You don't have anything to worry about either," Taryn said softly.

Absurdly, Paul felt like crying in the midst of his laughter. "You think so?"

In that moment, Taryn was ancient, looking out of a handsome boy's face with the sadness and wisdom that love engenders. "Yeah. The place you have in her life. You'll always have that. And you will be the only one that ever will."

Misha finished his match with Joe in a resounding defeat. Drink had sanded his voice back down to his youth, leaving his accent rich as loam. Joe held Misha up as they walked out into the parking lot. Egyptia held his left arm to keep him from spinning into the cars.

"Honey, you ain't nothing but dead weight right now. Try to stand up," Egyptia said.

"Only in Buffalo do the dead stand up," Misha said.

Paul and Taryn walked a few steps behind the parade.

"I don't know about you, but watching Misha makes me feel sober," Paul said.

An alley ran parallel to the parking lot, a ribbon of black between dull red and dirty gray office buildings. During the day this was a business district, adjacent to downtown. At night it was a wasteland. The parking lot was nearly empty in the scoured brainpan of a weeknight. Joe had parked his massive red convertible under the metal stalk of a streetlight. For a moment it looked like an apple waiting to be plucked, seductive. Joe and Egyptia carried Misha to the car and upended him in the backseat. "Close enough," Joe said.

Taryn and Paul were lagging behind, standing under the bar's neon sign.

The scream of tires slashed across the lot, the sound of rubber being scorched. A car roared down the alley at a sickening speed. It happened so quickly that all Paul got was a handful of images, a dark-colored car with the windows rolled down, young men leaning crazily out, shouting. He heard the words *fucking faggots*, then a peculiarly hollow sound like a hammer meeting a cement block. Or a bottle meeting a skull.

Next to him, Taryn dropped like a star flaming out.

He heard a shout of disbelief, ripped from a raw throat. It was his own voice. Egyptia responded to the threat first, kicking off her high heels and holding them like railroad spikes, ready to fight. She and Joe ran to his side. The car stopped, spun in a fishtail arc, the bumper scoring the brick wall. Taryn lay on her back, bleeding onto the pavement.

Joe went down on one knee, hovering protectively over the body as the car turned. Paul could feel Egyptia at his shoulder, making a wall of their bodies. Joe had his hand under Taryn's neck. There was more yelling from the car—*cocksuckers, queers, die, assfuckers*—spaced with sounds less human. The words came wet and hard as hail, thrown with mouthfuls of spit and beer. There was laughter sprinkled in, floating in the air.

"Come over here and say that, Nazi boys!" Egyptia called out, her voice rising with stress.

The engine revved.

"Be ready." Joe stood up, adding his body to the line.

The absurdity of it washed over Paul, the bull-necked brave stupidity of three people facing down a car. They didn't have a prayer. Even if the car stopped and the young men decided to beat them by hand, he counted at least six of them. Fear made him sober. He'd read about attacks like these, the sudden, irrational violence. He never expected the assailants to be laughing.

The show of resistance must have been enough. The car fishtailed again. Another bottle was hurled, shattering into a glittering spray fifteen feet from them. The car turned and sped off.

Paul's blood was on fire. Every nerve ending jumped and twitched, calling for combat. His senses were sharper than they'd ever been. Joe and Egyptia had already broken their defensive stance and were examining Taryn. *They must be more used to this,* Paul thought, from the speed with which they shifted gears. Taryn's eyes were open but unfocussed. Blood ran freely through her hair where the bottle had struck above and behind her right ear, matting it down.

"Oh my Lord, my sweet Lord," Egyptia said, her hand covering her mouth.

"Don't panic. Head wounds bleed. Egyptia, you drive. You're the only sober one. Buffalo General is closest." Joe stood up, cradling Taryn in his arms. "Paul, move Misha."

Paul took Misha's feet off the backseat and sat him up. Misha opened his eyes. "What?"

"We were jumped," Joe said, shoving him aside. He sat in the back, holding Taryn across his lap.

Misha swore. "Are they still here?"

"We got lucky. They took off. We have to get T to the hospital."

Egyptia slipped into the driver's seat. She took a look at the shoes in her hand, then tossed them over the door. "Never liked those heels anyway. Hang on, baby boy. We're on the way."

"Make a right on High Street," Joe said.

Paul rode in the front with Egyptia as she drove, her wig straining at the pins holding it down. There was a flash of streets, two quick turns and they were there. Egyptia made a sharp left into the drive marked Emergency. A security guard in a blue uniform came out of the sliding glass doors, shouting at them. "Hey! You can't park that thing here!"

"We have a person that needs emergency care," Paul said.

Egyptia held up her hand. "You take Taryn and go in, honey. I'll go park."

Joe carried Taryn through the glass doors. All emergency rooms he'd ever visited were the same, Paul thought. Orange or green plastic chairs stolen from a high school cafeteria. Admissions desks set up like Cold War checkpoints. Designed by Darwin to thin out the sick. Only those in great need would suffer through the emergency room. Joe carried Taryn up to the desk, right past the yellow line. The woman behind the desk put her hand over the phone she had balanced on her shoulder and pointed behind the line. "Do not cross the line."

Joe took a half step back. "We need to see a doctor."

"Fill out the forms."

"She was hit in the head. She can't fill anything out," Joe said, exasperated.

The woman took the phone off her shoulder. "Fill out the forms on the clipboard."

"I'll get it," Paul said. He could see that Joe was starting to crack. Standing with a bleeding Taryn in his arms was undoing him. Paul took the clipboard and guided Joe to the hideous chairs, where he sat with Taryn across his lap. "Do you know her information? I'll write it out." Paul took the pen off the rotted string. "Last name?"

"Cullen. Even I don't know if she has a middle name."

"I'll put 34 Mariner as her home address. Insurance?" Paul asked. Joe shook his head, jaw tight.

"We'll leave that blank." He got to next of kin and his hand stopped. Biological family wasn't an option. Rhea would certainly do, or Joe. Paul glanced at the man seated next to him. There was no physical resemblance to Taryn. "You're her stepfather, right?" Paul asked.

Relief was in Joe's brown eyes when he looked up. "Yes. Joseph Fregoe."

Blood had filled the cloth Joe held against Taryn's wound. "We need to see somebody. This is ridiculous," Joe snapped. "Sorry, I'm a little burned out on hospitals. Too much inept medical intervention in my life."

"Leave it to me," Paul said.

Taryn groaned. Joe stood up and sat her up in the chair. "Taryn. Hey. Can you open your eyes?"

Taryn's lids moved. One eye opened; the enlarged pupil left only a rim of blue.

"She's not talking." Joe crouched by the chair, gingerly holding the soaked cloth against Taryn's head.

The door banged open and Egyptia came in, six feet tall in her stocking feet. Misha was reeling behind her. In their wake came a security guard. "There they are. Oh Lord, look at our boy. He's covered in blood. Oh, Joe. What are we going to do? Have they seen you yet? We need a nurse over here!" Egyptia yelled. Misha collapsed into the chair next to Taryn. The guard paused behind them, not sure if he should throw them out. The man with his hair in a ponytail was reeking drunk, and the barefoot man in the dress was frightening him. Egyptia turned around. "You run along now. We made it in just fine."

The woman behind the desk was still on the phone.

"I have the patient's information. We need to see a doctor," Paul said, setting the clipboard back down.

"Have a seat until we call your name."

"We need to see a doctor," Paul repeated.

"Patients are not seen in the order they arrive. The average wait time is three hours. Thank you for your patience."

Paul leaned on the desk until the woman looked at him. "A girl was struck in the head and is bleeding and not fully conscious. I see six other people in the waiting room, none of them in her condition."

The woman looked the clipboard over. "The insurance information is missing."

He'd never felt lower in his life, the way this woman was talking to him. He saw her look over at Joe and Egyptia and Misha and form an ironclad opinion about them. He could imagine what kind of health care they would receive now. "She doesn't have any," Paul said.

"I'm sorry. Payment is expected at the time services are rendered. How does the patient plan on paying?" The woman held the clipboard up.

He could feel the desperation at his back, Joe and Egyptia's eyes on him. Paul took a certain satisfaction in reaching into his pocket. "Platinum," he said, tossing the card to her.

"We will call your name in a minute."

Paul went back to the chairs. "I think it will go more quickly now."

Egyptia kissed him on the cheek, nearly knocking him over. "That was the sweetest thing I've ever seen."

"Cullen, Torvin," the voice announced.

"*Taryn*," Joe said. He lifted Taryn to her feet. "Come on, kid."

They watched Joe and Taryn disappear behind swinging doors.

"We should get comfortable. It might be a long night," Paul said.

"Somebody should call Rosalind, and Rhea," Egyptia said.

"Ros is with Ellie. I will call." Misha lumbered to his feet.

"Sit back down before you hurt yourself. Let Paul do it," Egyptia said, grabbing Misha's hand. It wasn't easy. The man was swaying.

"I said I will call." Misha glared down at the drag queen.

"Misha, sit down."

A dangerous light shone in Misha's eyes. "You think I can't handle it? Hah? Because I missed the fight, yes?"

Egyptia stood up and draped her arms around Misha's shoulders. "Let's just say you and Uncle Jack have been very close tonight. It's a bad enough scene without Rosalind thinking her Taryn is dead in a gutter with his head stove in."

"I'll do it," Paul said quickly.

"Miss Ellie's number is in my bag. Pay phones are down the hall. Listen, give Rhea a call, too. Thanks, honey." Egyptia stayed focused on Misha as she spoke. The man's face started to crumple.

Paul took the bag and headed for the hall.

"Egyptia, am I a bad man?" Misha asked.

"No, baby. You just drunk. We all get down sometime."

The last thing Paul saw was Misha's head resting on Egyptia's shoulder.

Paul found the bank of pay phones. He opened Egyptia's scarlet sequined bag, getting some of the fringe caught in the clasp. He swore at the bag, then started to laugh at himself. "I'm cursing a purse." He found Egyptia's little black book, so proclaimed in bright gold lettering. It was a temptation he couldn't resist, thumbing through the names on the search for Ellie. Egyptia's system was hard to decipher, with people listed under first names, nicknames, even physical descriptions. He found Ellie under her first name, with a smiley face etched in lip liner. He dialed the number.

"Hi, you have reached Ellie. Actually, you haven't reached me because I'm not here. It's a machine talking to you. I might be here, but the machine doesn't know that. For all it knows, I'm in the Bahamas. Leave me a message, suggestion, or proposal after the beep."

Paul spoke quickly. "Ellie? It's Paul. I need to find Rosalind. It's urgent. If you're there, please pick up the—"

"Whoa! I'm here. We both are, actually. What's up?" Ellie asked.

"We're down at Buffalo General. We got jumped outside the bar," Paul said.

"Is everyone okay?" Ellie asked. He could hear the strain in her voice.

"Taryn got hit in the head with a bottle."

"Paul?" It was Rosalind. She'd taken the phone from Ellie.

"I...there was a fight outside the bar. Taryn got hit. We're at the emergency room." It was a flat series of statements. He found he couldn't summon any emotion. It must be shock, he thought. He was afraid of Rosalind's reaction. How had he ended up bearing this news?

Rosalind's voice was deadly calm. "How is she?"

"She was sitting up and her eyes were open. They're seeing her now," Paul said.

"Is she in there alone?" Rosalind asked, the first hint of emotion bleeding into her voice.

He said the most comforting thing he could. "Joe's with her." He thought he heard her sigh.

"Did anyone else get hurt?" Rosalind asked.

"No."

"We'll be right there."

Rhea was easier. He dialed the number, she picked up on the first ring.

"How bad?" Rhea asked. It was to be expected.

"We don't know yet. Joe is with her."

"Good. I'm on the way."

❖

"The cavalry has arrived," Egyptia said as Ellie and Rosalind came in. Rhea followed, a slim shark carving their wake. Rosalind looked composed, but it was the composure of a woman after a tornado, listening for the last brick to fall. Ellie saw Misha sprawled out in the chair, resting his head on Egyptia's sequined shoulder. Rhea went and stood behind Misha, arms folded tightly across her chest.

"How is everyone?" Ellie asked with a show of her usual wattage, looking at Egyptia. Egyptia shook her head, a small motion, and glanced at Misha. An understanding passed between the two. Ellie sat down on Misha's right. Rosalind went to Paul, who was pacing.

"Are they still in there?" she asked.

"No word yet. Joe hasn't come out. The factotum at the desk quoted an estimate of three hours, give or take."

"I want to see her," Rosalind said.

"Checkpoint is that way," Paul said.

Egpytia waved her hand, light struck on the crimson and gold nails. "Honey, a word of advice. You're her sister."

Rosalind stopped. "What? I look nothing like Taryn."

"Well, you ain't old enough to be her mother. Only immediate family gets in," Egyptia said.

"I'll just tell them that…" Rosalind trailed off, lost for words.

Egyptia's smile was sad. This was Rosalind's first time. She hadn't grown a thick skin yet. "Baby, I've been through enough emergency rooms, and intensive care units, and hospitals. You tell them the truth, you will be cooling your heels out here until hell freezes over and the angels go ice skating. Our families don't get recognized."

Paul watched the information settle on Rosalind. She hadn't thought of that. He could see it in her face. She had never needed to think of it before. Some things you don't notice until you slam into them headlong.

"Sister," Rosalind said. In that word was a doorway. There were concessions to make to be able to operate in the world as she now was, with the lover she had chosen. A few of these she had imagined. This was one she hadn't. The social stigma had presented itself to her, that her family and the people she worked with might not react well. But that implied, at worst, a break in relationship, certain disappointments. There would be emotional consequences, moral judgments. She hadn't imagined that the world would care beyond that who she loved, or exact such a price. That love had its limits, she was well aware, even with her romantic nature. That strangers, with the power of law and ignorance behind them, could limit her life in such a basic way was unimagined. That they would actively work to do so, based on whom she loved, was a revelation. Rosalind knew in the abstract that bigotry existed. Meeting it armed to the teeth was another matter.

Rosalind squared her shoulders. "If that's how it's going to be, we use what we can. I'm her sister." She marched to the front desk.

"Fill out the forms on the clipboard," the woman behind the desk said automatically.

"I'm not a patient. I need to see one of your patients, Taryn Cullen."

The woman looked up at Rosalind and squinted. "Only relatives allowed back." She shuffled through a pile of forms. "Miss Cullen's stepfather is with her now."

"I'm her sister," Rosalind said sweetly. "She'd feel much better having me there. You know how girls are."

The woman looked blankly at Rosalind for a moment. Rosalind gave her a dazzling smile.

"You can go back. Follow the blue line," the woman said.

Through the swinging doors, down a corridor painted with colored stripes, three lefts into the labyrinth to get to the room. She found Joe pacing in the hallway, chewing on his thumbnail. His eyebrows arched up when he saw her. She'd managed to hold herself in check until that moment, until she saw the concern in Joe's brown eyes. It was a split second before he composed his look, but she had seen it. He knew what effect he'd had when Rosalind started to cry.

"Aw, hey now. Don't worry. She's going to be fine." Joe gathered her into a bear hug.

Rosalind pressed against his chest. He was a solid wall of muscle under the flannel shirt. She allowed herself the comfort of leaning on him. "What happened, Joe?"

"We got jumped outside the bar. It was a car full of frat boys. She got clipped on the head by a bottle. They're doing the CAT scan now," Joe said. "She was sitting up and her eyes were open when she went in. You know she's gonna be all macho when you see her. The only thing that will undo her is if she sees you upset. You don't want to ruin Taryn's image, do you?"

Rosalind sniffed. "Of course not."

"That's right. We have to be strong. Always, so they can be."

The door opened. The doctor who came out looked calm and tired, but her ready smile eased some of the tightness in Rosalind's chest. The doctor looked too young on first glance, a college student masquerading, a resident. It was her eyes that gave the lie to her youth, the steady look of authority, the framing of fine lines gathered over years of study and research. "I'm Dr. Sucharita Paul. Who's responsible for Taryn Cullen?"

Joe and Rosalind responded as one. "I am."

"You're like a Greek chorus. The first thing I have to tell you is to breathe. She's doing fine. No fractures or severe damage showed up on the scan. What we are dealing with is a concussion," Dr. Paul said.

Rosalind felt the air squeeze out through her teeth. "She's okay?" she said in perfect disbelief. Her body refused to relax from its readiness for tragedy, from the bone-deep conviction that the love she felt could only be a prelude to ghastly loss. It was the memory of someone else's grief, carried down like a whisper in her blood, bereavement she was born expecting.

"There's some memory loss. That's typical with concussions. But she doesn't have to stay. You can take her home. You'll need to watch her for a few days. It's common to have headaches, to be extra sleepy or experience a change in mood, be unusually irritable or short tempered."

"That won't be a change in mood. That'll be a normal day," Joe said in pure relief.

Dr. Paul laid her hand on Rosalind's arm. "She's fine. Do you want to see her?"

"Yes."

It was twilight in the room, the dimmed lemon of industrial lights. Taryn was sitting on an exam table swinging her bare feet. Her head turned at the minute creak of the door, her forehead wrinkled in concentration or in pain. There was a square white bandage standing out like a plaque of bone in the thatch of black hair. The blood was gone from the side of her head. Rosalind noticed this as soon as she embraced her boy. It had been someone's small kindness to wash it away, even from the matted hair.

"Hey," Taryn said into her ear. The pitch was right, low and easy. It made her cry, after she promised Joe she wouldn't. She couldn't let Taryn see her crying, so she held on. "Don't cry. It's not that bad. It's just a knock on the head," Taryn said, stroking her back.

"I take knocks to your head seriously," Rosalind said, abandoning her posture. "How'd you know I was crying?"

"You got my neck wet," Taryn said reasonably.

"Where are your boots?" Rosalind asked. The oddest details caught her attention, pulling her away from the weight of her emotion.

"They took them off before putting me in that doughnut thing. The big X-ray, you know?"

"I know. How do you feel?" Rosalind asked.

"Like I got hit in the head. The doctor said it was a good thing I'd been drinking. It kept me from really hurting myself when I fell down." Taryn smiled. "I don't remember it. Last thing I remember was standing there talking to Paul. The gay bashers must've thought I was his boyfriend." Taryn started to laugh.

"It's not funny," Rosalind said, feeling a wave of fury threaten to swamp her.

"Sure it is. It'd be a perfect excuse for him to clip me in the head. You sure he didn't do it?" Taryn said.

"Stop laughing. I can't believe you find this funny. You could have been seriously hurt, or—" Rosalind said, directing her anger at Taryn.

"Hey." Taryn reached out and caught Rosalind's arm. "I wasn't. It's just another beating. I can be pissed about it, but my head already hurts. It's easier to laugh."

The anger couldn't stand in the focus of that direct gaze. The passionate, angry boy was subsumed in something else, a steadiness and humor that was deeply attractive. For a moment Rosalind felt a window open on the person Taryn would become. "You're starting to sound like Joe," Rosalind said.

Taryn's lips quirked. "You always end up sounding like your parents."

"If you're going to be reasonable, that leaves a void. I have to be the one to be pissed off. I want to go out and kill anyone who hurts you." Rosalind touched the bandage with a gentle hand.

Taryn tilted her head. "I think pissed off would suit you. You can join the Lesbian Avengers. Go out and scare the queer bashers. Shave your head. Get a few more tattoos and some strategic piercings—"

"Can't I be an activist and have hair?" Rosalind asked.

Taryn shrugged, then winced. "Ow. Bad idea. Headache."

"Come on. Lean on me. I'm taking you home."

Paul looked up when the doors opened. Joe had come back into the waiting room several minutes earlier, looking calm. Egyptia and Misha had half risen from their chairs. A glance at his face sat them back down. Everything might not be fine yet, but it was going to be. Joe managed to communicate this with a smile, with the way his thumbs were hooked into his pockets, the looseness of his stride. The patriarch exuded confidence. The tribe responded. Even Rhea seemed to uncoil. When Taryn came back, one long arm draped around Rosalind's shoulders, the waiting happiness was unleashed. He watched everyone mob the wounded girl, touching her, speaking in tripping layers, all but eating her alive. One person can be the touchstone of a group, can be elected to carry its heart. Taryn seemed to feed on the affection, growing stronger at each step, the familiar arrogant gleam back in her eye, the hint of a swagger in her walk. She wore her lover's supporting arm like a badge of honor.

And Rosalind…a casual glance in her direction was enough to see the change. She glowed like she'd been gilded with fire, burnished with it. Paul felt it, even as he hung back, felt the giddiness of the moment. Taryn was all right. The disaster had brushed them but passed them by. Paul felt the amplification of emotion, tossed back and forth from face to face, rising. It was too much to stand apart from.

They'd started to recall the attack, make it over into a story. With the disaster receding, the adrenaline lent the tale flavor, heightened their pleasure. It was the joy of cheating death, of the narrow escape, now it had to be boasted of and ritualized.

Joe spoke of Misha being upended into the car, of hearing the squeal of tires in the narrow alley. Paul heard his name mentioned. It hauled him in.

"I saw Taryn go down. The next thing I knew, there were Egyptia and Paul at my side, like the cavalry charging to the rescue. You should have seen Egyptia with her high heels ready, looking like avenging Isis. And Paul…" Here Joe paused and clapped Paul on the shoulder. "Paul lost his mind. He stood over Taryn's body and stared that car down. Nothing was getting through him. And he convinced that car. It turned right around and took off. Stonewall Paul."

Joe said it with his hand resting on Paul's shoulder. It was like the sky opening up. Paul felt, for the first time, what it was like to be at the center. He belonged. The story was about him. He was the hero. Rhea smiled. He saw Misha looking at him with envy, Egyptia looking at him with something else again. Rosalind gave him such a soft look he nearly broke down. She'd never looked at him like that before, like he was brave. Even Taryn smiled at him with admiration.

"That was a godawful stupid thing to do," Taryn said approvingly. "Thanks. Um, we're having this drag show thing. You want to come?"

CHAPTER NINETEEN

"Where the hell is my jacket?" The cry echoed from the second floor, down the back stairs and into the kitchen, ringing with frustration and anxiety. Angry footsteps clomped down the hall. Rhea raised her eyebrow and sipped at her tea.

"Aren't you going to answer her?" Paul asked, setting his teacup down.

"No. In a moment, she will recall that she left it across the back of the chair in her room, and she will feel foolish for throwing a fit. I'm sparing both of us the trouble of escalating the event," Rhea said serenely.

"Rhea, where are my shoes?" Joe bellowed from the front of the house.

"Right where you left them," Rhea said in a normal tone of voice.

"Oh, right. Sorry." Joe popped his head into the kitchen, then ducked up the back stairs.

"You're the only one not losing your head. Between the show and the wedding tonight, everyone has gone nuts. I'd expect you to be at least a little nervous," Paul said, looking at Rhea.

"Why?" Rhea asked.

"Well, you are the bride."

Rhea laughed. "I picked the right man. I'm sure of my choice.

The ritual will be great fun. There's no reason to be distressed. Now Joe—" There was a crash from the second floor. Rhea ignored it. "This is Joe's second marriage. But his first as a man. It means more to him. He's as nervous as I've ever seen him."

Paul considered this. "Is Joe's ex-husband coming to the wedding?"

Rhea paused and smiled at him as if he'd made progress. "Oh, yes. Ray is coming. It will be nice to see him. Stephan, his lover, should be there as well. It would be good for Misha to see him."

Paul found himself nodding as if this were perfectly natural. He caught himself and laughed. The laugh grew, pulling his head forward. He collapsed on the table. His head propped on his arms, laughing until his ribs felt like they were separating.

Goblin walked into the kitchen, munching on an apple. She looked at the man collapsed on the table, laughing his lungs out. "He all right?" she asked Rhea.

"Yes. He just got the joke for the first time. He'll be fine," Rhea said.

Goblin shrugged and wandered to the sink.

"You should get into the bathroom as soon as Taryn vacates, before the men use all the hot water," Rhea said calmly. The table shook from Paul's continued convulsions.

Goblin walked over and leaned on the back of Rhea's chair, watching Paul with interest. "Is it the tattoo?"

"I expect so. I finished it this morning. He's been floating for hours. I'm rather proud of this one. The bear came out well," Rhea said.

Goblin shook her head. "I hope he peaks before the show. Taryn'll belt him if he's laughing during the performance."

Paul rolled his head on the table. "Nothing ever goes. Everything changes and nothing ever goes. Not divorce, not death. Your ex just comes to your wedding, dead or not." He started laughing again.

"You're finally getting it," Rhea said, patting him on the arm.

Paul rested his cheek on the table and looked askance at Rhea. "How is it that you don't go around laughing all the time? It's absurd!"

"For the same reason I don't go around crying all the time. My nature is to see the sorrow, to seek it out and embrace it. To defeat it without flinching. But some see the joy, seek out the rock with the view of the sky and launch like eagles. Like Rosalind, who sees so much of the love. We need both. The pain and the joy are the sides of the madness. At the heart, at the center of everything is...a hub. Like the center of a wheel. You're caught out on the spokes, spinning. You will come to rest at the center in time," Rhea said.

Paul raised his head. "That's one of the most direct things you've ever said to me."

"You're ready to hear me now. Why waste words on a man who refuses to understand the language? But you've spent time immersed. Your ears are open."

"What I did with my semester abroad: I lived in a witch's house until I lost my mind, and nothing hurt anymore," Paul said with the edge of laughter.

"Things will still hurt, Paul. But now you will know that beneath all, nothing ever goes. Change is painful, but nothing ends. Nothing is wasted. Deep peace lies at the heart of the wheel." Rhea's eyes were coals of ebony, ringed with the yellow dance of flames. "Tonight, at the wedding, I would like you to stand up for me."

"You're kidding," Paul said, shocked and thrilled.

"Do I ever kid?" Rhea asked.

"I guess not. I'd be honored, Rhea."

"Good," Rhea said crisply. "Joe gets Taryn. I get Rosalind and you. It's fitting that you should be on the same side."

"What will I have to do?" Paul asked.

"When the priestess binds our hands, you will hand me the goblet. I would like you to say a prayer. You get to create the prayer, no limits." Rhea pushed a piece of heavy yellow paper and a pen toward Paul. "I have to help Goblin choose a dress. We'll be leaving for the show in a few hours. Joe has set aside a suit for you."

Paul took up the pen. "Thanks, Rhea," he said absently. He opened the paper as the witch left the room, soft-footed as a cat.

The heavy yellow paper stayed in Paul's hand as he jotted down notes while he watched Joe get ready. Joe's normally sure hands were clumsy with haste and heightened emotion, making a hash of his bow tie. Paul finally pushed the folded square of paper into his pocket and stood up.

"Here. Let me do that," Paul said, taking the tie away from Joe.

The man smiled, embarrassed and charming in his helplessness. "Thanks. I'm usually good at this."

Paul bent down to the tie. Joe arched his neck. Paul was close enough to smell the man's cologne, something with the notes of wood and musk. He could see the skin on Joe's neck where he had shaved close. Joe's beard had been fiercely shaped and touched with oil. He had no Adam's apple. Paul spoke, his breath touching the man's skin. "I had to learn how to do this for my wedding. A bow tie is not an easy thing. But when the day came, I was such a mess my father had to do it for me." Paul felt his ribs constrict, squeezing his heart. It was the first casual mention he'd made of his father, the first time a memory had come as a natural thing. He stood up, lips pressed together. Joe hadn't noticed.

"That's perfect. I always hoped my father would be able to do something like that for me. Life don't always work out the way we think it will," Joe said, looking into the mirror on the dresser. He saw a handsome man of thirty-four, broad through the shoulders, not particularly tall but well built, going rapidly bald. He smiled at his reflection.

"I'm sorry. Did he pass on?" Paul asked.

Joe looked over his shoulder and grinned. "No, I did."

"Ah. He wasn't good with your change," Paul said, coming to stand next to Joe. They faced themselves in the mirror, two men of a similar age, wearing identical black tuxedos.

"No," Joe said calmly. "I miss them, but they weren't able to accept it. Parents aren't always ready for their children to change. Makes me pretty damn determined never to do that to Goblin, not even if she wants to marry the next Jesse Helms."

"She's lucky. She's got a great dad," Paul said. "Two of them, I guess?"

"Ray's her dad. But I'm partial to being her papa. I'm growing into it." Joe squared his bow tie. "That's a handsome knot."

"When I was a boy I never thought of my parents as growing. They just were there, frozen in time. Eternal." Paul's voice cracked like a boy's.

"You miss him, don't you?" Joe set his hand on Paul's shoulder.

"Yes," Paul said with relief like the sight of shore. "Yes. I do miss him." The truth of the emotion was quiet but sure. He missed his father. For the first time since the funeral. In that moment Paul felt the ice in the chambers of his heart crack into a white spray, sending the powder along his veins. He missed his father.

"That's good. He'll be happy to hear that," Joe said with a mysterious smile.

"Gentlemen! If you do not get down here right now, we are going to the show without you!" Egyptia called in a high falsetto.

"Come on. The night's about to start."

The theater had to be approached through the waxed concrete corridors of a hairpin factory. He could make an artful metaphor out of it, Paul could, the trek through the factory halls on the way to the creation, but this evening didn't need metaphor. The facts were colorful enough. The freight elevator added atmosphere, Paul thought absently, but the crowd was the real decoration. There, in a hall of blinding white walls and shining gray floors, under florescent lights that hung from wire stalks, gathered a crowd of gypsies. Color flared in silk waterfalls from women far too tall for nature, standing out above many short men with hands in the pockets of their secondhand suits. The men were women, or female boys, beardless and eager. The women were crafted. The gender markers were convoluted, but weeks in the witch's house had readied him.

"Funny. I think we're the only normal guys here," Paul said to Joe, from the corner of his mouth.

"The only men in suits?" Joe asked in sheer delight. Paul seemed unaware of what he'd said. He was busy looking down the expanse of corridor at the crowd spilling over from the open doors of the arts center. The mass of people surprised him. He'd thought this was a minor show, something friends and immediate family patronized out of love. It was a drag show, for goodness sake, in a resolutely blue-collar town. All the publicity had been low key, fliers handed out in bars, posters along Elmwood Avenue, word of mouth. Joe had filled him in. Ellie and the cast had done most of it themselves.

"I wouldn't worry. The women will be here soon. In the proper context even we make perfect sense," Joe said.

"Even we," Paul repeated as the elevator doors opened and the metal gate was thrown back. Even overeducated, suburban white guys in their thirties, going bald, looking wholly unremarkable in this Mardi Gras crowd. He and Joe looked like two of a kind.

Egyptia strolled up the hall, her scintillating bright golden gown sweeping the floor. The queen spied them and broke into a brilliant smile, and Paul thought: context. He offered Egyptia his arm.

"Why thank you, honey. Don't you look smart in your tux? Who would have guessed he cleaned up well?" Egyptia asked Joe over Paul's head.

Rosalind and Rhea came up the corridor, Rhea in blue that hovered near the edge of black, Rosalind in a dress of scarlet. Crimson, bright as fresh blood, a shade he'd never imagined her wearing. Her hair was up, a style Egyptia must have done for her, but it was willful, escaping in lines that caught the light like rain. She looked remarkable, Paul thought, without the usual stab of pain. Paul looked at the people he stood with in a moment of pride. Everyone looked remarkable, dressed for a celebration.

"We better get in there. It looks sold out," Joe said.

"Ellie told me we have a few seats reserved in the front row," Rosalind said.

"We'd better," Egyptia said, looking shocked. "We are that boy's family. And they don't have a show without their king." A female boy handed him a program. Paul looked at her. She was shining. She wore a white T-shirt with a gray vest over it, buttoned closed, loose on her thin frame. Her brown hair was cropped close. She wore wire frame glasses and multiple small hoops in her ears. Paul smiled at her. She might have been one of his students. The enthusiasm with which she returned the smile was like a torch being lit. Something extraordinary was happening tonight. She was in on it, so was he. He felt the fire pass to him as she went away through the crowd, glowing. The soldiers that followed Joan of Arc could have looked no surer, facing down the English.

"I think that's one of Linda's students. They're doing the door and the ushering tonight," Rosalind said.

"She looked pretty excited," Paul said.

The usher at the door was a handsome, manly young woman in a pinstripe suit, complete with a white carnation in the buttonhole and a hat set at a jaunty angle. She looked rather like the groom at an Italian wedding. "Standing room only, sorry," she said, holding her arm across the door.

Egyptia looked down at her. The usher was half the queen's elevated height. "You don't understand. This…" Egyptia paused, indicating Rosalind with a wave of her hand, "is Rosalind Olchawski."

The queen waited for the information to sink in.

The effect, when it came, was gratifying. The usher's eyes grew very round, fixing in enchanted disbelief on the woman in the heart's blood dress. "Dr. Olchawski? Taryn's girl?"

"Yes," Rosalind said with a faint blush.

The usher beamed, lighting up the way the other young woman had. "We saved the front row for you. Right this way. Taryn made sure to get you the best seats in the house."

They took their seats in the front row, intimate distance from the stage. The back wall of the house was matte black. The facing walls were of a deep royal blue. Misha sat at the light board, a half-seen gargoyle above the back row. The house lights dimmed down. The noise of the crowd rose. Excitement sparked up. The room was full to capacity. People stood along the walls. The handsome woman at the door pulled it shut.

Okay, Paul thought. *I'm open, I'm ready. Let the games begin.*

He saw Taryn appear in a blaze of light. Even her tie had a perfect Windsor knot. Her goatee was perfect. Her jacket hung in a smooth line from her shoulders. Paul was puzzled. Something was going on, from the way the audience drew in its breath, sharp, scandalized.

His eye traveled down and saw that the coal black pants were open. The zipper was down. She was standing in such a way that he caught her right side. What was that in her left hand, hanging down loosely against her leg? It couldn't be…

Next to him, Rosalind shifted in her seat and crossed her legs. Taryn let her hand be seen, then, casually, slid it into her pants. A few minor adjustments, then a devilish grin as she zipped her trousers up.

Lights went to black. The show became a dazzling spectacle

that blurred past him, music, lights, scenes that slipped like phantasms through his fingers when he tried to grasp at their meaning. Some comedy he expected, sure. Drag was historically used for that. The two boys doing an Abbott and Costello routine made him laugh. They'd chosen to dress more obviously for that number, loose ties and unbound breasts, hair under fedoras. Girls looking like girls playing boys. Some lip-synching, also, he expected that. Drag queens did that. Fun, but not earth shattering. Was there nothing else to this than a little bit of play with the boundaries, a little bit of a joke?

Then the light broke. Sheer white, bouncing off the sharp white shirts of the boys, now circling the stage in a single file. All were clad exactly alike, dress shirts, black trousers with a length of rope for a belt. More lip-synching? No, they were moving. Now each of them had a chair. The music kicked up, from slow and building, to a driving beat. The boys all broke from the stage and went into the audience.

Now he understood why they were sitting in the front row. It wasn't just a place of honor. Taryn strolled toward them, and Paul felt himself anchored into his chair. From the quick look of confusion Rosalind tossed at him, she didn't know what was going on either.

Taryn took Rosalind's hand and led her up onstage. The seat next to Paul's felt very empty. All around him the kings selected women from the audience and led them up onstage and sat them in the chairs.

With military precision, they snapped the rope free of their belt loops. Another snap, and it went around the woman in the chair before them. Held captive, the women shrieked in delight as the kings danced for them. The look on Rosalind's face transfixed him. Such desire, from a woman. Everything was backward. He could imagine Rosalind dancing for Taryn, sprawled out and lustful in a chair. Dancing was female. Being danced for was male. But this? The boys danced for the women and the women gave themselves over to hunger. If not for the rope, some of the women might just have stood up and seized their boys.

One crack of a heel, like a drumbeat, and all the kings straddled the women. It was easy for Taryn, with the length of her legs, to stand astride Rosalind, to offer then refuse, her hips to her captive. He never would have imagined it, a butch lap dance.

The house lights coming up were a shock. Egyptia patted him on the knee.

"Intermission. Come on, honey. We can beat the crowd."

Egyptia took Paul's hand and led him out into the gallery.

"You have to move fast if you want to get a good space."

Egyptia sat down on one of the few bar stools lined up against the far wall of the gallery space. Paul gratefully sat down next to the queen. Someone to anchor him, to share a space in that sea of heightened emotion.

The doors opened and the audience flooded out. They massed around the bar, buying beer and water, wine and soda. The noise was deafening. Egyptia leaned over and shouted into Paul's ear. "Well?"

Paul frowned, puzzled. "Well what?"

Egyptia leaned back in. He could feel the queen's breath on his skin. "What do you think?"

Paul nodded, understanding the question. "You want the virgin's opinion? It's wonderful. I had no idea. Is it like this when you perform?"

Egyptia smiled seductively. "I should make you come and find out for yourself. But if I can't have you as a virgin, I'm not sure I want you."

"Virginity is overrated," Paul said earnestly.

"Well, I sure don't miss mine," Egyptia said.

"Seriously, Joe told me Taryn performs with you. What's it like?" Paul asked.

Egyptia shook her head. "Performed, I think. I don't expect I'll get that boy back now that all these girls have their hands on him. I think he's going in a new direction. When we do it, it has much more grandeur, more style. Let me put it this way. A queen is larger than life. We show life what it could be by being just too much." Egyptia's hand drifted up and made a minute adjustment to her wig.

Paul watched the gesture, mesmerized. It was languid, offhand, but perfectly timed. Too perfectly timed to be anything but art. "I get it."

"I think you do." Egyptia smiled at him. "Like the cigarette people say, 'You've come a long way, baby.'"

Rosalind, Joe, and Rhea fought their way through the crowd to a spot by the wall.

"I'll get drinks. Wine all around?" Joe asked.

"Water for me. I will be drunk enough later, on you and your wine," Rhea said.

Joe grinned and kissed her.

"Wine, Ros?"

"That sounds good. I feel a little flushed," Rosalind said.

The press of the crowd surged around them and carried Joe off.

"I don't wonder why. Elvis has that effect on women," Rhea said smiling.

"Don't I know it. I could hear some of the audience talking on the way out. I'll be lucky if I ever see her again," Rosalind said.

"Yes, that's the problem. Taryn has to be dragged, kicking and screaming, to your bed," Rhea said.

Rosalind laughed. "Maybe not that bad."

"If anything stood in her way she would go right through it," Rhea said.

Rosalind caught sight of a familiar platinum wig above the crowd. "There's Paul and Egyptia. I bet he's a little overwhelmed. I'm going to grab them. Wait here."

Paul was leaning in close to Egyptia, his head tilted in concentration, as the queen spoke into his ear. They looked very involved.

"Hey, Paul! We have a spot over by the wall. Care to join us?"

Paul looked up. "No, I think we're fine here. I'm talking to Egyptia."

"Okay." Rosalind walked back to Rhea.

"Are they joining us?" Rhea asked.

Rosalind blinked and shook her head. "No. They were having a conversation. Paul said he was fine."

"Hmm," Rhea said.

Joe came back, balancing cups. "Savages, all of them. Get them all whipped up and turn them loose on the bar."

"Ellie! Hey!" Rosalind called out, motioning her over. Ellie, head to toe in black with a headset loose around her neck, slid like a knife between packed people.

"Hey, darling. You enjoying it so far?" Ellie asked.

"It's wonderful. I had no idea she was going to drag me up onstage," Rosalind said.

"Some idea. Come on, you're dating Elvis."

"Yeah," Rosalind said wistfully. "Hey, are you going to see her before the second half?"

"I am the stage manager," Ellie said.

Rosalind beamed. "Good. I want you to give her something for me."

Ellie burst into the dressing room. "Okay, this is your ten-minute warning. I'll be flashing the lights to get them back in. Very good response, guys. They're loving it."

"That mean we have time for a cigarette?" Wolf asked.

Ellie took her head set off and stared at Wolf. "If you can smoke it and be back here, in costume for the street scene, in five. Don't make me hunt you down, little boy. I'm in full bitch mode."

"The best stage managers always are. Did you see Rosalind?" Taryn asked.

Ellie strolled over to Taryn, who was taking her jacket off the costume rack. She looked Taryn over from slicked hair to motorcycle boots.

"I sure did."

"Is she liking it?" Taryn asked, her back to Ellie.

"Very much. She wanted me to give you something from her," Ellie said.

Taryn looked over her shoulder. "What?"

Ellie spun Taryn around and wrapped her arms around her neck. The dressing room was suddenly quiet as a church as Ellie gave Taryn a monumental, gigantic, world-class kiss.

"Whoa," Sam said, looking at Wolf.

Ellie came up for air. "That's from your girl. And I have to say, I finally got a good excuse to kiss both of you. Any more messages you want to send, you know where to find me. Now get dressed. You have seven minutes."

It was when he stopped trying to understand that the show became intelligible to him, Paul thought. Girls as boys, girls as girls, switch or change or hide or reveal, illusion or revelation, it was all magic. It was comedy, and dancing, and lip-synching, but it was all celebration. Here, in this context, everybody made sense. Freedom was there to be had for the asking. Desire was lauded. Masculinity was spoofed, and revealed.

Taryn was performing a monologue about going to the gynecologist that had been quite funny when she stopped, he thought, directly in front of him. The audience vanished, the stage vanished, she was just talking, directly to him.

"What do you see when you look at me?" Taryn demanded. It seemed like a ridiculous question; she was a handsome boy, tall, broad shouldered, lean hipped, dangerous and sexy and thrilling.

"Some people take off their clothes and get naked. I take off my clothes and strip away layers of meaning, of context and desire. I strip off my clothes, and I'm invisible." Her hands moved to the buttons on her shirt, undoing them, one by one. "I don't trade marshmallow recipes, and I don't have kids, and no, I'm not pregnant. Yes, I'm very sure. No, I don't use birth control. No, not even condoms. Invisible."

❖

Tattoos writhed from her neck, down her back and arms, disappearing into the thin white shell of the tank top. Ink and muscle sheathing bone. A body that did not speak to expectations. Here, with just this much skin revealed, she was still a boy. Would she be, if the tank top came off? The jeans? The black shirt trailed on the stage like a banner with the wind gone out. Her hand flashed forward, the shirt arched through the air, landing in Paul's lap.

Afterward, Paul could tell from the clapping that punctured his thoughts that Robbie and Grace had delivered monologues, but he couldn't recall a word. The black shirt stayed in his knotted fists.

Invisible. The word resonated in his skull, shaking him like a rung bell. It was how he'd felt all his life. It made becoming an observer easy. He was already removed from the action, outside the mainstream. Only when Rosalind, who was the center of attention and warmth, turned her eyes on him was he visible. Like a satellite seen by reflected light.

But Taryn? Taryn was the center of attention, magnetic, dangerous. He couldn't conceive of her being invisible. Yet there it was, the outline of a situation with the cold ring of truth. Even she, even that arrogant, charismatic swaggering boy, became invisible out of her context.

In that moment it came to him. Anybody seemed perfectly at home in their own environment. That was the only way he'd seen Taryn. He had tried to compare his experience with hers, but he had been a fish out of water when he'd landed at 34 Mariner, lost beyond all finding. Her ironclad sense of self had aroused envy and a grudging admiration. Taryn knew who she was. Hell, most of the denizens of the witch's house seemed to know exactly who they were. They made it look easy, even Joe, secure in his genial masculinity.

Paul's mind turned to Joe, to helping him dress for the evening. He glanced down the row of seats, past Rosalind, glowing with pride, to Egyptia, regal and amused, her endless legs crossed, displaying graceful ankles just a hint too strong for expectation. Joe sat with a delighted smile on his face, holding Rhea's hand in his lap. A man about to be married. A man. The journey he had undertaken to become the man he was could have crushed him. Instead, it had given him an endless reserve of humor and love. That had been his choice. Down the row, his ex-wife, shining with love for her girlfriend. A drag queen, a transman, and a witch.

They were at home here, but none of them had been born into their place. They had come to it, created it, out of years of pain and searching, out of stubborn refusal to be only what was expected, out of desire. Rosalind had been struggling then. How had he not seen it? *Sometimes it is willful, our refusal to see,* he thought. *I wasn't ready to see her. She still had to be what I needed.*

He could feel her, next to him, radiating warmth. She felt his look and smiled at him, tearing herself away from the stage for a moment. Just as she'd always done, felt his need and answered it, even when she longed to be looking elsewhere. He felt the weight, then, of the expectations he had always placed on her. How had she carried them and never broken? Only after they had ended had she started to seek herself out, a woman in her thirties starting the work of identity. She'd moved off to Buffalo, alone. *Look at her now,* younger than he recalled, burnished by the love she'd found. *No,* Paul thought, *not just that.* She'd also found herself.

It hadn't been easy for any of them. It couldn't have been. But they were here. It was survivable. Everyone went through it. Not just queer people, though coming out was a hallmark of creating identity. Everyone. He sat with that thought while the drag show ended, while the applause started to shake the walls. He wasn't any different than anyone else and perhaps, at the center, nobody was. What was intrinsic stayed intrinsic. He felt it, for the first time, the profundity of the connection between himself and the people around him. He'd always wanted to belong. What he hadn't known was that he already did.

❖

In the dressing room some of the other kings were changing. Taryn buttoned up her spare black shirt quickly.

"You heading out there, T?" Robbie asked her.

"Have to meet my adoring public." Taryn slipped out the door with a grin.

They were all there, Egyptia, Rhea, Joe, Misha down from the tech booth, Ellie still in her backstage black, Linda holding the flowers the kings had gotten for her. Even Paul, who looked dazed, leaning on Egyptia's arm.

Taryn raised an eyebrow at that, but Egyptia just blew her a kiss. And Rosalind. Her lover's look took Taryn's breath for a moment. *This is why we do this.* That look, pride and desire and recognition. A woman who knew what she wanted and you just knew it was you. That look, from a woman who saw all of you and reached for you, hands open. There was nothing else to do but take Rosalind in her arms and kiss her.

Taryn felt Rosalind's arms wind around her neck, felt her lover's hands comb through her hair. This was what mattered, being able to turn from the spotlight and still be seen. To have Rosalind there, waiting for her. They parted slowly from the kiss, Rosalind's arms still around Taryn's neck.

"Don't know who I bribed in heaven to have you look at me like that," Taryn said softly.

"I'll always look at you like this. You're my boy," Rosalind answered.

Taryn felt the hands on her back, tugging at her arms, a horde of people congratulating her, all seeking her attention. She smiled helplessly at Rosalind, who slid an arm around Taryn's waist, opening up, allowing the crowd to greet the drag king.

When the greeting had ebbed a bit, when most of the crowd was filing out, the family remained in a circle.

"Time to be off! We have a wedding to throw, in another country, at midnight. We can fawn over the pretty boy on the way," Misha said.

Ellie poked him in the ribs. "Hey, we all worked on the show. I think we all deserve a little fawning."

"Very well. Come with me to the wedding, and I will fawn over you," Misha said, grinning.

"I'm coming to the wedding either way. But with you? I'll think about it."

Egyptia dangled a set of keys. "Enough out of the both of you. Come on, boys and girls, Egyptia's driving."

Joe shook his head. "I don't think we're even going to make it across dressed as we are, all still high from the show. The guards are gonna take one look at the van full of us and close the border."

"It is Halloween. Tonight we have free passage across all borders," Rhea said.

Taryn slipped out of Rosalind's arm. "You guys go on ahead. There's one thing I have to do."

Taryn ducked away from the circle. In the midst of the crowd, her eye had caught someone standing by the bar, watching her but not approaching. It was easy to pick out the bright flame of metallic red hair.

Taryn hadn't seen Colleen since the first night she'd brought Rosalind into Spot Coffee. From the look on Colleen's face, seeing Taryn was tying her stomach in knots.

When Taryn walked right up to her, Colleen stood, nervously pulling at the sleeves of her shirt.

"Hey," Taryn said gently.

"Hi."

"I'm glad you could make it to the show."

Colleen looked away, at the bar, at her feet, at Taryn's hands. "Well, you know I'm in Linda's class and everyone came and all. It was great. Everybody was great. You were…" She let the sentence die, unable to imagine how to finish it.

"Colleen." Taryn's voice was warm, but insistent. It was time to grow up a little.

"Yeah?"

"I owe you an apology. I was a jackass to you, the way I treated you. It was cruel and stupid. You are a great girl, sweet and generous. I don't want you thinking it was your fault or anything."

"You never promised me anything. I knew how it was."

Taryn shook her head. "It was wrong. I didn't pay any attention to how you felt. You deserve a lot better than that."

Tears started down Colleen's cheeks. "I never thought I'd ever hear you say anything like that."

"I keep getting reminded, people change."

"So I guess you are still seeing Dr. Olchawski."

Taryn nodded. "Yeah."

"Never woulda figured that. I mean, she's really nice," Colleen said.

"Yes. She is." Taryn reached out and cupped Collen's chin. "So are you. You'll make some lucky girl very happy. Don't let anybody step on your heart, okay?"

"Yeah. Okay."

"Good. I'll see you around?" Taryn asked, smiling.

"Yes. I'd like that."

Taryn jogged into the lobby, where Egyptia was pointedly waiting, tapping her wicked nails against Paul's shoulder in a tiger's display of impatience.

"Do I look like the kind of woman who has all night to be waiting around?"

"No, you look like the kind of woman who has to be the center of attention. Which is gonna be hard, seeing as it's not your wedding we're going to," Taryn said.

Egyptia waved her nails like a steel fan closing. "I don't think I'll have any trouble being the center of attention. If a certain ham can get off his 'I'm the ghost of Elvis' trip long enough for anyone else to get warm in the light."

"I am not a spotlight hog," Taryn said, wounded.

"Whatever, Mr. Thing. You sure didn't look too much like you were sharing up there."

Taryn let her lower lip quiver. "Egyptia, you know I have issues. I have trouble sharing my toys."

"Depends on whom you're sharing them with," Paul said from behind the screen of Egyptia's extravagant gestures.

Egyptia and Taryn stopped dead.

"What? I can't make a crack? Everyone else in this madhouse does," Paul said.

"Didn't expect it out of you. That was actually funny," Taryn said.

"You never know what people are capable of in the right moment," Paul said, oblivious to the smile Egyptia flashed at Taryn.

CHAPTER TWENTY

They walked down the cut stone path to the sound of drums, bells, singing, and a chant weaving throughout all the other noise like a snake in the long summer grass.

Isis, Astarte, Diana, Hecate, Demeter, Kali, Innanna
Isis, Astarte, Diana, Hecate, Demeter, Kali, Innanna
Isis, Astarte, Diana, Hecate, Demeter, Kali, Innanna

It was the Worm Ouroboros. It ended and began and ended without seam, the shell of an egg. Women ringed around the bonfire, dancing. Men and women circled about the edge of the dance, drumming.

Rhea's former coven had been setting up for hours, so that when the company arrived from the drag show, the wedding would be ready to go. The circle had been cast, the directions called. Sage and sweet grass burned. Music now called forth both spirit and the spirits. It was Samhain, the witch's New Year, the night of all the long year when the veil between the worlds grew thin and permeable as gauze. Here, on the lakeshore, near the border between nations and elements, the border between life and death grew thin like stretched gold wire. Ceramic dishes of apples and red-dyed eggs were set out on long wooden tables hastily constructed from planks. Ale, beer, hard cider, and hot wine flowed. Women danced, children ran back and forth on the sand. Into this walked Rhea, at the head of her company.

After the drive across the border, fortuitously without incident, the group had split along the groom's side and the bride's. Egyptia,

Rosalind, and Ellie went with Rhea. Taryn and Misha went with Joe. They separated in the grassy spot used for parking, without word, before the arching wooden gate. There would be time for talking. This wasn't it. The women went to prepare the bride. The men and the boy went to ready the groom.

Weddings divide along gender lines by ancient custom, the separation of the two worlds emphasized before their hopeful joining.

The compound was as Rhea remembered it, enough so that it bit at her when she walked up the path between the houses. She took the house on the left, her house. Joe had the house on the right, her cousin's house. A simple matter of forging keys gave them access. It caused her pain in the most familiar way, the way visiting this spot always did, the pain of a past that she never let go of. Rhea was not a woman to let go.

Taryn hadn't understood, in her teens, why Rhea hated going up to the cabin, to the lake house. It was, for Rhea, like visiting the scene of an accident where someone she'd loved died. The dried blood was still on the floor. That was the feeling that radiated from the lake house for her, the trapped rejection of her birth family. Yes, it was externally beautiful. Yes, it was the one place that Taryn seemed to fully relax. It was only that last thing, the good it did for Taryn, that enabled Rhea to endure the spot at all while they were lovers. As soon as their romantic relationship faded into the bonds of family, Rhea had abandoned coming here.

It was then that Taryn started to understand. She would feel the same way, if she ever went back to Lackawanna, to the house on Pine and Lincoln. Memory can be very tied to a certain place. Both the memory and the place can be avoided. Not forever, Rhea thought. But what was truly forever? All things moved on the Wheel. All seasons passed. She was living proof. She was living, proof.

Egyptia scuttled past, her skirt held up to avoid tripping on the hem. "Let me. I know how to make an entrance. Now, Rhea, you haven't been up here since the menfolk have been working, so I want you to close your eyes and walk in." Egyptia held her hand on the door.

Rhea smiled. "Very well. I will be surprised."

Certainly there was a taste of humor in the words. If she wanted, Rhea could know what the inside of the house looked like. It took effort not to know, but it was a choice Rhea was learning how to make.

Pretend you don't know what is in the child's hand. The importance was in the way it was held out to you.

So she closed her eyes, and other things, and let Egyptia open the door and Rosalind call her in.

Ellie and Egyptia guided her into the center of the living room. She knew the layout of the house, had walked it in darkness for decades.

"Okay, honey. Open them!" Egyptia cried.

Rhea opened. The wood stove was familiar; beyond that, nothing was. The smoky gray-green paneling was gone. The room glowed like garnets in the softened light. The color of the dress he had given her, she knew it at once. Joe's touch, it had to be, that subtle attention. It was a house she didn't know.

She turned in a full circle, taking everything in, feeling the work that had gone into this moment, feeling the affection behind the work, and the hope. Gradually, she opened and felt the house itself. The pain was gone. Whatever they had done here had been inadvertent, a side effect of the work they did together. There was no Craft in it, no lingering taste of a spell or a cleansing. But it was magic nonetheless.

Egyptia clapped her hands. "You like?"

"Unbelievable," Rhea said.

"You should see the bedroom. Taryn's bride gift," Rosalind said softly.

"Yes," Rhea said and walked down the hall.

This time, she cheated, feeling the room before she went in. She opened the door with tears in her eyes.

Rosalind gave her a moment and then followed her in. Rhea was standing transfixed between the two murals: Demeter and Persephone; Cernunnos, the Green Man. "They worked on it together," Rhea said when Rosalind stood behind her. Her voice was full of wonder.

"Yes, they did. It was Paul's idea to add something for Joe, and he helped Taryn paint it."

"He helped create something, through knowing us. Through joining the family. Does he have any idea what he's done?" Rhea asked, touching the image of the handsome, bearded man with the open hands.

"I don't think so. Not yet. Does it matter?"

"Not at all. Magic can happen with and without knowing. In his case, I think it is entirely appropriate it happens without knowledge," Rhea said. She looked at Rosalind, the tears still on her cheeks as she smiled. "I can feel the night you and that impossible boy spent here, you know."

Rosalind blushed and tucked her hair behind her ear. "Ah, well..."

"It's lovely. A good blessing for the room."

Rosalind ducked her head and then looked back up at Rhea. "This is entirely inappropriate to be saying on your wedding night, but I should tell you something. I heard the talk you had with Taryn, in the kitchen. You know the one."

"Yes, I do," Rhea said calmly.

"I heard what you said, about it being time to move on. Time for her to accept not being the center of, well, everything to you."

"Yes," Rhea said.

"You said that to her. But she never got a chance to answer you before I came in. I want, I mean, I need to—" Rosalind stopped, unable to finish the sentence.

"To know what I think she would have said?" Rhea asked. Rosalind nodded, her throat closing with the threat of tears.

"I took a tomcat into my house once, a stray. Street cat, a real fighter, used to scavenging for everything. I would keep his dish full twice a day, and he would still attack it as if he would never see food again. He could not accept that he didn't live out of want anymore," Rhea said.

"So what happened to the cat?" Rosalind asked, feeling tears start to slide from the corner of her eyes.

"He grew up, settled down a little, and fell in love with an English professor," Rhea said with a perfectly straight face.

Rosalind laughed as the tears fell.

Rhea took her hands. "She loves you more than I've ever seen her love anyone or anything. She still comes from hunger. Be patient with her. You'll need to be. You two have a long time left to fight things out."

"That an observation?" Rosalind asked.

"No, that is a prediction. You belong to one another. This time around, you got lucky enough to both realize it at the same time."

Rhea released Rosalind's hands and looked at the bed. Her eyebrow rose in question.

"My bride gift," Rosalind said simply.

After the torturous night she'd spent on the old bed, made tolerable only by Taryn wrapped around her, Rosalind had known what she was getting for Rhea and Joe's union. It was a grand bed, mahogany with inlaid panels of cherry, piled with pillows and down comforters deep enough to drown in. "There's a spare quilt I brought up in the closet. Just in case you get cold."

"A bed fit for a king," Rhea said.

"For a goddess," Rosalind said without thinking, looking at the mural of Demeter.

She missed the dark humor of Rhea's sidelong glance. "*Hieros gamos*. I'd thought you'd forgotten before you were born."

"Pardon?" Rosalind asked, looking back at her.

"Fit for the union of the goddess and the god," Rhea said, her gesture including both murals.

Something Rhea had said struck a chord in her memory, something she'd heard often, long ago. Some mystery she'd once known. "What was that you—"

"Where is Paul?" Rhea asked abruptly.

Rosalind looked around, as if he might be in the room, overlooked. "I assumed he was with the men."

"He's standing for me. Poor man might not know where he's supposed to be."

"Should I go get him?" Rosalind asked.

"No, let Egyptia do it. I'd like a few minutes with you, if you would allow it," Rhea said.

Rosalind ducked back down the hall. Egyptia was showing her dress to Ellie.

"Whoa. I didn't know Marie Antoinette set the dress code. I'm feeling way underdressed," Ellie said, taking it in.

"Egyptia, would you go get Paul? Rhea wanted to have him here," Rosalind asked.

"Sure, honey. I can do that."

Egyptia found Paul standing on the lawn of the second house, staring down at the bonfire and the dancing on the beach below. The wind had picked up, driving the scent of brack, sage, and crushed flowers to crest against the edge of the grassy overhang.

Paul lifted his head into the wind, inhaling the mixture. Nothing else had ever smelled like this, this complex layering. A month ago, he'd have turned away in disgust at the first note, unable to get past the thick oily green scent. Now it was something to be endured, a momentary sting before the subtler layer of sandalwood and the pungency of the sage met him like old friends. His work with Rhea had taught him that. The limestone firepit was behind him, the smaller blaze a welcome hand on his lower back, steadying. Like a cat curled up to him on a cold night. He heard Egyptia's heels clatter on the stone path.

"You can see the lights from Buffalo. That cindery glow every city has," Paul said, glancing back over his shoulder at the queen.

"Buffalo is not every city, sugar. Trust me on this. But sometimes it is right nice to get away and look back at it," Egyptia said.

"I could say the same about marriage. In fact, I will. It is right nice to get away and look back on it, to watch other people and how they take it on. I wonder what they will do differently," Paul said.

"Just about everything. Joe and Rhea are not like anybody else. Aw, hell, nobody is like anybody else."

"You ever think about getting married?" Paul asked, tilting his head.

"You askin' me?" Egyptia pushed at his shoulder.

"No, I—"

"Relax, baby, I'm playing with you. I've thought about it. And if Denzel Washington ever wakes up and gives me a call, I'll be picking out my veil."

"So Denzel's your type?"

"Tall, chocolate, and handsome? Ooh, yeah. But if some *muy macho papi* comes along I could be persuaded. What about you? What's your type?"

"I used to say Rosalind. She was the incarnation of my type. But that wouldn't make a lot of sense to say nowadays, unless I want to be that guy that always dates girls who are about to come out." Paul shook his head.

Egyptia threaded her arm through his. "If it helps, honey, I'm already out. Come on, Miss Rhea sent me to fetch you."

❖

"Egyptia went after Paul. You wanted some time with me?" Rosalind asked.

Rhea sat down on the bed, perched like a sparrow. She patted the surface next to her. Rosalind took this as an invitation and joined her.

"I'm not much good at this," Rhea said, looking at the mural of Persephone and Demeter. "It has always been easier for me to live with hard emotions. Grief, loss, anger. In this, Taryn should have been my daughter." Rhea smiled at Rosalind.

"Taryn can be pretty hard. And that has its charm. But you know the moment I first knew I was in deep trouble with that boy?" Rosalind asked. She accepted the older woman's attentive silence as permission to continue. "Our first night together I burst into tears on her. She didn't make me explain, or pull away. She just held me. Tenderness was the last thing I expected from her. I knew right then that I'd fall for her hard."

"This is why I need you here. I have no idea of how to be. I've never been married. I thought it wouldn't faze me, but I find myself actually...scared," Rhea said.

"It's normal to get nervous."

"No, you misunderstand. I have *never* been married. I'm not sure it is even possible."

Rosalind listened carefully to where Rhea placed her emphasis. In it was the echo of thousands of years, dust gathered under syllables unmoved since a priestess had last gazed out of a plain brick gate in a city of enameled tiles.

"Oh. You mean...*never*, never."

"Yes."

"How can I help?" Rosalind asked.

Rhea smiled at her. "That has always been your nature, you know.

Presented with a challenge you accept it as personal and ask how you can help. What do you remember about the *hieros gamos*?"

"Er, yes. Greek, 'sacred marriage.' I know this. We've been through this," Rosalind said.

"We have been through this more times than you can number, more than the myriad fires of heaven, since the wind first lifted the birds above the waters, since the first hero took up his bronze-tipped arrows to slay monsters. You and your academic ancestors were always priestesses of the temple," Rhea said.

"I know you're going to tell me to just say the first thing that pops into my head without censoring it."

"You're psychic," Rhea said dryly.

"No life can exist without the blessing of heaven. The way the high priest of a city showed the favor of heaven is to marry the Great Goddess. The sacred marriage took place under the sky, at the top of the temple. One of the priestesses stood in for the goddess. The marriage was consummated before witnesses. It was the union of earth and sky, mortal and immortal. It renewed vegetation, guaranteed rain, foretold peace and prosperity for the city."

"How do we achieve it?"

"You have to tend the garden," Rosalind blurted out. "Follow the seasons, and even with their variations, the pattern remains. And the setting matters. For people in a desert city, surrounded with the yellow dust, the magic of growing things, of life renewed, is so much more potent."

"Setting matters." Rhea turned her head toward the lake, as if she could see straight through the wall.

"If they are wounded, let them rest. If they hunger, give them meat and wine. If they long, satisfy their longing, but if they desire, increase their desire. Ride with it on wings into the sun," Rosalind recited, from someone's memory.

"That's it!" Rhea jumped up, her thin body drawn up tight, a sinew under exertion.

"What's it?"

Rhea's dark eyes glowed. "Desire. Abundance. Symbols. We have a spell to cast, you and I."

"Okay."

"It will be intense for everyone," Rhea cautioned. "The sacred marriage is symbolic of joining and renewal for the whole community. If we do this properly, everyone in attendance will be swept up in it. There will be consequences. Desire will be unleashed."

"Hmm. If I follow you, and I think I do, everyone will be trying on their wings and mounting toward the sun, so to speak."

"Can we, in good conscience, do this?" Rhea asked.

Rosalind stood up and took Rhea's hand. "This is exactly what the celebration is for. Uniting across the boundaries. You have to take on the solemn responsibility of setting a good example and encouraging everyone to have a lot of sex."

Rhea doubled over laughing. "Me?"

"You."

"On Samhain?"

"It's the time you chose for the wedding, and with all the borders being crossed, what better time?" Rosalind asked.

There was a gleam of deviltry in Rhea's eyes. "Should we warn everyone?"

"Oh, I think they'll catch on soon enough."

The two women were laughing hysterically when Paul knocked on the door.

"What flowers are you carrying?" Rosalind asked.

"Red anemones. Blood lilies, from the spilled blood of Adonis as he died," Rhea said.

"Oh yeah, that's not too heavy-handed at all. A flower sprung from the blood of a beautiful youth slain in front of his grieving lover," Rosalind said, reclining on the bed.

"Sorry, they were fresh out of upbeat, cheerful flowers related to death and love."

"I say we send you out there in a necklace of skulls. That's holiday appropriate."

"Taking nakedness well past the flesh?"

Paul cleared his throat. "Sorry. Egyptia said you wanted to see me."

"Yes, Paul, please come in," Rhea said warmly.

"I'll go pester the groom's side," Rosalind said, rolling off the bed.

Rhea caught her arm. "You know what you need to do?"

"I know exactly what I need to do," Rosalind said and winked at her.

Rosalind knocked politely on the door of the cabin, even though it was half open. Misha met her, leaning his arm on the frame.

"May I come in?" Rosalind asked.

"Abandon hope all ye who enter here," Misha said as a form of welcome, and stepped away from the door.

Taryn looked up at her, surprised. She was sitting on the couch, putting the finishing touches on her polished shoes. "I thought the women weren't supposed to see us till the ceremony."

"There have been a few minor changes. Rhea sent me over to tell you guys about them."

Joe came out of the bedroom, pulling at his tie. "Be easier if you'd just hand me a rope and tell me to choke myself. I never liked ties."

"But it's such a guy thing," Taryn said, standing up.

"Your kind of guy thing, GQ boy. I'm more of a Home Depot guy. Hello, Rosalind. You look stunning." He leaned in and kissed Rosalind's cheek.

"I'm glad somebody noticed," Rosalind said, glancing pointedly at Taryn.

"It is not like Rhea to make last-minute changes to anything. She must be careful. She might end up impulsive," Misha said.

"What sort of changes?" Joe asked.

Rosalind handed out sheets of paper. "A quick rewrite to the ceremony. We have things that we'd like each of you to say. Look over them and see if you have any questions."

Misha took his with indifference, Taryn with interest, Joe with puzzlement.

Rosalind watched them with great satisfaction as their expressions changed. Joe looked up at her, did a double take, and clutched the paper in his hand.

"Rosalind, you know what this is, don't you?"

"Explicitly." Rosalind smiled on the word.

"I mean, of course you do. You wouldn't do anything like this without meaning to, or without knowing what the consequences will be, or could be, or the Rule of Three, calling it back on you. It's a lot to take on for the caster. Not that you're not up to it, of course you are—"

Taryn slapped him on the back. "You're babbling."

Joe looked at her, askance. Then back to Rosalind. He smiled, slowly, and started to nod. "Yes. Of course you are."

Misha squinted at the paper. "All I have to do is say this?"

Rosalind nodded. "And let the ceremony take its course."

He shrugged and folded the paper. "Nothing to it."

"Oh, you'd be surprised," Joe said, catching Rosalind's eye. They both burst out laughing in the same moment.

"Everyone is in on this?" Joe asked when he could breathe again.

"Everyone has a part to play, yes. Not everyone has fully absorbed their part. We haven't had a lot of briefing time. But Rhea and I thought it would explain itself once it begins," Rosalind said, the picture of sweetness and reason.

"Mighty Aphrodite." Joe shook his head. "This will be a night to remember."

"Okay, gentlemen. Sorry to interrupt and run, but we have a ceremony to start. I'll see you out by the fire. Good luck, Joe." She kissed Joe on the cheek.

"Wait a minute." Taryn's voice had dropped down into a growl. "That's it? No explanation?"

Rosalind stopped at the sound and faced Taryn. "Come here," she said pleasantly.

She took Taryn's hand. Rosalind threw a smile over her shoulder at Joe and Misha as she pulled her out the door. "I'll give her back in a minute."

Two long strides brought them to the back of the cabin, facing the distant road through a screen of pines.

"So what's this all about?" Taryn asked.

Rosalind stopped, pivoted, and took Taryn's hands and placed them on her waist. She leaned back against the wall, drawing Taryn in with her, kissing her passionately.

The smooth fabric of the dress ran like water through Taryn's hands, guided down over Rosalind's hips, called forth, raised, challenged, and met. Fingers curled into flesh, pulling like a new gravity. When they paused, hinted at stopping, they were nudged, urged on, pressed downward. Rosalind took Taryn's hand and guided it, lifting her dress like a veil.

She felt Taryn hesitate, aware of the path that ran by them, of the circle of light from the houses, of the people gathered on the lawn in front of the house. Voices filled the air around them, from a window they could hear Joe and Misha. None of that mattered.

She had to get Taryn's attention and she knew how. The wood caught on her dress as she turned against it, lifting her skirt.

"Come on, baby. Touch me."

In answer Taryn moaned, slid fingers under and around layers of cloth.

"Yes, baby. Just like that. I just want you to feel me. I want you to feel me."

The touch was light, experimental, tracing, gilding, calling waves. Rosalind arched her neck and pressed her head back against the wall, her hands fumbling around in Taryn's hair, grasping the back of her neck.

"I want you to feel me." She was wet, and Taryn's open mouth was in the curve between her neck and shoulder.

"Oh. Yes, baby. Sweet."

It was agony to take Taryn's wrist, to slow her motion, to softly pull those beloved fingers away. She could feel Taryn's question as she raised her head, eyes coming back into focus reluctantly.

"Just a taste. For now." Rosalind lightly kissed her lips.

An eyebrow rose, Taryn's look mingled arousal and frustration.

"More," Taryn said, biting at Rosalind's neck.

"Later," Rosalind said gently.

She watched the flare up of challenge in Taryn's eyes and it made her melt. Maybe they did have enough time for—

"Rosalind? T? Where'd you guys run off to? The processional is starting." It was Goblin, walking up the lawn. In a moment she would round the corner and learn more about the world than she needed to know just yet.

Rosalind hastily smoothed down her skirt, with no help from Taryn. Taryn leaned over her, one arm resting on the wall, covering Rosalind.

"I want to be inside you," Taryn whispered in her ear.

Goblin rounded the corner. "Oh, hey guys. Listen, the torches have gone down to the fire. We have to start the processional."

"Okay, Goblin. We're right behind you," Rosalind said. When Goblin's back was turned, Taryn lazily drew her hand up to her mouth and took her fingers in, one by one.

The processional started at the top of the lawn and followed down, past the limestone firepit, down the pale wooden stairs to the beach, where a bonfire raged up into the night. October 31, All Hallows' Eve, Samhain. Torchbearers had gone down first and stood in a loose ring. The coven had called the directions and cast the circle. Now all who came entered sacred space. The altar was set close enough to take heat from the fire. The previous nights had been cold as pain. Tonight there was a loosening of the bitterness, nothing resembling warm, merely less cold.

Rhea's side entered first, Goblin at the head of the line in a gown of brown and green, her hair unbraided. Rosalind followed. Her dress, of the friendly, accommodating skirt, was red as blood, red as the anemones that Rhea carried. Egyptia came next in a glory of cream and saffron, with a bemused Paul close at hand. Ellie wore black.

They stopped at the altar and turned, facing the assembled crowd. It was a small shock to Rosalind to see how many people were actually assembled on the beach. A rough estimate gave her nearly one hundred.

Goblin stepped forward into the space before the altar. "The circle has been cast. The community gathers to witness. Bring the betrothed forward to the altar. Who speaks for Rhea?"

"I speak for Rhea. It is her desire to stand before the altar with this man. Open the way," Paul said.

Rhea came into the circle as Paul spoke, in a long sleeved robe of white closed with bone toggles. She stood at the altar as Joe's side came down the steps, all in black tie.

Taryn walked first, a born performer, her step graceful and unhurried. She took the torch to the altar and set it in a sconce. Misha followed. He'd shaved. His brown hair was bound back and tucked into his collar. He looked younger than Rosalind ever remembered seeing him. Following him she recognized Ray, Joe's ex-husband and Goblin's father.

"Who speaks for Joe?" Goblin asked.

Misha stepped forward and spoke as Joe came down. "I speak for Joe. It is his desire to stand before the altar with this woman. Open the way."

On the altar, draped in red and gold, was a two-handed goblet with the base of a silver tree winding up around the cup of red glass. A dagger lay across the top, the hilt set toward the groom's side of the circle. The blade was twelve inches long and broad, rising to a point that caught the light. The hilt was in the shape of a man: his outstretched arms formed the guard, his legs the pommel. Beside them a loaf of bread rested on a ceramic plate, surrounded with red-dyed eggs and apples. A crystal skull with sapphire glass set in the eye sockets stood behind, wreathed in a garland of red and orange leaves.

The groom's side faced the bride's, divided by the altar between them. The silence was sudden. Rosalind had grown so used to the drumming that she no longer registered it, any more than she registered her own heartbeat moment to moment.

She knew the next steps of the ritual, knew that Taryn would take Joe's hand and lead him to the altar, then turn to the bride's side. It was her function in the ritual to bring the bride and groom together, leave them standing in the space that they would declare themselves united. Rosalind knew the ritual. She'd helped to design it.

What she hadn't known was how it would tear at her heart, watching the handsome boy walk toward Rhea. The gathered crowd knew they were watching something end, something profound and deep and worthy of mourning. It was a formal moment, a crafted moment, a ritual. Rosalind let the tears come down her cheeks. She knew the nature of ritual, now, after spending time with Rhea: a sacred space crafted to contain and symbolize emotion too great for anything less.

Ritual called for sacrifice. The larger the moment, the greater the sacrifice. Now, on the altar of Joe and Rhea's marriage, the sacrifice was her lover, her beloved boy, Taryn, who had been Rhea's lover and child and friend. *Nothing ever ends,* she reminded herself. *It changes form. Slowly, in fits and starts, all or nothing or as gradually as the ice age retreating, it changes, one thing into another.*

Here, intrinsically, the center would remain the same, a great love between a woman and a girl that had lasted lifetimes. Yet the Wheel had turned. From this moment it was acknowledged that it would never be the same between them. Something new was beginning.

This had to end, this end had to be recognized, before her love for Taryn could grow, but still she felt it, the weight of what was passing. She felt the grief on Taryn's behalf, loving her enough to mourn anything that caused her pain, even pain that would set her free.

She wanted to reach out to her when she saw the look on Taryn's face. Wanted to gather her up in her arms and tell her she would always be loved. Rosalind could feel the effort, the straining of Taryn's heart. Often in her life had Taryn been abandoned or thrown away by love. Security, and the peace that allows new things to blossom, had never been hers. What life offered had to be seized with both hands and devoured quickly before it vanished. What had Rhea told her? *Taryn comes from hunger.* It was agony to have every instinct backed by experience tell her that love was not a place she would ever rest, then deliberately hand away the only home she had ever known.

Taryn walked to Rhea and knelt before her, head bowed. Rhea set her hand on Taryn's head, took a red anemone from the flowers she carried, and pinned it to Taryn's jacket.

Taryn stood, suppliant transformed into knight. They were aware of the people watching, of the nature of the ritual, of the bruised tenderness between them that needed, at last, to have a formal way of passing. Taryn held out her arm, a gentleman at the end. Rhea took it and they walked to the altar, a short journey. Taryn stepped away and left Rhea facing Joe.

She'd done it. Taryn had given Rhea away. Rosalind saw the tear fall before Taryn turned away.

Taryn walked back to the groom's side and stood next to Misha.

Joe took up the goblet in his left hand and the dagger in his right.

"From now I am not halved, I am doubled. I am we, we are multitudes."

Rhea answered him. "You called me forth from sleep, you banished winter. Life came in your wake."

Joe held the dagger out to her, hilt first. The knife was placed in the goblet.

Goblin stepped up to the altar with a cord of braided scarlet and gold and green. She grinned and took Joe and Rhea's joined hands in hers.

"I don't have anything pretty to say. But you guys belong together, and you love each other, and I'm proud to have you as parents. Everybody, we come together to stand for these two people, for this couple as they continue their life together." She took the cord and bound them together by the wrist.

"Thank you, sweetheart," Joe said, kissing her.

It was Paul's turn to speak. He felt his hands tremble as he opened the piece of paper. "When I first came here, nothing made any sense. Rhea cried for me. Joe offered me the shirt off his back and a place in his household. I wore the ashes of my divorce like a mark on my forehead. I thought anybody who was willing to get married deserved a psych exam. But you two give me hope, an almost impossible, ephemeral transcendent hope, that this can be done. By the two of you, this can be done right, and that gives the rest of us hope."

Egyptia struck a pose with a flourish, the curve of her hip speaking in tongues. "I give you Rhea and Joe! Now, we celebrate!"

Drumming kicked up like the surf followed hard by the roar from the crowd, the cheering overlapping. The dancing started on the sand, churning the brack and bed of small shells like millstones. Up on the lawn, by the limestone firepit, the great cauldron of hot wine was set on its own tripod.

The bride's side and the groom's lost their definition and flowed, one into another, as if designed so. Taryn stood by the altar near the crystal skull, her hands on Rosalind's hips, pulling Rosalind against her.

The hearty greeting and cheer Paul expected, the level of ribaldry he did not. This wedding was progressing very swiftly into a lusty affair.

What did I expect? Paul thought. *Bunch of pagans getting married on Samhain.* He stopped dead in his tracks. Samhain. He'd called it by the witch's name. It wasn't Halloween to him anymore. He pronounced it, slowly. *Sow-en.*

"What you muttering, honey?" Egyptia asked him, slipping his hand through her arm.

"Just the holiday name. Caught myself calling it Samhain. I've been here too long, Egyptia. Not only is all this normal, it's automatic. I don't think the same way anymore."

"Well thank the Goddess for that," Egyptia said decisively. She kissed him on the cheek. It took her bending down to do it.

"Joe's put me in charge of the hot wine. You want to come help out?"

Egyptia was clearly puzzled. "Joe put you in charge of the hot wine?"

"He said I'm ready, or some other cryptic thing."

"Well then. If Joe says you are ready, why are we waiting?" Egyptia took his hand and pulled him toward the stairs.

By the altar Rosalind twined her arms around Taryn's neck, amazed and delighted with the ceremony, the night, the wedding, the splendid drunken feeling that was on her before she had a drop of wine.

"I know what you two are up to," Taryn said.

All innocence, Rosalind asked, "What might that be?"

"You're enacting the sacred marriage. You cast the spell. I can't believe Rhea went for it."

"It was her idea." Rosalind managed not to smirk when she said it.

Taryn's eyebrows climbed up, surprised. "Rhea? The blessing is unparalleled, but to bring that back on everyone, to not only allow but cause that many people getting laid on her wedding night? Then times have changed."

"Oh yes, my beautiful boy. Times have changed. Think you can stand being only my beloved?"

The kiss wasn't exactly a surprise, but the intensity of it was, the hunger unsheathed, the demand of it. The kiss slowed. Rosalind thought Taryn would pull away, but she didn't. Taryn kept her lips pressed against Rosalind's and changed the urgency, turning the kiss from demand to invitation. At length, Taryn pulled away, knowing she would be missed.

"Nothing less," Taryn whispered against Rosalind's mouth.

"You can be my Adonis, but no boar hunting for you. I am not having you die on me."

"It's Samhain, sweet love. We have to watch what we say," Taryn said in mock seriousness, glancing at the altar.

Rosalind took her hand and laid it on the top of the crystal skull. "You think I'm kidding? Your life is mine. You don't get to die without me saying it's okay."

"Guess I'm sticking around for a while, then."

Rhea and Joe walked through the crowd, greeting all guests and well-wishers, their right hands still bound together.

"Now you form a line, you rude boys," Egyptia said to Wolf, Robbie, and Sam.

"What if we're not all boys here, Egyptia?" Wolf asked.

The queen looked down a long way to reach Wolf. "My apology to the lady hiding behind you thugs. You still line up and take turns. Were you raised in a barn?"

"Raised by wolves."

"That explains a lot," Egyptia said.

Paul stood at the cauldron, stirring. The wine seemed perfect to him, the heat exactly right, but how he knew such a thing was outside of his experience. "Step right up. It's a cold night. We all need a little something warm in us." Only after Egyptia started laughing madly did he realize what he'd said. He started to speak. The queen put her fingers on his lips, halting him.

"You said it right the first time, baby."

Paul raised the ladle and filled goblets for the line. Wolf pushed at Robbie's shoulder.

"Where's Laurel?"

"Dancing. I'm bringing the wine back to her," Robbie said.

The white-haired boy looked at Robbie, grinning at her with a self-satisfied air, at Paul and Egyptia as they doled out the wine. "Am I the only single bastard here?" Wolf asked in disgust.

"Bastard, yeah. Don't know about single," Robbie said.

"Go fight down on the sand, boys." Egyptia shooed them along.

Paul stirred the wine in lazy circular motions. He'd thought more people would be lining up for the wine, but maybe the wine was an acquired taste. He lifted his own goblet to his lips and supposed he'd acquired it somewhere along the way.

The rhythm of the drumming changed. The queen raised her head. "That's one of the songs for the dead," Egyptia said, looking down the beach toward the dancing.

"How can you tell?" Paul asked.

"West African rhythm. It's after midnight. It's time to welcome them in."

"Huh."

"Do you know about Samhain?" Egyptia walked back to the cauldron and tilted her glass at Paul. He filled it, obligingly. *Some things are easier without words,* he thought. *Reduce a moment to its purest elements—hunger, thirst, desire—and let them speak for themselves.* Aloud, he said, "Rhea and Joe both have been preparing me."

"Do you have anybody coming?" Egyptia asked.

"Pardon?" Paul looked around, as if there were people in the crowd he was supposed to know.

"People that have passed, usually in the last year."

Paul smiled. "You don't know? That's how I ended up here."

"Honey, there ain't much I do know about you, except you were married to Miss Rosalind."

"That's funny. I feel like I've been through so much since I came here, so many intense things have happened. I've changed. And it feels like everyone here has shared them. But it's only been a month of my life. How much do I know about any of you?" Paul said. How had his goblet gotten empty?

"Sometimes it's nice to have a little mystery. To be able to take a vacation from yourself," Egyptia said.

"Like going to Canada to look back at Buffalo?"

"Just like that." Egyptia leaned down and kissed him. Not a peck on the cheek, not a quick kiss. He recognized this, as he was kissing her. Had to be the drumming, or the wine, or the wedding, but it made sense of its own. She pulled away. He felt the blush creep up his neck.

"Um, Egyptia. This isn't exactly—"

Her smile was knowing and brilliant. "Look. You ain't exactly my type. I ain't exactly your type. But maybe, just for tonight, we won't think on all that."

And she kissed him again.

The fire was naked women dancing. The wine was sex and the promise of sex, well past the invitation. There was no more summoning. It had arrived. The spell was set. It was the middle hours of the night of Samhain and everyone was mad.

Taryn had been sent for hot wine. It was the only way Rosalind could keep from hauling Taryn behind a pile of driftwood and giving the stars a show.

They had been kissing and talking. The talking was gone and the kissing wasn't stopping. Something rattled about in Rosalind's skull, some moment of importance still to be met, before giving in to this tide. Taryn had been perfectly willing to discount the wedding guests, the sand, the shells, and the brack and urge Rosalind to stretch out on the beach with her.

"Come on, baby. I'll lie down first. You won't get any sand on you."

"Not. Sand. I. Am. Worried. About," Rosalind said, punctuating each word with a kiss.

"What are you worried about?" Taryn asked, unfairly, from the space just under Rosalind's ear. There was something left undone, and this boy was not helping her focus. Rather, she was lost every time Taryn touched her. She had to think.

Rosalind set her hands on Taryn's shoulders and pushed her away. "Go get us some wine."

"You sure you want me gone?" Taryn murmured, teeth closing on her ear with a cat's affection.

"I never want you gone," Rosalind said in agony. The thought was too much to bear. She leaned into Taryn, then caught herself. Focus. What would Taryn respond to?

Rosalind caressed the line of Taryn's jaw, trailing down her neck.

Taryn groaned, and her eyes drifted closed.

"My sweet boy. My knight, my king. I want to taste the hot wine with you, drink from the same cup your lips have touched. Have you taste the wine from my lips. Would you go get us some, baby?"

Blue eyes snapped open and glared at her, caught, a unicorn with its head in a virgin's lap. "Your wish is my command."

"I'll test that theory a little later tonight," Rosalind said.

Taryn sprinted up the sand toward the stairs.

The air was cold enough to bring her blood down. She inhaled deeply, leaning her head back to look at the stars. What was it? She felt it, the spell they had cast, the call of abandon. A quick glance up the beach, at the fire, up to the lawn showed that everyone was feeling it. Dancers had wandered away from the fire. The darkness was studded with the shapes of people embracing.

The stars started to pinwheel. Rosalind closed her eyes. What was it that was missing? She reviewed the spell they'd cast. All seemed in place there. She didn't even need to open her eyes to know this. The drift of song was spiced with sighs. The sacred marriage was working. Her mind turned to the people involved. Rhea's voice sounded in her brain. *If the symbols are right, look to the participants. In the end, all spells are about the people.*

Rosalind sat up abruptly. That was it. She had to see Joe.

She sprinted down the beach.

Joe was standing by the fire. The red cord that bound him to Rhea had been loosened to a tie of three feet. He stood at a small distance from Rhea with the cord a red snake reclining between them. A goblet of wine was in his free hand, used to toast the crowd around him. He saw Rosalind run up the beach, barefoot, saw the grains of sand spark like stars in the red field of her dress, intermixed with the strands of her hair. He had a full idea of how they got there, and so grinned at her and saluted with the goblet.

"Rosalind! Come stand here between the bonfire and the wine. The night's cold has no sway. Though it looks like you've found your own way of stoking the internal fire. Where is Taryn?"

Rosalind took his arm and walked him the length of the cord. "The spell isn't finished."

"What do you mean? Look around. Everyone is in its sway, even the people abstaining."

"It's incomplete. I know what we have to do." Rosalind glanced at Rhea, who was deep in conversation with Laurel.

"Tell me," Joe said.

"The turning was right. The joining was right. The symbols are right, up to a point. But the ending isn't right yet. What was missing from Rhea's relationship with Taryn? When they were lovers."

Joe frowned. "Nothing that I know of. Rhea loved Taryn deeply, was fierce about protecting her."

Rosalind gestured decisively. "Exactly. Rhea loved Taryn. I know Taryn loved her, but there was always a recognition between them that certain walls needed to be up, for each to preserve themselves. Half of the dynamic between them was Rhea looking after Taryn, so they could move to being family after they were no longer lovers. Rhea still got to look after Taryn."

"I think I get it. No one has ever looked after Rhea."

"Ever. I think we could go back to the beginning of recorded history and not find it. She's never had her equal."

Joe's eyes opened a bit wider. "A lot more is being healed here than just the sacred marriage."

"All part of it, I think. The generation of new things begins with this night," Rosalind said.

"So as the stand-in for the god, I need to...?" Joe said.

"Take her. Sweep her off her feet. Not let her think, or be in control, of anything until dawn. Let Rhea meet your strength and be allowed, finally, to surrender."

Joe nodded at Rosalind and rubbed his chin. "You are a whole new brand of wicked. Rhea has no idea what she wrought, letting you into the house that first night."

"I think it was Taryn who hauled me in," Rosalind said.

"You think anyone could enter Rhea's house if she didn't allow it?" He winked at her and took up the red cord. "Spells need balance. Go find your boy. Tonight we unleash joy."

It pains us to hear that we are as large as life, that at any moment joy could tear through us and still leave us standing. That we are not the shell of a house, but the inhabitants. We are capable of all things and meant for them. There is nothing small about any of us. We are born with the divine in us and can wake to it at any point. To stand in the feeling of love and give yourself over to that drunkenness is falling with your eyes toward the sun. Ganymede knew that the eagle would sweep him up, and he held his arms out in embrace.

It would serve the sons of his sons to remember this.

The cabin was covered in people sprawled in a patchwork, looking to Rosalind as if someone had taken armloads of blankets and tossed them into the air. This was the cousin's house, the last stop for all the guests staying for the night. The main house was reserved for Rhea and Joe, so every available space in the second house was due to be draped over with humanity as the night wound down, as the wine kicked in, as the magic happened.

The bedrooms were all taken by the people gathered around Taryn. Ellie and Misha had taken one room and were already ensconced. The second room was reserved for her and Taryn; no one would think of disturbing that. The third was empty.

Halfway to the door, Rosalind had to admit that she was drunk. That couldn't be Egyptia, delicately lifting her high heels between sprawled bodies, leading Paul by the hand. And that certainly couldn't be Paul kissing Egyptia. Falling back against the door to the unclaimed room, pushing it open. Vanishing from sight. Rosalind shook her head to clear her vision. It didn't help.

There was just so much. So much soft, perfect chocolate skin, legs everywhere, longer than the span of his imagination and beautiful. Paul ran his hand down Egyptia's leg and felt the muscle under the skin, a hint more muscle than he'd ever felt in a woman's leg. Her long arms draped across his back. Excess of everything.

"I don't even know your real name," Paul said.

"Egyptia."

"I don't know who I am. I don't know what I need."

"It's okay, honey. Tonight, I'll see you the way you want me to see you. Even if nobody ever has. I'll take care of you, baby."

He kissed her and she sighed and pulled him in. She knew how to respond to him, how to make him feel strong, and in charge, and generous. When had a woman last made him feel this way? He'd thought it would be so different, but not different this way, not such an affirmation of his own maleness. Contrast, chiaroscuro, perspective. Looking back at himself from the shore of her eyes and liking what he saw. Maybe it was heightened, maybe it was a mix of illusion and reality, but it made him feel real. Seen.

Not an observer anymore.

So, in the last hours of the last night of the witch's year, when all boundaries became veils, the walls inside him fell, and Paul traveled where he had never been. There was no more need for signs, or symbols, or mazes. He came face-to-face with himself at last.

He'd fallen asleep without meaning to, without recognizing the transition. It had to be sleep, because he was seeing his father. Nothing like an apparition, just a man walking into the room. Dressed for running, as he looked every morning when he woke Paul up for high school. As he'd looked the morning of his death.

Paul sat up in bed.

"Are you here?" he asked, surprised at the steadiness of his own voice. It was easy to accept this moment without knowing everything about it after the time he'd spent here. Just another part of the journey.

"No, I'm over at Aunt Helen's. Of course I'm here. You're talking to me." His father's voice, no mistaking it, and his father's sense of humor.

"If it looks like a duck and walks like a duck—" Paul said automatically.

"It should stay out of the pond during hunting season." His father sat down on the bed.

"Are you all right?" Paul asked.

"Just fine. I was checking in on you." He looked at the sheet his son was wearing, at the queen asleep next to him. "I'm glad to see you're loosening up a little. I like the tattoo."

"Thanks. There are a lot of things I've tried in the last month I never thought I would," Paul said.

"Can't take life too seriously. You don't get out alive. Go on and roll your eyes, you always did."

"Was the funeral what you wanted?" Paul asked.

His father smiled at him. "You're not sure I'm here, but you're willing to talk to me anyway. That's new. You've made a lot of new choices and none of them were easy. I'm proud of you."

"After you…weren't here anymore, I didn't know what to do. I was lost."

"You've done a good job of finding yourself."

"I had a lot of help."

His father lifted his head, as if hearing something Paul couldn't register. "You had to choose to accept the help. It takes a strong man to do that. We don't have a lot of time. It's almost dawn. They'll be putting out the fires soon."

"Wait! You can't go. We haven't had any time. There's so much I need to tell you."

His father stood up. "I've been watching. That Rosalind always did look out for you. You're doing just fine."

"Dad, wait—"

"Can't. The fires are going out. Remember our talk, whether you believe it or not. Come from love, and everything else will work out. I love you, Paul."

He felt his father's kiss press to his forehead, then fade away. There were tears in his eyes, but he felt a profound sense of peace. If there were no more questions to ask, he'd gotten the answer his father wanted him to have. He was smiling and sitting up in bed when Egyptia woke up and found him.

Rosalind was wrestling with the ancient coffeemaker in the kitchen of the cabin, trying not to wake the horde of people sleeping in the front room. It was just dawn, but she was wide awake, clear eyed, filled with an energy that made sleep seem wasteful. She wasn't the only one, evidently. Taryn was gone. There had been stirrings from Ellie and Misha's room.

The door to the third room, Egyptia's room, opened. Paul walked out barefoot, his white shirt open, his tuxedo coat over his arm, his hair a halo. Rosalind managed not to drop the can of coffee. He saw her and smiled in greeting, not seeming to care at all that he'd been spotted. He came and joined her in the kitchen. He leaned against the counter, looking relaxed and calm as she'd never seen him. There had always been a tightness about Paul as long as she could remember. He smiled at her, and there was a softness to him, nothing coiled, nothing wrapped beyond endurance. He looked like a different man.

"Good morning," he said softly.

"Good morning. I'm trying to convince this thing to make us coffee, but it isn't cooperating," Rosalind said.

"Let me take a look at it. The plug is loose. Try it now."

"Thanks. I'm lucky you're up early, too."

"I didn't think anyone else would be after a night like last night."

"What kind of a night was it?" Rosalind asked, glancing at the third bedroom.

"A journey. A chance to look back, from another country."

"Are you applying for a passport?" she asked lightly, setting the coffeemaker back on the counter. She looked up to see his face. He was trying not laugh.

"You can ask me more directly. No, I don't think I'm applying for a passport. It was something I needed, and am glad for, but my citizenship is still the same."

"And Egyptia?"

"She's putting her face on, as she says. Shooed me out of the room. We talked about it this morning. She told me she had fun, and we can be friends and leave it at that. I'm not exactly her type. But she was sweet to me."

Rosalind started to laugh. "This is not a conversation I ever pictured us having."

"You think I did? I never would have pictured any of this." Paul glanced out the kitchen window. "Taryn's out on the beach."

Rosalind looked. "She must be putting the fires out. Samhain's over. Oh, for goodness sake, she's barefoot. Walking in Lake Erie. In October."

"November," Paul corrected.

"Right, the month is over. You're free to go back to Poughkeepsie."

"I think I'll stick around a few more days, get a chance to say good-bye to everyone. Thank Rhea and Joe," Paul said.

"You know you're always welcome to come back."

"I will. I think Buffalo would be a fine place to spend some time." Paul leaned down and kissed Rosalind on the cheek. "Thank you. For everything."

"Happy New Year, Paul."

Taryn stood on the sand, emptying a bucket filled with lake water over the last coals of the bonfire. Rosalind walked down the steps to the beach, the blanket from their bed in the cabin wrapped over her clothing like a cape. In her right hand she carried Taryn's boots.

"It's too cold to be out here barefoot. Are you insane?" Rosalind asked.

Taryn nodded. "Completely insane. Took you long enough to notice. I had to walk into the lake for the water to douse the fires."

"Put these on. Idiot." She slapped the boots into Taryn's stomach.

"I love you too."

"I'm going to spend my life looking after you. You do know that?" Rosalind opened the blanket and drew Taryn in. Taryn kissed her.

"Of course I know. I'm going to spend my life looking after you, too."

"I woke up and thought I'd make everyone coffee, and you weren't there. Have you slept at all?" Rosalind asked.

"Some, yeah. I usually don't sleep on Samhain. I had the dream again," Taryn said.

"Same one?"

Taryn nodded. "It started out the same. The darkness and the sounds of sawing, the grass against the sky. But then it changed. The wood was burnt, but when I picked it up the ash fell away. I didn't make a cross out of it. I had the wood there in my hand, and I felt like I could choose what to do with it. I didn't burn myself alive. I made a fire out of it. That was it."

"It sounds to me like you are finally finished with that dream. Purged of it. That cycle has ended. The cloud is gone. No more burning alive," Rosalind said.

"There are other ways I'd rather burn."

Rosalind took Taryn's face in her hands and kissed her tenderly. "You will."

"I'm done down here. Samhain is officially over."

"Come on back up to the house. The coffee should be ready. And do I have a story to tell you about Paul and Egyptia."

Rosalind took her hand and they walked up the stairs. The sun rose over the lake, warming their backs, casting light from one shore over to the next. It was morning in Buffalo.

About the Author

Susan Smith was a founding member of the HAG Theatre Company in Buffalo, New York. After a decade of performing and writing for the stage, Smitty turned back to her first love, writing novels. Like most of the artists in hardworking Buffalo, Smitty keeps a full-time day job as a librarian and college instructor, while occasionally being enticed by drag shows and theater projects. Along with her partner, the drag king Johnny Class, Smitty divides her time between Toronto and Buffalo. Traveling is good for the soul and borders are made to be crossed.

Books Available From Bold Strokes Books

The Devil Unleashed by Ali Vali. As the heat of violence rises, so does the passion. A Casey Clan crime saga. (1-933110-61-9)

Burning Dreams by Susan Smith. The chronicle of the challenges faced by a young drag king and an older woman who share a love "outside the bounds." (1-933110-62-7)

Fresh Tracks by Georgia Beers. Seven women, seven days. A lot can happen when old friends, lovers, and a new girl in town get together in the mountains. (1-933110-63-5)

The Empress and the Acolyte by Jane Fletcher. Jemeryl and Tevi fight to protect the very fabric of their world...time. Lyremouth Chronicles Book Three (1-933110-60-0)

First Instinct by JLee Meyer. When high-stakes security fraud leads to murder, one woman flees for her life while another risks her heart to protect her. (1-933110-59-7)

Erotic Interludes 4: Extreme Passions. Thirty of today's hottest erotica writers set the pages aflame with love, lust, and steamy liaisons. (1-933110-58-9)

Storms of Change by Radclyffe. In the continuing saga of the Provincetown Tales, duty and love are at odds as Reese and Tory face their greatest challenge. (1-933110-57-0)

Unexpected Ties by Gina L. Dartt. With death before dessert, Kate Shannon and Nikki Harris are swept up in another tale of danger and romance. (1-933110-56-2)

Sleep of Reason by Rose Beecham. While Detective Jude Devine searches for a lost boy, her rocky relationship with Dr. Mercy Westmoreland gets a lot harder. (1-933110-53-8)

Passion's Bright Fury by Radclyffe. Passion strikes without warning when a trauma surgeon and a filmmaker become reluctant allies. (1-933110-54-6)

Broken Wings by L-J Baker. When Rye Woods meets beautiful dryad Flora Withe, her libido, as hidden as her wings, reawakens along with her heart. (1-933110-55-4)

Combust the Sun by Andrews & Austin. A Richfield and Rivers mystery set in L.A. Murder among the stars. (1-933110-52-X)

Of Drag Kings and the Wheel of Fate by Susan Smith. A blind date in a drag club leads to an unlikely romance. (1-933110-51-1)

Tristaine Rises by Cate Culpepper. Brenna, Jesstin, and the Amazons of Tristaine face their greatest challenge for survival. (1-933110-50-3)

Too Close to Touch by Georgia Beers. Kylie O'Brien believes in true love and is willing to wait for it, even though Gretchen, her new boss, is off-limits. (1-933110-47-3)

100th Generation by Justine Saracen. Ancient curses, modern-day villains, and an intriguing woman lead archeologist Valerie Foret on the adventure of her life. (1-933110-48-1)

Battle for Tristaine by Cate Culpepper. While Brenna struggles to find her place in the clan, Tristaine is threatened with destruction. Second in the Tristaine series. (1-933110-49-X)

The Traitor and the Chalice by Jane Fletcher. Tevi and Jemeryl risk all in the race to uncover a traitor. The Lyremouth Chronicles Book Two. (1-933110-43-0)

Promising Hearts by Radclyffe. Dr. Vance Phelps arrives in New Hope, Montana, with no hope of happiness—until she meets Mae. (1-933110-44-9)

Carly's Sound by Ali Vali. Poppy Valente and Julia Johnson form a bond of friendship that becomes something far more. A poignant romance about love and renewal. (1-933110-45-7)

Unexpected Sparks by Gina L. Dartt. Kate Shannon's attraction to much younger Nikki Harris is complication enough without a fatal fire that Kate can't ignore. (1-933110-46-5)

Whitewater Rendezvous by Kim Baldwin. Two women on a wilderness kayak adventure discover that true love may be nothing at all like they imagined. (1-933110-38-4)

Erotic Interludes 3: Lessons in Love ed. by Radclyffe and Stacia Seaman. Sign on for a class in love…the best lesbian erotica writers take us to "school." (1-9331100-39-2)

Punk Like Me by JD Glass. Twenty-one-year-old Nina has a way with the girls, and she doesn't always play by the rules. (1-933110-40-6)

Coffee Sonata by Gun Brooke. Four women whose lives unexpectedly intersect in a small town by the sea share one thing in common—they all have secrets. (1-933110-41-4)

The Clinic: Tristaine Book One by Cate Culpepper. Brenna, a prison medic, finds herself drawn to Jesstin, a warrior reputed to be descended from ancient Amazons. (1-933110-42-2)

Forever Found by JLee Meyer. Can time, tragedy, and shattered trust destroy a love that seemed destined? Chance reunites childhood friends separated by tragedy. (1-933110-37-6)

Sword of the Guardian by Merry Shannon. Princess Shasta's bold new bodyguard has a secret that could change both of their lives. He is actually a *she*. (1-933110-36-8)

Wild Abandon by Ronica Black. Dr. Chandler Brogan and Officer Sarah Monroe are drawn together by their common obsessions—sex, speed, and danger. (1-933110-35-X)

Turn Back Time by Radclyffe. Pearce Rifkin and Wynter Thompson have nothing in common but a shared passion for surgery—and unexpected attraction. (1-933110-34-1)

Chance by Grace Lennox. A sexy, funny, touching story of two women who, in finding themselves, also find one another. (1-933110-31-7)

The Exile and the Sorcerer by Jane Fletcher. First in the Lyremouth Chronicles. Tevi and a shy young sorcerer face monsters, magic, and the challenge of loving. (1-933110-32-5)

A Matter of Trust by Radclyffe. When what should be just business turns into much more, two women struggle to trust the unexpected. (1-933110-33-3)

Sweet Creek by Lee Lynch. A celebration of the enduring nature of love, friendship, and community in the heart-warming lesbian community of Waterfall Falls. (1-933110-29-5)

The Devil Inside by Ali Vali. The head of a New Orleans crime organization falls for a woman who turns her world upside down. (1-933110-30-9)

Grave Silence by Rose Beecham. Detective Jude Devine's investigation of ritual murders is complicated by her torrid affair with pathologist Dr. Mercy Westmoreland. (1-933110-25-2)

Honor Reclaimed by Radclyffe. Secret Service Agent Cameron Roberts and Blair Powell close ranks to find the would-be assassins who nearly claimed Blair's life. (1-933110-18-X)

Honor Bound by Radclyffe. Secret Service Agent Cameron Roberts and Blair Powell face political intrigue, a clandestine threat to Blair's safety, and the seemingly irreconcilable differences that force them ever further apart. (1-933110-20-1)

Innocent Hearts by Radclyffe. In a wild and unforgiving land, two women learn about love, passion, and the wonders of the heart. (1-933110-21-X)

The Temple at Landfall by Jane Fletcher. An imprinter, one of Celaeno's most revered servants of the Goddess, is also a prisoner to the faith—until a Ranger frees her by claiming her heart. The Celaeno series. (1-933110-27-9)

Protector of the Realm: Supreme Constellations Book One by Gun Brooke. A space adventure filled with suspense and a daring intergalactic romance. (1-933110-26-0)

Force of Nature by Kim Baldwin. From tornados to forest fires, the forces of nature conspire to bring Gable McCoy and Erin Richards close to danger, and closer to each other. (1-933110-23-6)

In Too Deep by Ronica Black. Undercover homicide cop Erin McKenzie tracks a femme fatale who just might be a real killer…with love and danger hot on her heels. (1-933110-17-1)

Stolen Moments: Erotic Interludes 2 ed. by Stacia Seaman and Radclyffe. Love on the run, in the office, in the shadows…Fast, furious, and almost too hot to handle. (1-933110-16-3)

Course of Action by Gun Brooke. Actress Carolyn Black desperately wants the starring role in an upcoming film produced by Annelie Peterson. Just how far will she go for the dream part of a lifetime? (1-933110-22-8)

Rangers at Roadsend by Jane Fletcher. Sergeant Chip Coppelli has learned to spot trouble coming, and that is exactly what she sees in her new recruit, Katryn Nagata. The Celaeno series. (1-933110-28-7)

Justice Served by Radclyffe. Lieutenant Rebecca Frye and her lover, Dr. Catherine Rawlings, embark on a deadly game of hide-and-seek with an underworld kingpin who traffics in human souls. (1-933110-15-5)

Distant Shores, Silent Thunder by Radclyffe. Dr. Tory King—along with the women who love her—is forced to examine the boundaries of love, friendship, and the ties that transcend time. (1-933110-08-2)

Hunter's Pursuit by Kim Baldwin. A raging blizzard, a mountain hideaway, and a killer-for-hire set a scene for disaster—or desire—when Katarzyna Demetrious rescues a beautiful stranger. (1-933110-09-0)

The Walls of Westernfort by Jane Fletcher. All Temple Guard Natasha Ionadis wants is to serve the Goddess—until she falls in love with one of the rebels she is sworn to destroy. The Celaeno series. (1-933110-24-4)

Change Of Pace: Erotic Interludes by Radclyffe. Twenty-five hot-wired encounters guaranteed to spark more than just your imagination. Erotica as you've always dreamed of it. (1-933110-07-4)

Honor Guards by Radclyffe. In a wild flight for their lives, the president's daughter and those who are sworn to protect her wage a desperate struggle for survival. (1-933110-01-5)

Fated Love by Radclyffe. Amidst the chaos and drama of a busy emergency room, two women must contend not only with the fragile nature of life, but also with the irresistible forces of fate. (1-933110-05-8)

Justice in the Shadows by Radclyffe. In a shadow world of secrets and lies, Detective Sergeant Rebecca Frye and her lover, Dr. Catherine Rawlings, join forces in the elusive search for justice. (1-933110-03-1)

shadowland by Radclyffe. In a world on the far edge of desire, two women are drawn together by power, passion, and dark pleasures. An erotic romance. (1-933110-11-2)

Love's Masquerade by Radclyffe. Plunged into the indistinguishable realms of fiction, fantasy, and hidden desires, Auden Frost is forced to question all she believes about the nature of love. (1-933110-14-7)

Love & Honor by Radclyffe. The president's daughter and her lover are faced with difficult choices as they battle a tangled web of Washington intrigue for...love and honor. (1-933110-10-4)

Beyond the Breakwater by Radclyffe. One Provincetown summer, three women learn the true meaning of love, friendship, and family. (1-933110-06-6)

Tomorrow's Promise by Radclyffe. One timeless summer, two very different women discover the power of passion to heal and the promise of hope that only love can bestow. (1-933110-12-0)

Love's Tender Warriors by Radclyffe. Two women who have accepted loneliness as a way of life learn that love is worth fighting for and a battle they cannot afford to lose. (1-933110-02-3)

Love's Melody Lost by Radclyffe. A secretive artist with a haunted past and a young woman escaping a life that has proved to be a lie find their destinies entwined. (1-933110-00-7)

Safe Harbor by Radclyffe. A mysterious newcomer, a reclusive doctor, and a troubled gay teenager learn about love, friendship, and trust during one tumultuous summer in Provincetown. (1-933110-13-9)

Above All, Honor by Radclyffe. Secret Service Agent Cameron Roberts fights her desire for the one woman she can't have—Blair Powell, the daughter of the president of the United States. (1-933110-04-X)